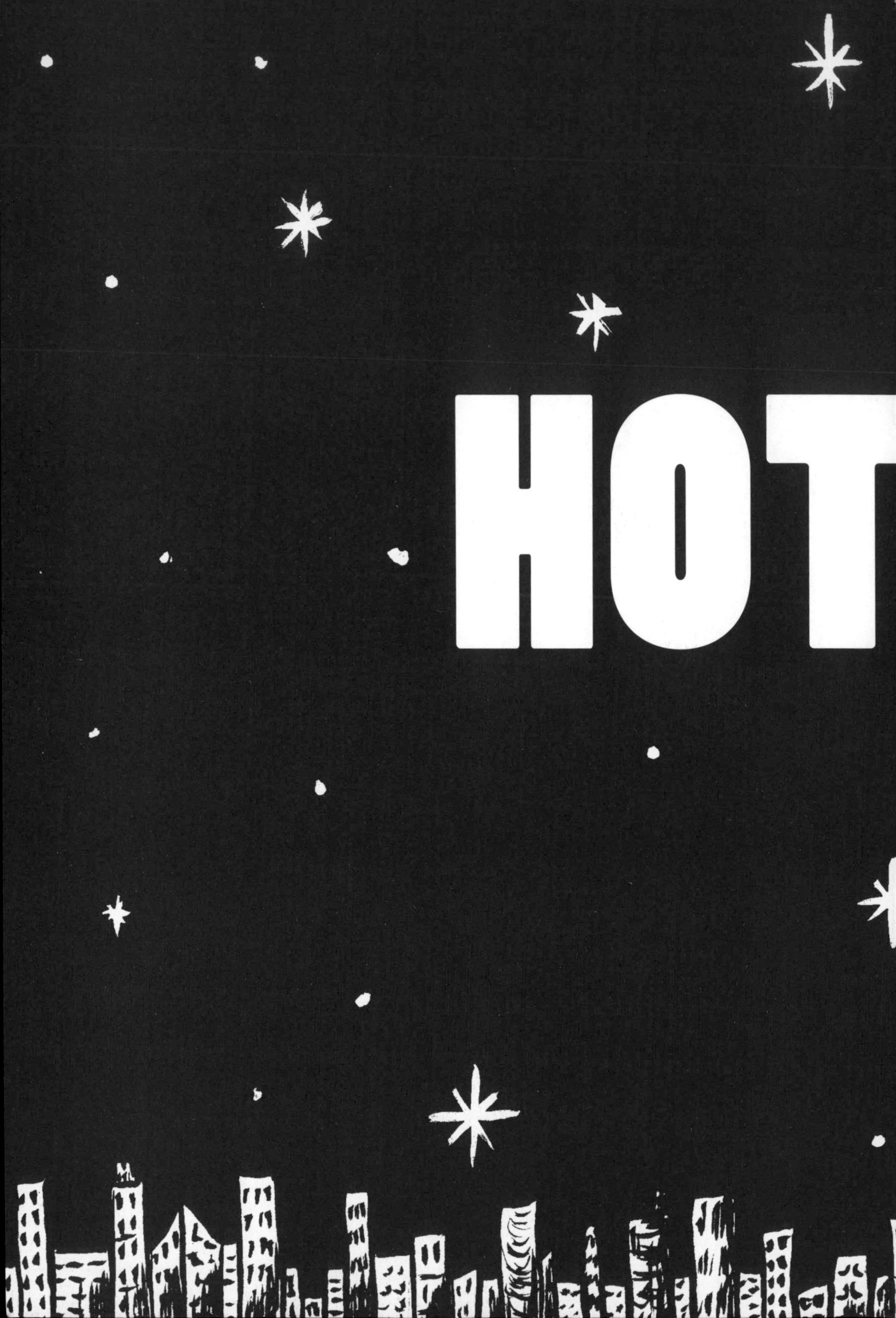
HOT

COMB

Ebony Flowers

Drawn & Quarterly

For my parents,
Phyllis, Diane, and Houston

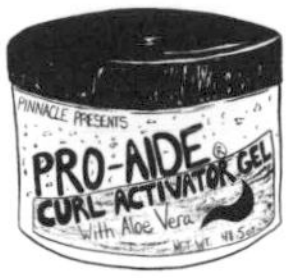
PINNACLE PRESENTS
PRO-AIDE®
CURL ACTIVATOR GEL
With Aloe Vera

Pinnacle Presents

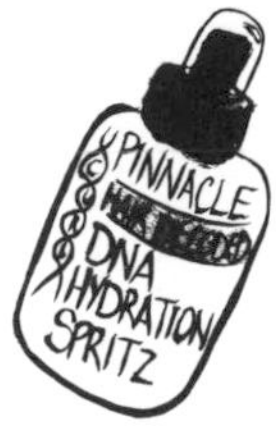
PINNACLE
DNA
HYDRATION
SPRITZ

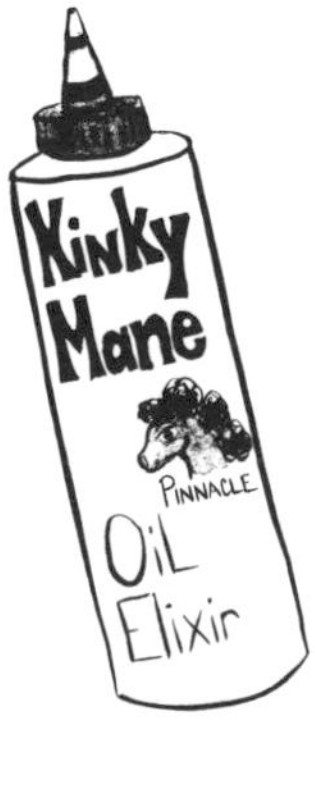
Kinky Mane
PINNACLE
Oil Elixir

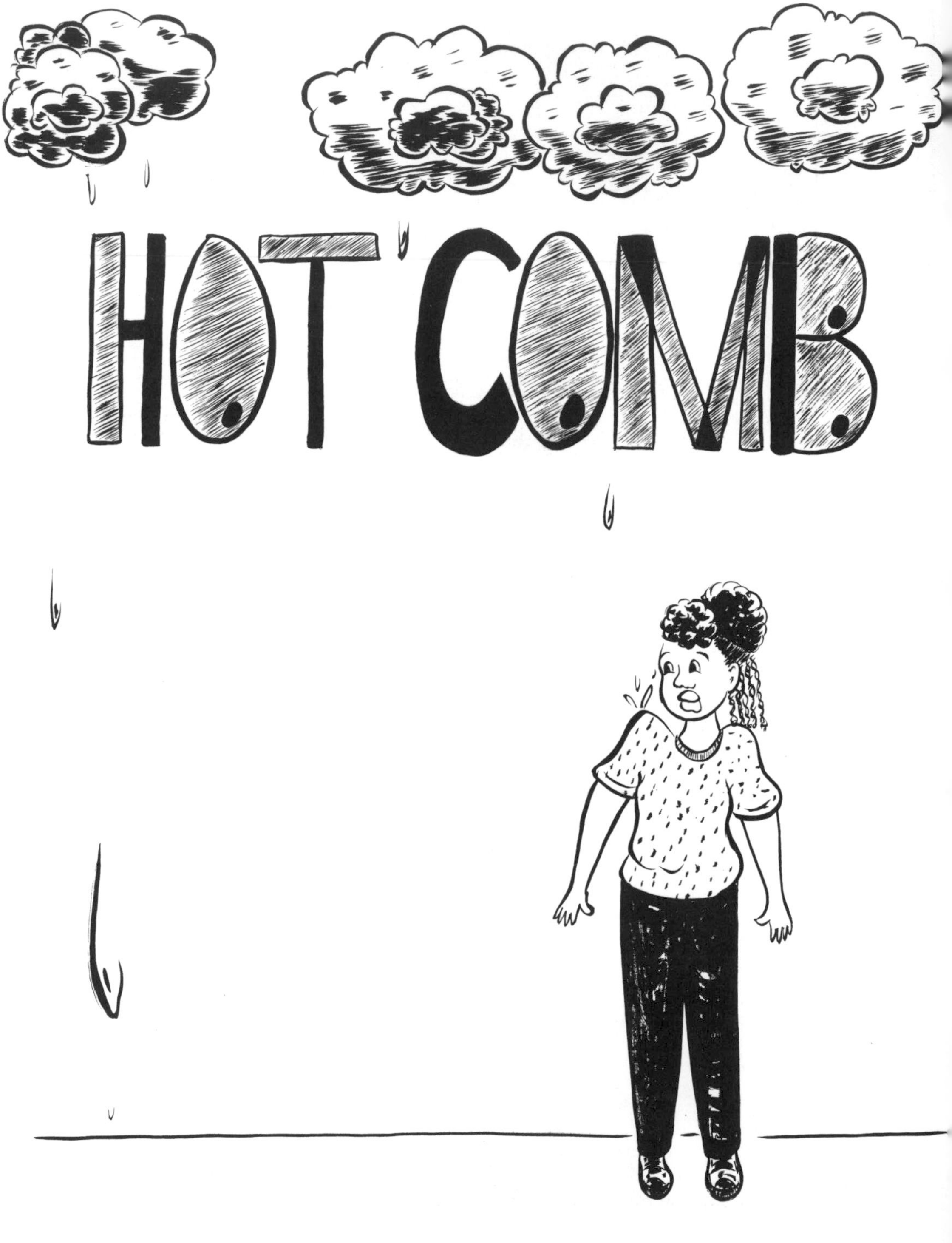
HOT COMB

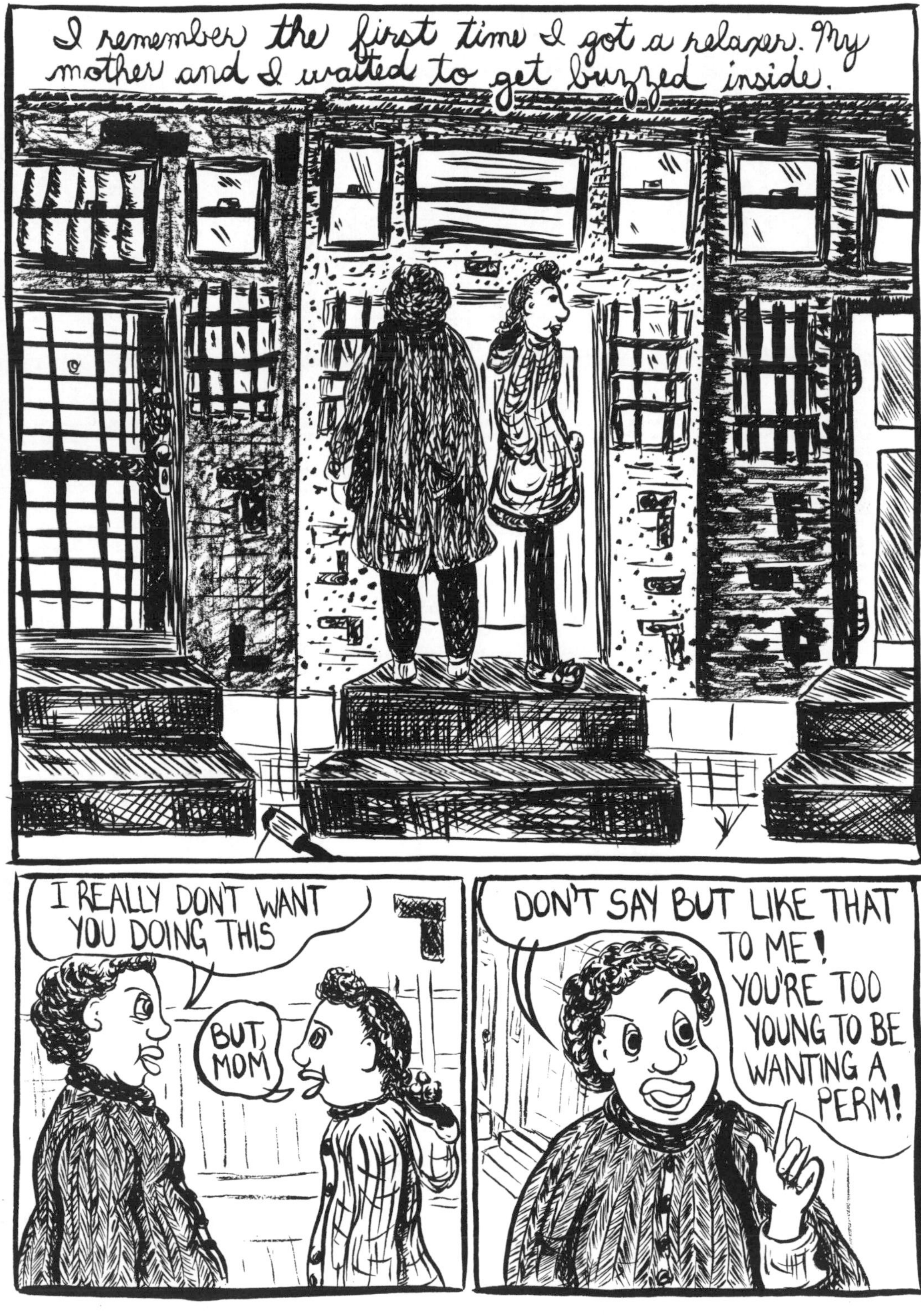
I remember the first time I got a relaxer. My mother and I waited to get buzzed inside.
I REALLY DON'T WANT YOU DOING THIS
BUT, MOM
DON'T SAY BUT LIKE THAT TO ME! YOU'RE TOO YOUNG TO BE WANTING A PERM!

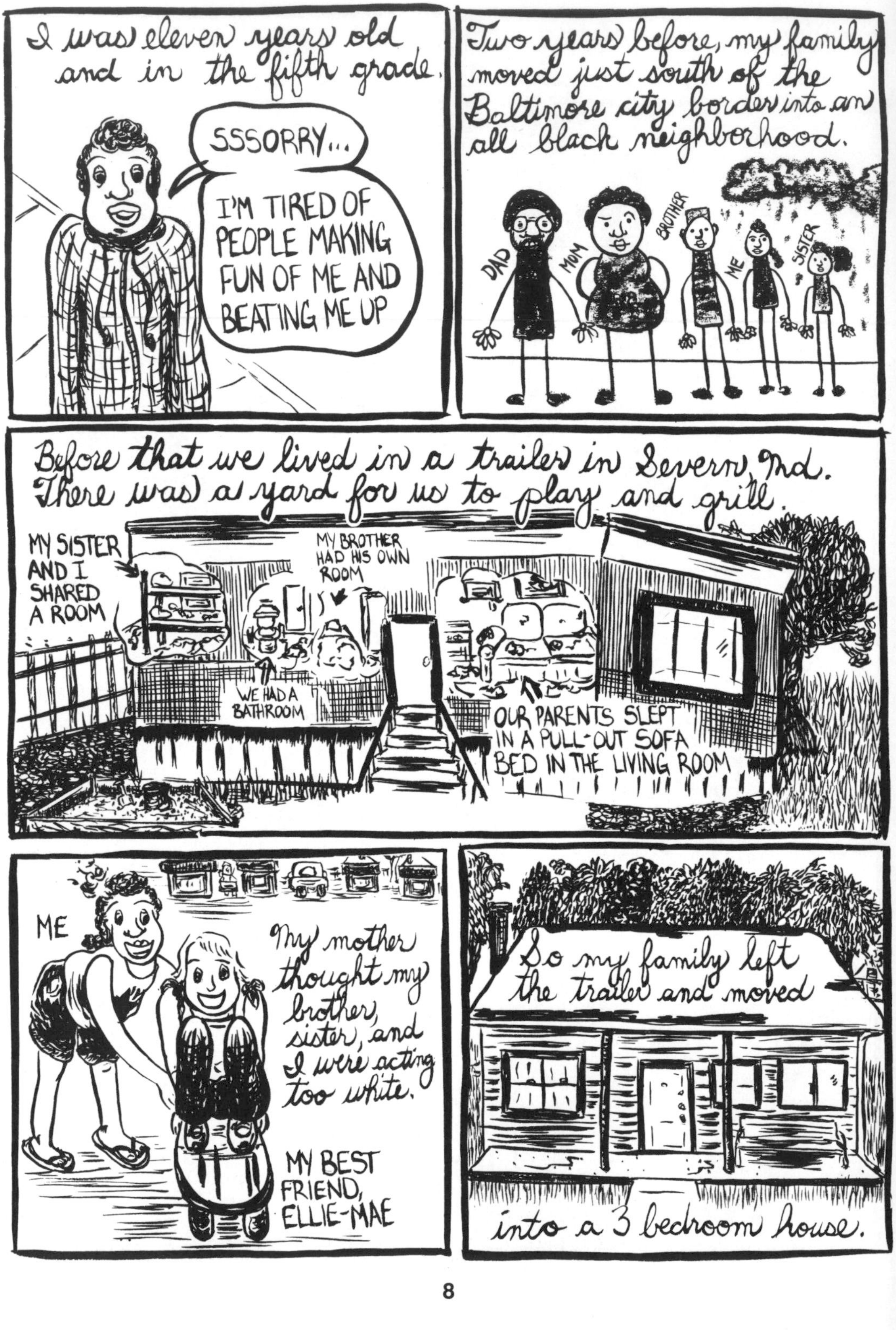

I was eleven years old and in the fifth grade.
SSSORRY...
I'M TIRED OF PEOPLE MAKING FUN OF ME AND BEATING ME UP
Two years before, my family moved just south of the Baltimore city border into an all black neighborhood.
DAD
MOM
BROTHER
ME
SISTER
Before that we lived in a trailer in Severn, Md. There was a yard for us to play and grill.
MY SISTER AND I SHARED A ROOM
MY BROTHER HAD HIS OWN ROOM
WE HAD A BATHROOM
OUR PARENTS SLEPT IN A PULL-OUT SOFA BED IN THE LIVING ROOM
ME
My mother thought my brother, sister, and I were acting too white.
MY BEST FRIEND, ELLIE-MAE
So my family left the trailer and moved
into a 3 bedroom house.

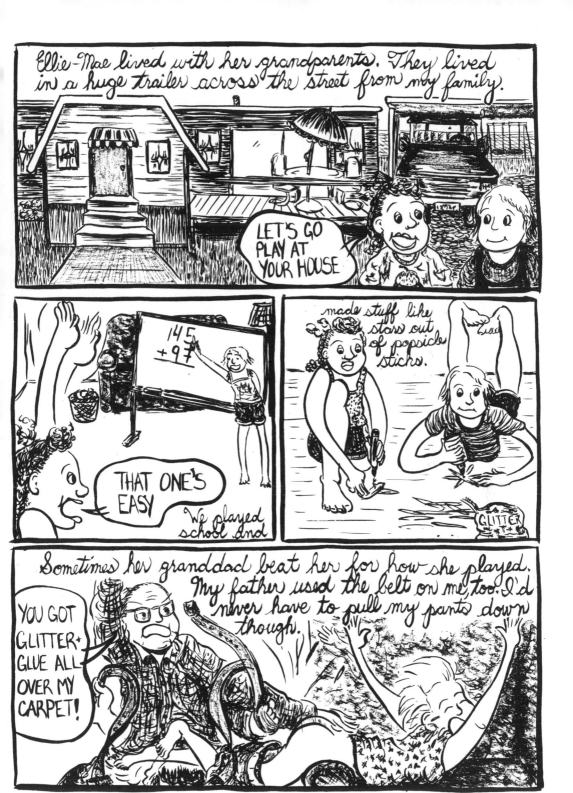

Ellie-Mae lived with her grandparents. They lived in a huge trailer across the street from my family.

LET'S GO PLAY AT YOUR HOUSE

14 5
+ 97

THAT ONE'S EASY

We played school and

made stuff like stars out of popsicle sticks.

GLITTER

Sometimes her granddad beat her for how she played. My father used the belt on me, too. I'd never have to pull my pants down though.

YOU GOT GLITTER + GLUE ALL OVER MY CARPET!

9

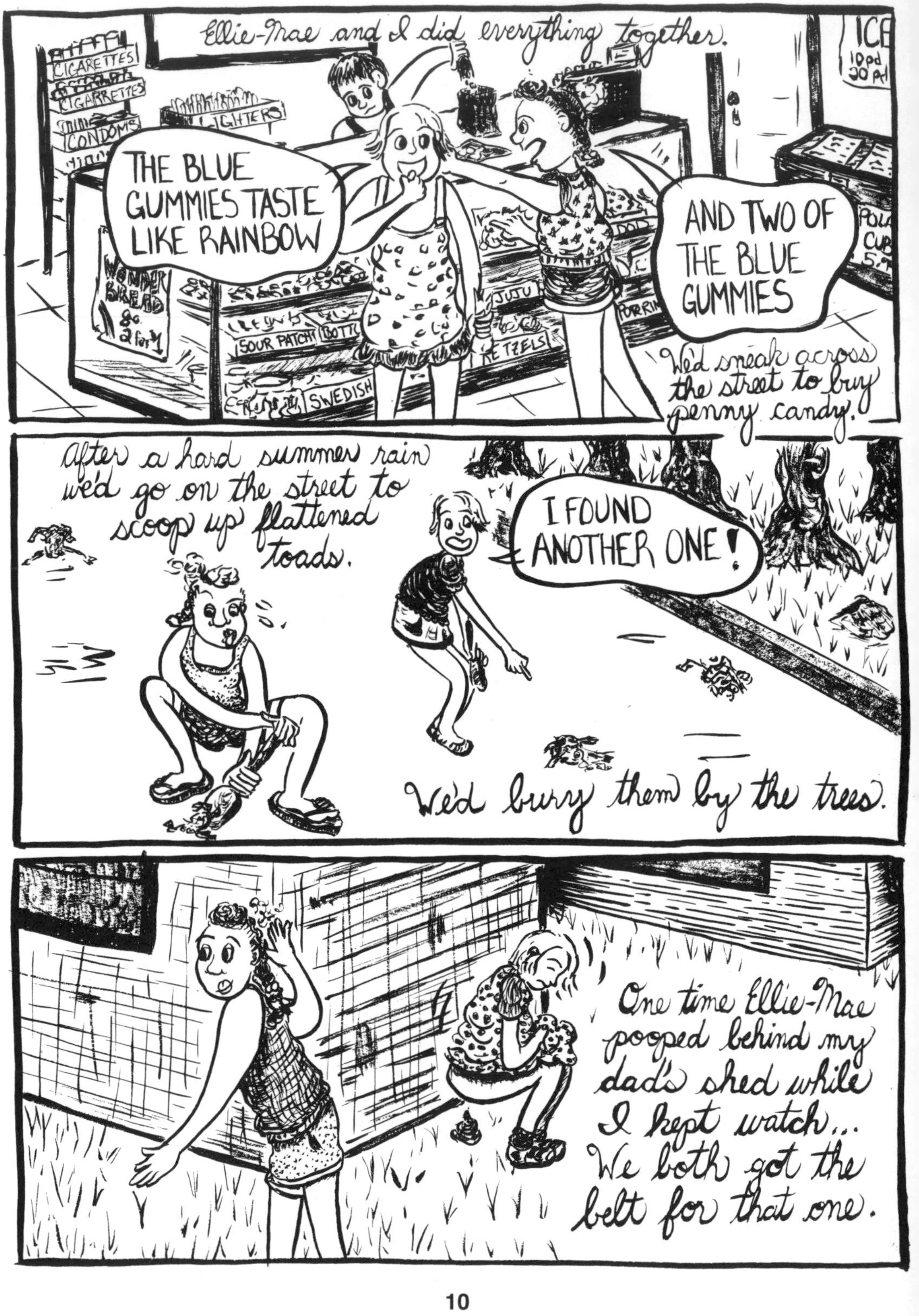
Ellie-Mae and I did everything together.
CIGARETTES
CIGARRETTES
CONDOMS
LIGHTERS
ICE
THE BLUE GUMMIES TASTE LIKE RAINBOW
AND TWO OF THE BLUE GUMMIES
SOUR PATCH
SWEDISH
JUJU
We'd sneak across the street to buy penny candy.
After a hard summer rain we'd go on the street to scoop up flattened toads.
I FOUND ANOTHER ONE!
We'd bury them by the trees.
One time Ellie-Mae pooped behind my dad's shed while I kept watch... We both got the belt for that one.

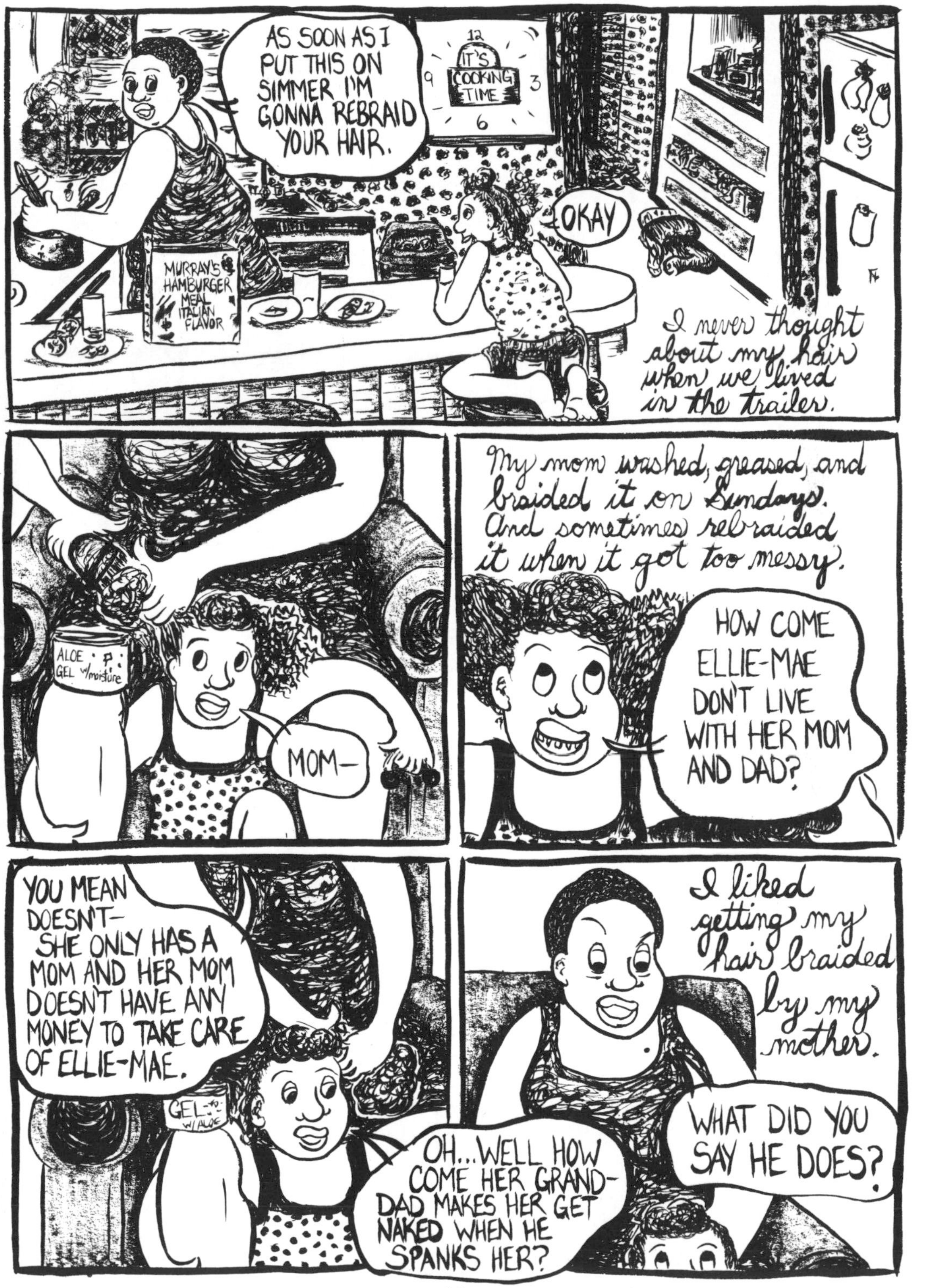
AS SOON AS I PUT THIS ON SIMMER I'M GONNA REBRAID YOUR HAIR.
IT'S COOKING TIME
MURRAY'S HAMBURGER MEAL ITALIAN FLAVOR
OKAY
I never thought about my hair when we lived in the trailer.
ALOE GEL w/moisture
MOM-
My mom washed, greased, and braided it on Sundays. And sometimes rebraided it when it got too messy.
HOW COME ELLIE-MAE DON'T LIVE WITH HER MOM AND DAD?
YOU MEAN DOESN'T- SHE ONLY HAS A MOM AND HER MOM DOESN'T HAVE ANY MONEY TO TAKE CARE OF ELLIE-MAE.
GEL w/ALOE
OH... WELL HOW COME HER GRAND-DAD MAKES HER GET NAKED WHEN HE SPANKS HER?
I liked getting my hair braided by my mother.
WHAT DID YOU SAY HE DOES?

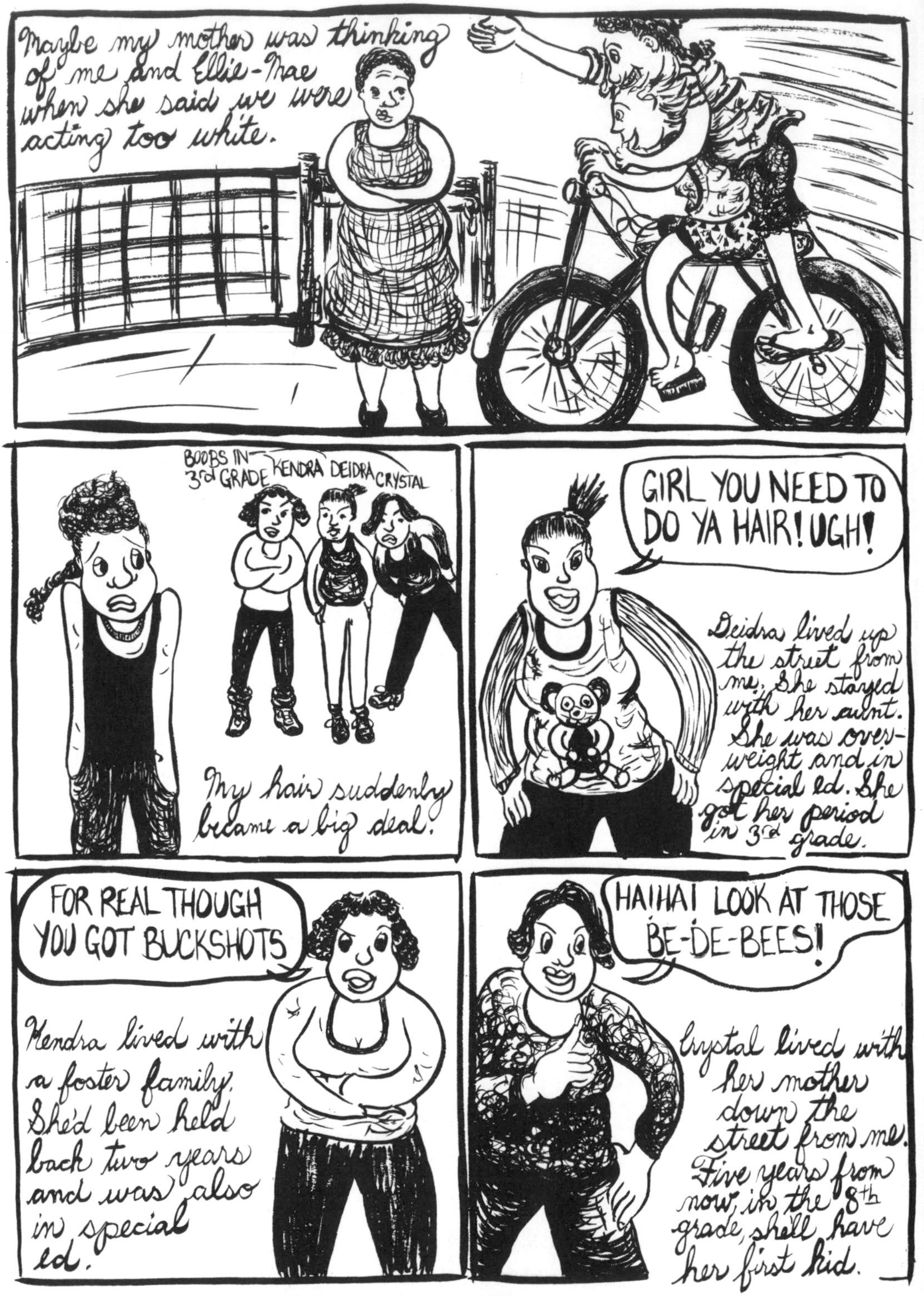

Maybe my mother was thinking of me and Ellie-Mae when she said we were acting too white.
BOOBS IN 3rd GRADE
KENDRA
DEIDRA
CRYSTAL
My hair suddenly became a big deal.
GIRL YOU NEED TO DO YA HAIR! UGH!
Deidra lived up the street from me. She stayed with her aunt. She was overweight and in special ed. She got her period in 3rd grade.
FOR REAL THOUGH YOU GOT BUCKSHOTS
Kendra lived with a foster family. She'd been held back two years and was also in special ed.
HAIHAI LOOK AT THOSE BE-DE-BEES!
Crystal lived with her mother down the street from me. Five years from now, in the 8th grade, she'll have her first kid.

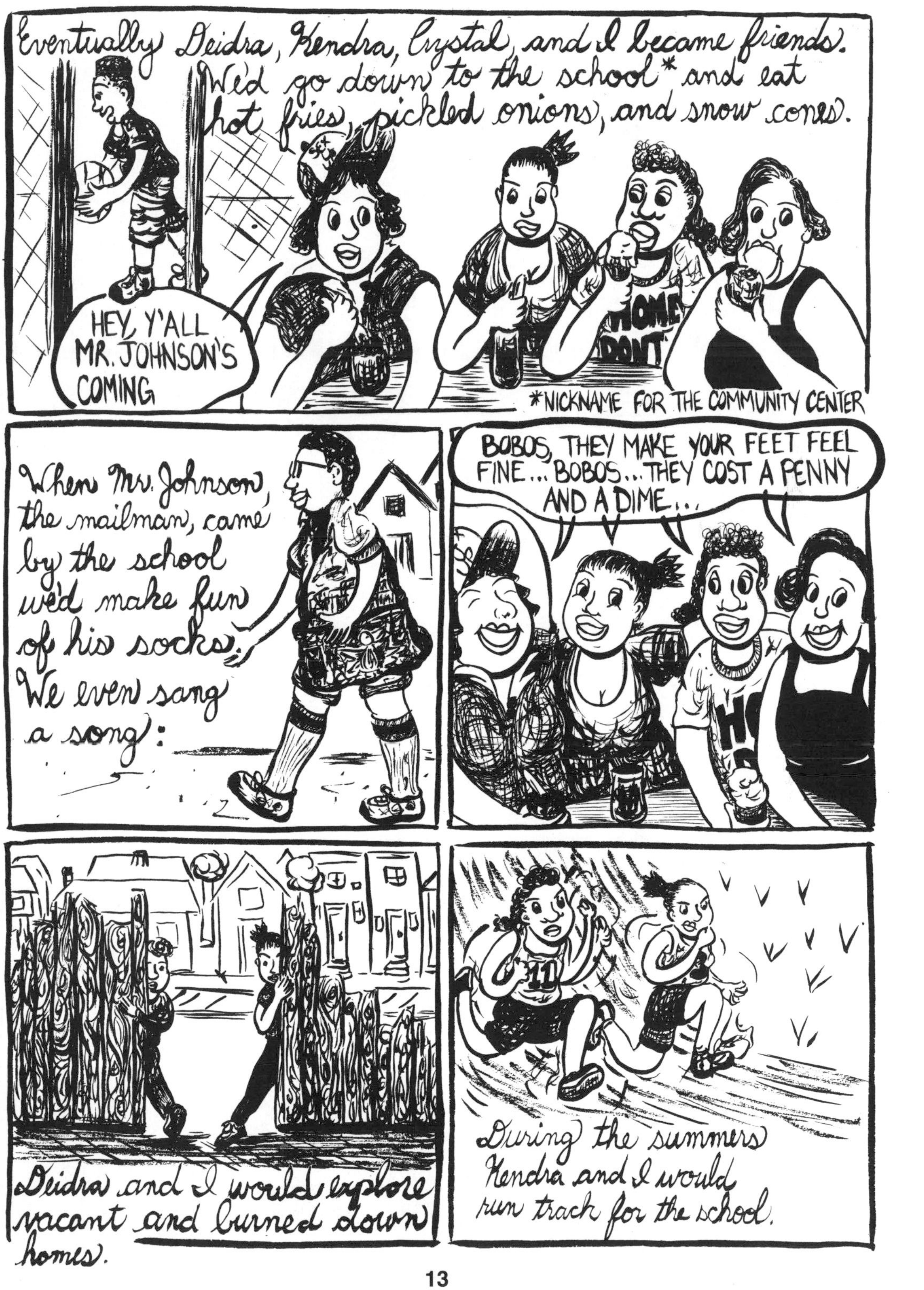
Eventually Deidra, Kendra, Crystal, and I became friends. We'd go down to the school* and eat hot fries, pickled onions, and snow cones.
HEY, Y'ALL MR. JOHNSON'S COMING
HOME DONT
*NICKNAME FOR THE COMMUNITY CENTER
When Mr. Johnson, the mailman, came by the school we'd make fun of his socks. We even sang a song:
BOBOS, THEY MAKE YOUR FEET FEEL FINE... BOBOS... THEY COST A PENNY AND A DIME...
Deidra and I would explore vacant and burned down homes.
During the summers Kendra and I would run track for the school.
11

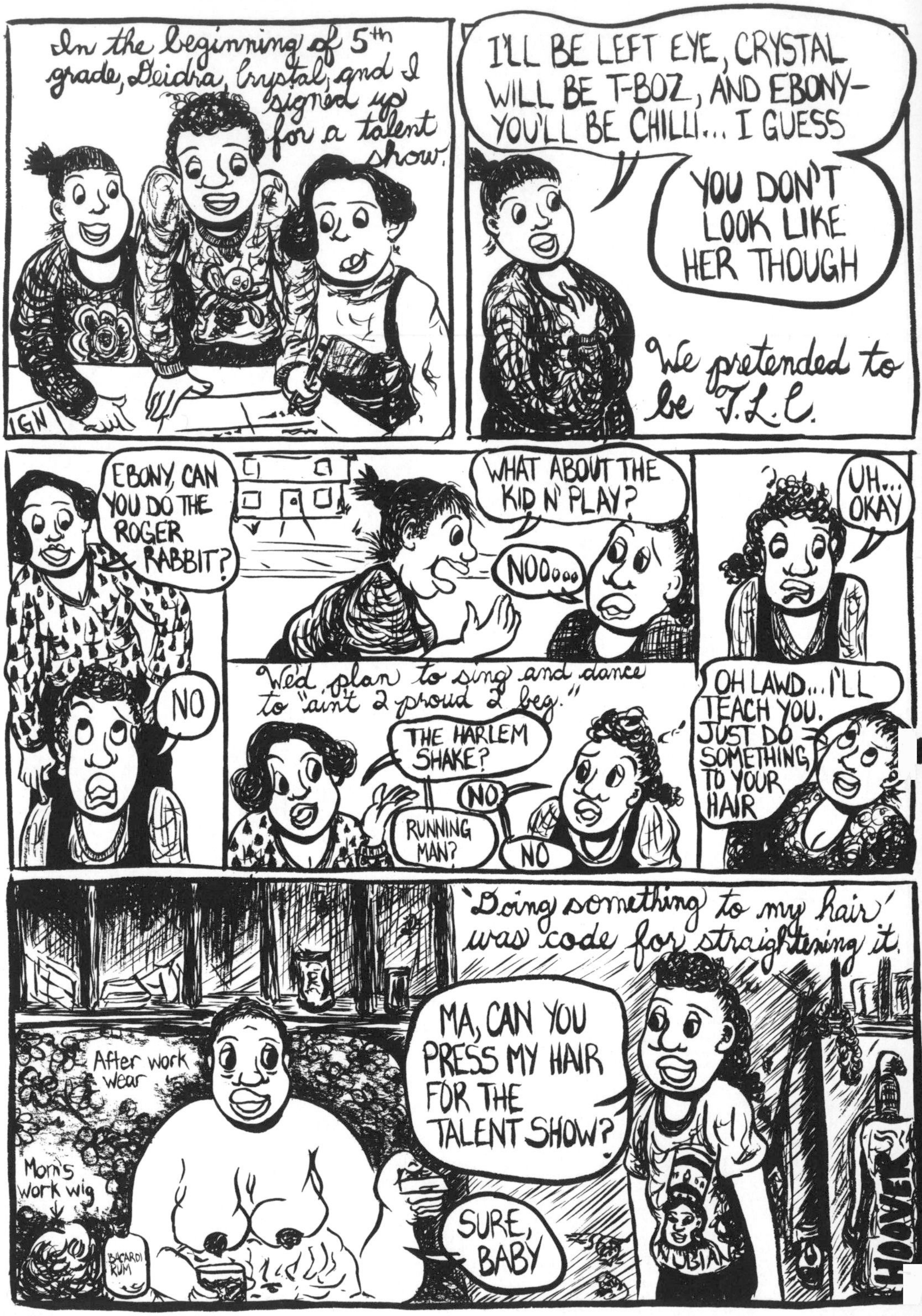
In the beginning of 5th grade, Deidra, Crystal, and I signed up for a talent show.
IGN
I'LL BE LEFT EYE, CRYSTAL WILL BE T-BOZ, AND EBONY- YOU'LL BE CHILLI... I GUESS
YOU DON'T LOOK LIKE HER THOUGH
We pretended to be T.L.C.
EBONY, CAN YOU DO THE ROGER RABBIT?
NO
WHAT ABOUT THE KID N' PLAY?
NOOooo
UH... OKAY
We'd plan to sing and dance to "ain't 2 proud 2 beg."
THE HARLEM SHAKE?
NO
RUNNING MAN?
NO
OH LAWD... I'LL TEACH YOU. JUST DO SOMETHING TO YOUR HAIR
'Doing something to my hair' was code for straightening it.
MA, CAN YOU PRESS MY HAIR FOR THE TALENT SHOW?
SURE, BABY
After work wear
Mom's work wig
BACARDI RUM
NUBIAN
HOOVER

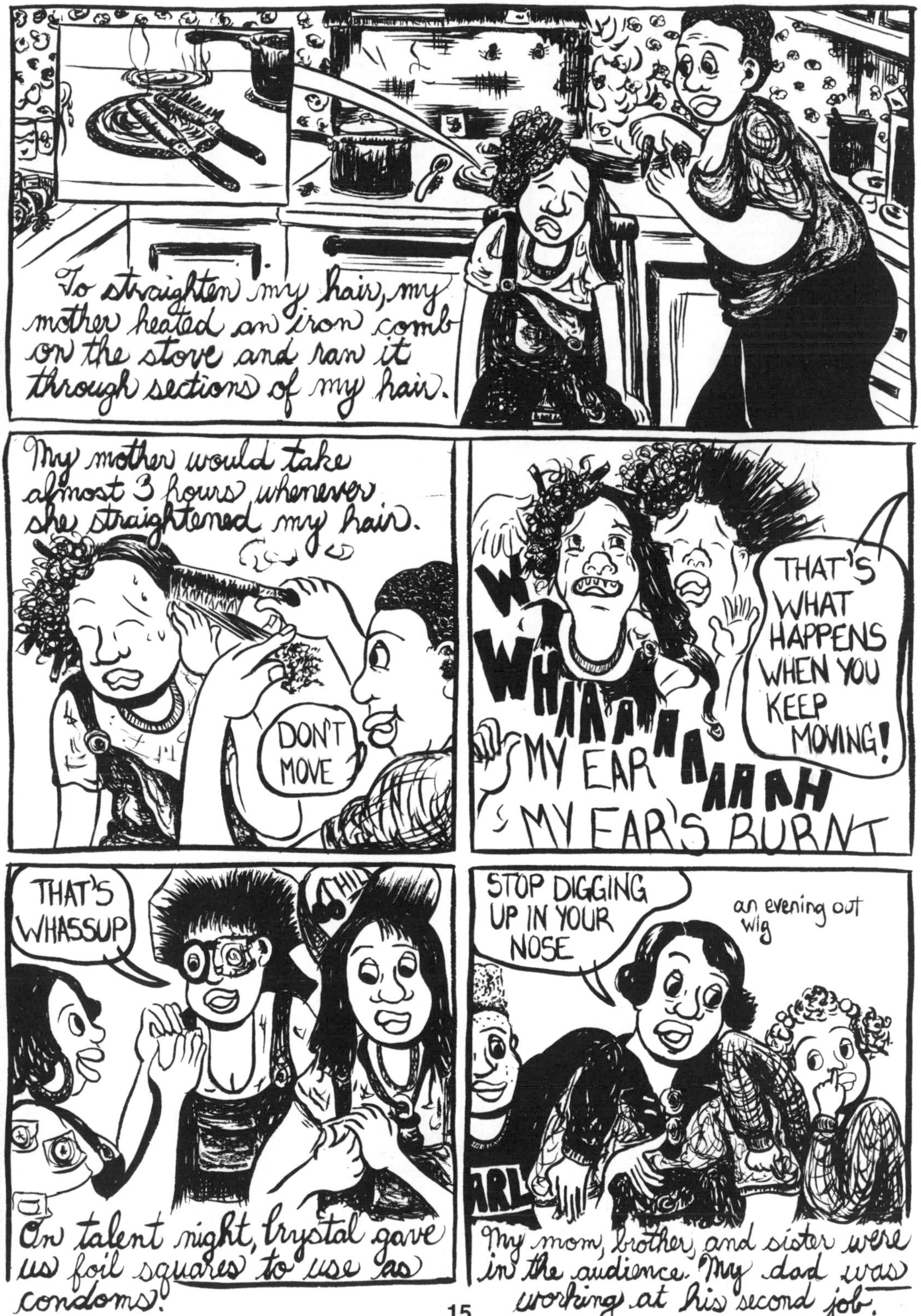
To straighten my hair, my mother heated an iron comb on the stove and ran it through sections of my hair.
My mother would take almost 3 hours whenever she straightened my hair.
DON'T MOVE
WHAAAAAAAAAH
MY EAR
MY EAR'S BURNT
THAT'S WHAT HAPPENS WHEN YOU KEEP MOVING!
THAT'S WHASSUP
On talent night, Crystal gave us foil squares to use as condoms.
STOP DIGGING UP IN YOUR NOSE
an evening out wig
My mom, brother, and sister were in the audience. My dad was working at his second job.

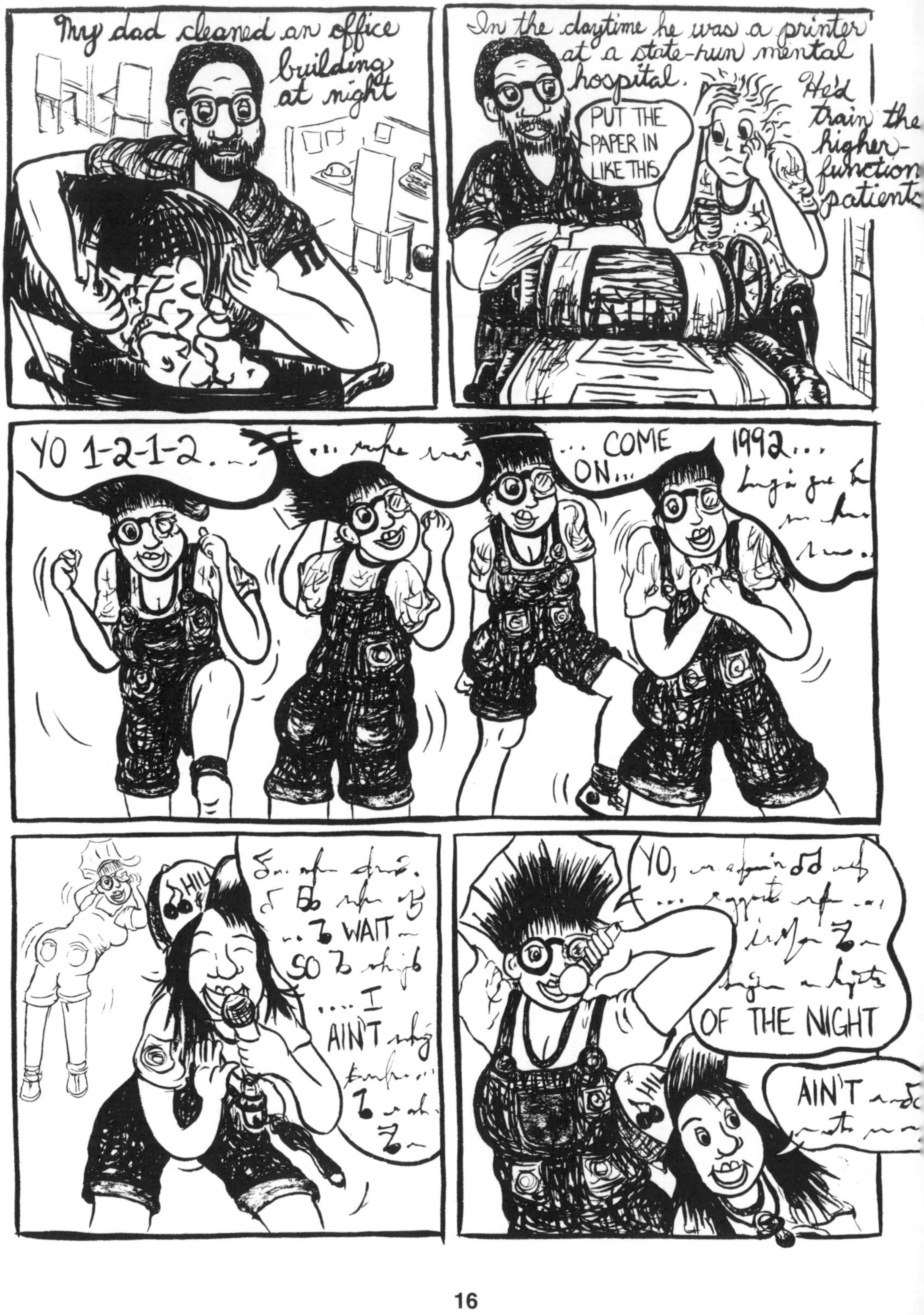
My dad cleaned an office building at night
In the daytime he was a printer at a state-run mental hospital.
PUT THE PAPER IN LIKE THIS
He'd train the higher-function patients
YO 1-2-1-2...
... COME ON...
1992...
WAIT
SO
I
AIN'T
YO,
OF THE NIGHT
AIN'T

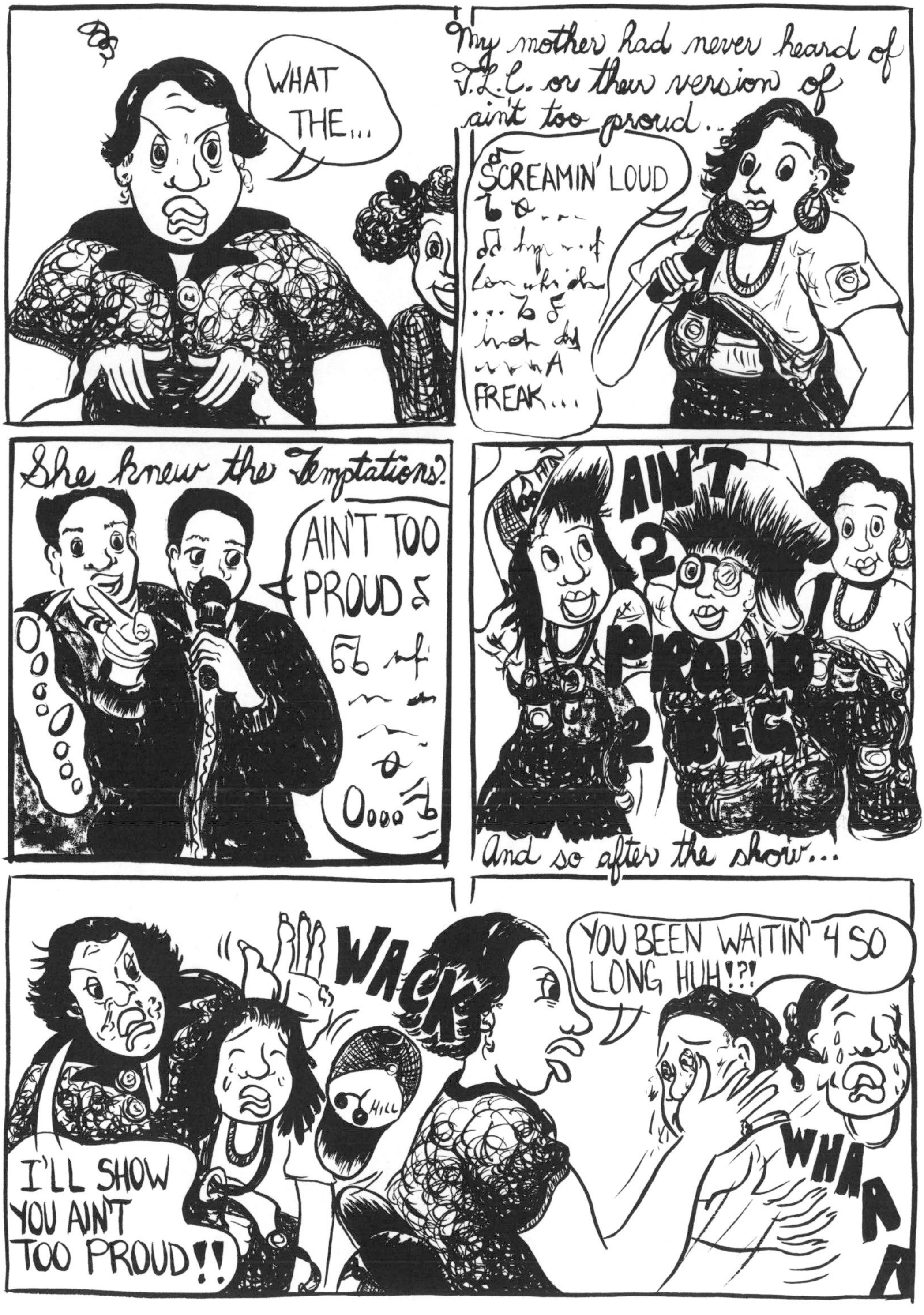
WHAT THE...
My mother had never heard of T.L.C. or their version of ain't too proud...
SCREAMIN' LOUD
FREAK...
She knew the Temptations?
AIN'T TOO PROUD
Oooo
AIN'T 2 PROUD 2 BEG
And so after the show...
WACK
YOU BEEN WAITIN' 4 SO LONG HUH!?!
I'LL SHOW YOU AIN'T TOO PROUD!!
WHAP

And when my dad got home EARLY the next morning..
WACK!
GET YA' BUTT OUTTA BED!
I SHOULD KNOCK YOU...
H.B.F.
GO GET A SWITCH!
HURRY UP! DON'T PICK NO SMALL ONE EITHER!
I'M SORRY I'M SORRY WHAAAA, I'M SORRR
SO YOU THINK YOU GROWN HUH!? TURN 'ROUND!
YOU OK, EB...
PEAS & MURRAY
GO AWAY!
I stopped asking about a perm after the talent show.

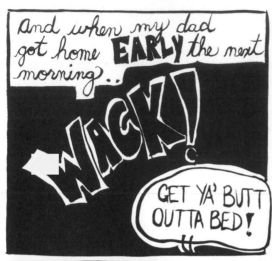

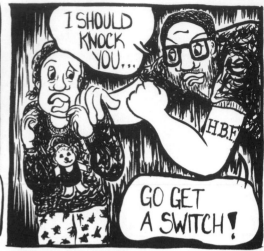

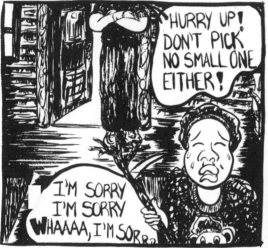

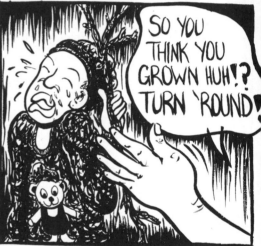

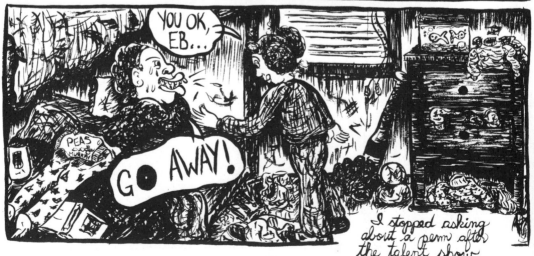

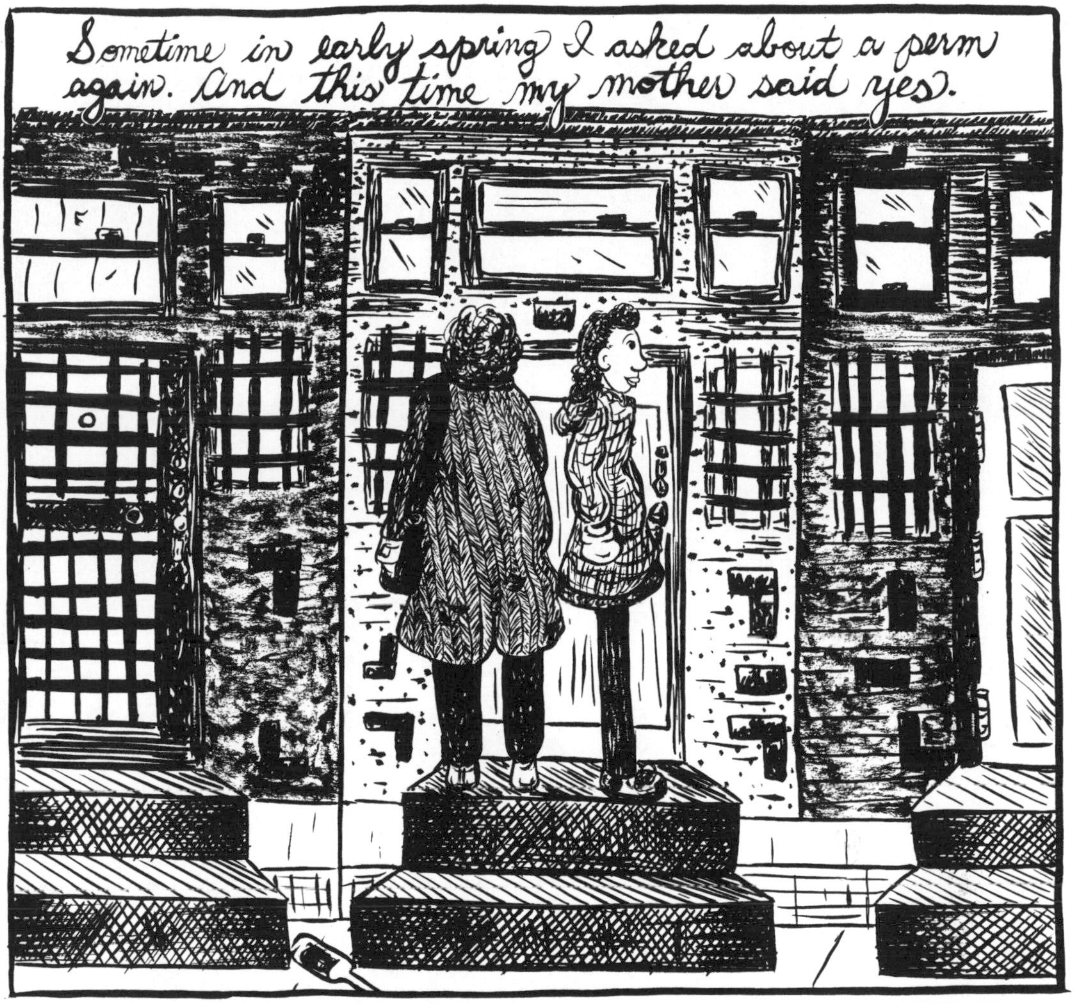
Sometime in early spring I asked about a perm again. And this time my mother said yes.

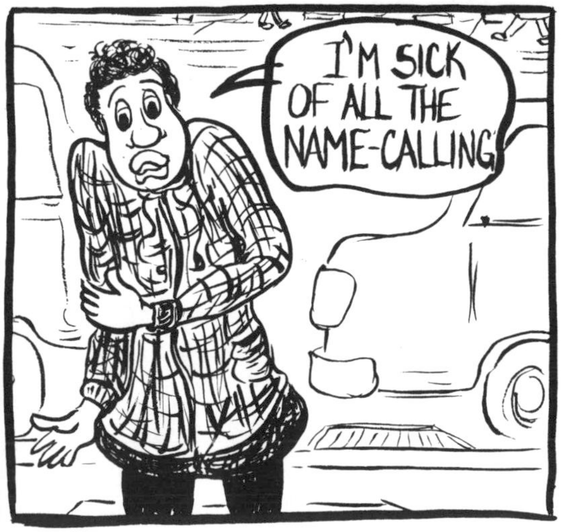
I'M SICK OF ALL THE NAME-CALLING

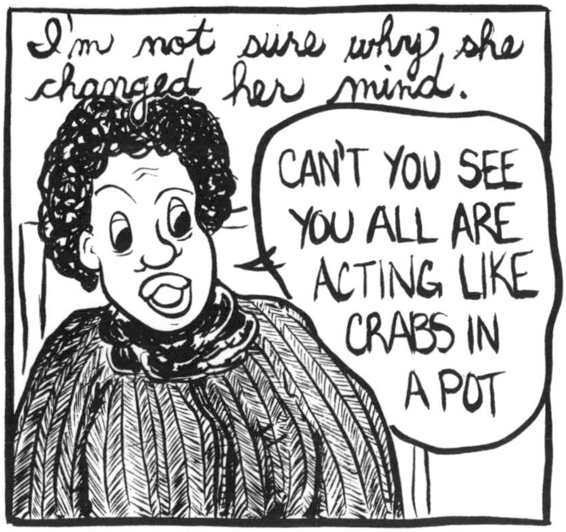
I'm not sure why she changed her mind.
CAN'T YOU SEE YOU ALL ARE ACTING LIKE CRABS IN A POT

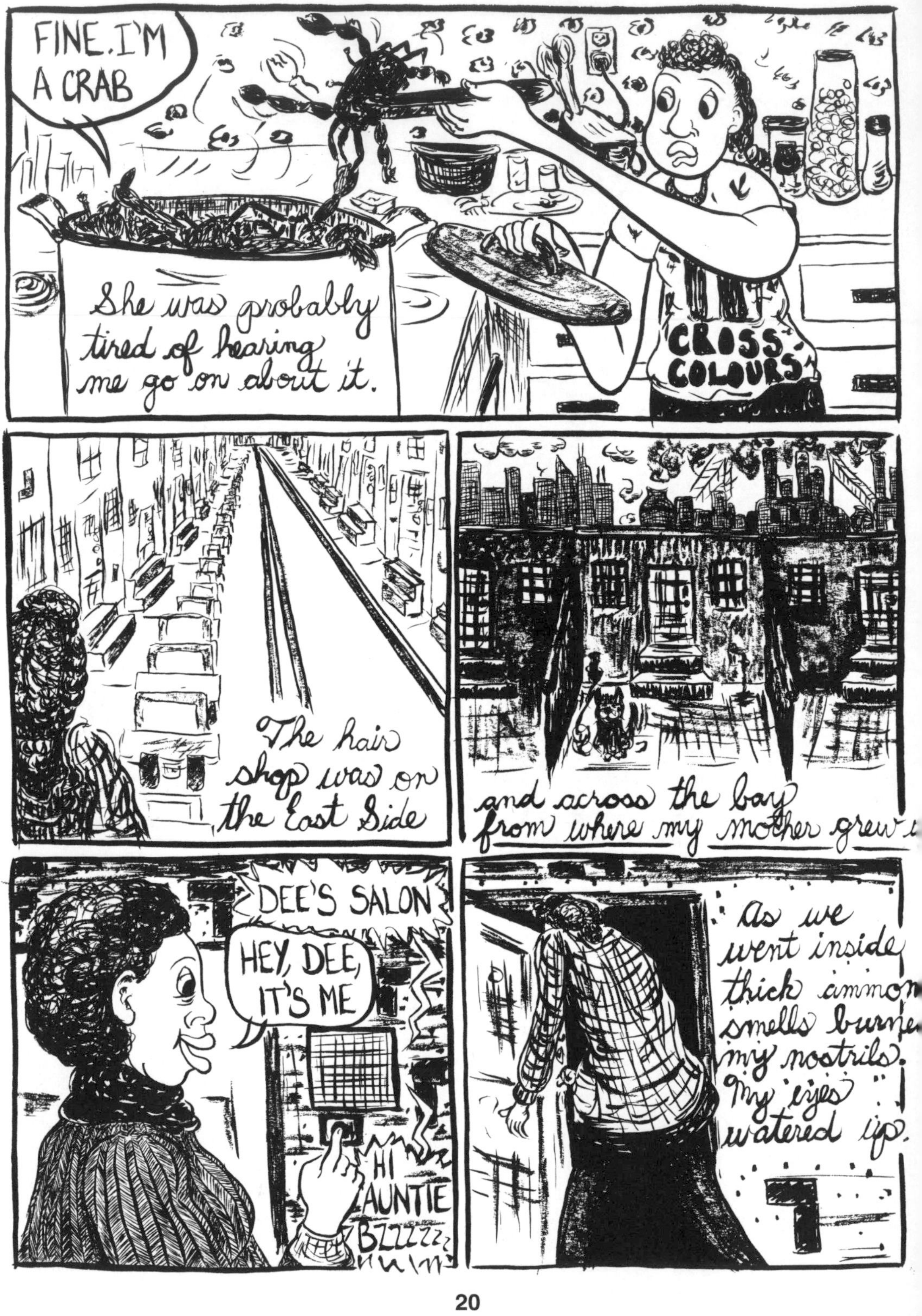
FINE. I'M A CRAB
CROSS COLOURS
She was probably tired of hearing me go on about it.
The hair shop was on the East Side
and across the bay from where my mother grew
DEE'S SALON
HEY, DEE, IT'S ME
HI AUNTIE
BZZZZZZ
As we went inside thick ammon smells burne my nostrils. My eyes watered up.

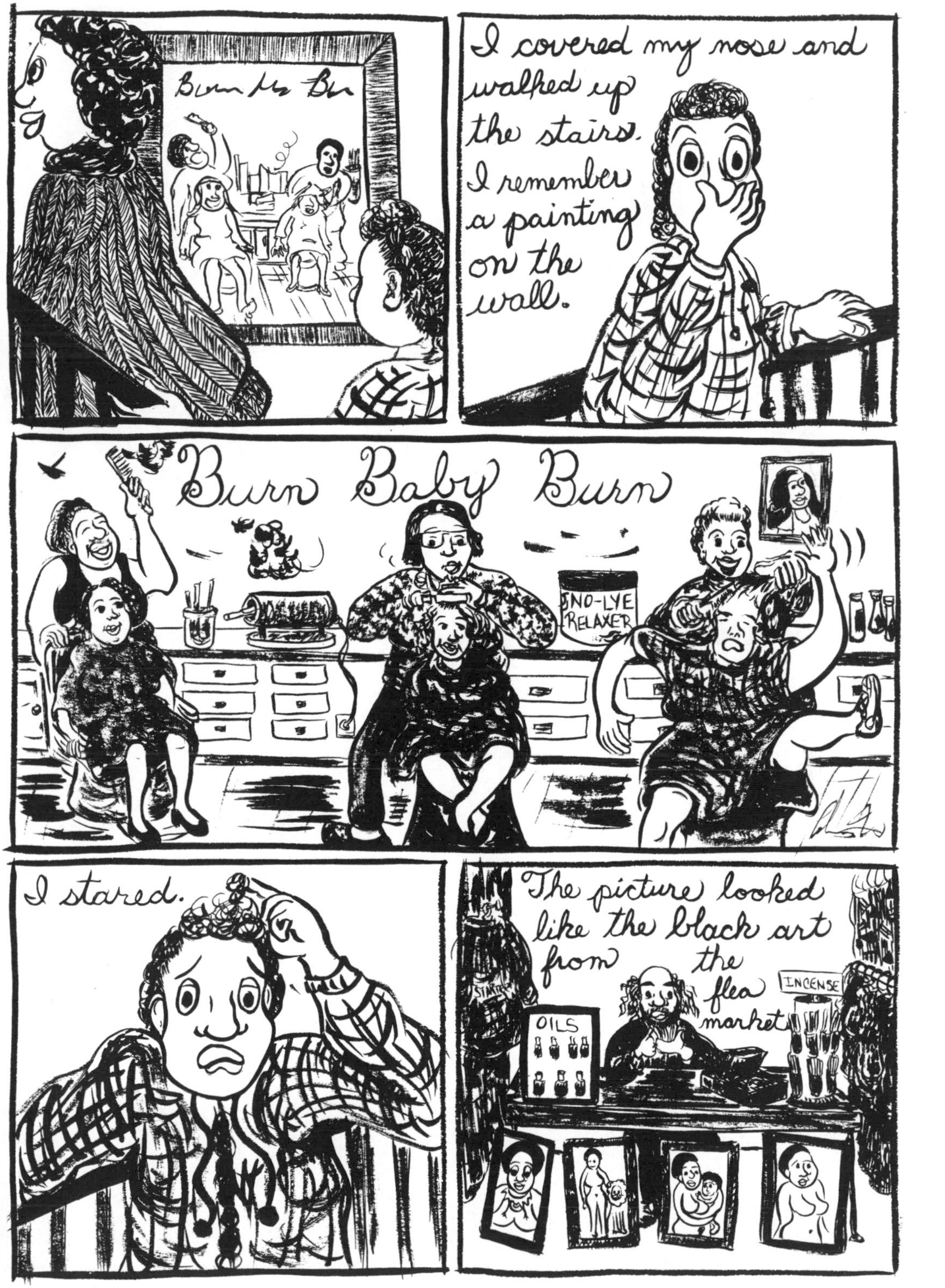
I covered my nose and walked up the stairs. I remember a painting on the wall.
Burn Baby Burn
SNO-LYE RELAXER
I stared.
The picture looked like the black art from the flea market
OILS
INCENSE

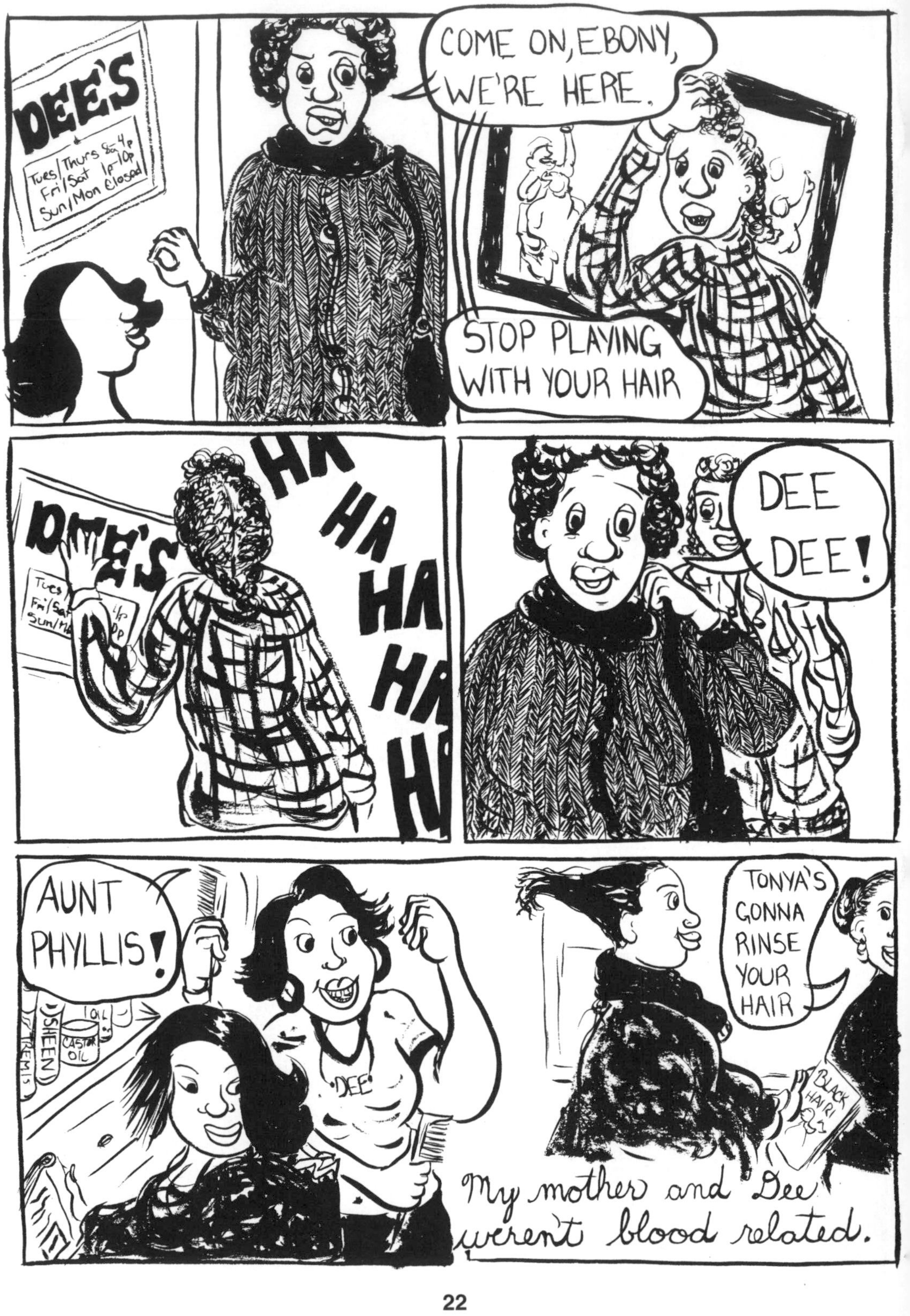
DEE'S
Tues/Thurs 8a-4p
Fri/Sat 1p-10p
Sun/Mon Closed
COME ON, EBONY, WE'RE HERE.
STOP PLAYING WITH YOUR HAIR
HA HA HA HA
DEE DEE!
AUNT PHYLLIS!
SHEEN
CASTOR OIL
OIL
DEE
TONYA'S GONNA RINSE YOUR HAIR
BLACK HAIR
My mother and Dee weren't blood related.

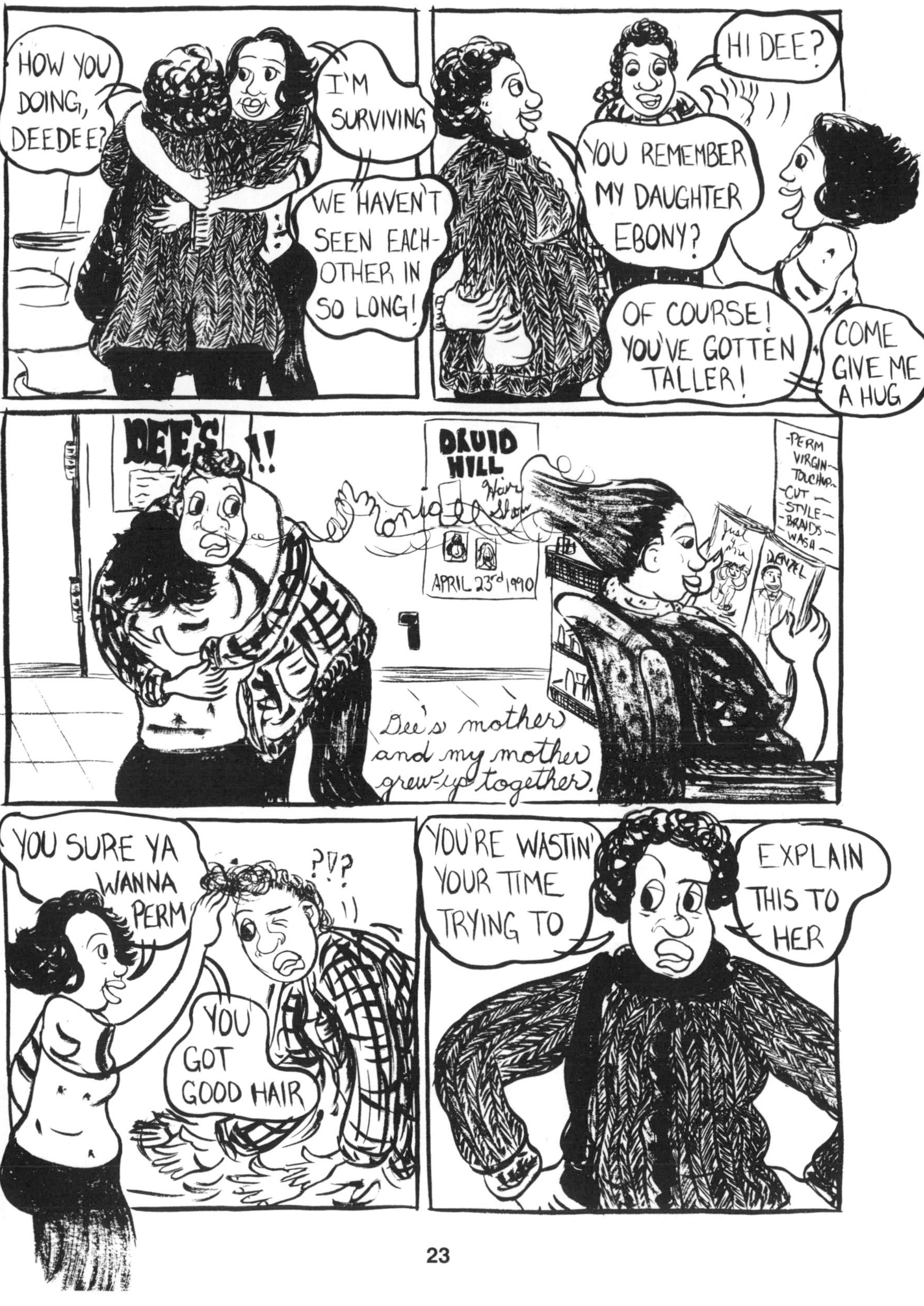
HOW YOU DOING, DEEDEE?
I'M SURVIVING
WE HAVEN'T SEEN EACH-OTHER IN SO LONG!
HI DEE?
YOU REMEMBER MY DAUGHTER EBONY?
OF COURSE! YOU'VE GOTTEN TALLER!
COME GIVE ME A HUG
DEE'S
!!
DRUID HILL Hair Show
APRIL 23rd 1990
-PERM
VIRGIN-
TOUCHUP-
-CUT -
-STYLE-
-BRAIDS-
-WASH -
DENZEL
Dee's mother and my mother grew-up together.
YOU SURE YA WANNA PERM
?!?
YOU GOT GOOD HAIR
YOU'RE WASTIN' YOUR TIME TRYING TO
EXPLAIN THIS TO HER

I BET YOU'RE TENDER-HEADED
I'LL USE THE KIDDY PERM ON YOU
Y'ALL HAVE A SEAT, RELAX AS SOON AS I FINISH MISS ATTACA'S HAIR YOU'RE NEXT
DEE
HOW'S YOUR MOTHE
While my mother talked with Dee...

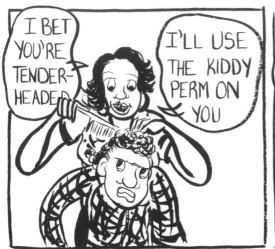

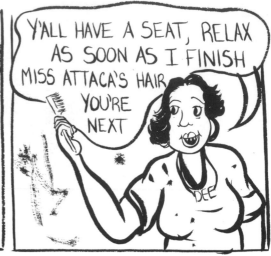

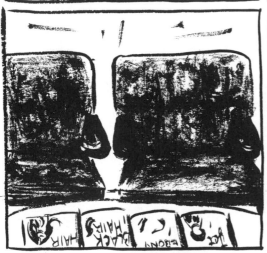

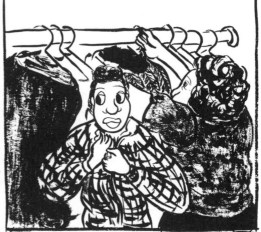

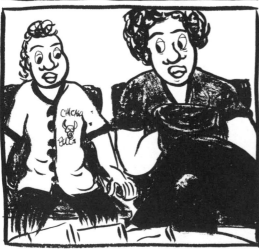

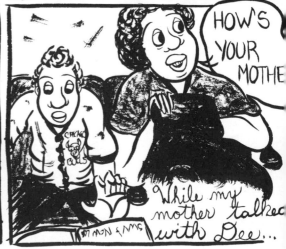

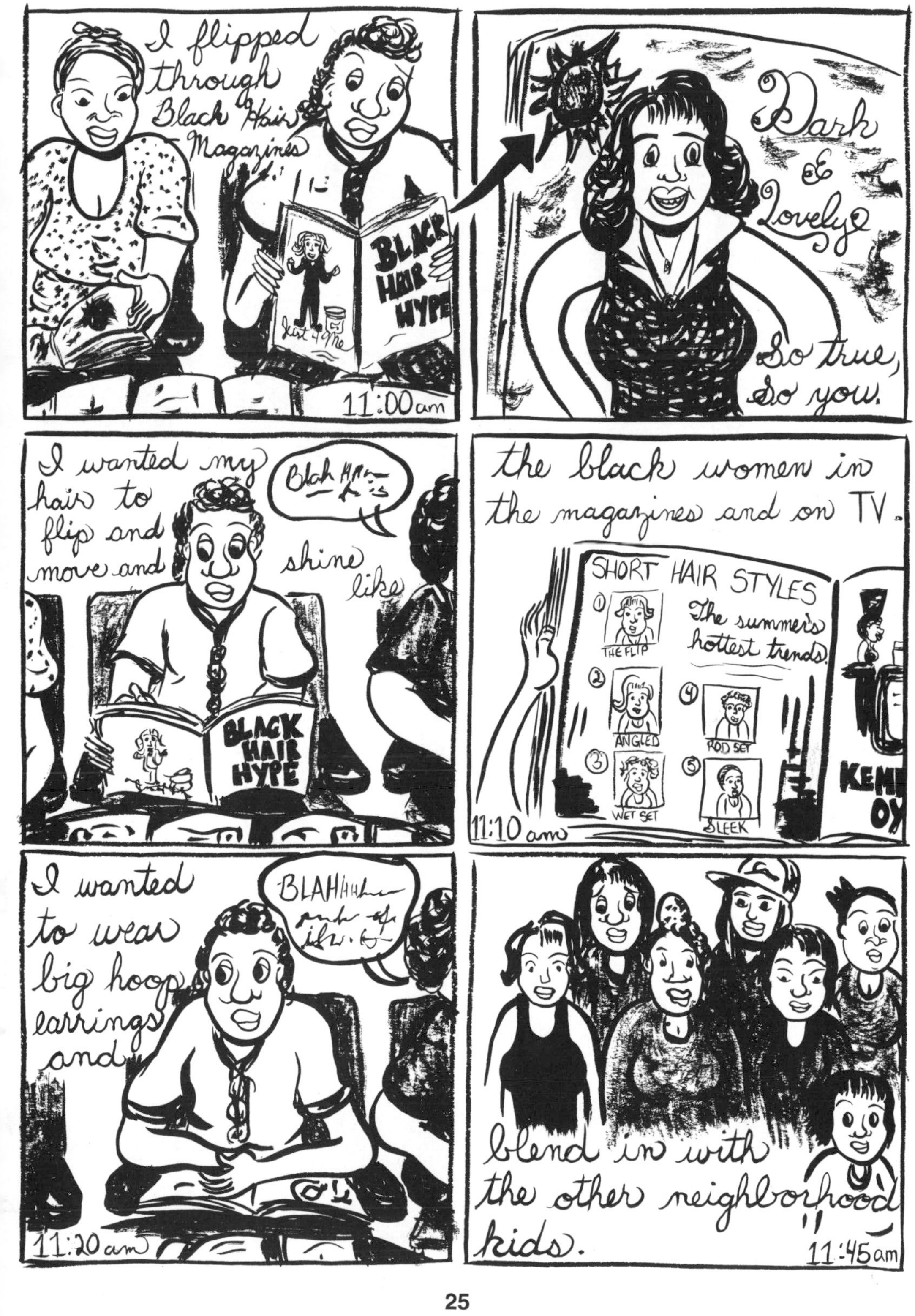
I flipped through Black Hair Magazines
BLACK HAIR HYPE
Just 4 Me
11:00am
Dark & Lovely
So true, So you.
I wanted my hair to flip and move and shine like
BLACK HAIR HYPE
the black women in the magazines and on TV.
SHORT HAIR STYLES
The summer's hottest trends
1 THE FLIP
2 ANGLED
4 ROD SET
3 WET SET
5 SLEEK
11:10 am
I wanted to wear big hoop earrings and
BLAH
11:20 am
blend in with the other neighborhood kids.
11:45am

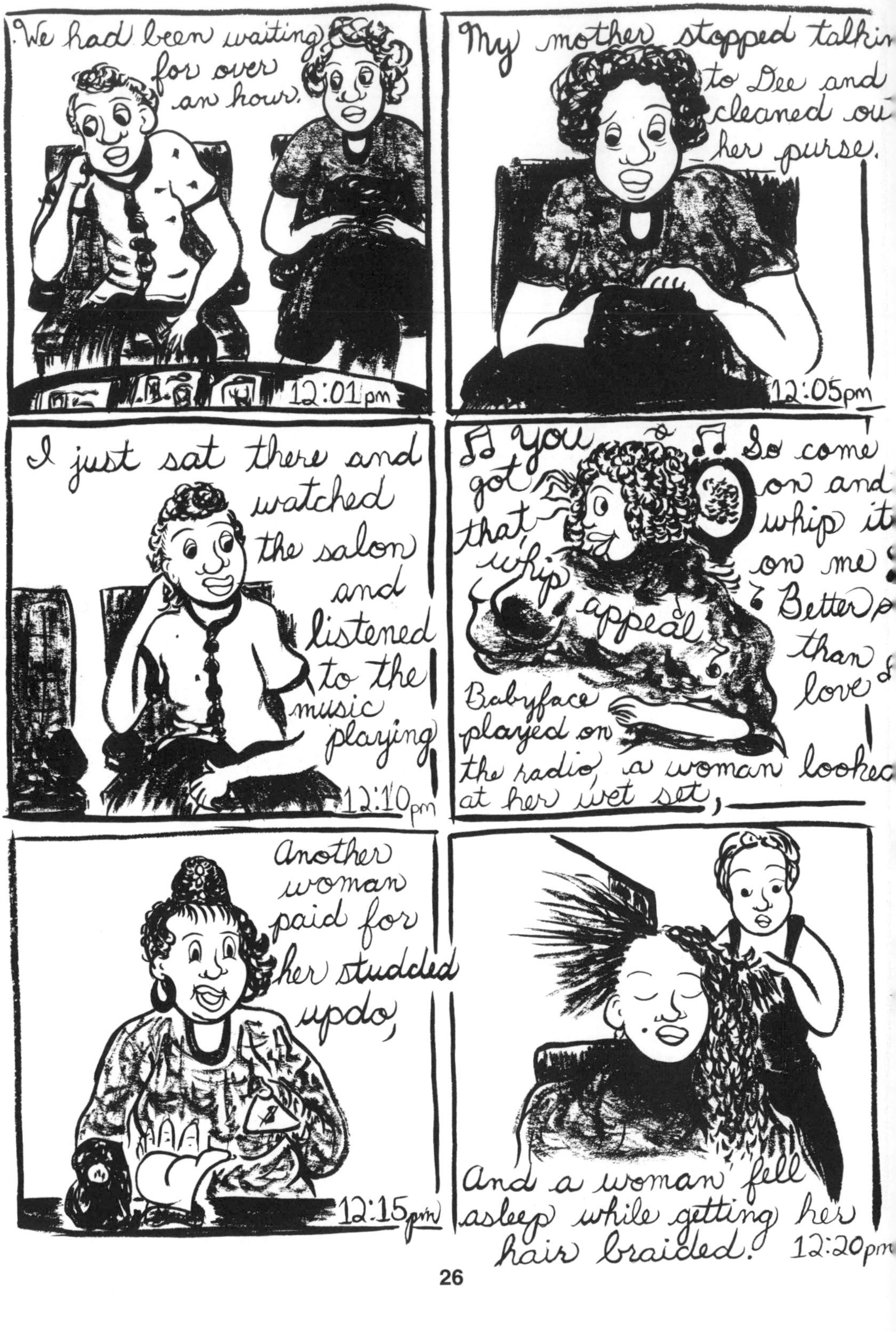
We had been waiting for over an hour.
12:01pm
My mother stopped talkin to Dee and cleaned ou her purse.
12:05pm
I just sat there and watched the salon and listened to the music playing
12:10pm
♫ You got that whip appeal ♫
So come on and whip it on me & Better than love
Babyface played on the radio, a woman looked at her wet set,
another woman paid for her studded updo,
12:15pm
And a woman fell asleep while getting her hair braided.
12:20pm

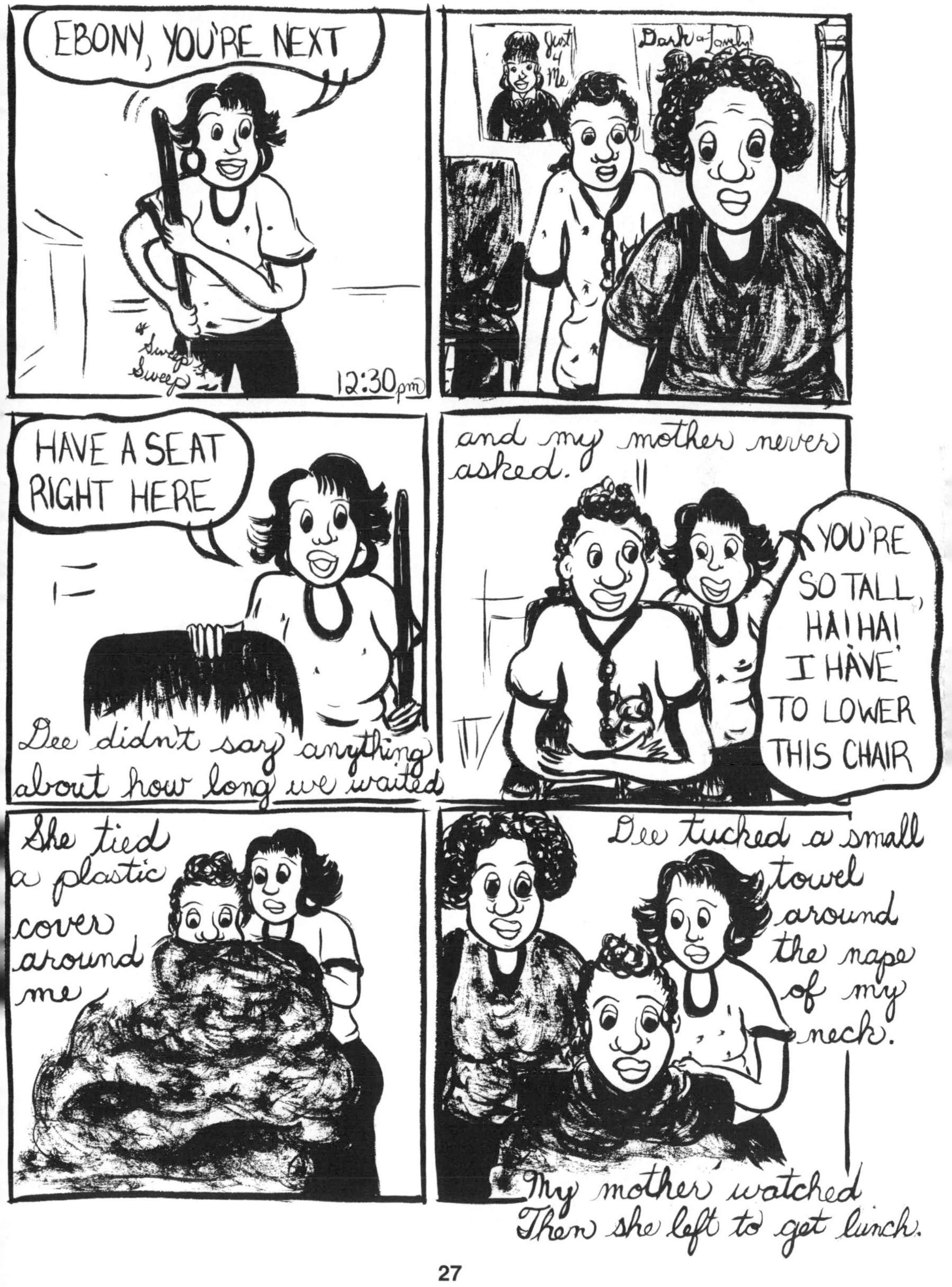
EBONY, YOU'RE NEXT
Sweep Sweep
12:30pm
Just 4 Me
Dark & Lovely
HAVE A SEAT RIGHT HERE
Dee didn't say anything about how long we waited
and my mother never asked.
YOU'RE SO TALL, HA! HA! I HAVE TO LOWER THIS CHAIR
She tied a plastic cover around me
Dee tucked a small towel around the nape of my neck.
My mother watched
Then she left to get lunch.

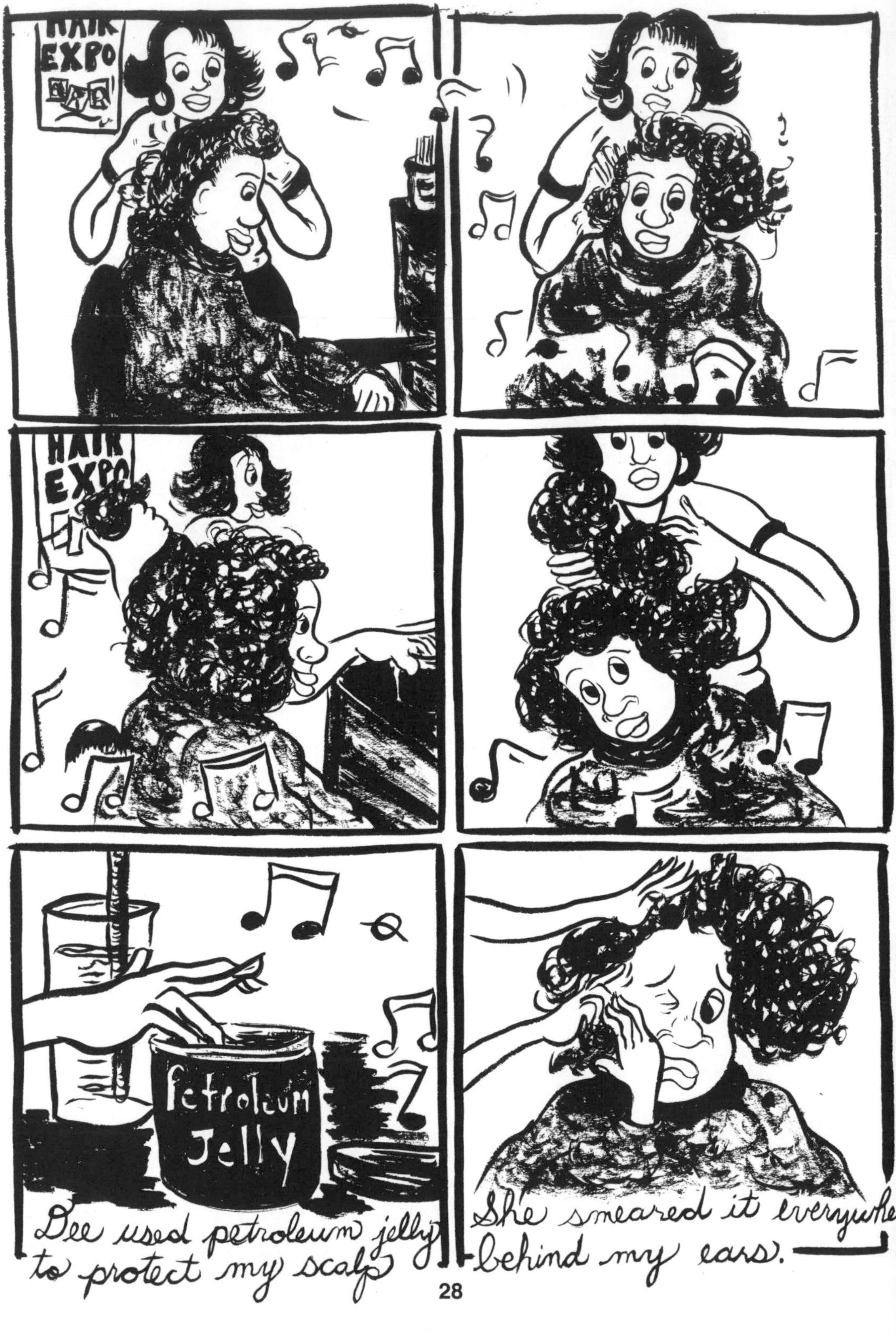
HAIR EXPO
Petroleum Jelly
Dee used petroleum jelly to protect my scalp
She smeared it everywhe
behind my ears.

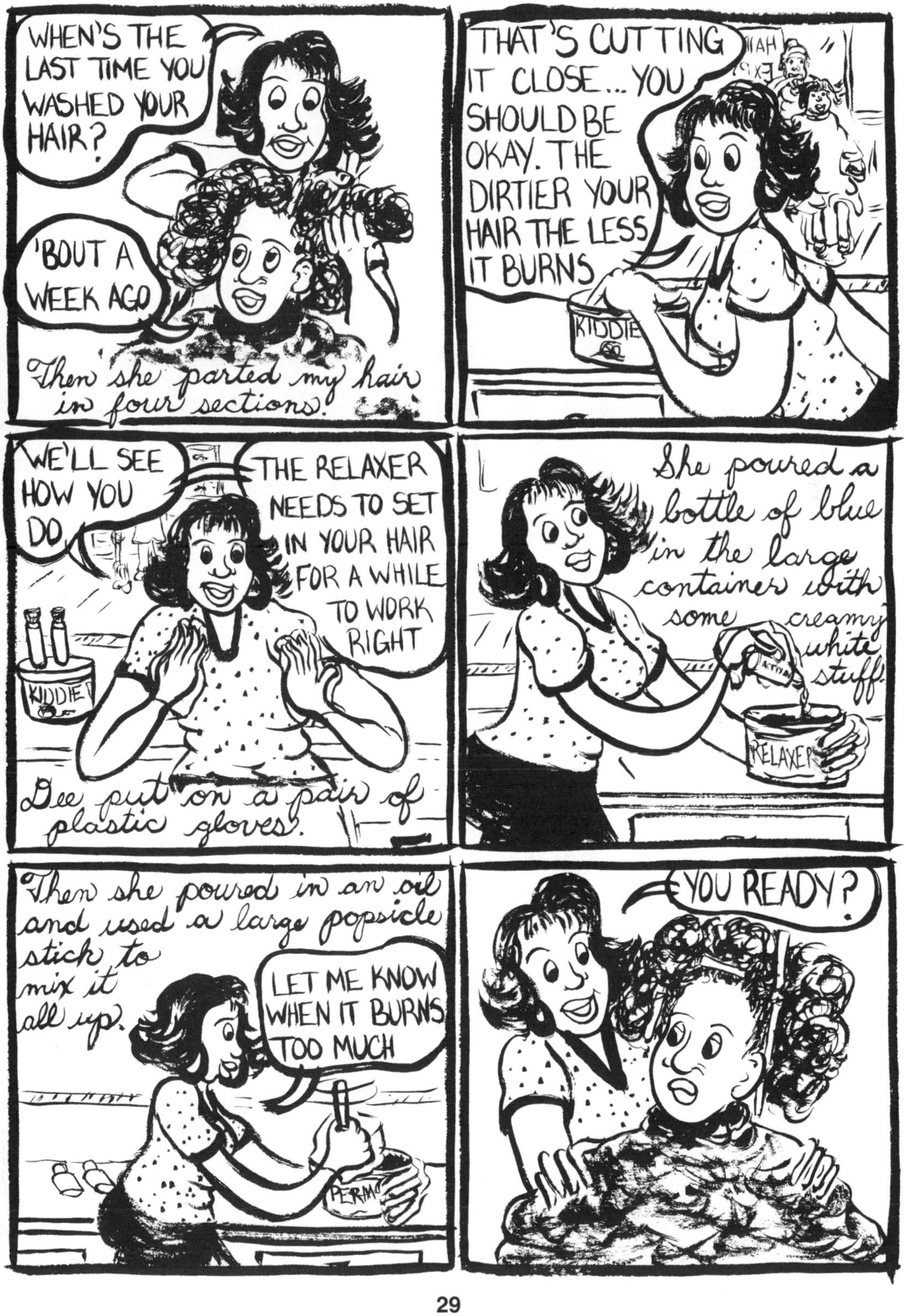
WHEN'S THE LAST TIME YOU WASHED YOUR HAIR?
'BOUT A WEEK AGO
Then she parted my hair in four sections.
THAT'S CUTTING IT CLOSE... YOU SHOULD BE OKAY. THE DIRTIER YOUR HAIR THE LESS IT BURNS
KIDDIE
WE'LL SEE HOW YOU DO.
THE RELAXER NEEDS TO SET IN YOUR HAIR FOR A WHILE TO WORK RIGHT
KIDDIE
Dee put on a pair of plastic gloves.
She poured a bottle of blue in the large container with some creamy white stuff.
RELAXER
Then she poured in an oil and used a large popsicle stick to mix it all up.
LET ME KNOW WHEN IT BURNS TOO MUCH
YOU READY?

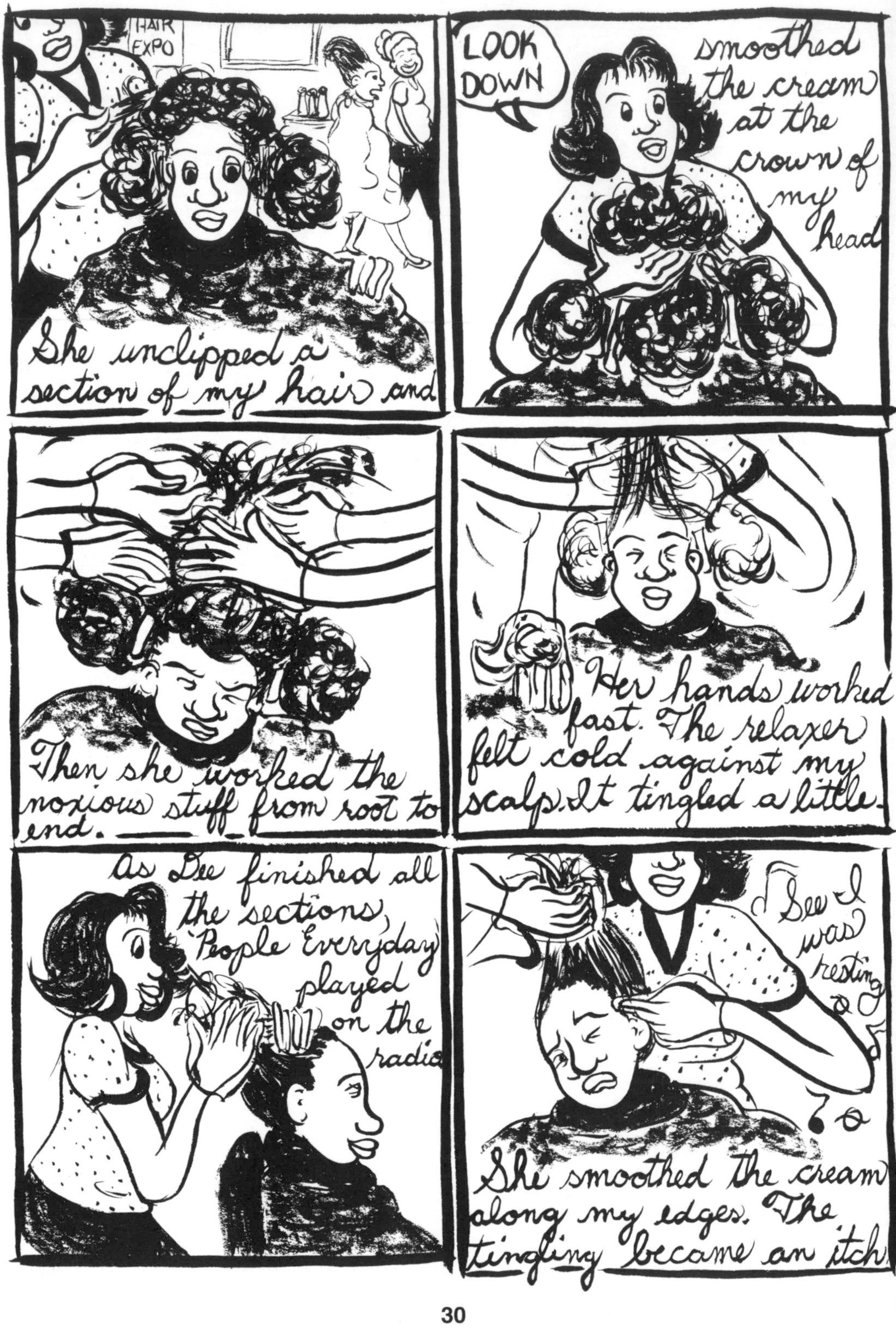
HAIR EXPO
She unclipped a section of my hair and
LOOK DOWN
smoothed the cream at the crown of my head
Then she worked the noxious stuff from root to end.
Her hands worked fast. The relaxer felt cold against my scalp. It tingled a little.
As Dee finished all the sections, "People Everyday" played on the radio
See I was resting
She smoothed the cream along my edges. The tingling became an itch

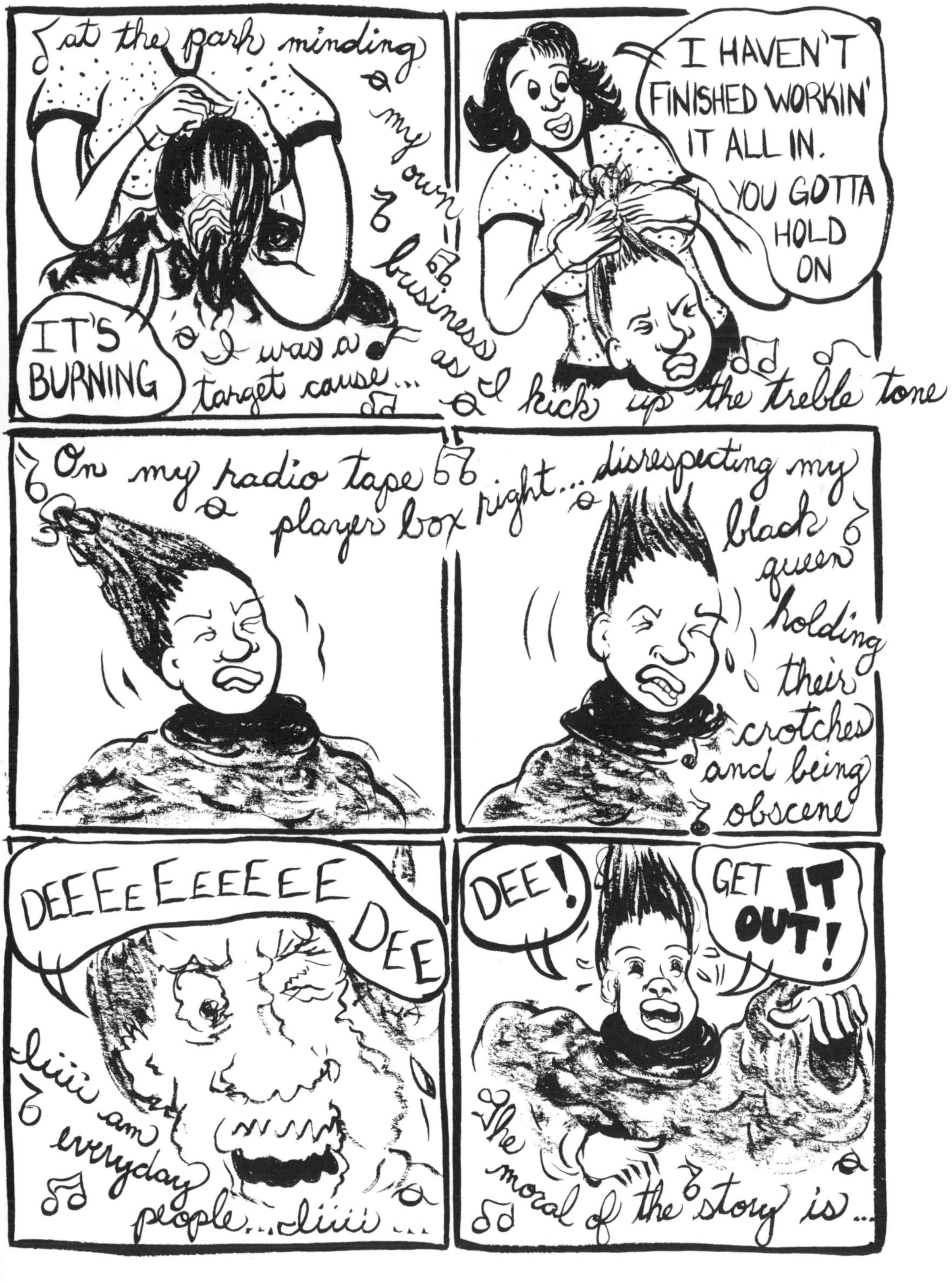
at the park minding my own business
IT'S BURNING
I was a target cause...
as I kick up the treble tone
I HAVEN'T FINISHED WORKIN' IT ALL IN. YOU GOTTA HOLD ON
On my radio tape player box right... disrespecting my black queen holding their crotches and being obscene
DEEEeEEEEEE DEE
liiii am everyday people... liiii...
DEE!
GET IT OUT!
The moral of the story is...

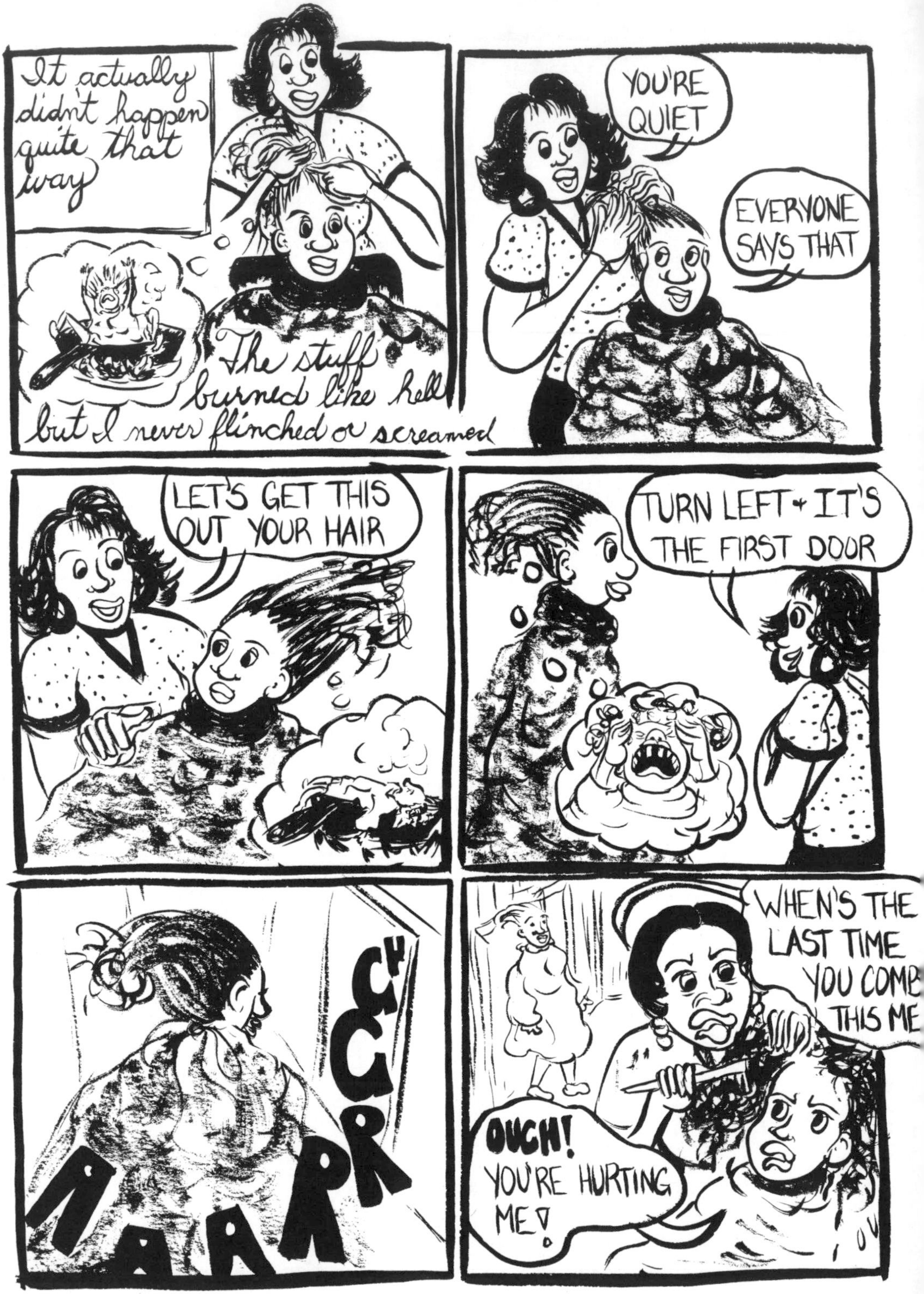

It actually didn't happen quite that way
The stuff burned like hell but I never flinched or screamed
YOU'RE QUIET
EVERYONE SAYS THAT
LET'S GET THIS OUT YOUR HAIR
TURN LEFT + IT'S THE FIRST DOOR
NARRRGGCH
WHEN'S THE LAST TIME YOU COMB THIS ME
OUCH! YOU'RE HURTING ME!

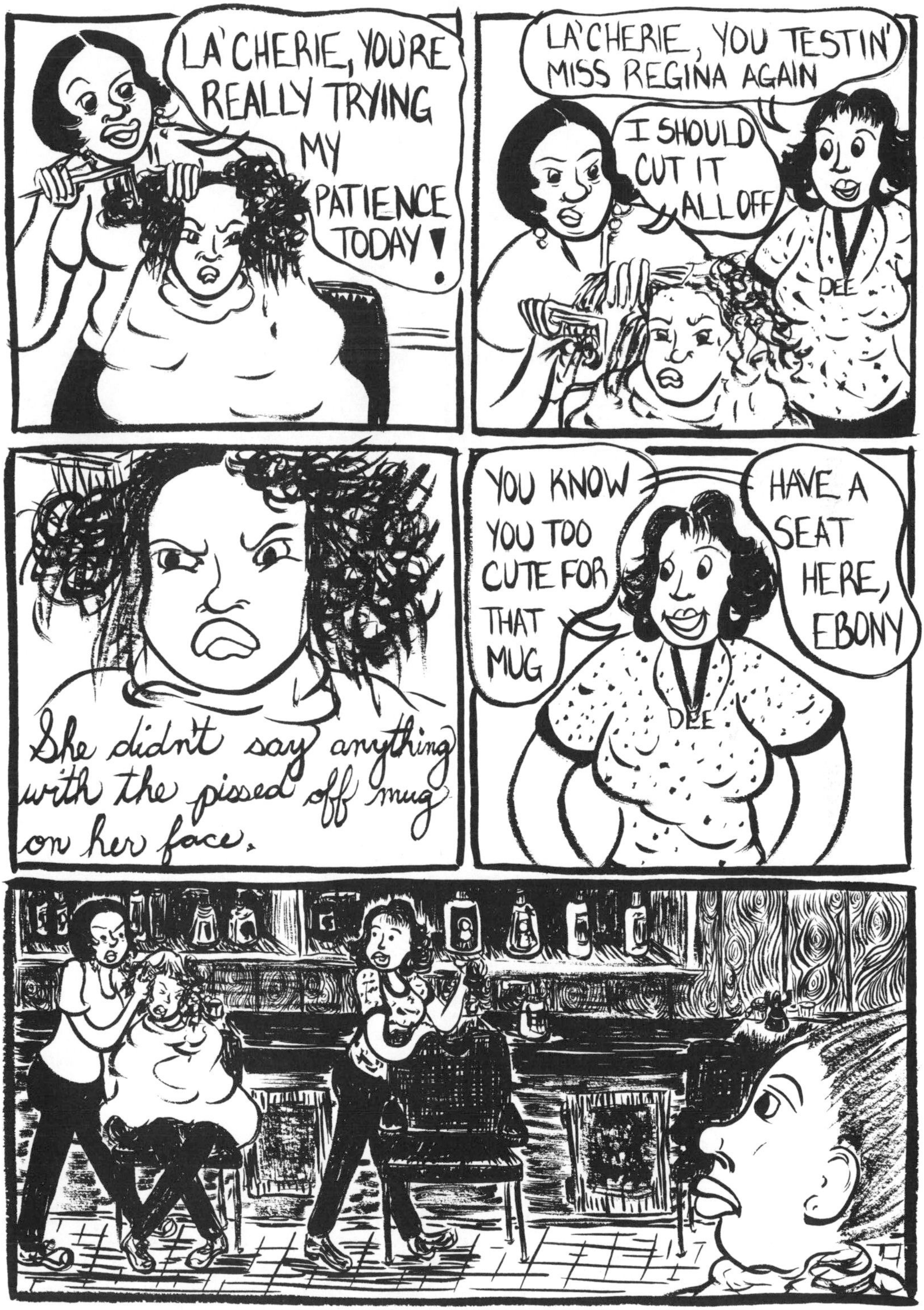
LA'CHERIE, YOU'RE REALLY TRYING MY PATIENCE TODAY!
LA'CHERIE, YOU TESTIN' MISS REGINA AGAIN
I SHOULD CUT IT ALL OFF
DEE
She didn't say anything with the pissed off mug on her face.
YOU KNOW YOU TOO CUTE FOR THAT MUG
HAVE A SEAT HERE, EBONY
DEE

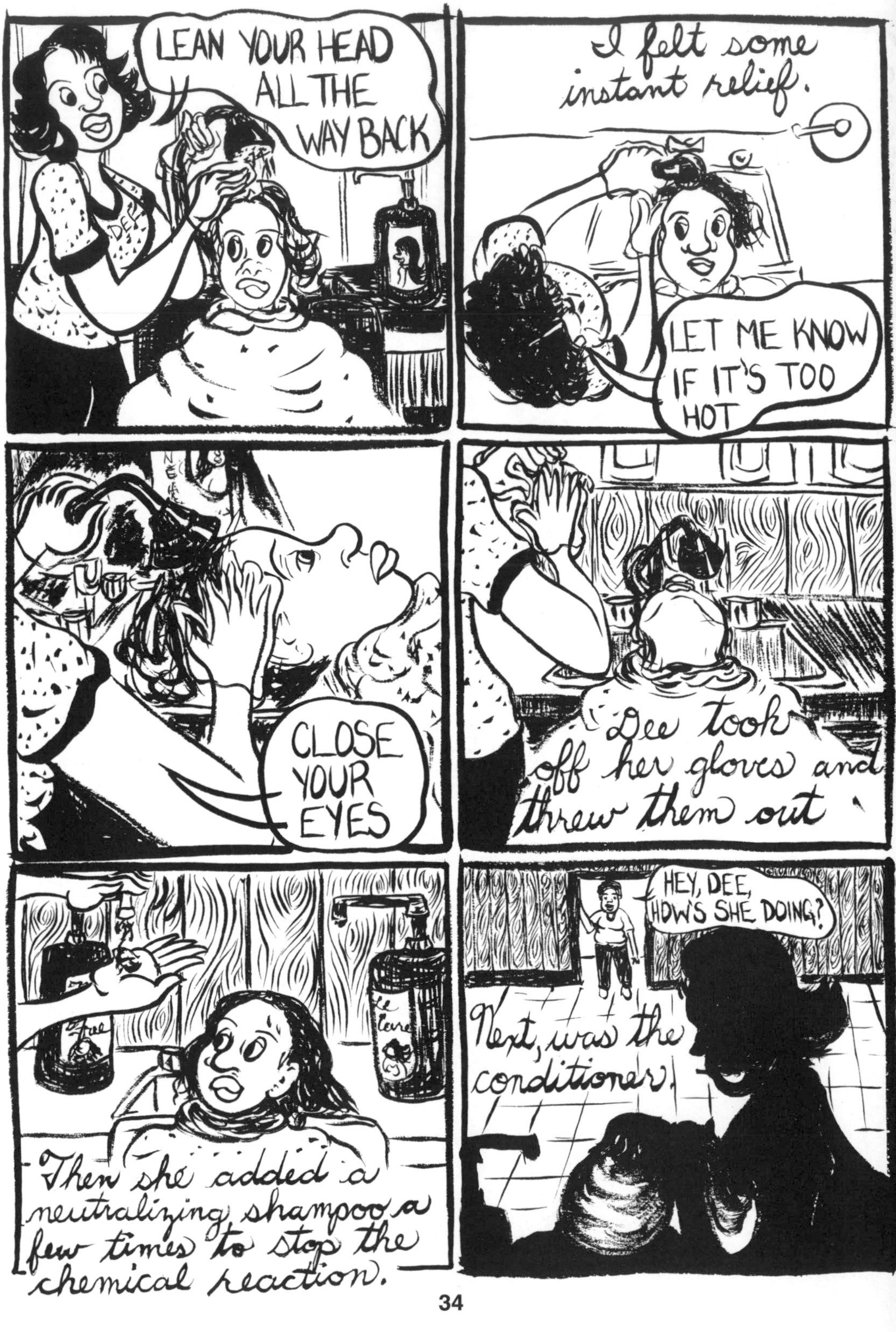
LEAN YOUR HEAD ALL THE WAY BACK
I felt some instant relief.
LET ME KNOW IF IT'S TOO HOT
CLOSE YOUR EYES
Dee took off her gloves and threw them out
Then she added a neutralizing shampoo a few times to stop the chemical reaction.
HEY, DEE, HOW'S SHE DOING?
Next, was the conditioner.

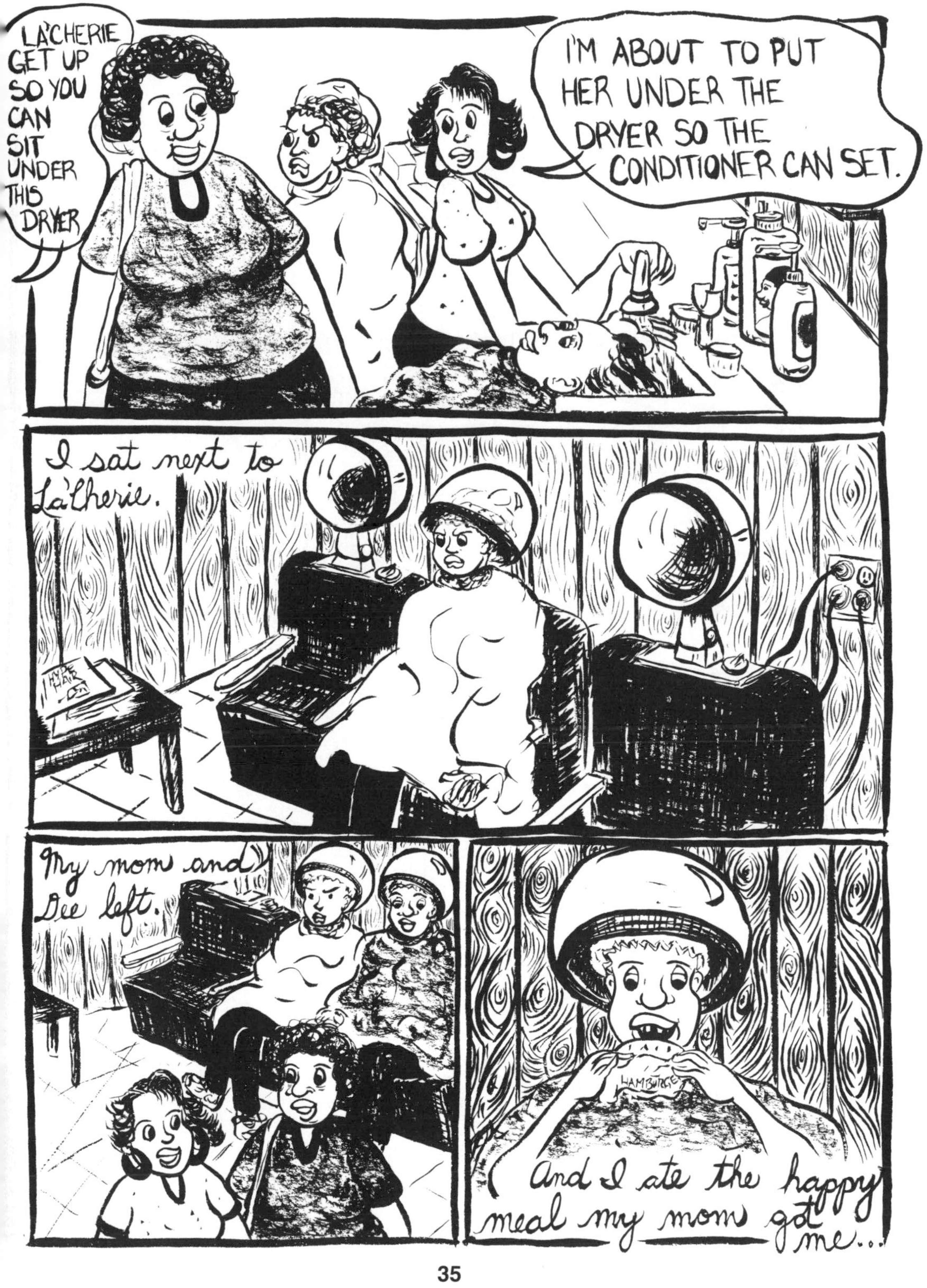
LA'CHERIE GET UP SO YOU CAN SIT UNDER THIS DRYER
I'M ABOUT TO PUT HER UNDER THE DRYER SO THE CONDITIONER CAN SET.
I sat next to La'Cherie.
My mom and Dee left.
And I ate the happy meal my mom got me...

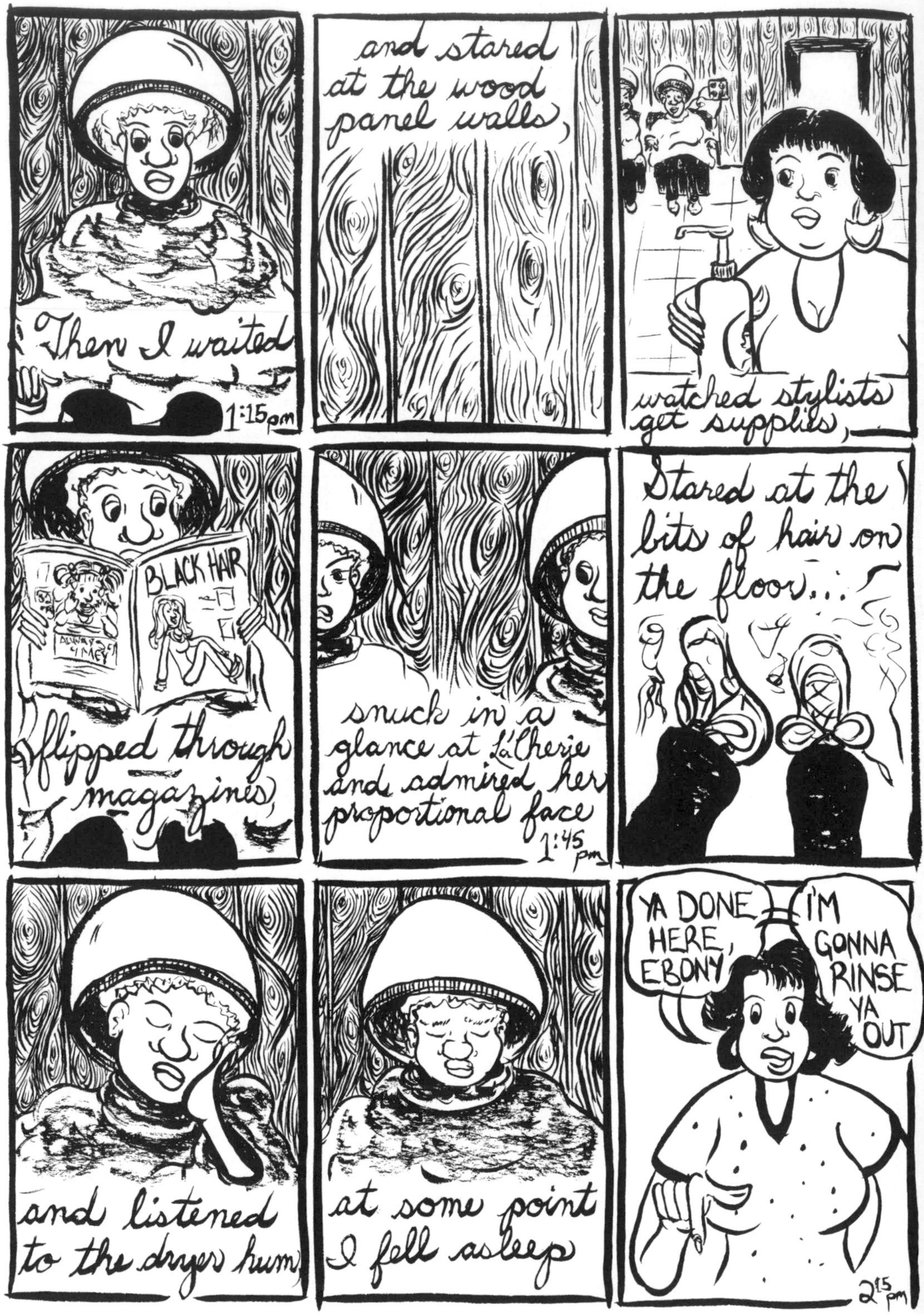
Then I waited
1:15pm
and stared at the wood panel walls,
watched stylists get supplies,
BLACK HAIR
flipped through magazines,
snuck in a glance at LaCherie and admired her proportional face
1:45pm
Stared at the bits of hair on the floor...
and listened to the dryer hum
at some point I fell asleep
YA DONE HERE, EBONY
I'M GONNA RINSE YA OUT
2:15pm

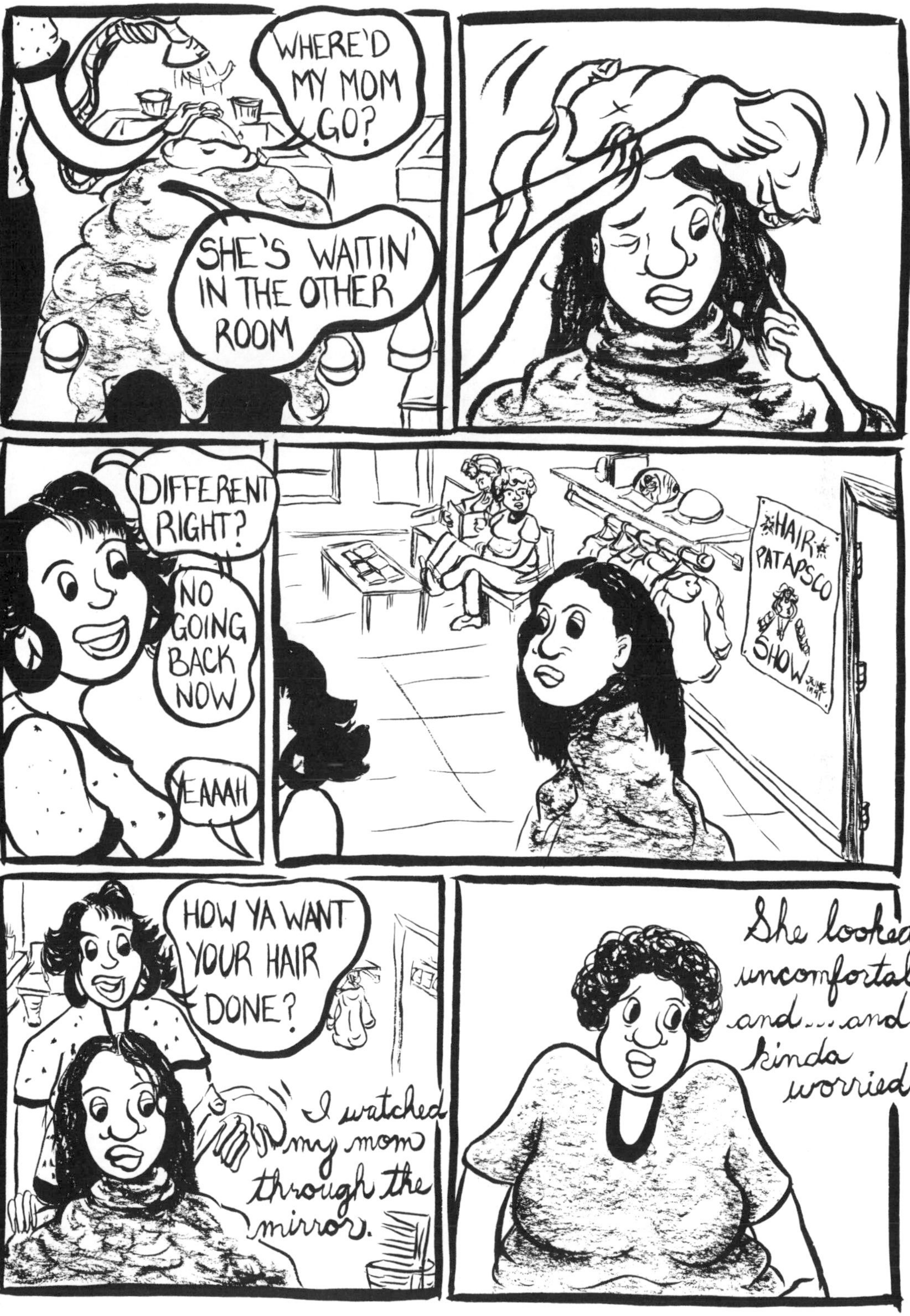

WHERE'D MY MOM GO?
SHE'S WAITIN' IN THE OTHER ROOM
DIFFERENT RIGHT?
NO GOING BACK NOW
YEAAAH
HAIR PATAPSCO SHOW
HOW YA WANT YOUR HAIR DONE?
I watched my mom through the mirror.
She looked uncomfortable and... and kinda worried

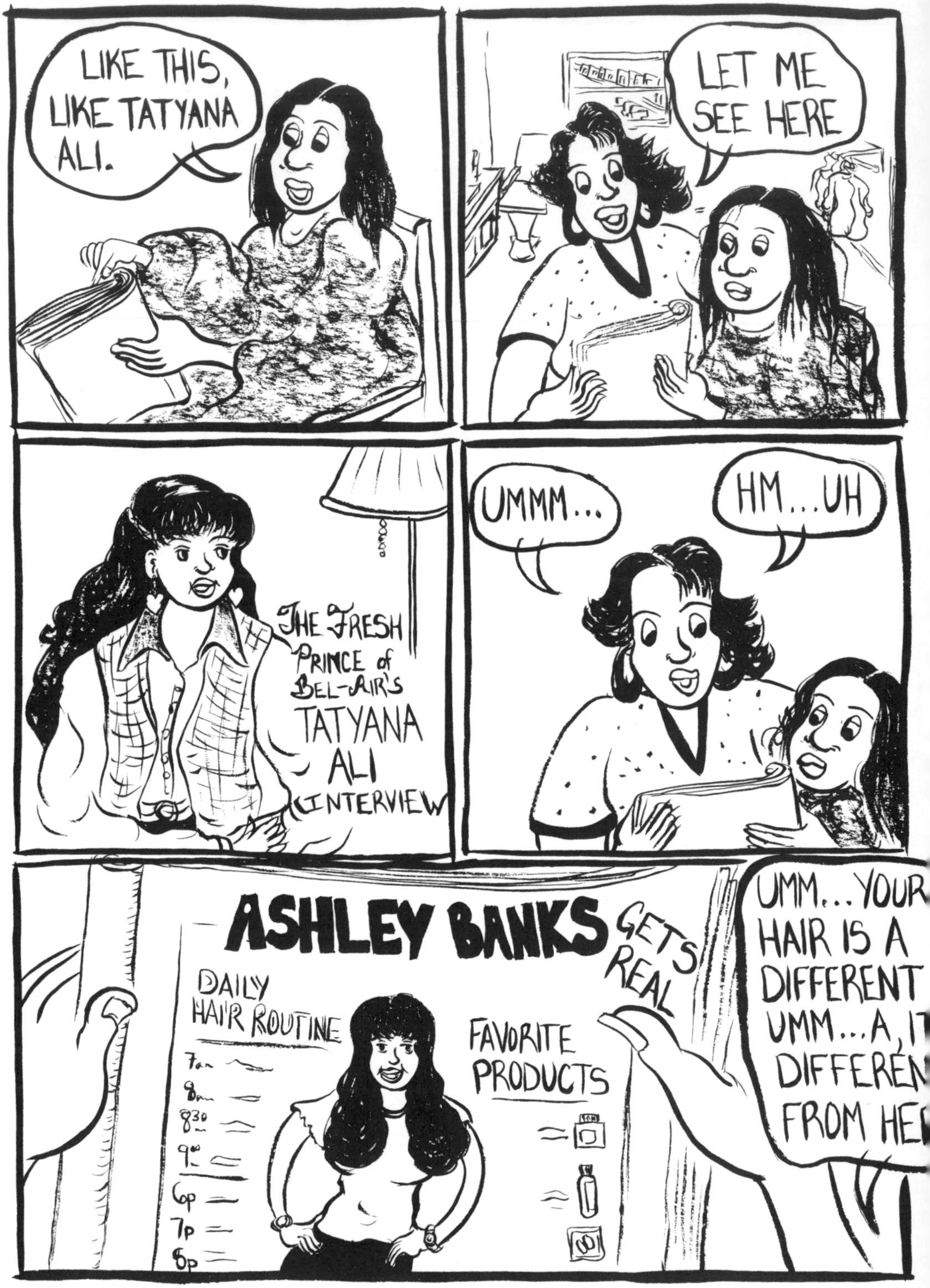
LIKE THIS, LIKE TATYANA ALI.
LET ME SEE HERE
THE FRESH PRINCE of BEL-AIR'S TATYANA ALI INTERVIEW
UMMM...
HM...UH
ASHLEY BANKS GETS REAL
DAILY HAIR ROUTINE
FAVORITE PRODUCTS
UMM... YOUR HAIR IS A DIFFERENT UMM...A, IT DIFFEREN FROM HE

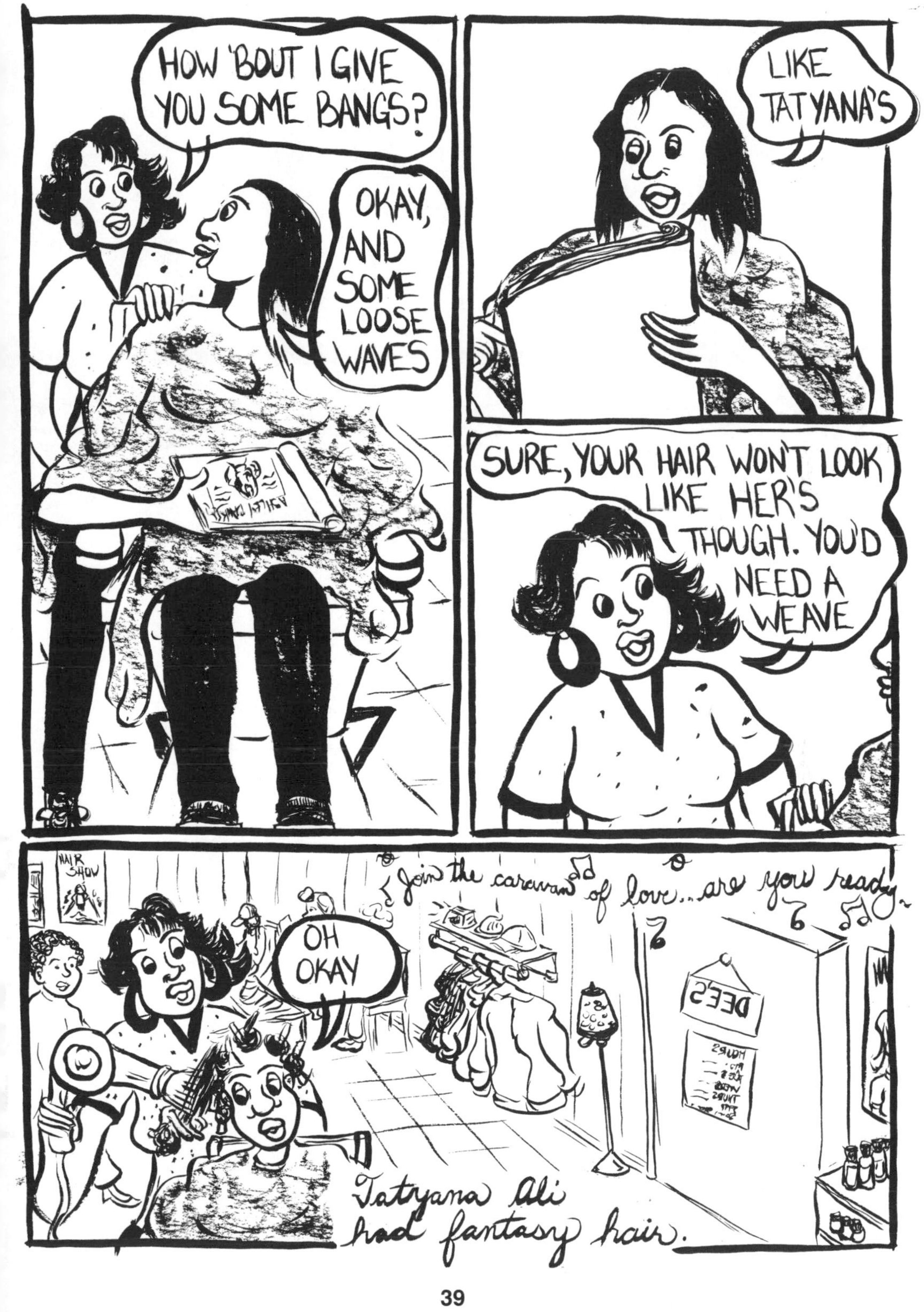
HOW 'BOUT I GIVE YOU SOME BANGS?
OKAY, AND SOME LOOSE WAVES
LIKE TATYANA'S
SURE, YOUR HAIR WON'T LOOK LIKE HER'S THOUGH. YOU'D NEED A WEAVE
HAIR SHOW
join the caravan of love... are you ready
OH OKAY
Tatyana Ali had fantasy hair.

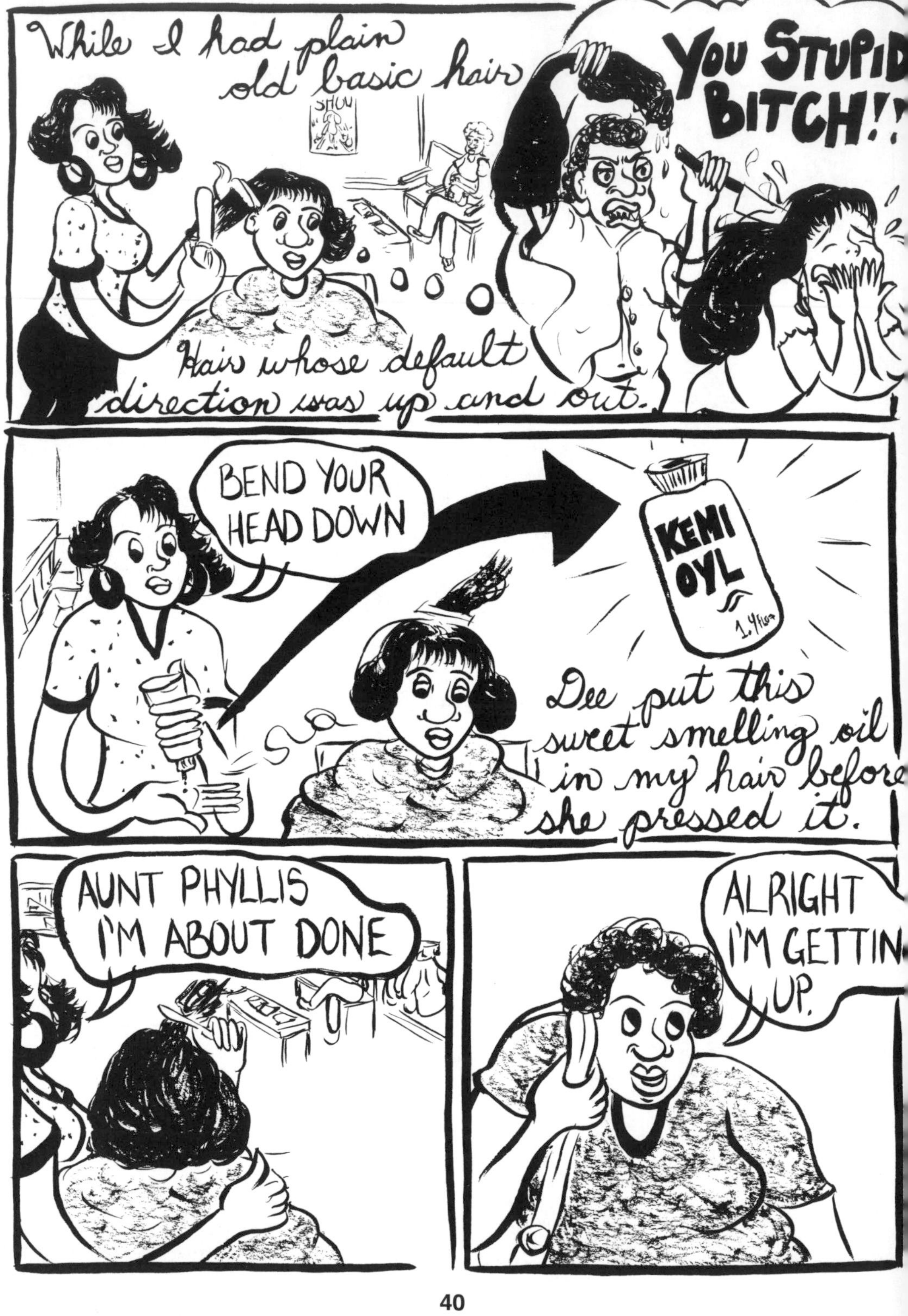
While I had plain old basic hair
SHOW
YOU STUPID BITCH!!
Hair whose default direction was up and out.
BEND YOUR HEAD DOWN
KEMI OYL
Dee put this sweet smelling oil in my hair before she pressed it.
AUNT PHYLLIS I'M ABOUT DONE
ALRIGHT I'M GETTIN UP.

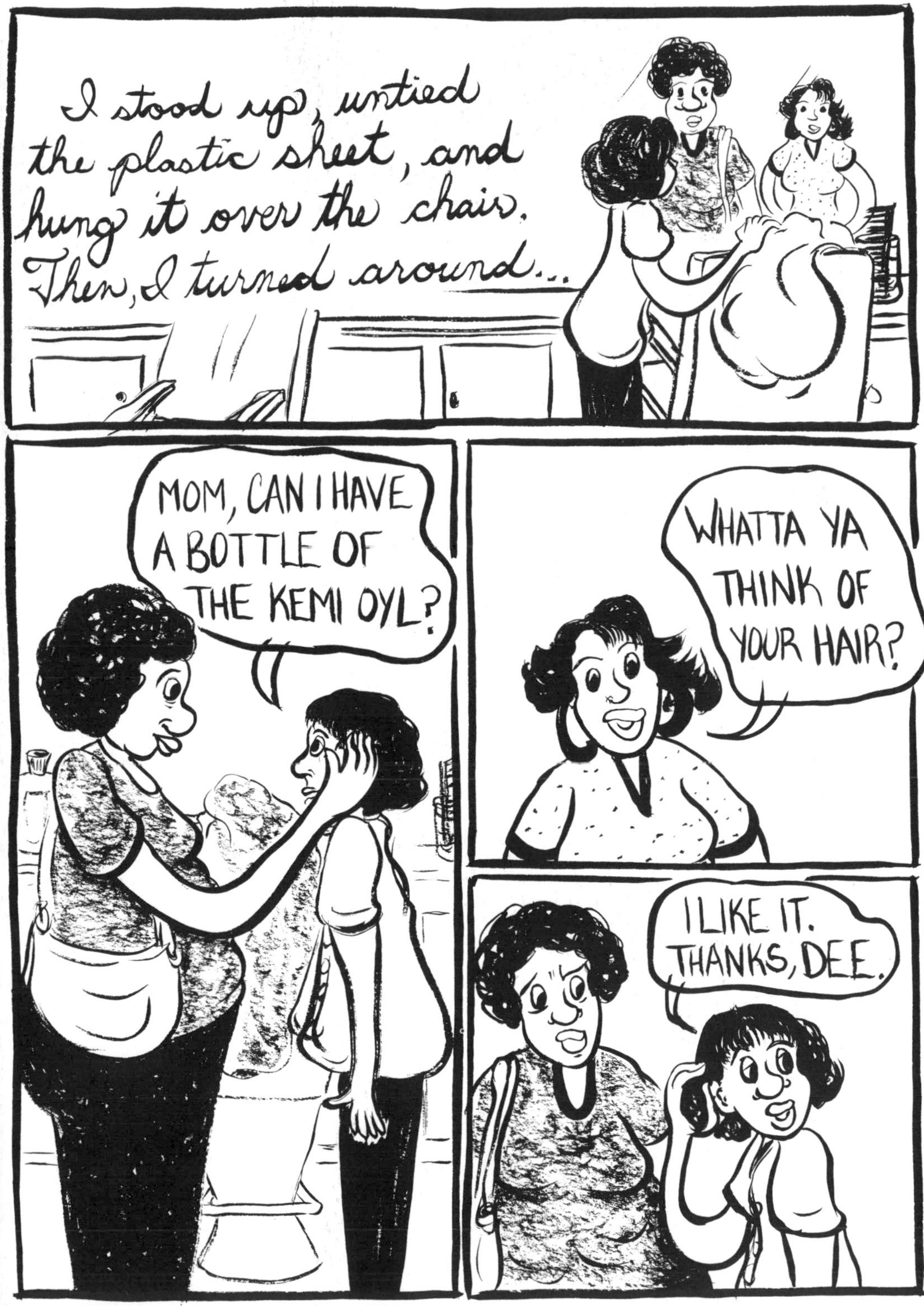
I stood up, untied the plastic sheet, and hung it over the chair. Then, I turned around...
MOM, CAN I HAVE A BOTTLE OF THE KEMI OYL?
WHATTA YA THINK OF YOUR HAIR?
I LIKE IT. THANKS, DEE.

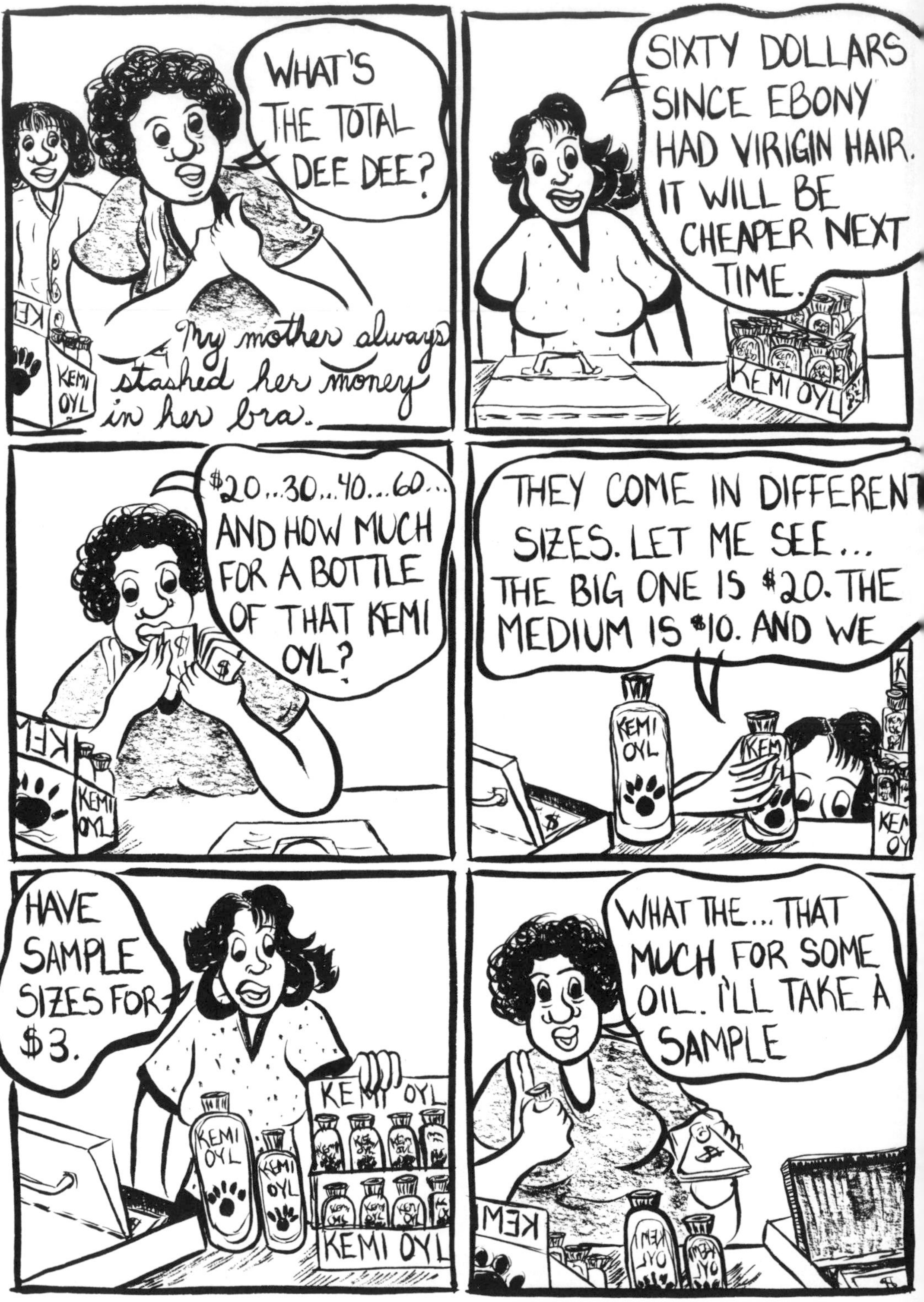
WHAT'S THE TOTAL DEE DEE?
KEMI OYL
My mother always stashed her money in her bra.
SIXTY DOLLARS SINCE EBONY HAD VIRIGIN HAIR. IT WILL BE CHEAPER NEXT TIME.
KEMI OYL
$20...30...40...60... AND HOW MUCH FOR A BOTTLE OF THAT KEMI OYL?
KEMI OYL
THEY COME IN DIFFERENT SIZES. LET ME SEE... THE BIG ONE IS $20. THE MEDIUM IS $10. AND WE
KEMI OYL
HAVE SAMPLE SIZES FOR $3.
KEMI OYL
WHAT THE... THAT MUCH FOR SOME OIL. I'LL TAKE A SAMPLE

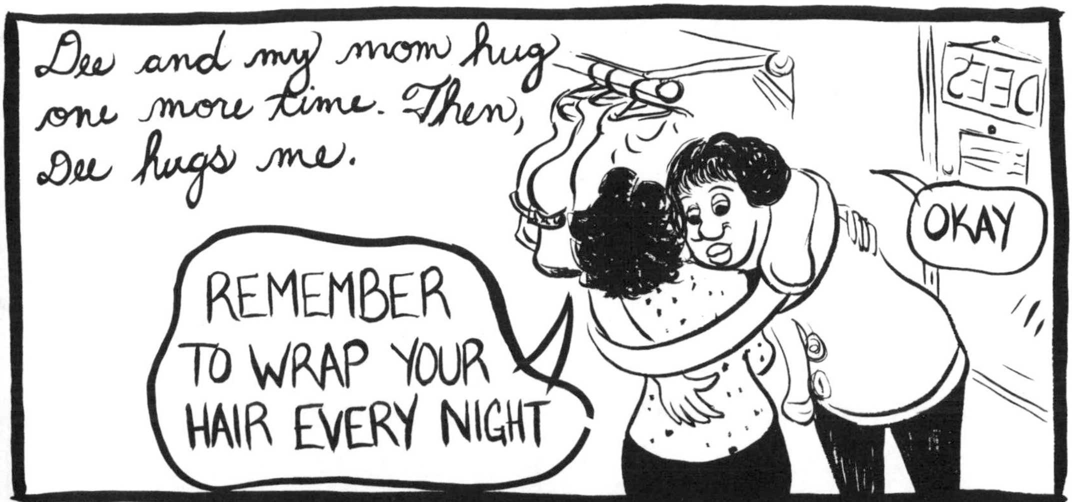
Dee and my mom hug one more time. Then, Dee hugs me.
OKAY
REMEMBER TO WRAP YOUR HAIR EVERY NIGHT
DEES

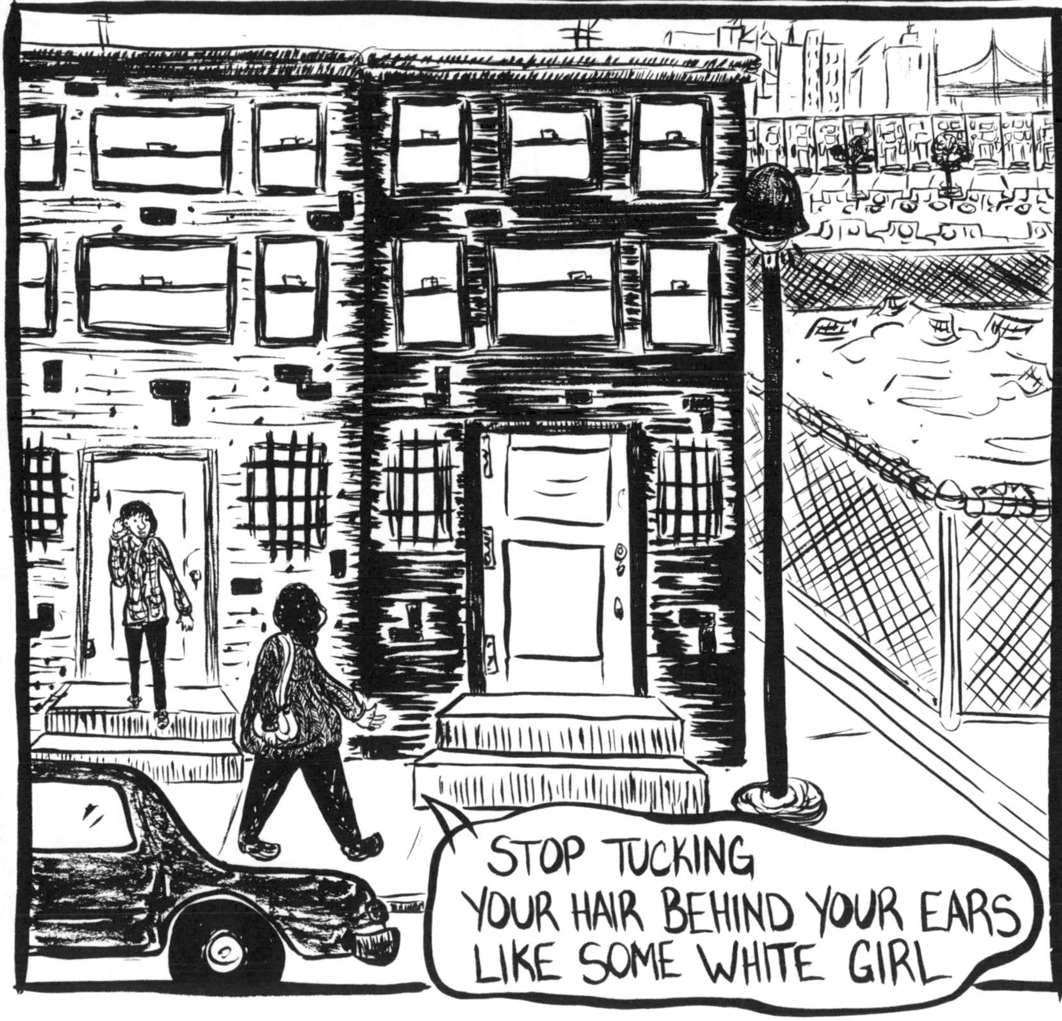
STOP TUCKING YOUR HAIR BEHIND YOUR EARS LIKE SOME WHITE GIRL

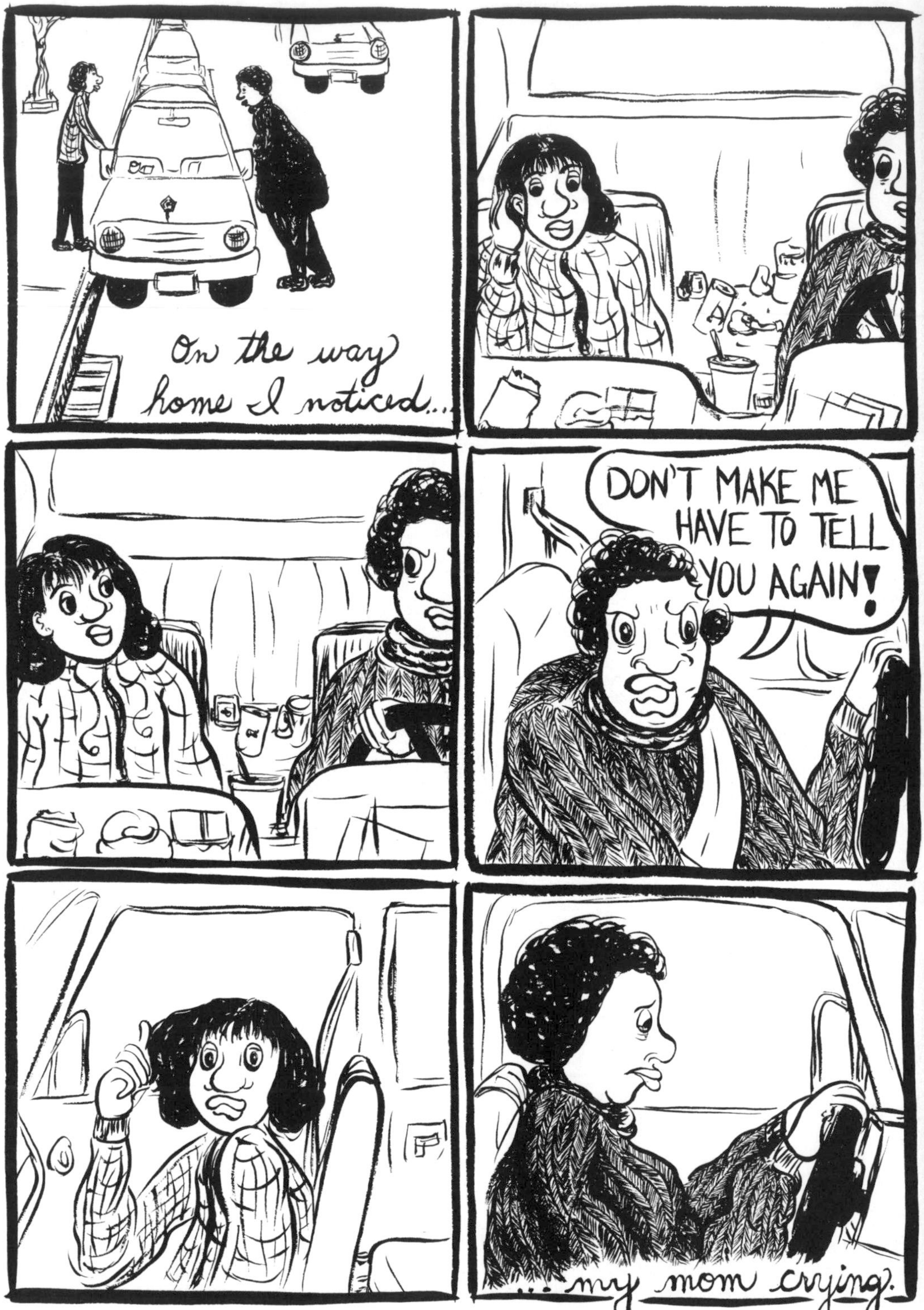
On the way home I noticed...
DON'T MAKE ME HAVE TO TELL YOU AGAIN!
...my mom crying.

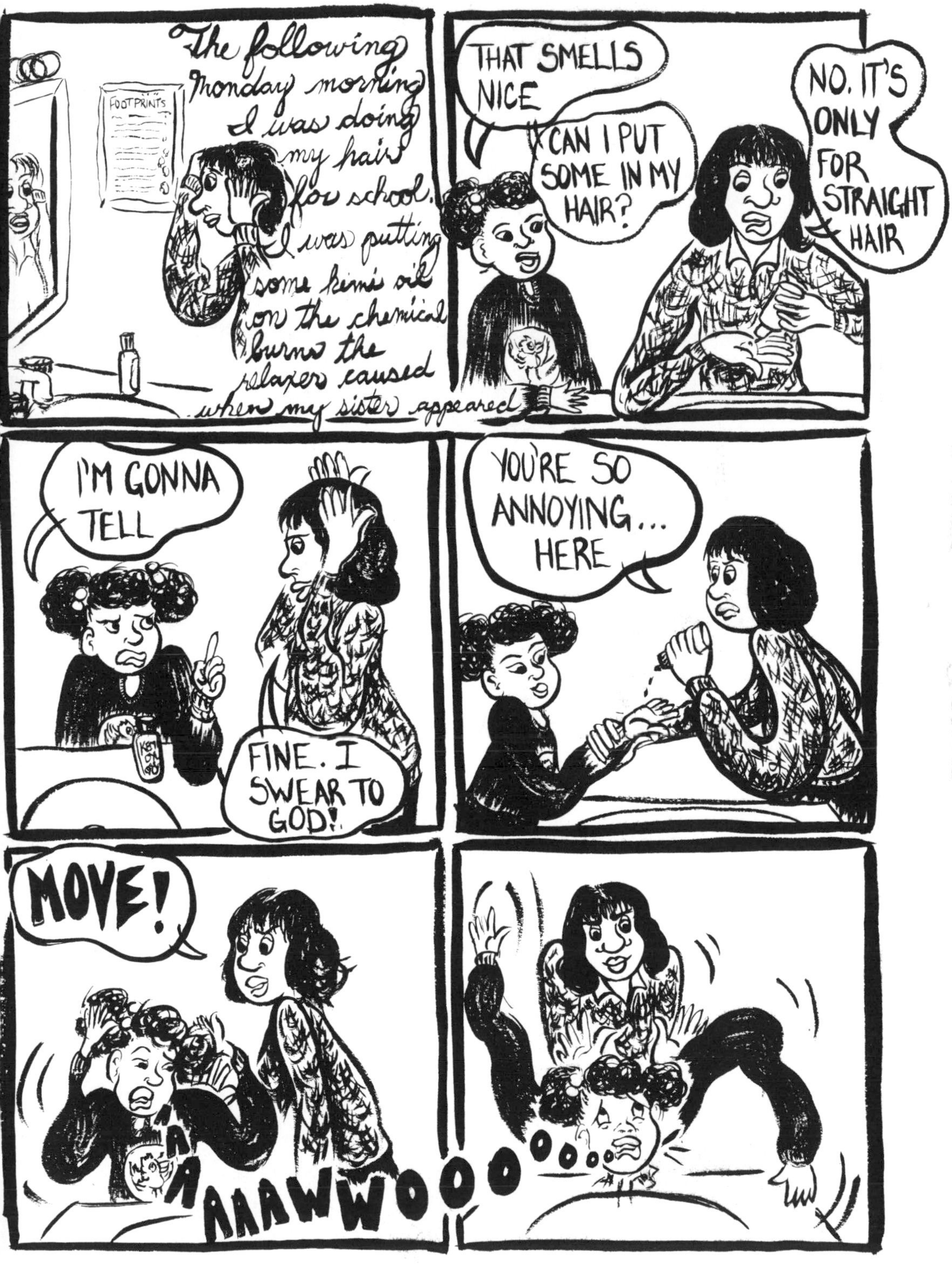
The following monday morning I was doing my hair for school. I was putting some kimi oil on the chemical burns the relaxer caused when my sister appeared
FOOTPRINTS
THAT SMELLS NICE
CAN I PUT SOME IN MY HAIR?
NO. IT'S ONLY FOR STRAIGHT HAIR
I'M GONNA TELL
FINE. I SWEAR TO GOD!
YOU'RE SO ANNOYING... HERE
MOVE!
AAAAAWWOOOOooooo

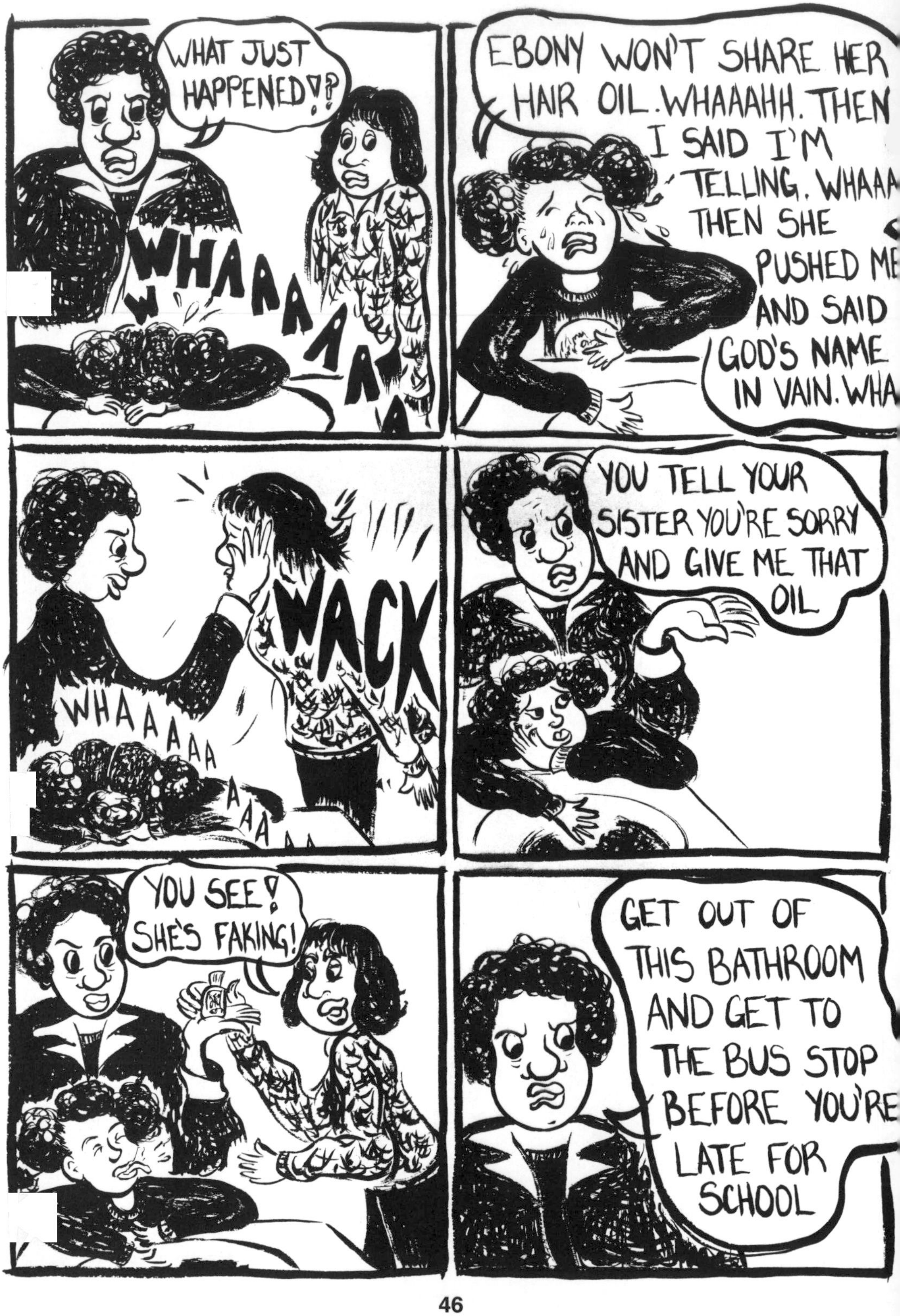
WHAT JUST HAPPENED!?
WHAAAAAAA
EBONY WON'T SHARE HER HAIR OIL. WHAAAHH. THEN I SAID I'M TELLING. WHAA THEN SHE PUSHED ME AND SAID GOD'S NAME IN VAIN. WHA
WACK
WHAAAAAAAAAA
YOU TELL YOUR SISTER YOU'RE SORRY AND GIVE ME THAT OIL
YOU SEE! SHE'S FAKING!
GET OUT OF THIS BATHROOM AND GET TO THE BUS STOP BEFORE YOU'RE LATE FOR SCHOOL

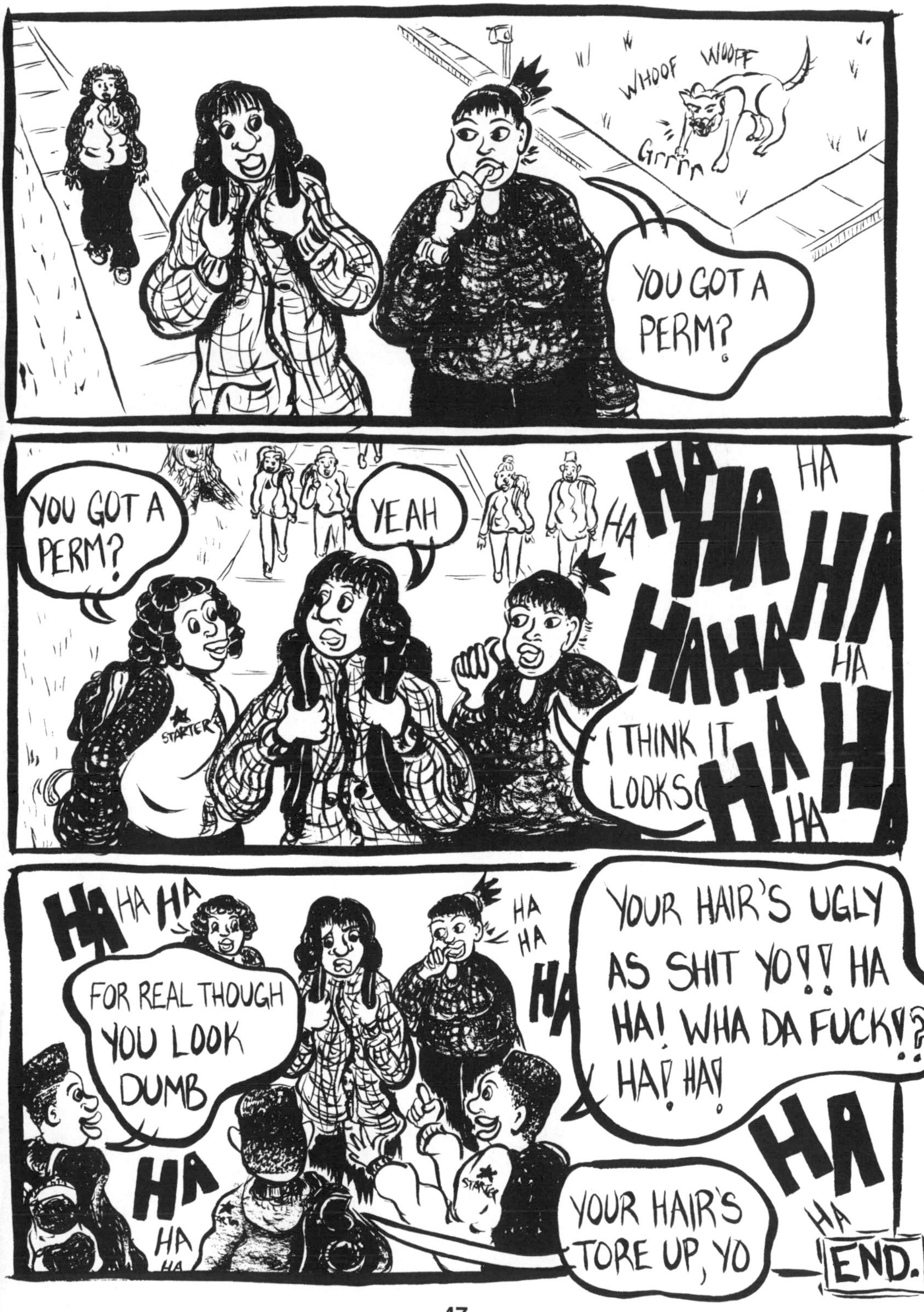
WHOOF WOOFF
Grrrrr
YOU GOT A PERM?
YOU GOT A PERM?
YEAH
HA HA HA HA HA HA HA HA
I THINK IT LOOKS
HA HA HA
HA HA HA
FOR REAL THOUGH YOU LOOK DUMB
YOUR HAIR'S UGLY AS SHIT YO!! HA HA! WHA DA FUCK!? HA! HA!
HA HA HA
YOUR HAIR'S TORE UP, YO
HA HA
END.

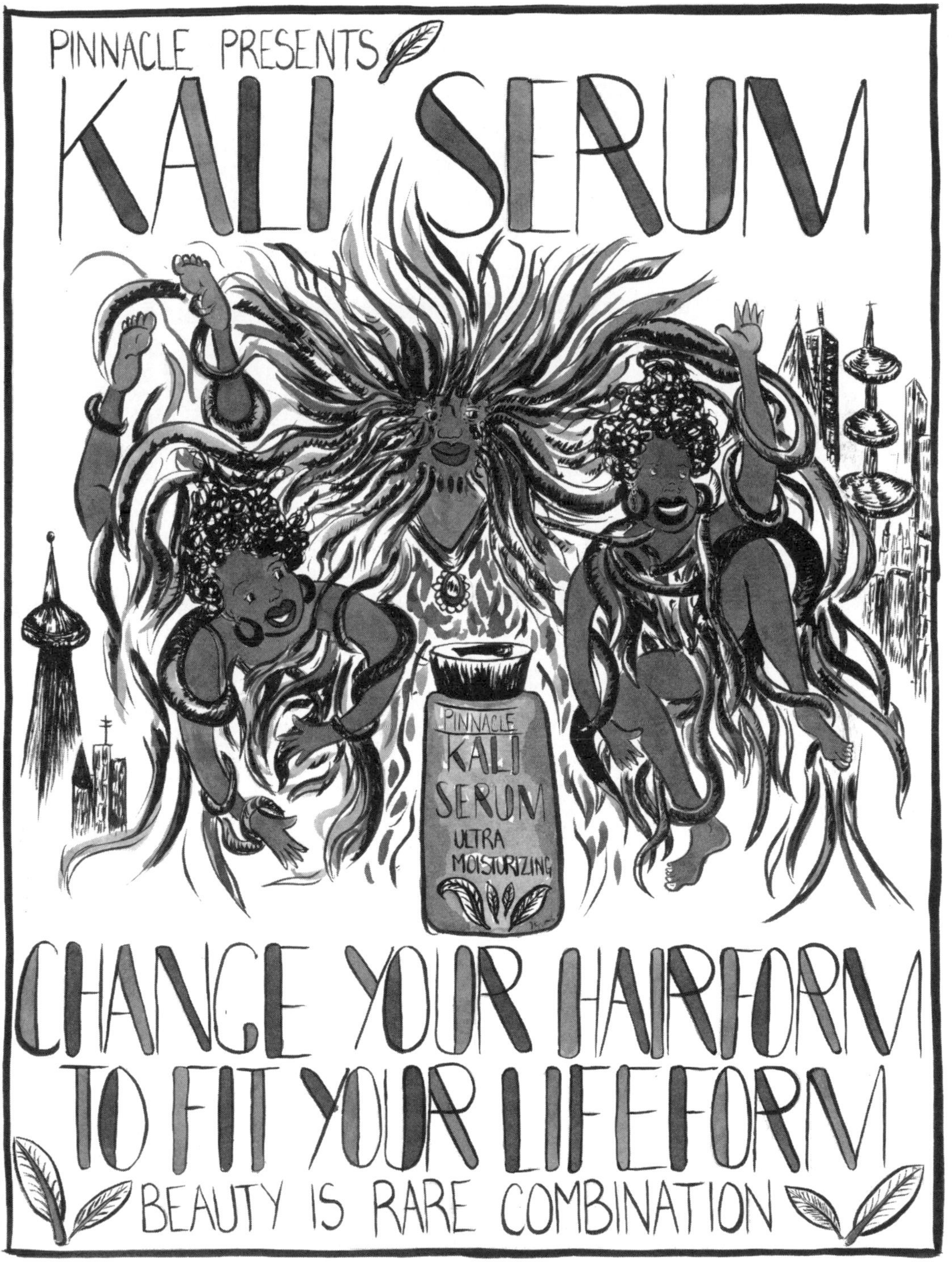
PINNACLE PRESENTS
KALI SERUM
PINNACLE
KALI
SERUM
ULTRA
MOISTURIZING
CHANGE YOUR HAIRFORM
TO FIT YOUR LIFEFORM
BEAUTY IS RARE COMBINATION

THE LADY ON THE TRAIN

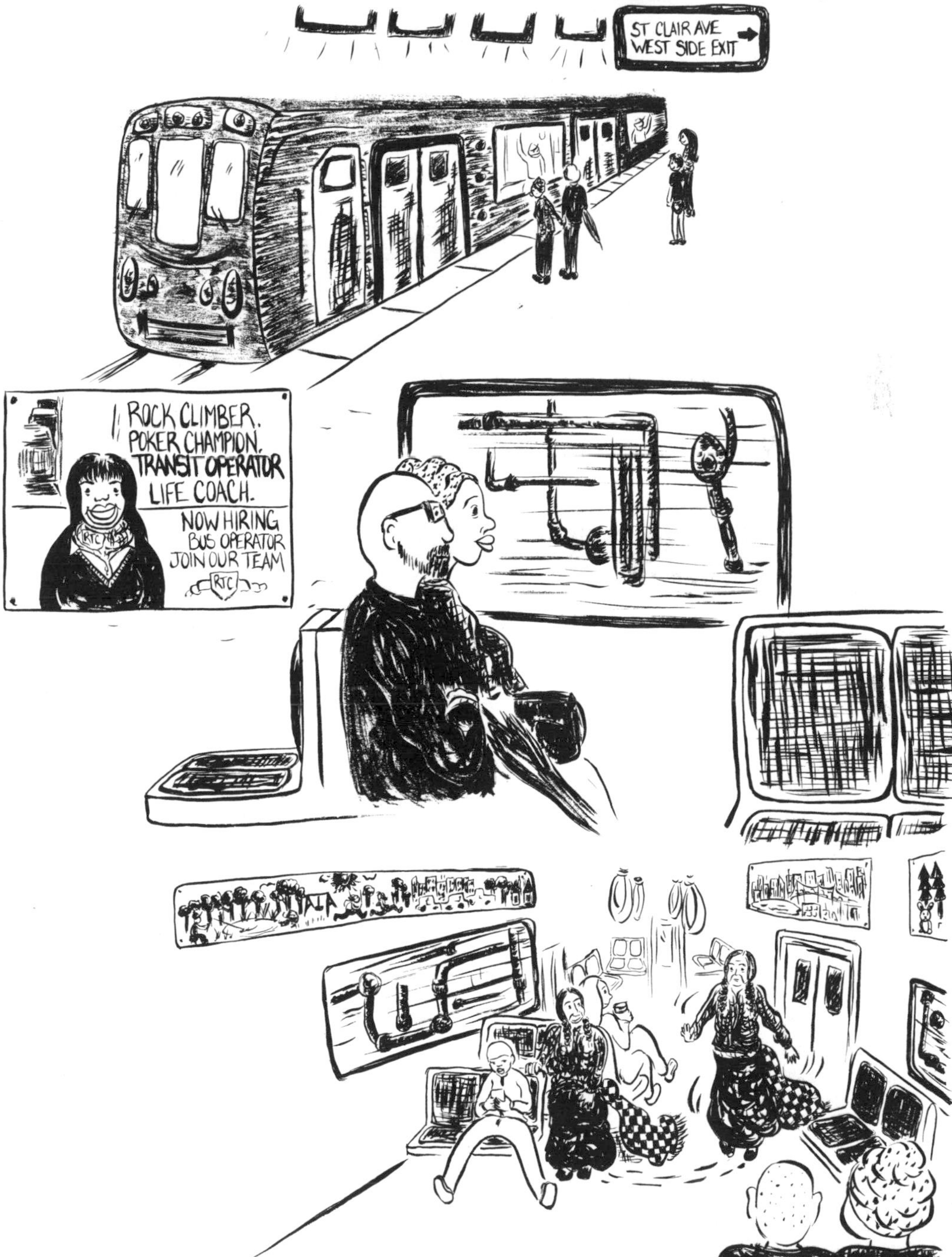
ST CLAIR AVE
WEST SIDE EXIT
ROCK CLIMBER.
POKER CHAMPION.
TRANSIT OPERATOR
LIFE COACH.
NOW HIRING
BUS OPERATOR
JOIN OUR TEAM
RTC

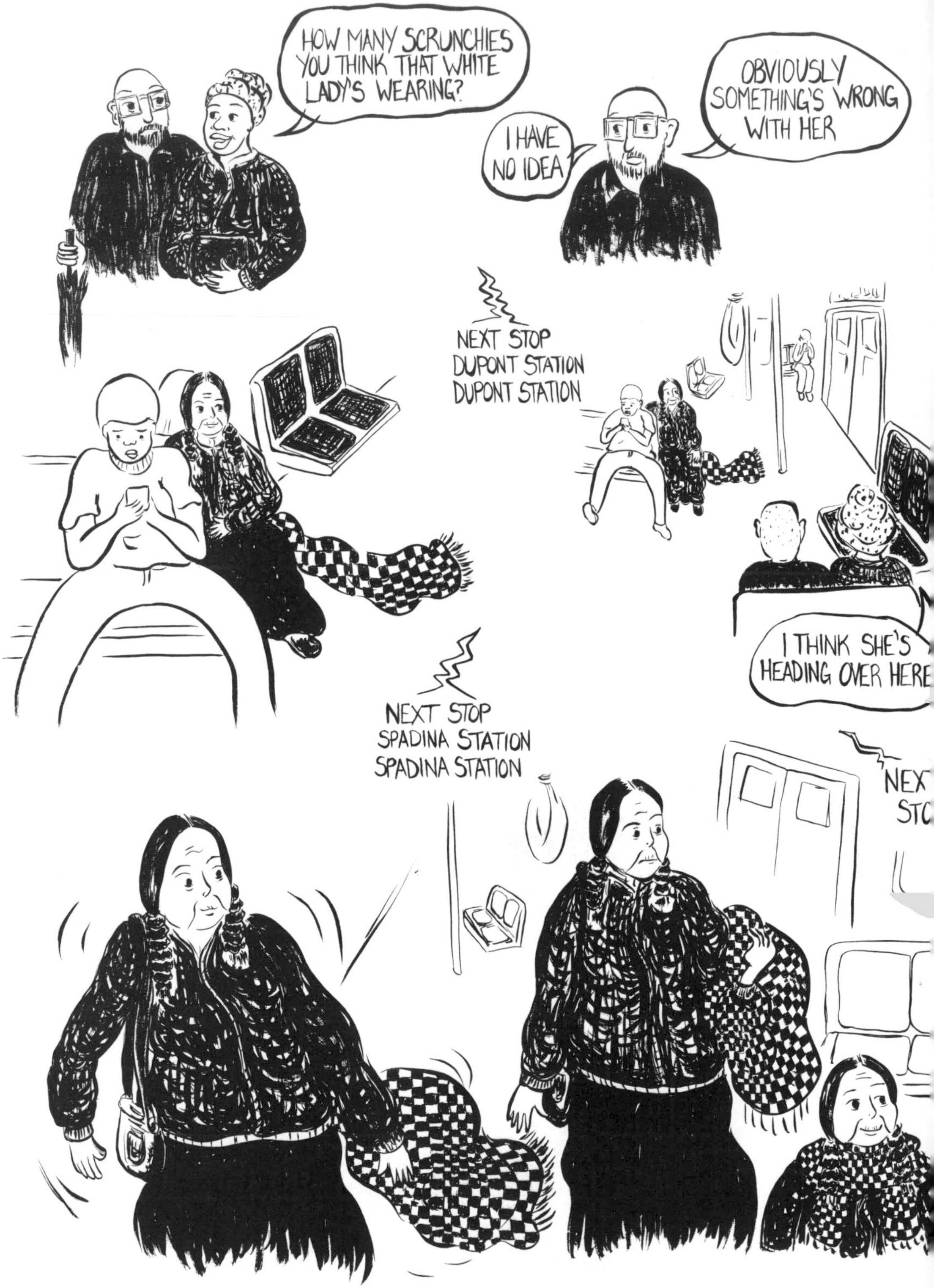
HOW MANY SCRUNCHIES YOU THINK THAT WHITE LADY'S WEARING?
I HAVE NO IDEA
OBVIOUSLY SOMETHING'S WRONG WITH HER
NEXT STOP DUPONT STATION DUPONT STATION
I THINK SHE'S HEADING OVER HERE
NEXT STOP SPADINA STATION SPADINA STATION

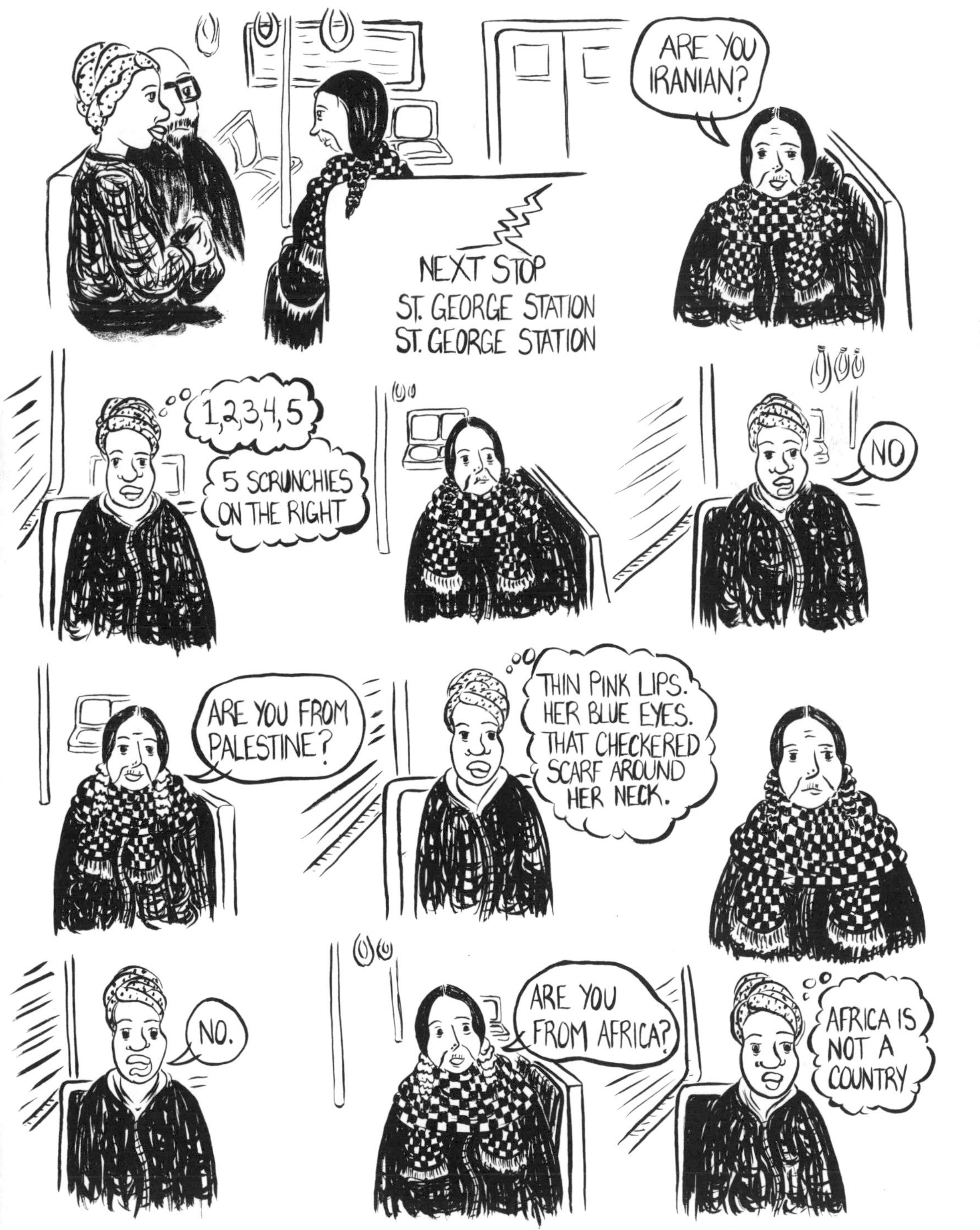
NEXT STOP
ST. GEORGE STATION
ST. GEORGE STATION
ARE YOU IRANIAN?
1,2,3,4,5
5 SCRUNCHIES ON THE RIGHT
NO
ARE YOU FROM PALESTINE?
THIN PINK LIPS. HER BLUE EYES. THAT CHECKERED SCARF AROUND HER NECK.
NO.
ARE YOU FROM AFRICA?
AFRICA IS NOT A COUNTRY

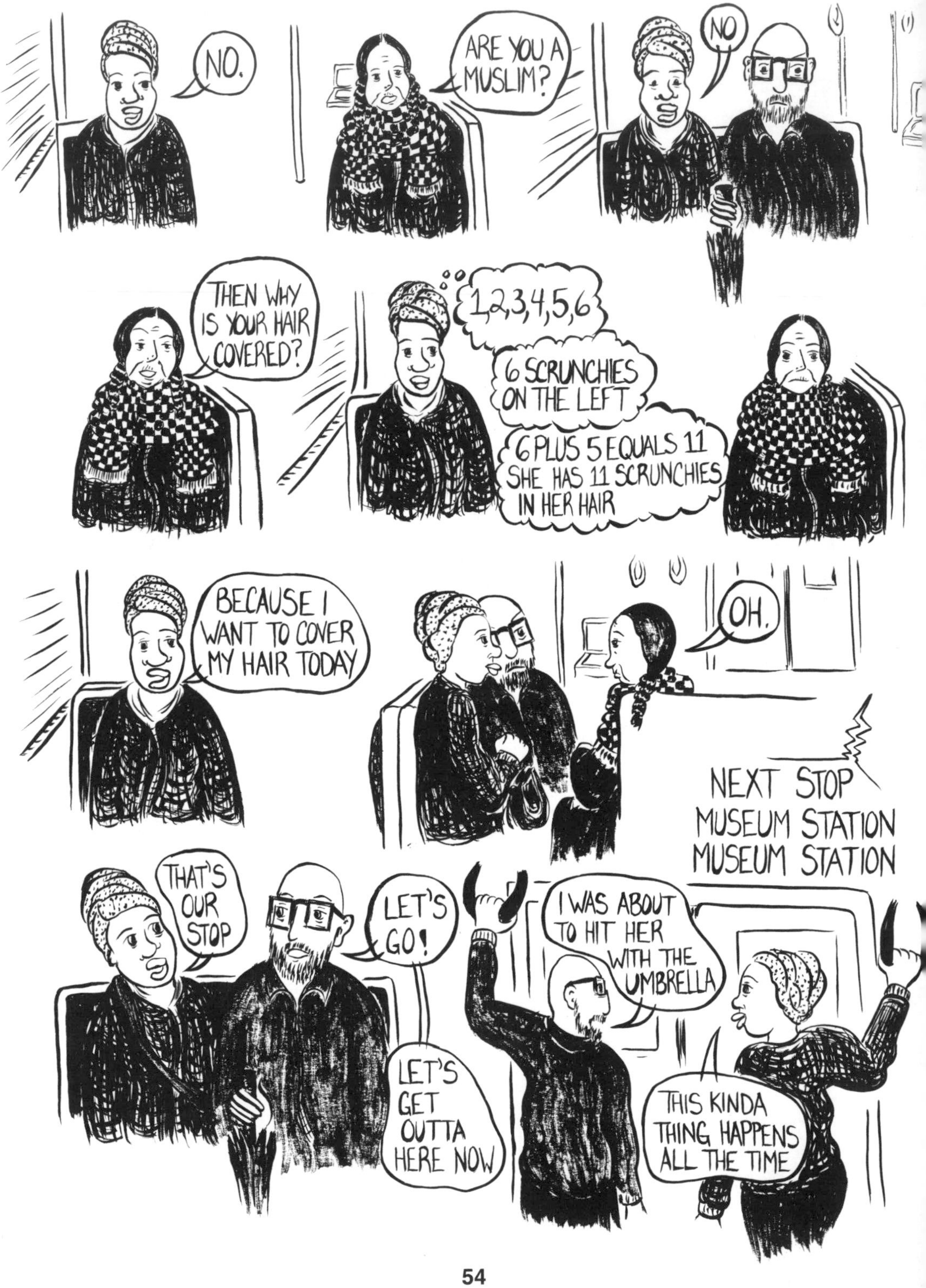
NO.
ARE YOU A MUSLIM?
NO
THEN WHY IS YOUR HAIR COVERED?
1,2,3,4,5,6
6 SCRUNCHIES ON THE LEFT
6 PLUS 5 EQUALS 11 SHE HAS 11 SCRUNCHIES IN HER HAIR
BECAUSE I WANT TO COVER MY HAIR TODAY
OH.
NEXT STOP MUSEUM STATION MUSEUM STATION
THAT'S OUR STOP
LET'S GO!
LET'S GET OUTTA HERE NOW
I WAS ABOUT TO HIT HER WITH THE UMBRELLA
THIS KINDA THING HAPPENS ALL THE TIME

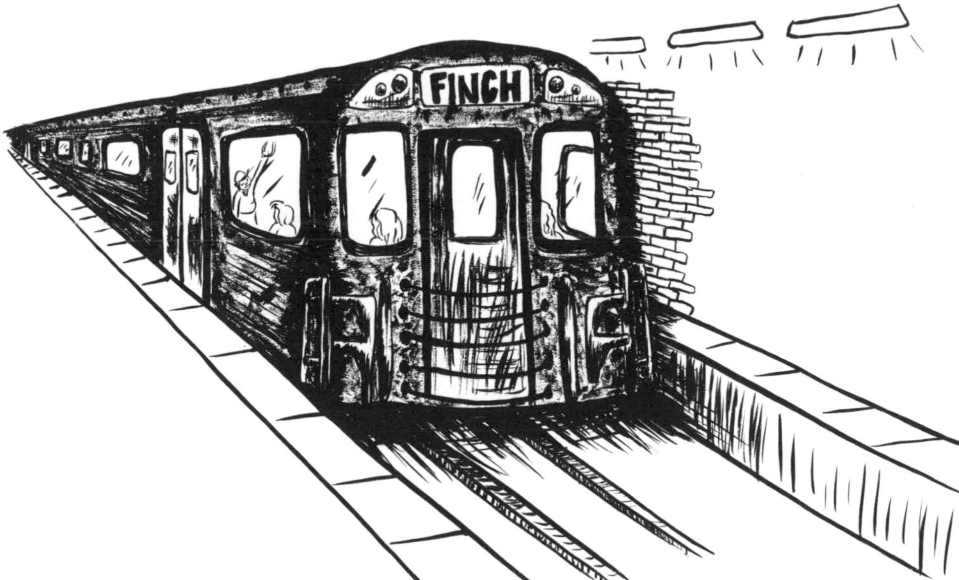
FINCH
END.

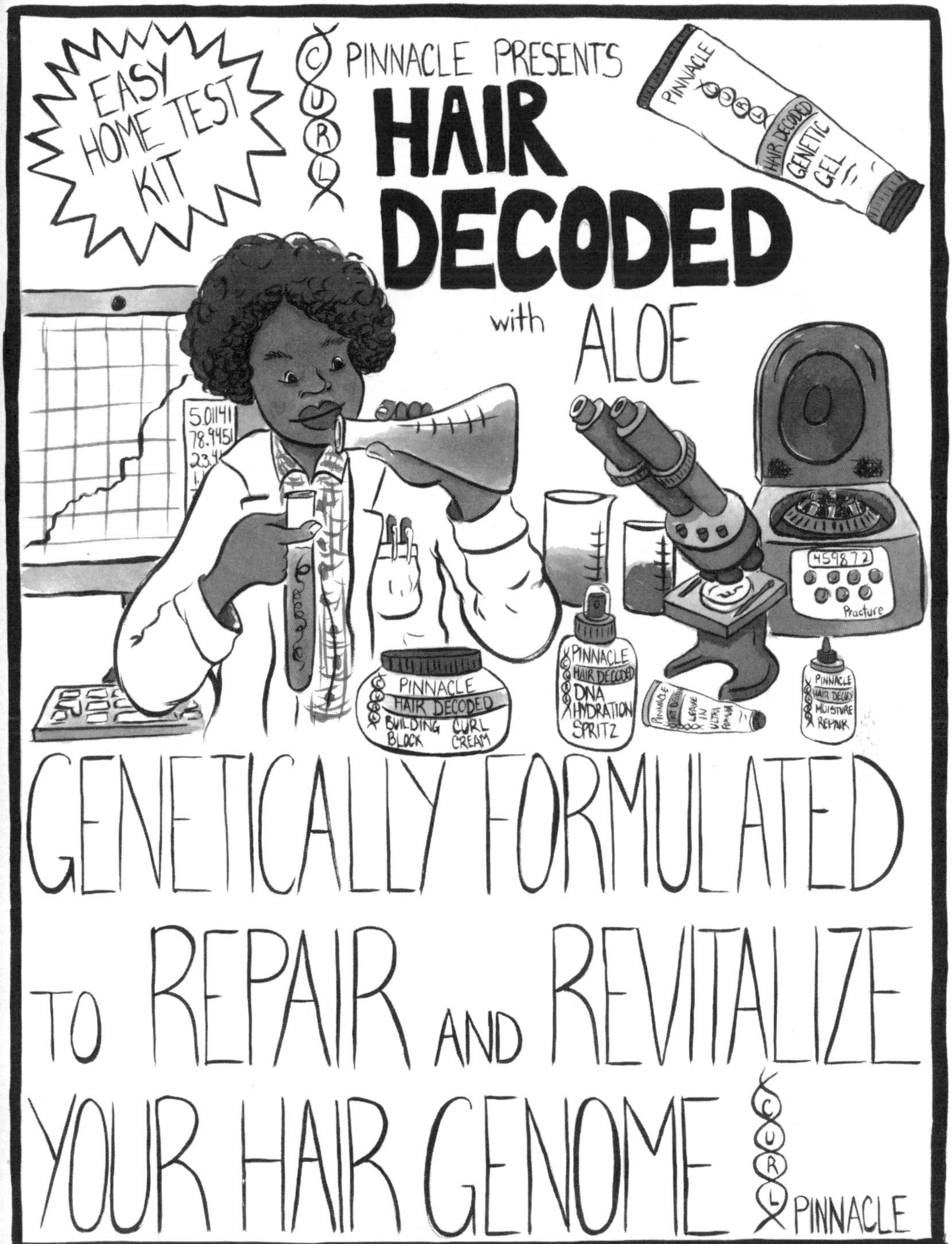
EASY HOME TEST KIT
CURL
PINNACLE PRESENTS
HAIR DECODED
with ALOE
PINNACLE HAIR DECODED GENETIC GEL
5.01141
78.9451
459872
Practure
PINNACLE HAIR DECODED BUILDING BLOCK CURL CREAM
PINNACLE HAIR DECODED DNA HYDRATION SPRITZ
PINNACLE LEAVE IN
PINNACLE HAIR DECODED MOISTURE REPAIR
GENETICALLY FORMULATED
TO REPAIR AND REVITALIZE
YOUR HAIR GENOME
CURL
PINNACLE

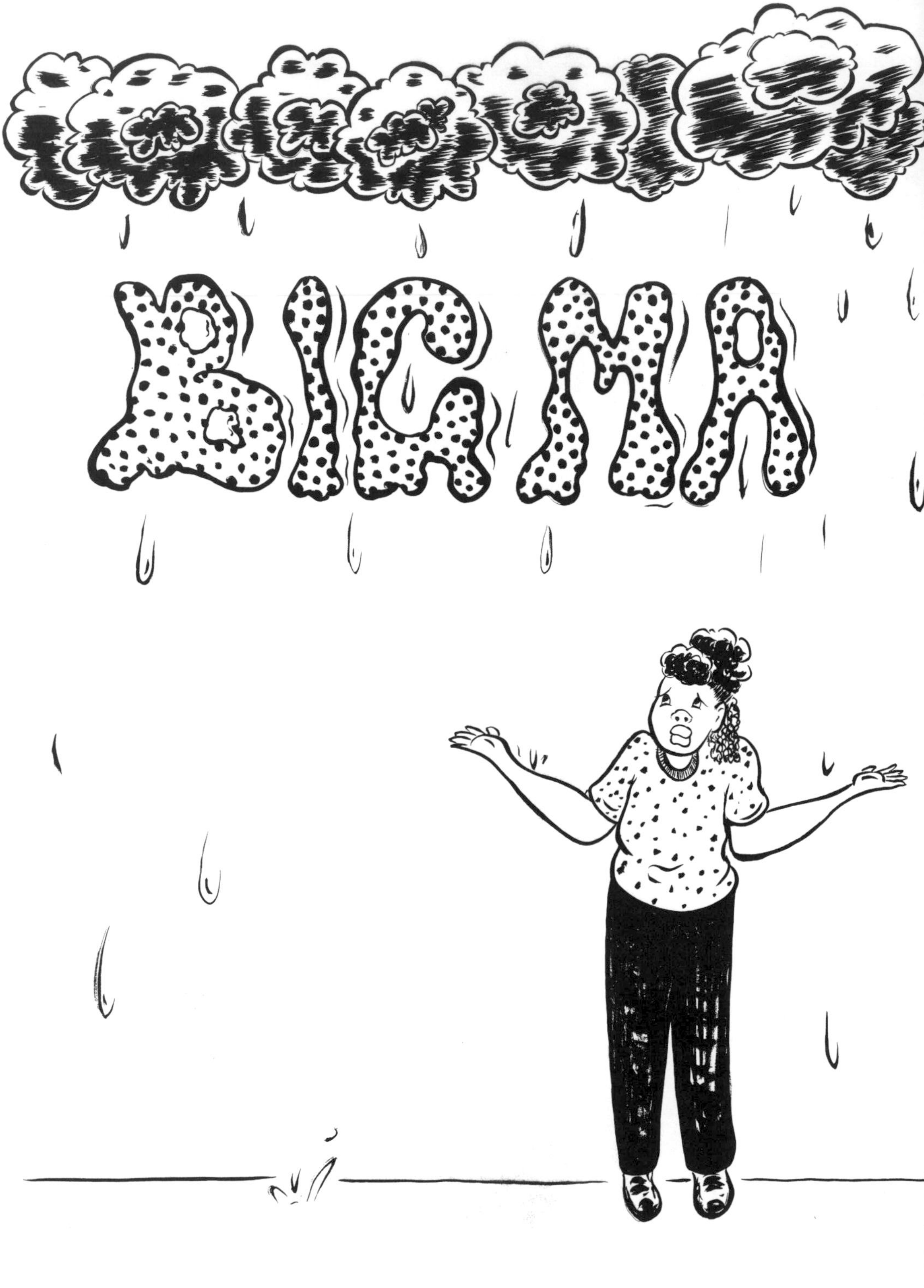
BIG MA

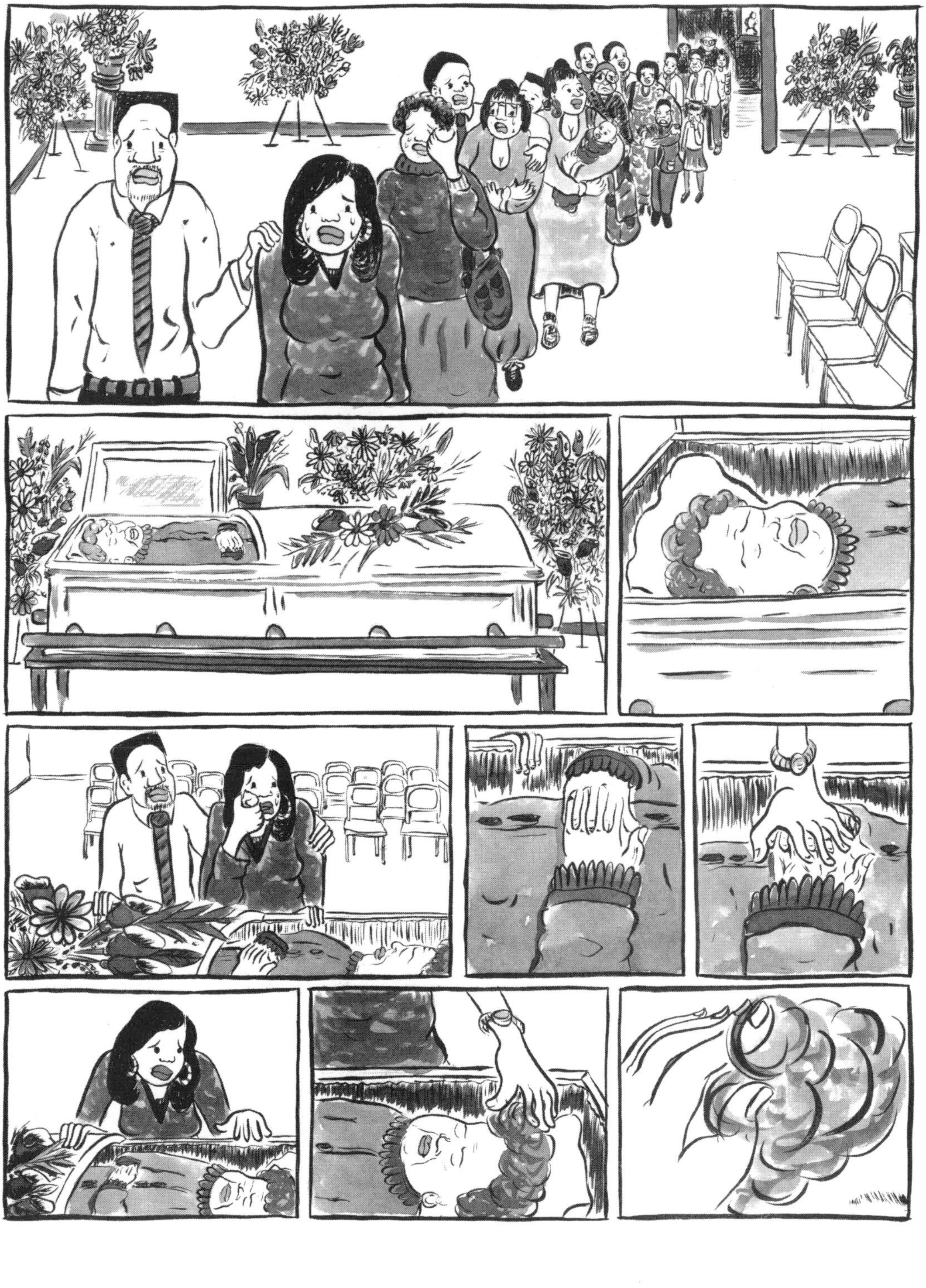

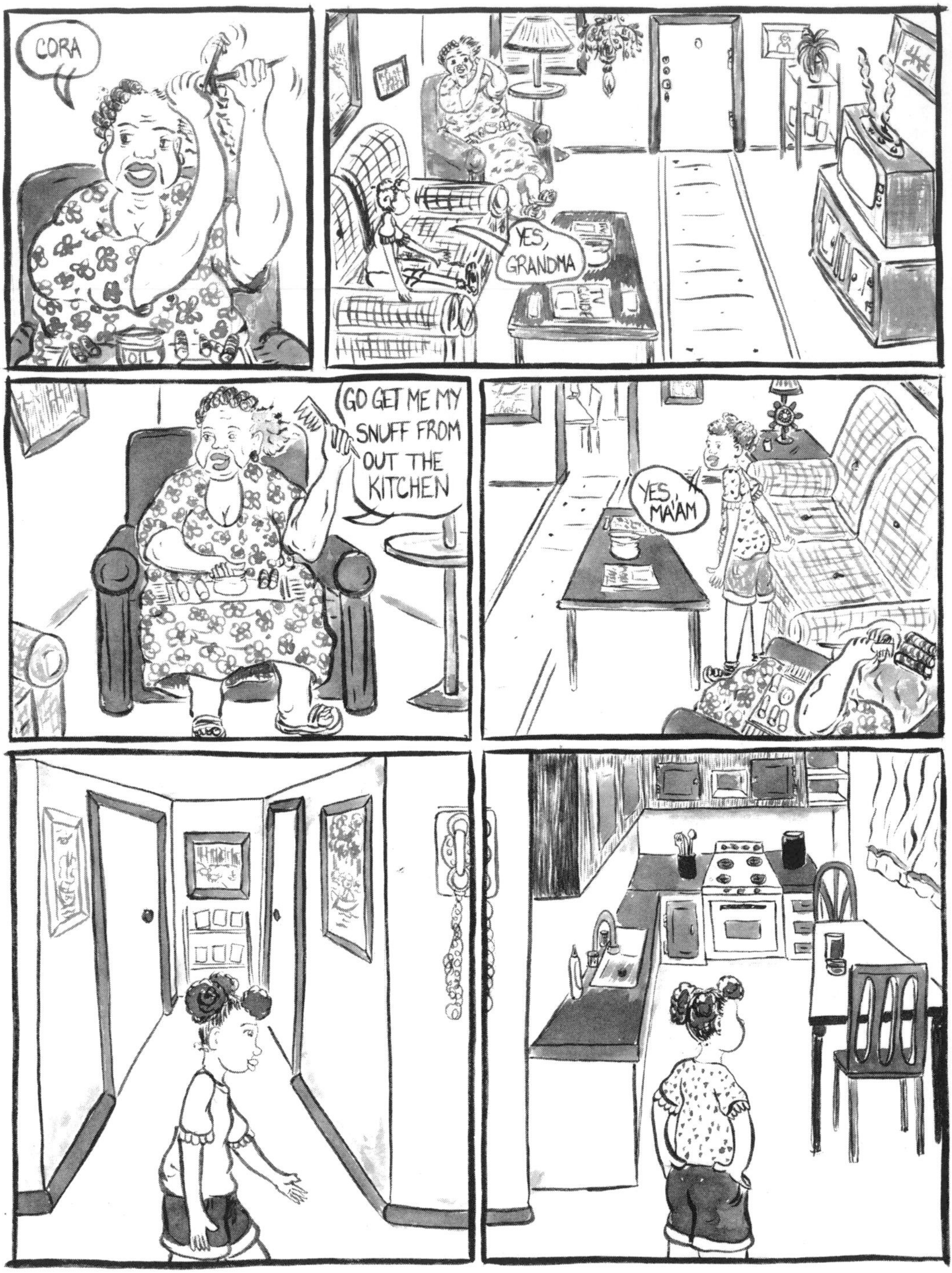
CORA
YES, GRANDMA
TV GUIDE
GO GET ME MY SNUFF FROM OUT THE KITCHEN
YES, MA'AM

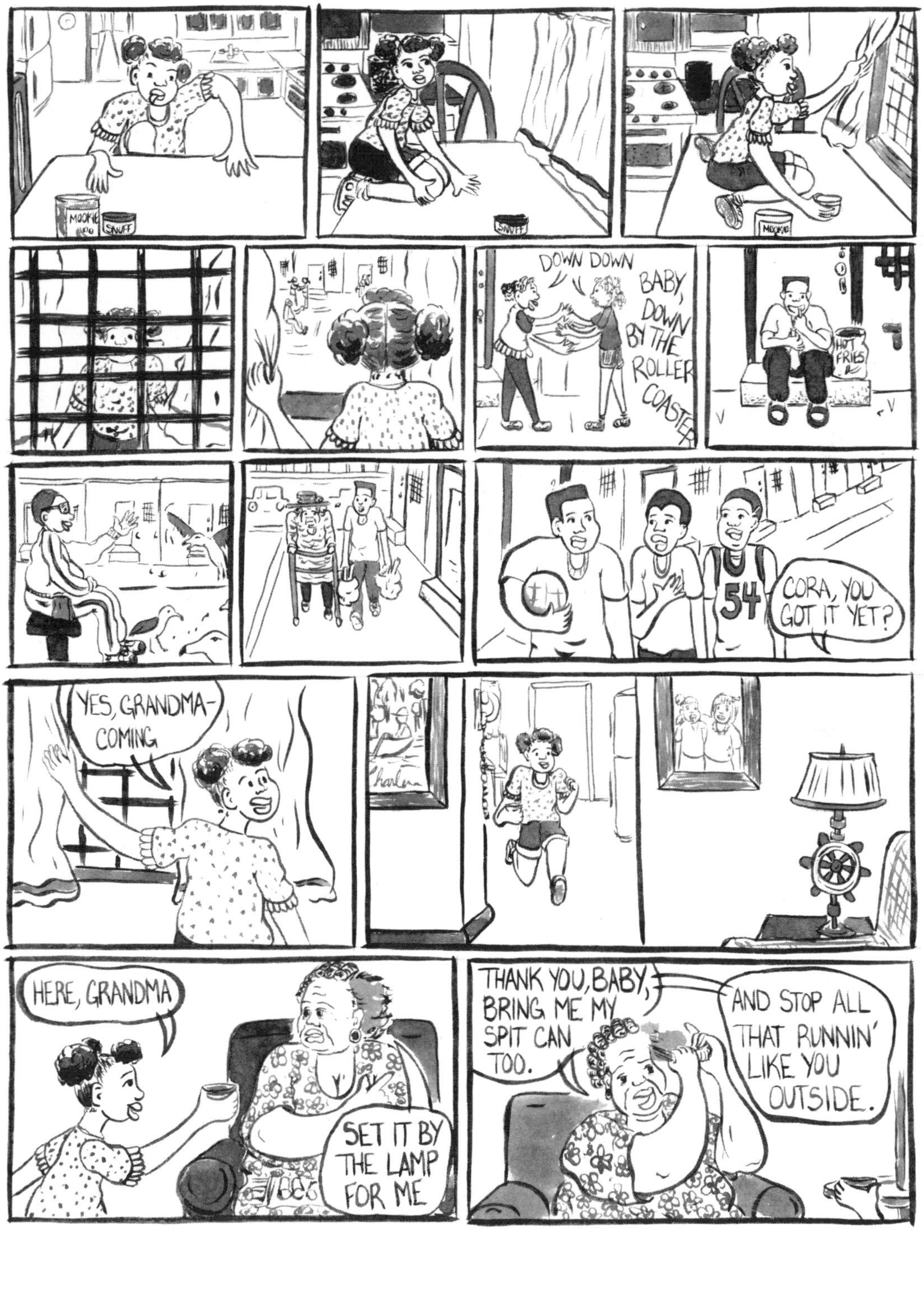
MOOKIE
SNUFF
SNUFF
MOOKIE
DOWN DOWN
BABY, DOWN BY THE ROLLER COASTER
HOT FRIES
54
CORA, YOU GOT IT YET?
YES, GRANDMA-COMING
HERE, GRANDMA
SET IT BY THE LAMP FOR ME
THANK YOU, BABY, BRING ME MY SPIT CAN TOO.
AND STOP ALL THAT RUNNIN' LIKE YOU OUTSIDE.

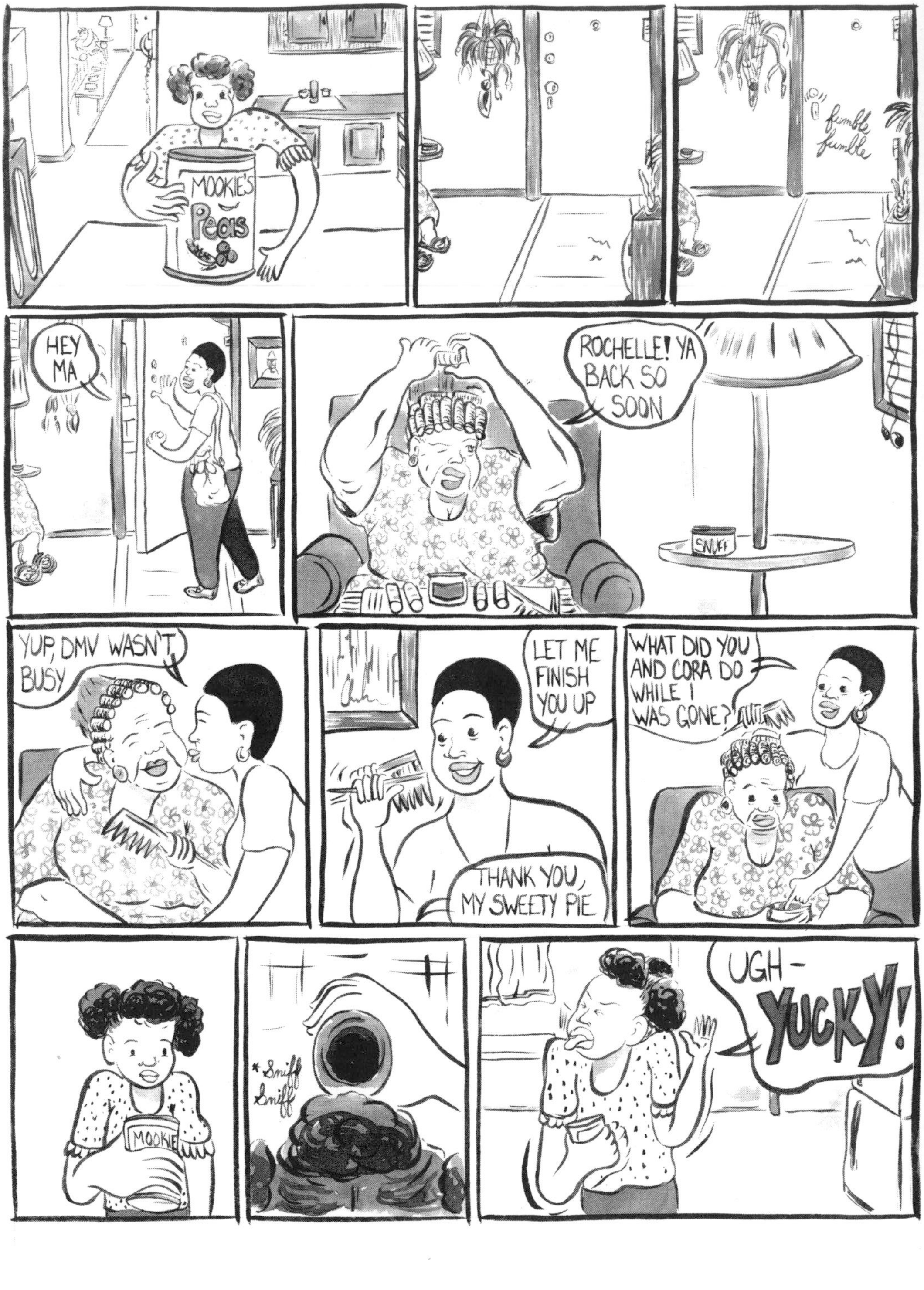
MOOKIE'S
Peas
fumble fumble
HEY MA
ROCHELLE! YA BACK SO SOON
SNUFF
YUP, DMV WASN'T BUSY
LET ME FINISH YOU UP
THANK YOU, MY SWEETY PIE
WHAT DID YOU AND CORA DO WHILE I WAS GONE?
MOOKIE
*Sniff Sniff
UGH - YUCKY!

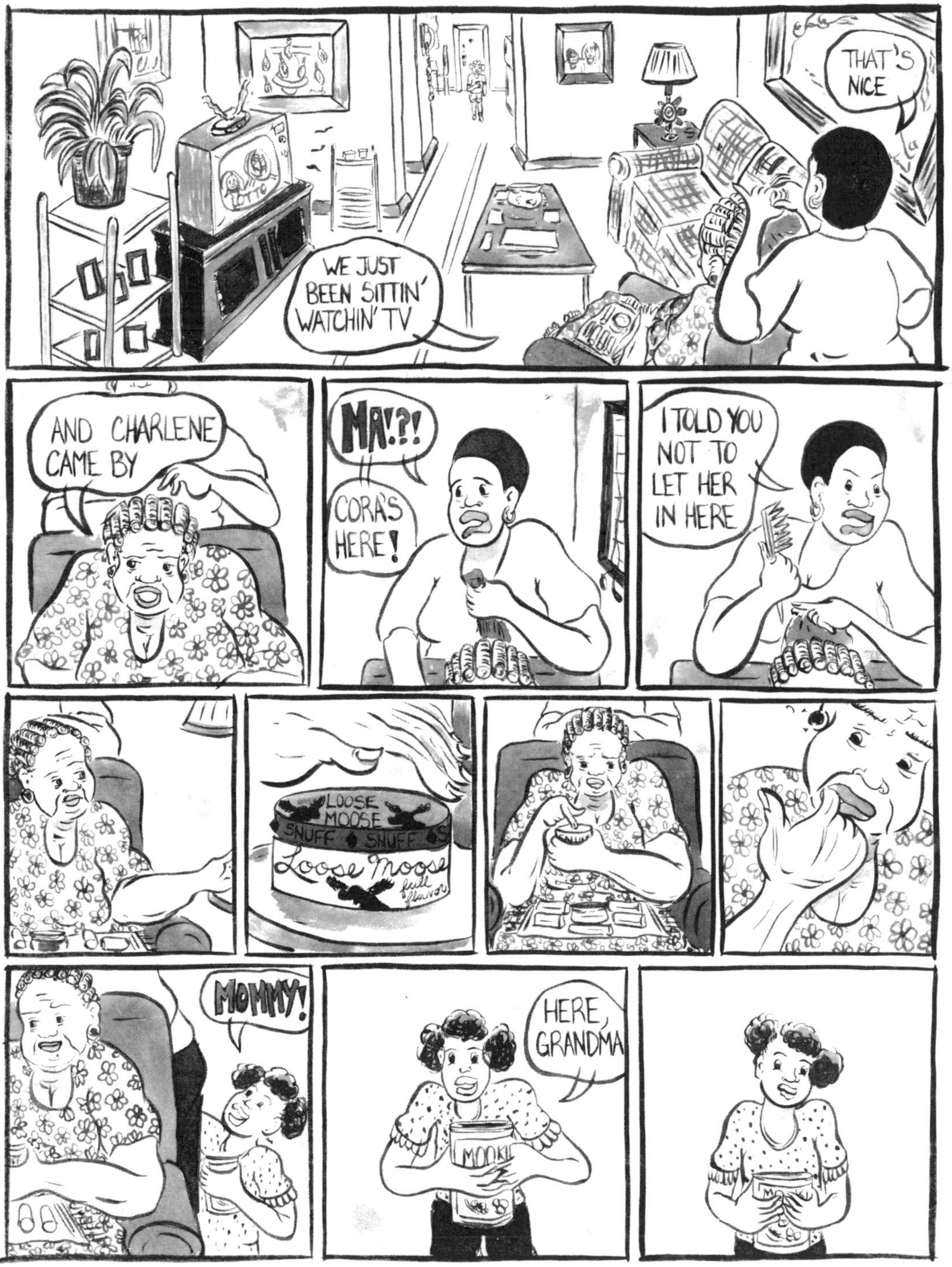
THAT'S NICE
WE JUST BEEN SITTIN' WATCHIN' TV
AND CHARLENE CAME BY
MA!?!
CORA'S HERE!
I TOLD YOU NOT TO LET HER IN HERE
LOOSE MOOSE
SNUFF SNUFF
Loose Moose
full flavor
MOMMY!
HERE, GRANDMA

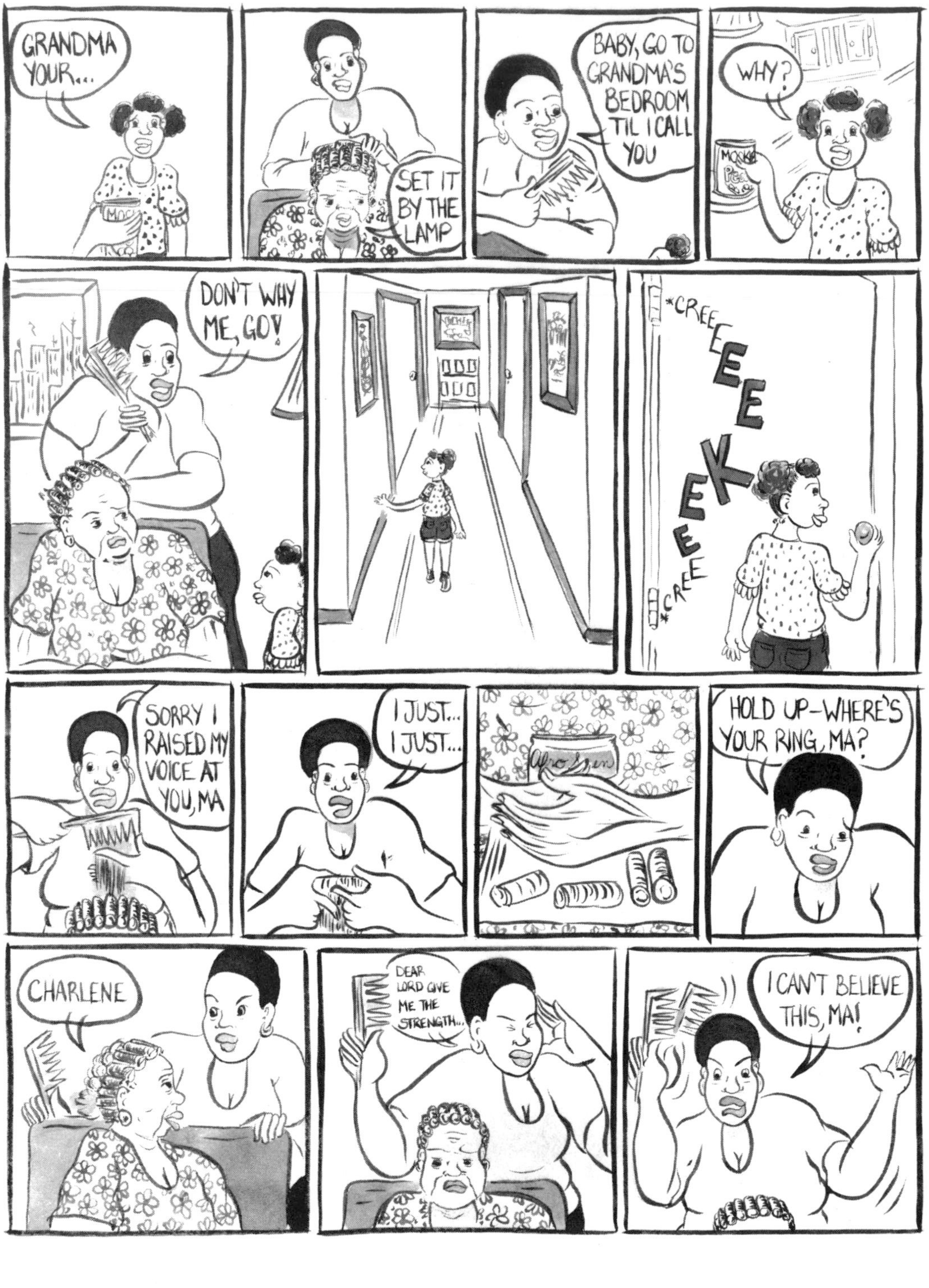
GRANDMA YOUR...
SET IT BY THE LAMP
BABY, GO TO GRANDMA'S BEDROOM TIL I CALL YOU
WHY?
DON'T WHY ME, GO!
*CREEEEEEKEEE
*CREE
SORRY I RAISED MY VOICE AT YOU, MA
I JUST... I JUST...
Afro Sheen
HOLD UP-WHERE'S YOUR RING, MA?
CHARLENE
DEAR LORD GIVE ME THE STRENGTH...
I CAN'T BELIEVE THIS, MA!

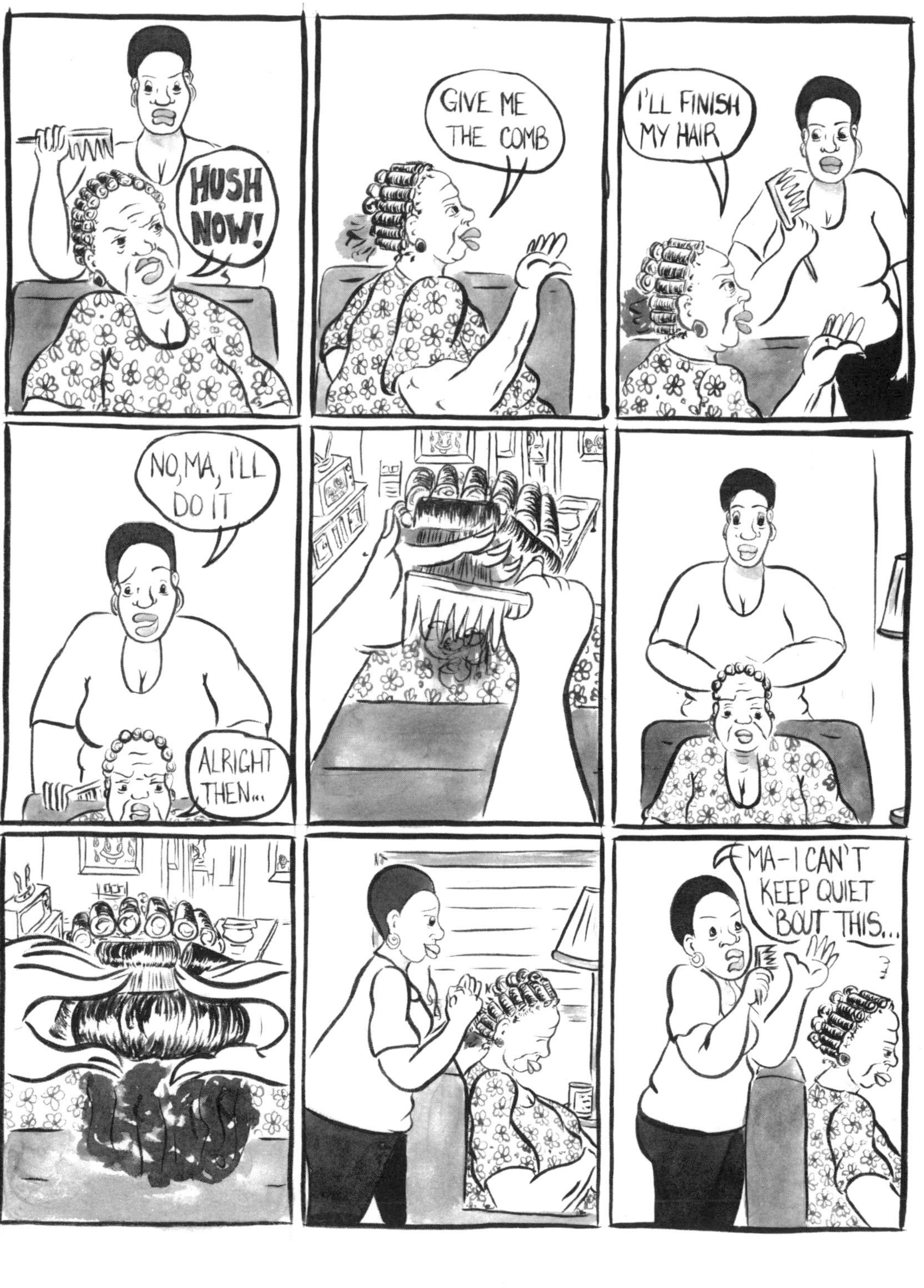
HUSH NOW!
GIVE ME THE COMB
I'LL FINISH MY HAIR
NO, MA, I'LL DO IT
ALRIGHT THEN...
MA- I CAN'T KEEP QUIET 'BOUT THIS...

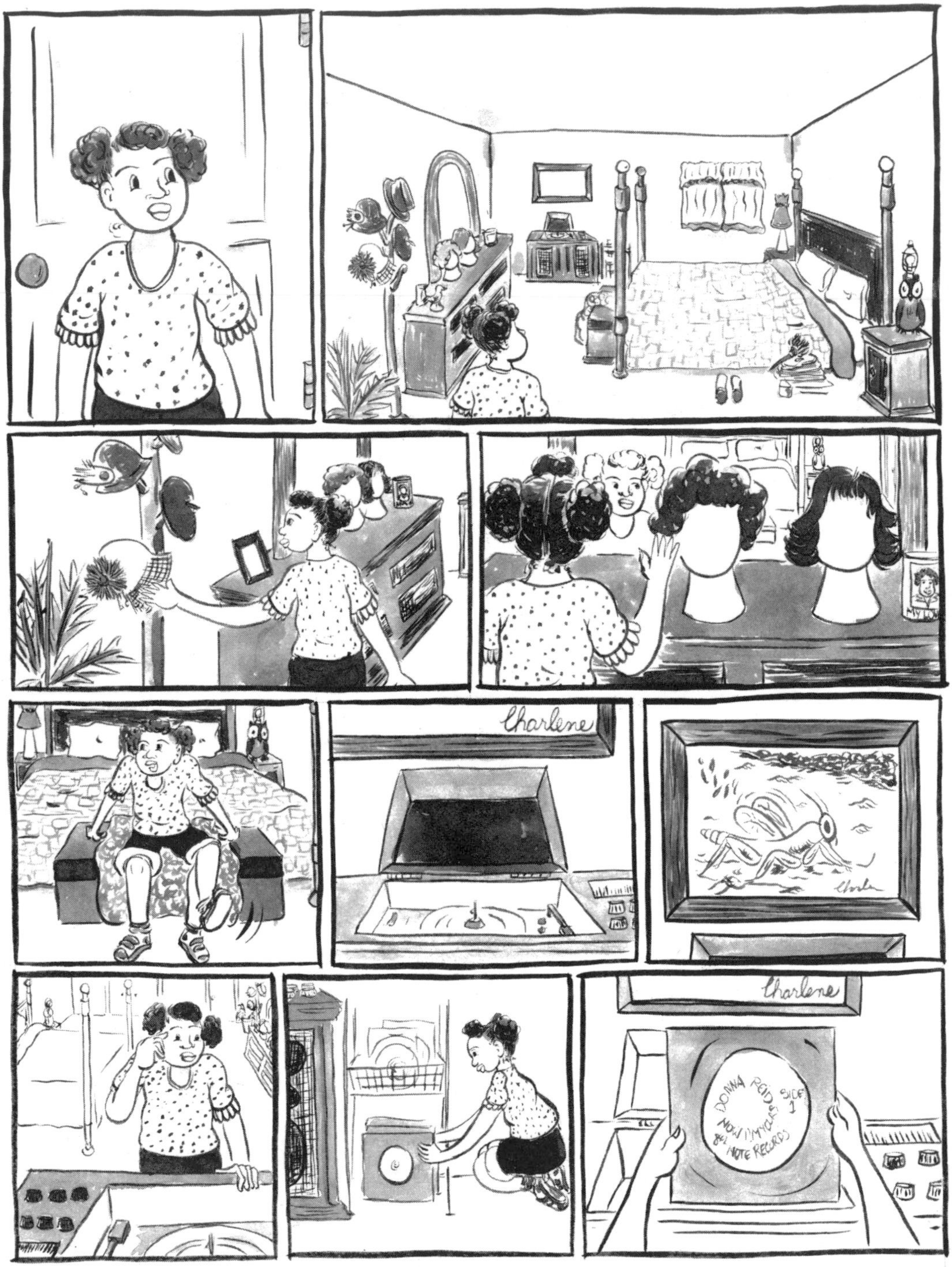
Charlene
Charlene
DONNA REID
NOW I'M YOURS
SIDE 1
8th NOTE RECORDS

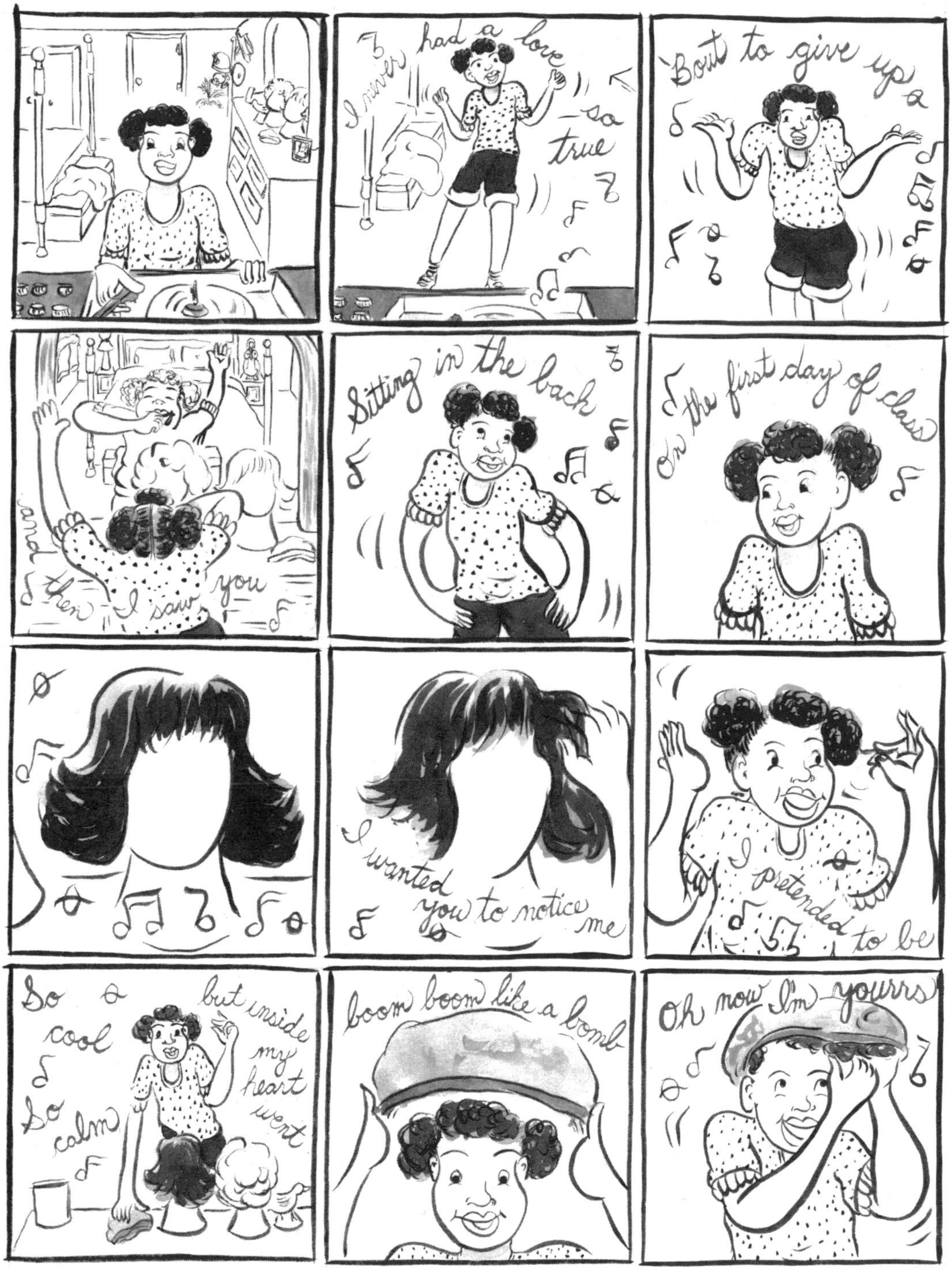
I never had a love
so true
'Bout to give up
and then I saw you
Sitting in the back
On the first day of class
I wanted you to notice me
I pretended to be
So cool
So calm
but inside my heart went
boom boom like a bomb
Oh now I'm yourrs

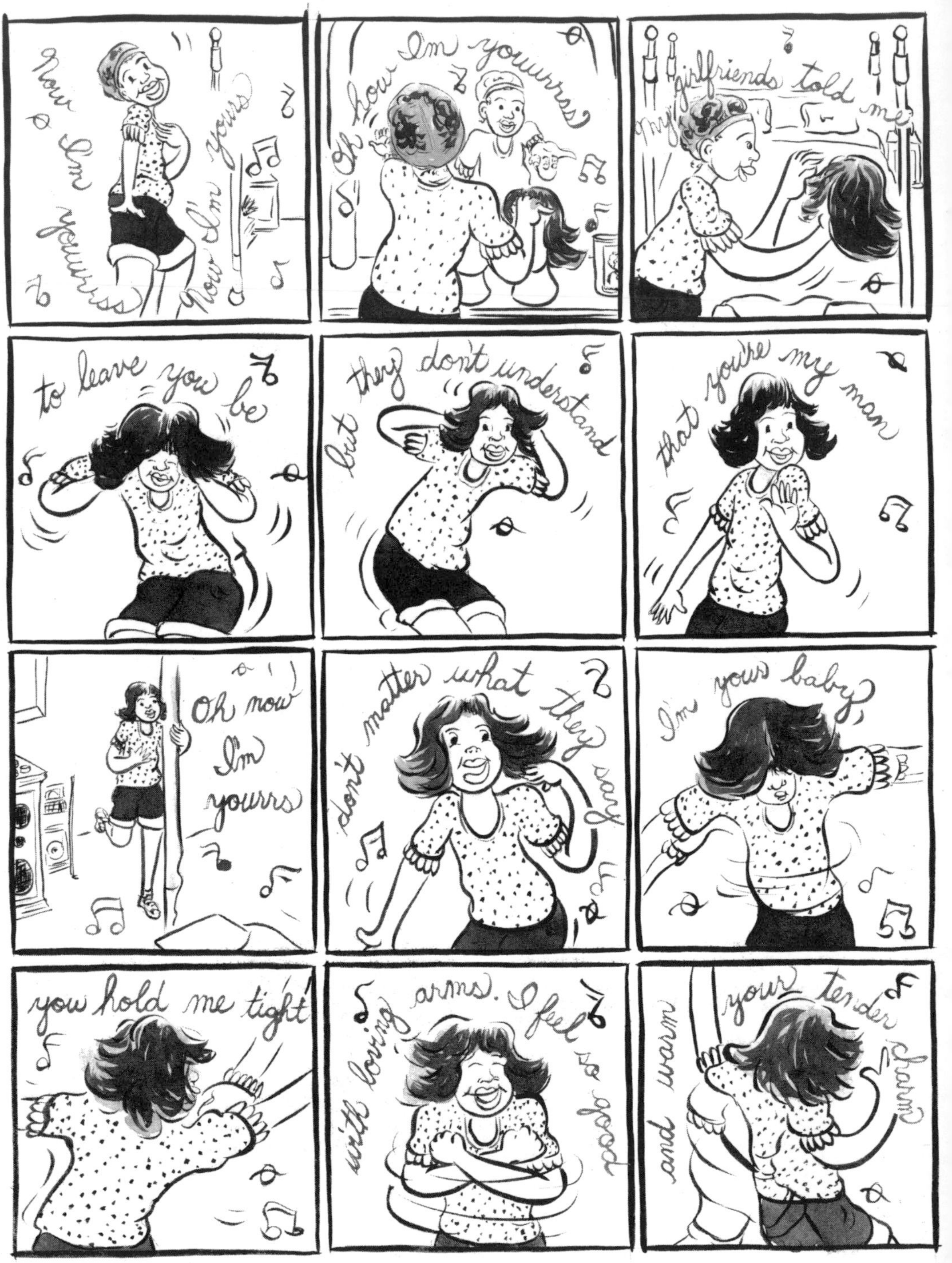
Now I'm yourrss
Now I'm yours
Oh now I'm yourrss
my girlfriends told me
to leave you be
but they don't understand
that you're my man
Oh now I'm yourrs
don't matter what they say
I'm your baby,
you hold me tight
with loving arms. I feel so good
and warm your tender charm

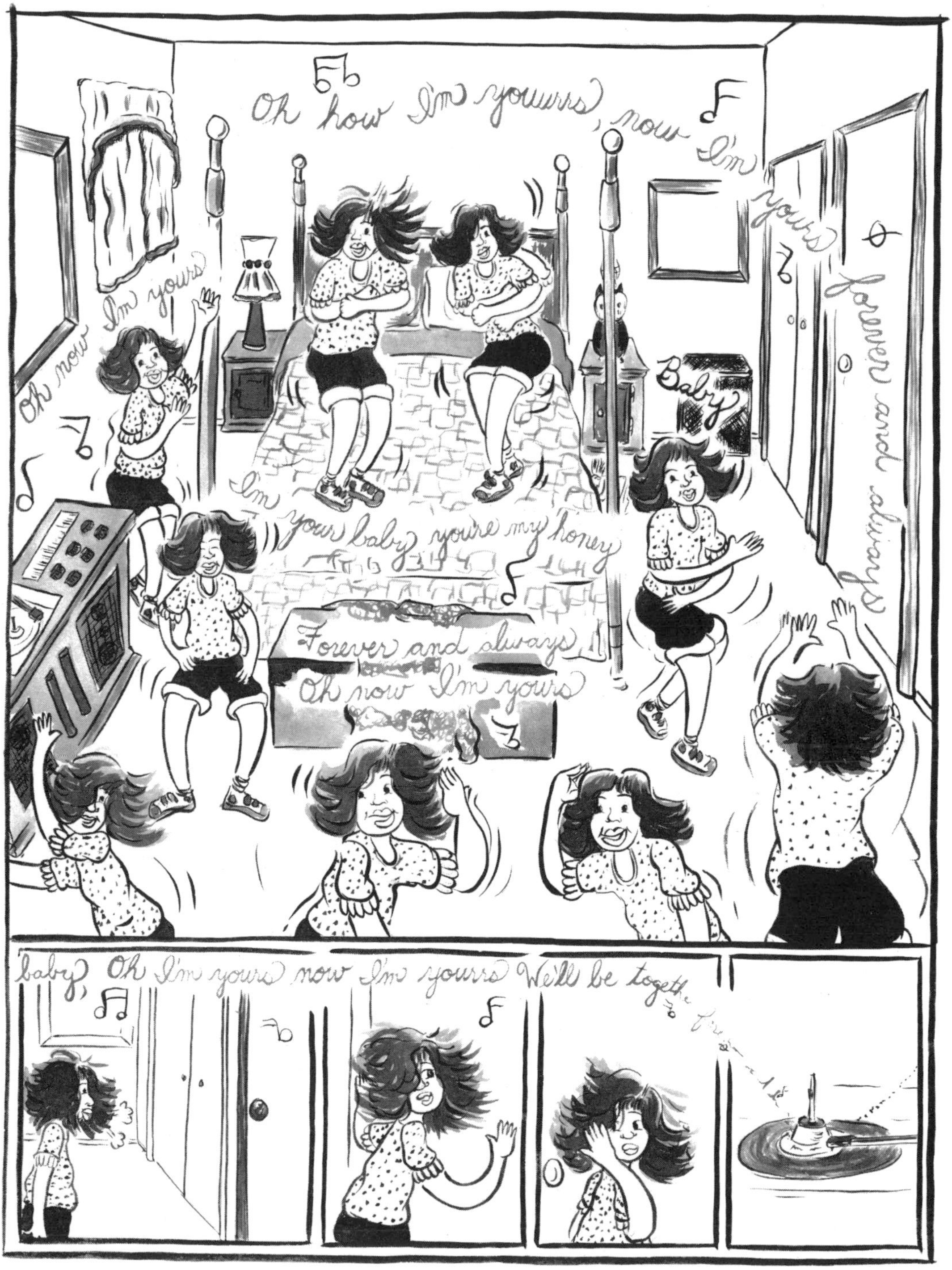
Oh how I'm yourrs, now I'm yours forever and always
Oh now I'm yours
Baby
I'm your baby you're my honey
Forever and always
Oh now I'm yours
baby, Oh I'm yours now I'm yourrs We'll be togethe

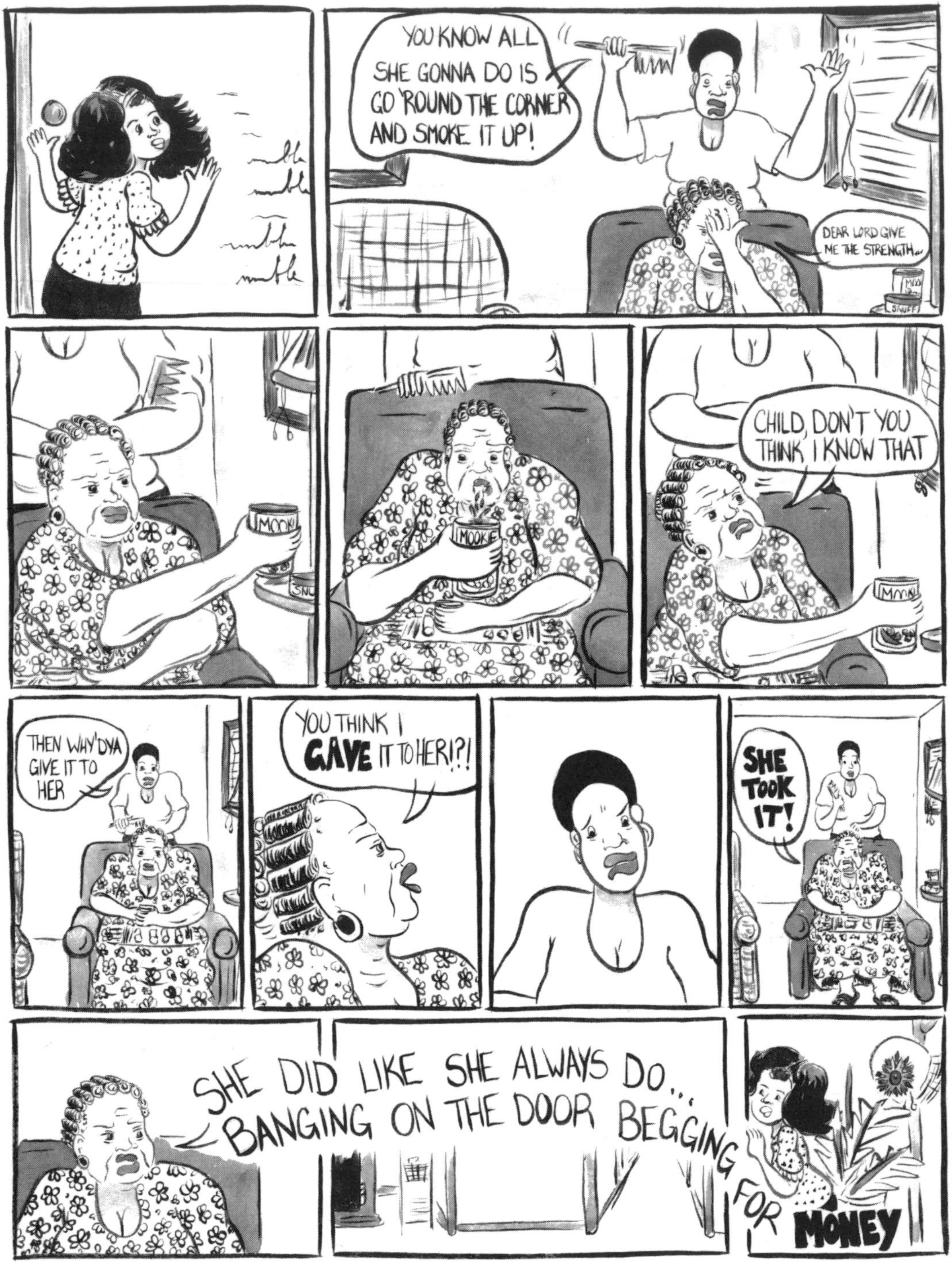
mumble
mumble
mumble
mumble
YOU KNOW ALL SHE GONNA DO IS GO 'ROUND THE CORNER AND SMOKE IT UP!
DEAR LORD GIVE ME THE STRENGTH...
SNUFF
MOOK
SNU
MOOKIE
CHILD, DON'T YOU THINK I KNOW THAT
THEN WHY'DYA GIVE IT TO HER
YOU THINK I GAVE IT TO HER!?!
SHE TOOK IT!
SHE DID LIKE SHE ALWAYS DO... BANGING ON THE DOOR BEGGING FOR MONEY

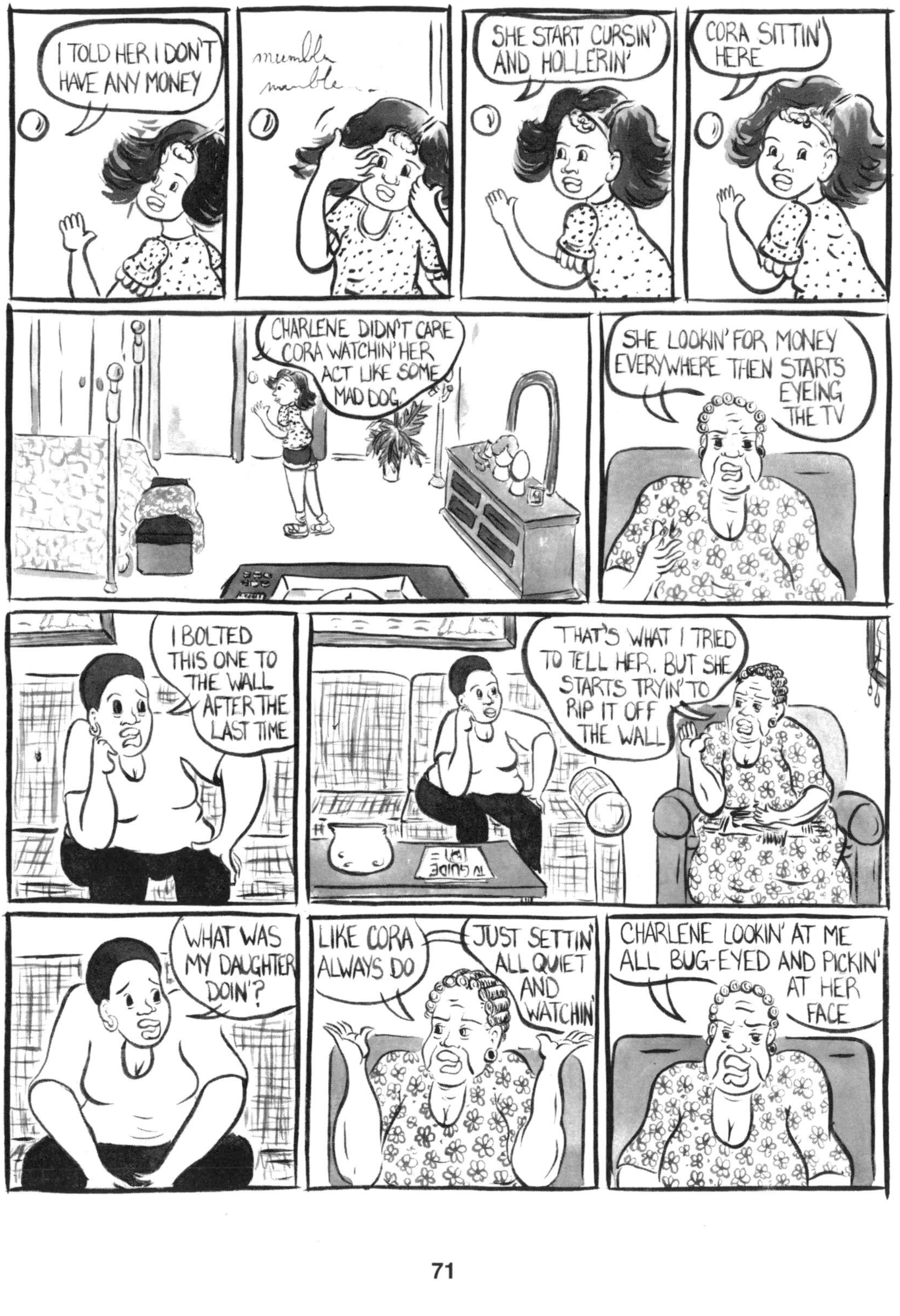
I TOLD HER I DON'T HAVE ANY MONEY
mumble mumble
SHE START CURSIN' AND HOLLERIN'
CORA SITTIN' HERE
CHARLENE DIDN'T CARE CORA WATCHIN' HER ACT LIKE SOME MAD DOG
SHE LOOKIN' FOR MONEY EVERYWHERE THEN STARTS EYEING THE TV
I BOLTED THIS ONE TO THE WALL AFTER THE LAST TIME
THAT'S WHAT I TRIED TO TELL HER. BUT SHE STARTS TRYIN' TO RIP IT OFF THE WALL
TV GUIDE
WHAT WAS MY DAUGHTER DOIN'?
LIKE CORA ALWAYS DO
JUST SETTIN' ALL QUIET AND WATCHIN'
CHARLENE LOOKIN' AT ME ALL BUG-EYED AND PICKIN' AT HER FACE

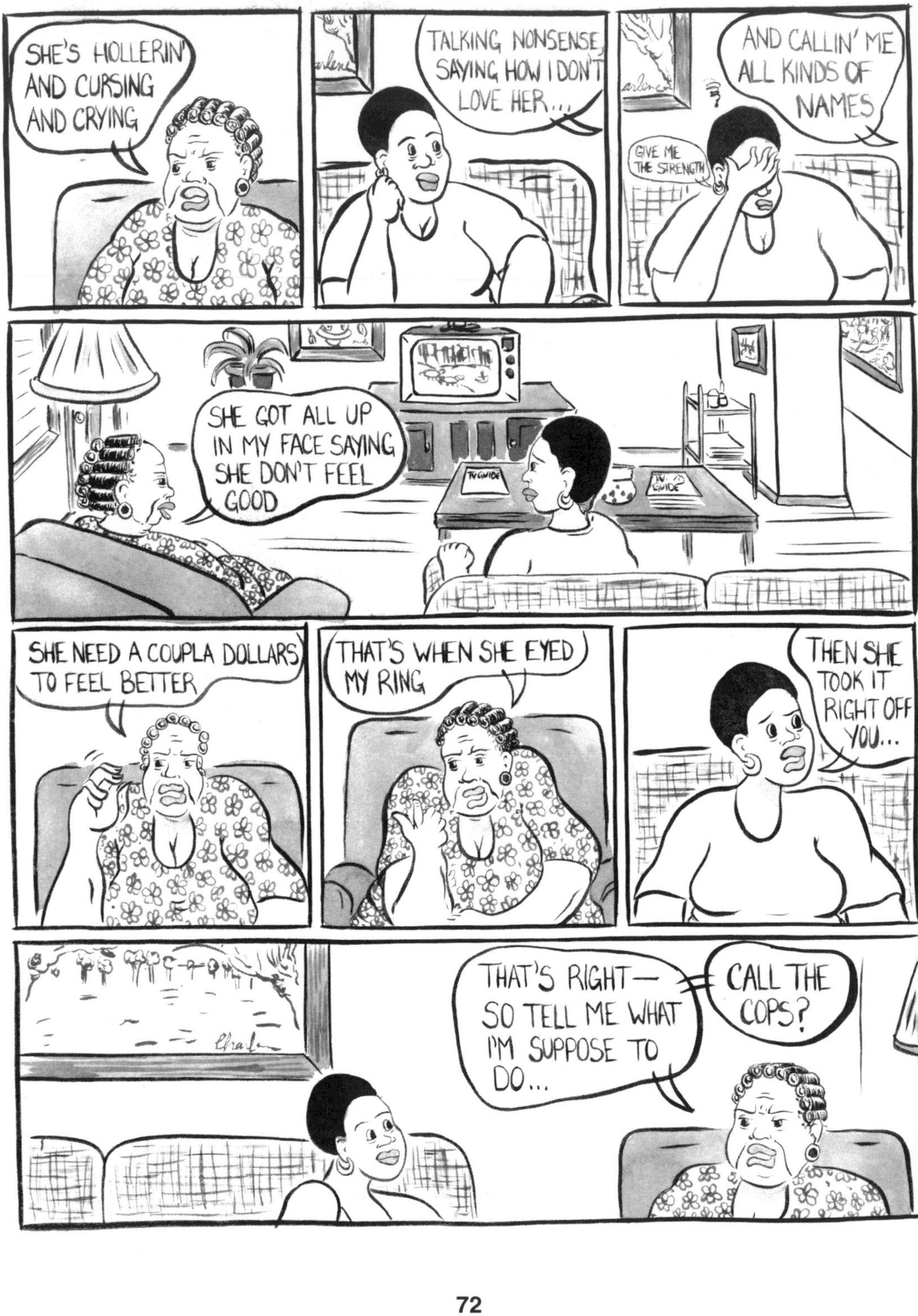
SHE'S HOLLERIN' AND CURSING AND CRYING
TALKING NONSENSE, SAYING HOW I DON'T LOVE HER...
AND CALLIN' ME ALL KINDS OF NAMES
GIVE ME THE STRENGTH
SHE GOT ALL UP IN MY FACE SAYING SHE DON'T FEEL GOOD
TV GUIDE
TV GUIDE
SHE NEED A COUPLA DOLLARS TO FEEL BETTER
THAT'S WHEN SHE EYED MY RING
THEN SHE TOOK IT RIGHT OFF YOU...
THAT'S RIGHT— SO TELL ME WHAT I'M SUPPOSE TO DO...
CALL THE COPS?

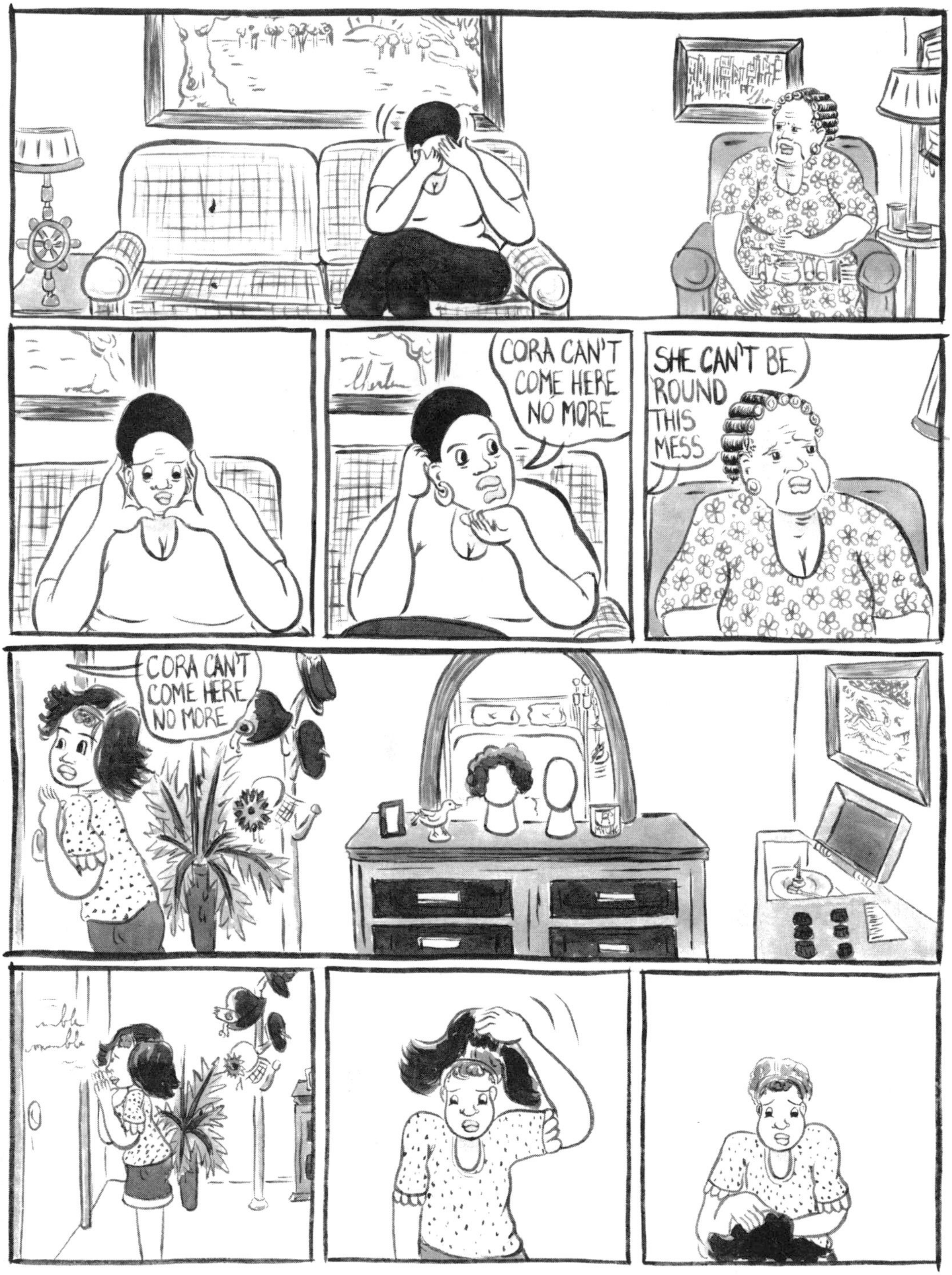
CORA CAN'T COME HERE NO MORE
SHE CAN'T BE ROUND THIS MESS
CORA CAN'T COME HERE NO MORE

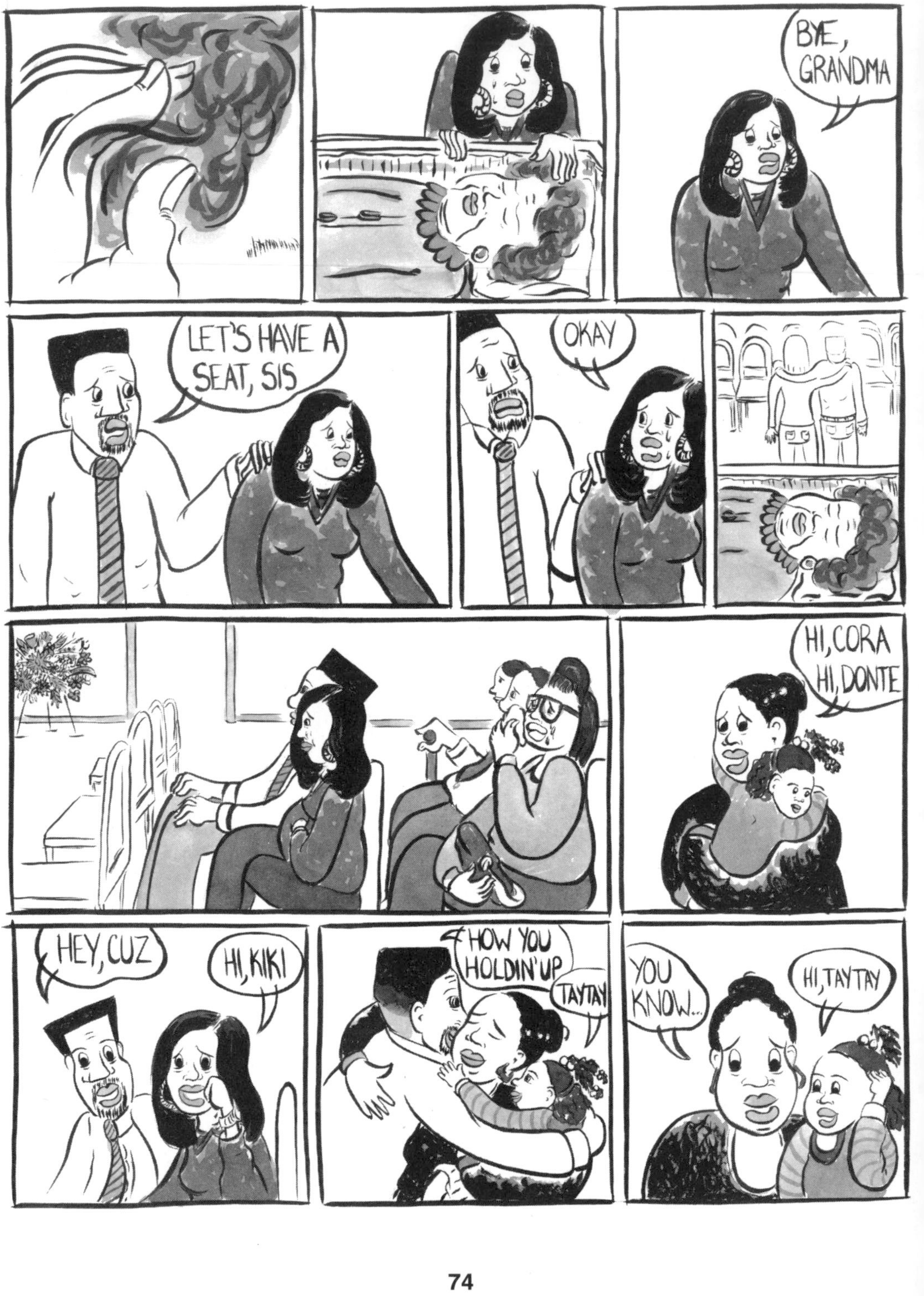
BYE, GRANDMA
LET'S HAVE A SEAT, SIS
OKAY
HI, CORA
HI, DONTE
HEY, CUZ
HI, KIKI
HOW YOU HOLDIN' UP
TAYTAY
YOU KNOW...
HI, TAYTAY

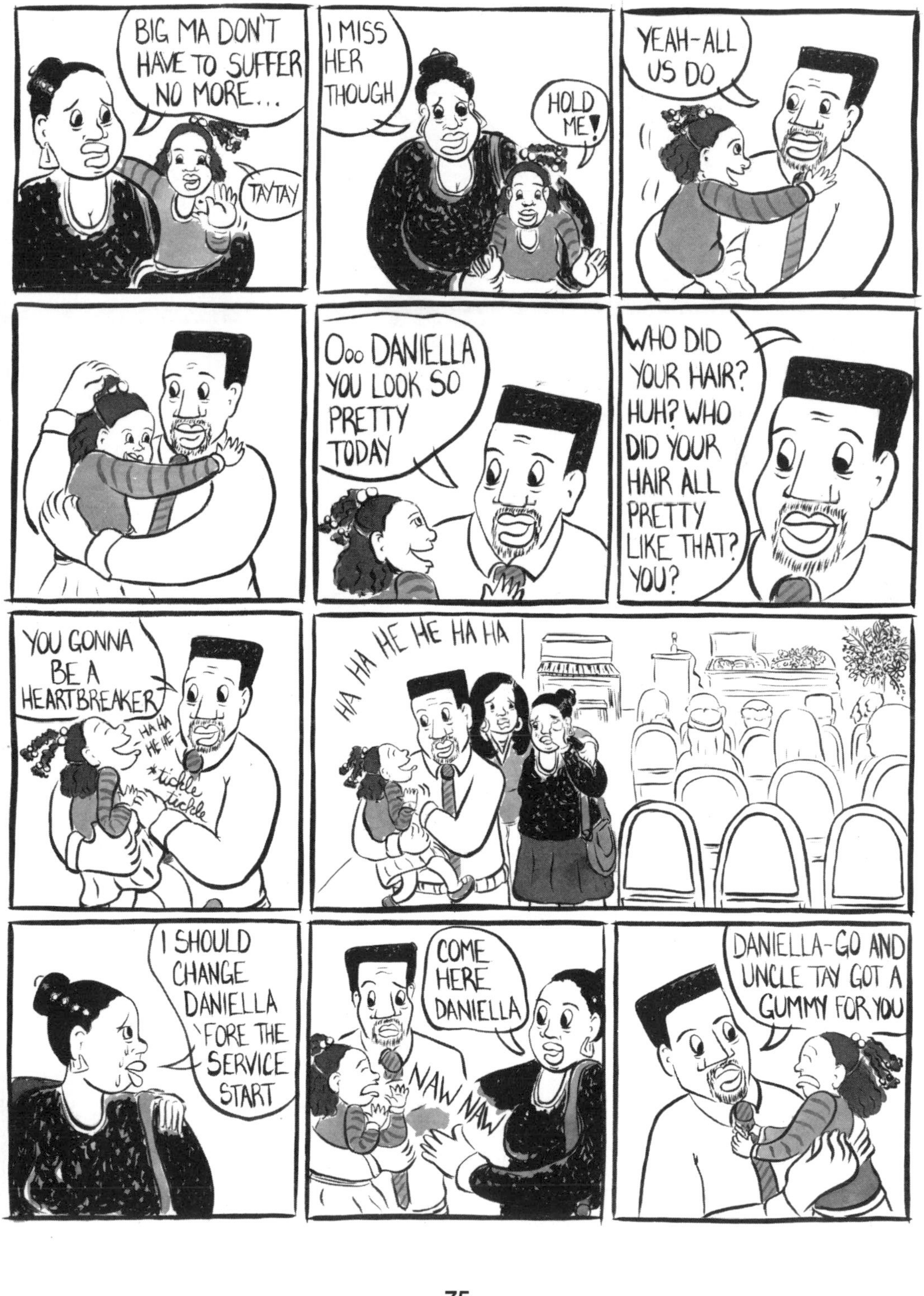
BIG MA DON'T HAVE TO SUFFER NO MORE...
TAYTAY
I MISS HER THOUGH
HOLD ME!
YEAH-ALL US DO
Ooo DANIELLA YOU LOOK SO PRETTY TODAY
WHO DID YOUR HAIR? HUH? WHO DID YOUR HAIR ALL PRETTY LIKE THAT? YOU?
YOU GONNA BE A HEARTBREAKER
HA HA HE HE
*tickle tickle
HA HA HE HE HA HA
I SHOULD CHANGE DANIELLA 'FORE THE SERVICE START
COME HERE DANIELLA
NAW NAW
DANIELLA-GO AND UNCLE TAY GOT A GUMMY FOR YOU

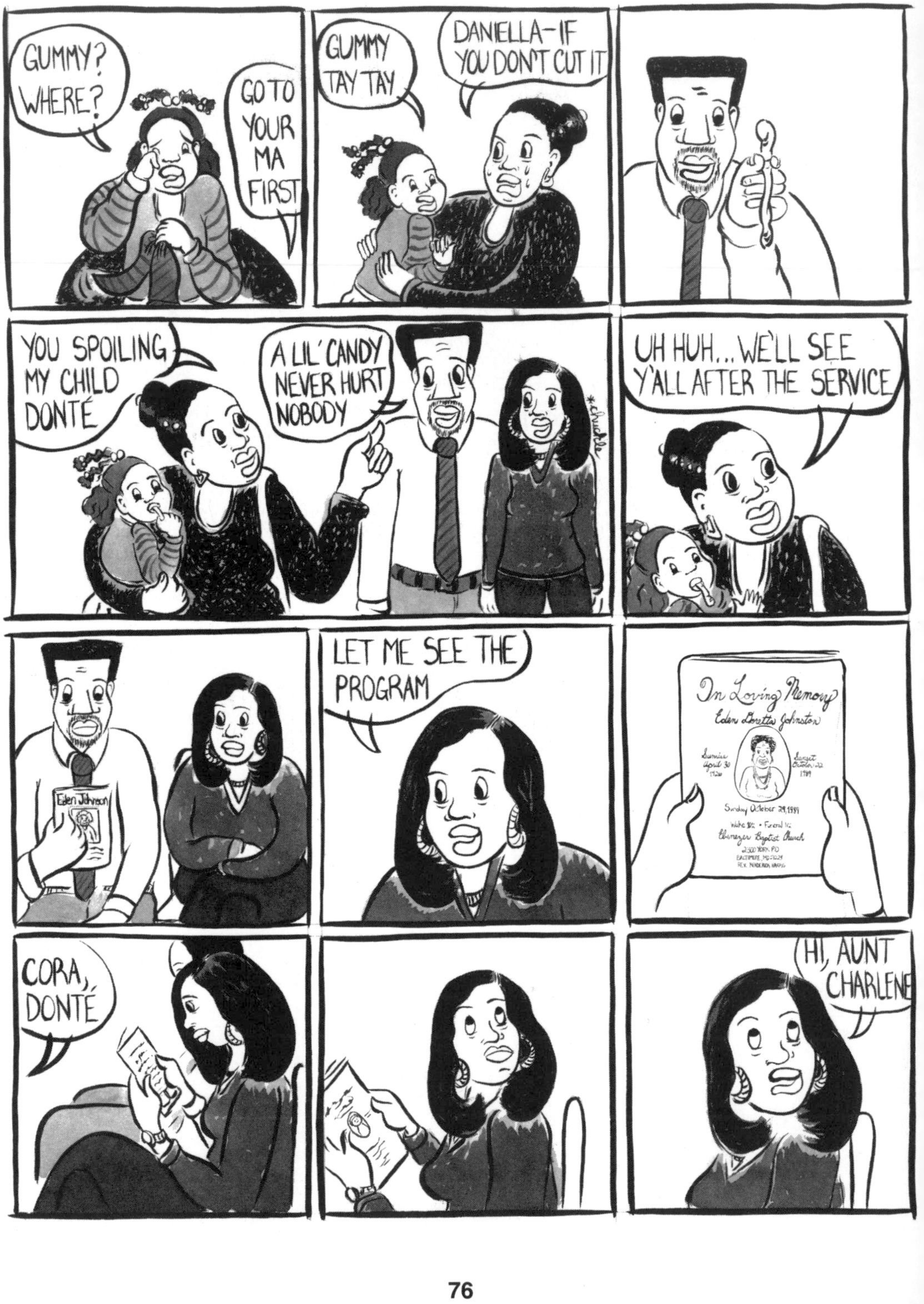
GUMMY? WHERE?
GO TO YOUR MA FIRST
GUMMY TAY TAY
DANIELLA–IF YOU DON'T CUT IT
YOU SPOILING MY CHILD DONTÉ
A LIL' CANDY NEVER HURT NOBODY
chuckle
UH HUH... WE'LL SEE Y'ALL AFTER THE SERVICE
Eden Johnson
LET ME SEE THE PROGRAM
In Loving Memory
Eden Doretta Johnston
Sunrise April 30
Sunset October 22 1989
Sunday October 29, 1989
Ebenezer Baptist Church
CORA, DONTÉ
HI, AUNT CHARLENE

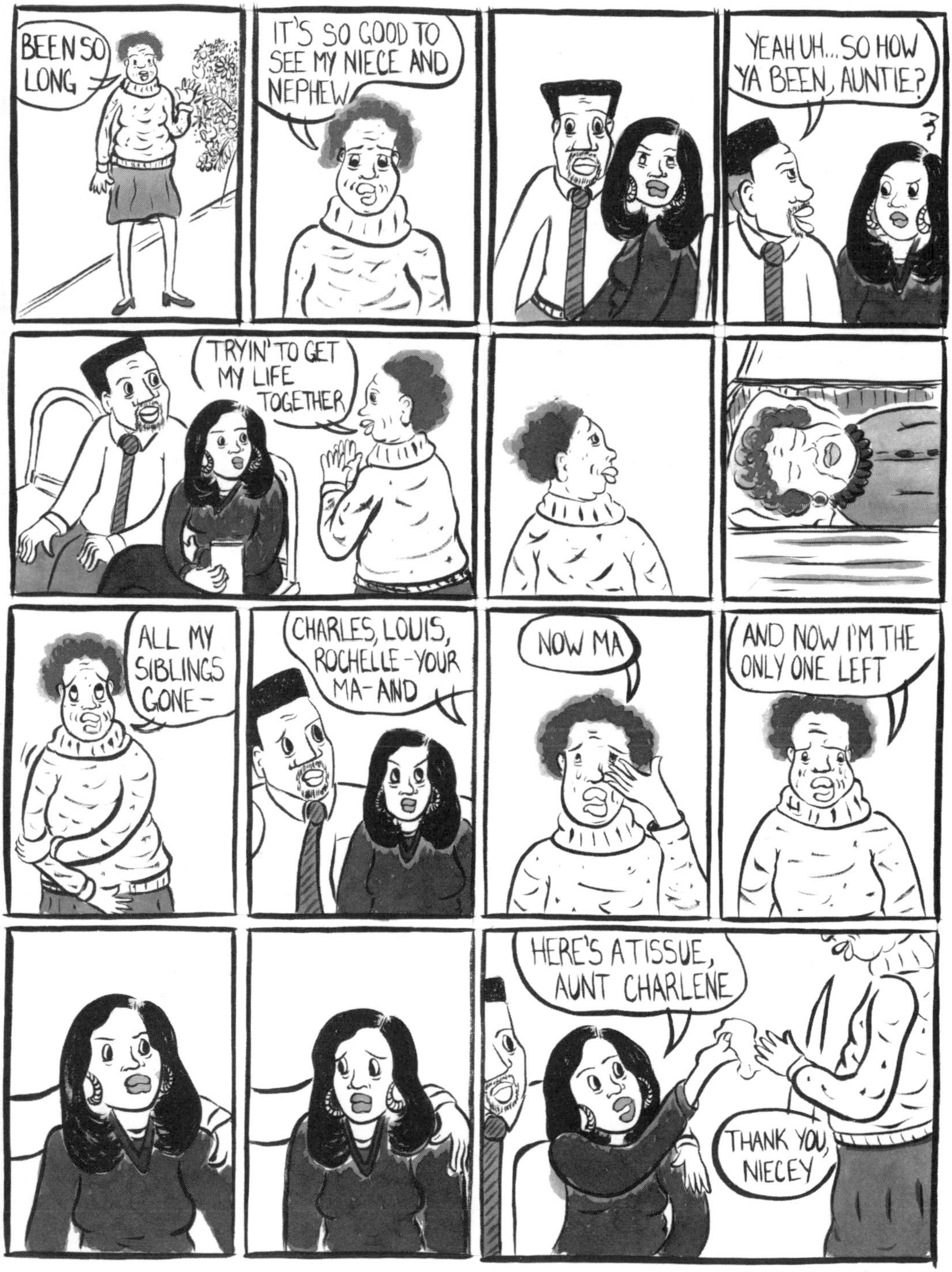
BEEN SO LONG
IT'S SO GOOD TO SEE MY NIECE AND NEPHEW
YEAH UH... SO HOW YA BEEN, AUNTIE?
TRYIN' TO GET MY LIFE TOGETHER
ALL MY SIBLINGS GONE-
CHARLES, LOUIS, ROCHELLE-YOUR MA-AND
NOW MA
AND NOW I'M THE ONLY ONE LEFT
HERE'S A TISSUE, AUNT CHARLENE
THANK YOU, NIECEY

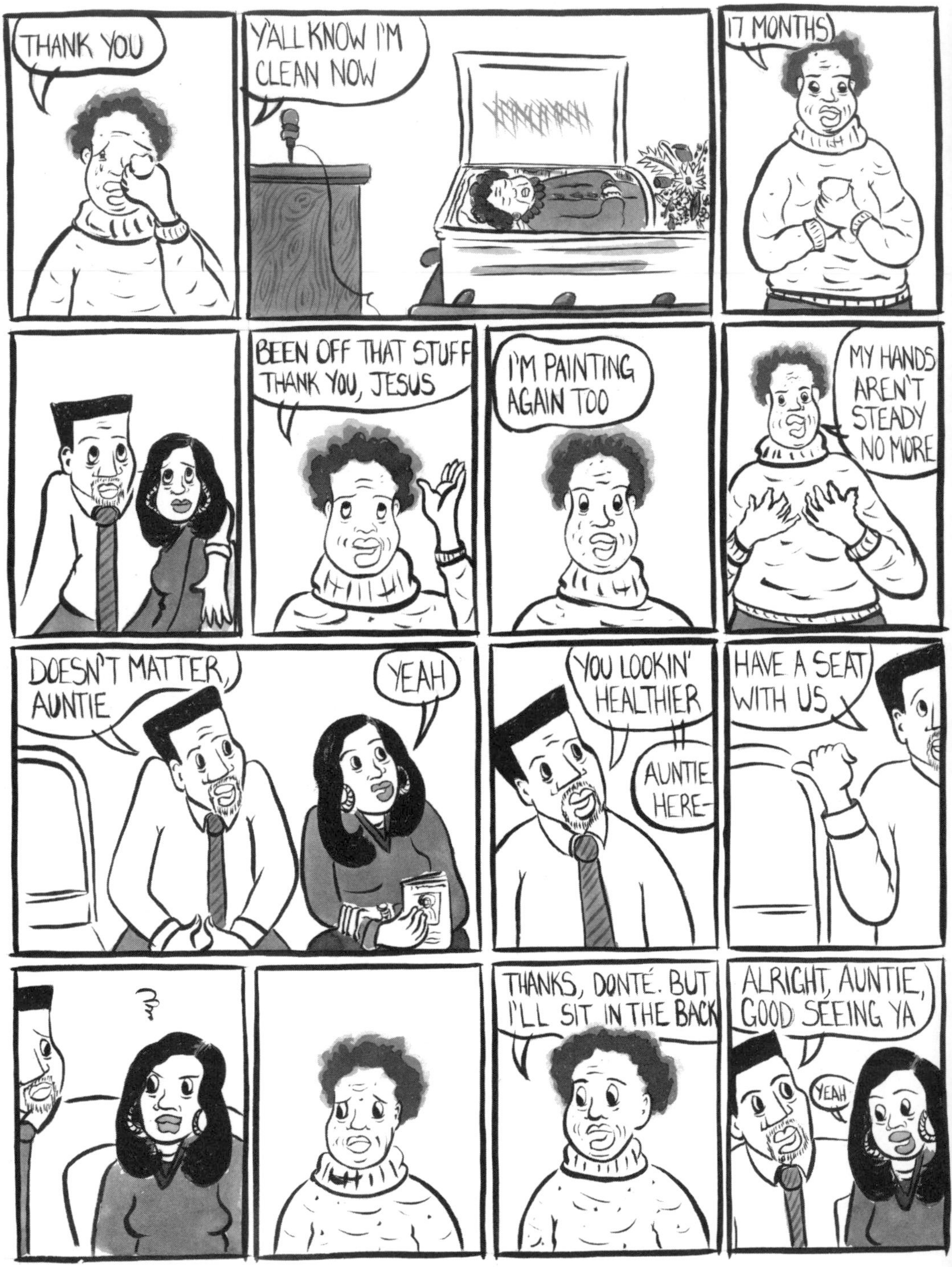
THANK YOU
Y'ALL KNOW I'M CLEAN NOW
17 MONTHS
BEEN OFF THAT STUFF THANK YOU, JESUS
I'M PAINTING AGAIN TOO
MY HANDS AREN'T STEADY NO MORE
DOESN'T MATTER, AUNTIE
YEAH
YOU LOOKIN' HEALTHIER
AUNTIE HERE-
HAVE A SEAT WITH US
THANKS, DONTÉ. BUT I'LL SIT IN THE BACK
ALRIGHT, AUNTIE, GOOD SEEING YA
YEAH

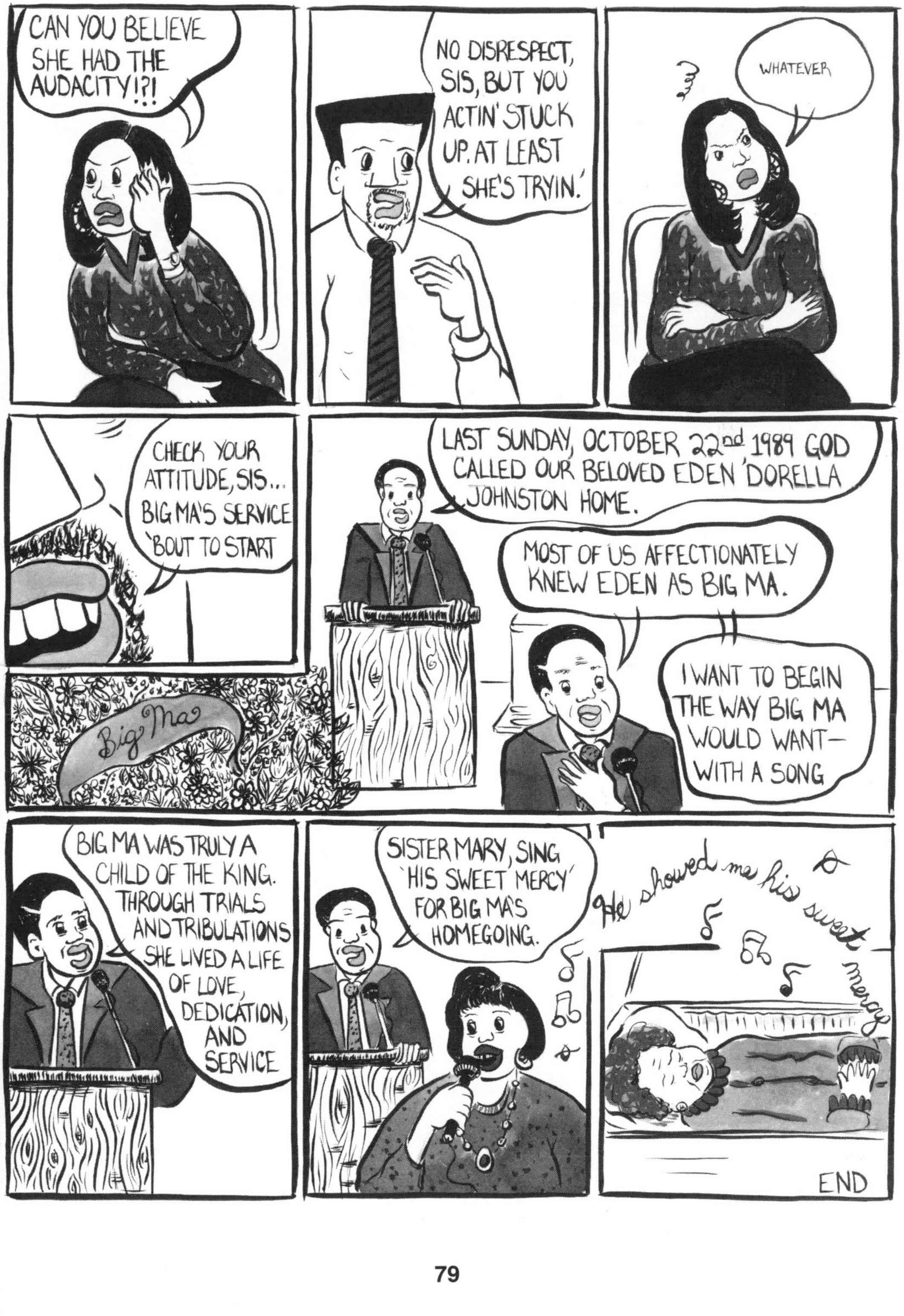
CAN YOU BELIEVE SHE HAD THE AUDACITY!?!
NO DISRESPECT, SIS, BUT YOU ACTIN' STUCK UP. AT LEAST SHE'S TRYIN.'
WHATEVER
CHECK YOUR ATTITUDE, SIS... BIG MA'S SERVICE 'BOUT TO START
Big Ma
LAST SUNDAY, OCTOBER 22nd 1989 GOD CALLED OUR BELOVED EDEN 'DORELLA' JOHNSTON HOME.
MOST OF US AFFECTIONATELY KNEW EDEN AS BIG MA.
I WANT TO BEGIN THE WAY BIG MA WOULD WANT— WITH A SONG
BIG MA WAS TRULY A CHILD OF THE KING. THROUGH TRIALS AND TRIBULATIONS SHE LIVED A LIFE OF LOVE, DEDICATION, AND SERVICE
SISTER MARY, SING 'HIS SWEET MERCY' FOR BIG MA'S HOMEGOING.
He showed me his sweet mercy
END

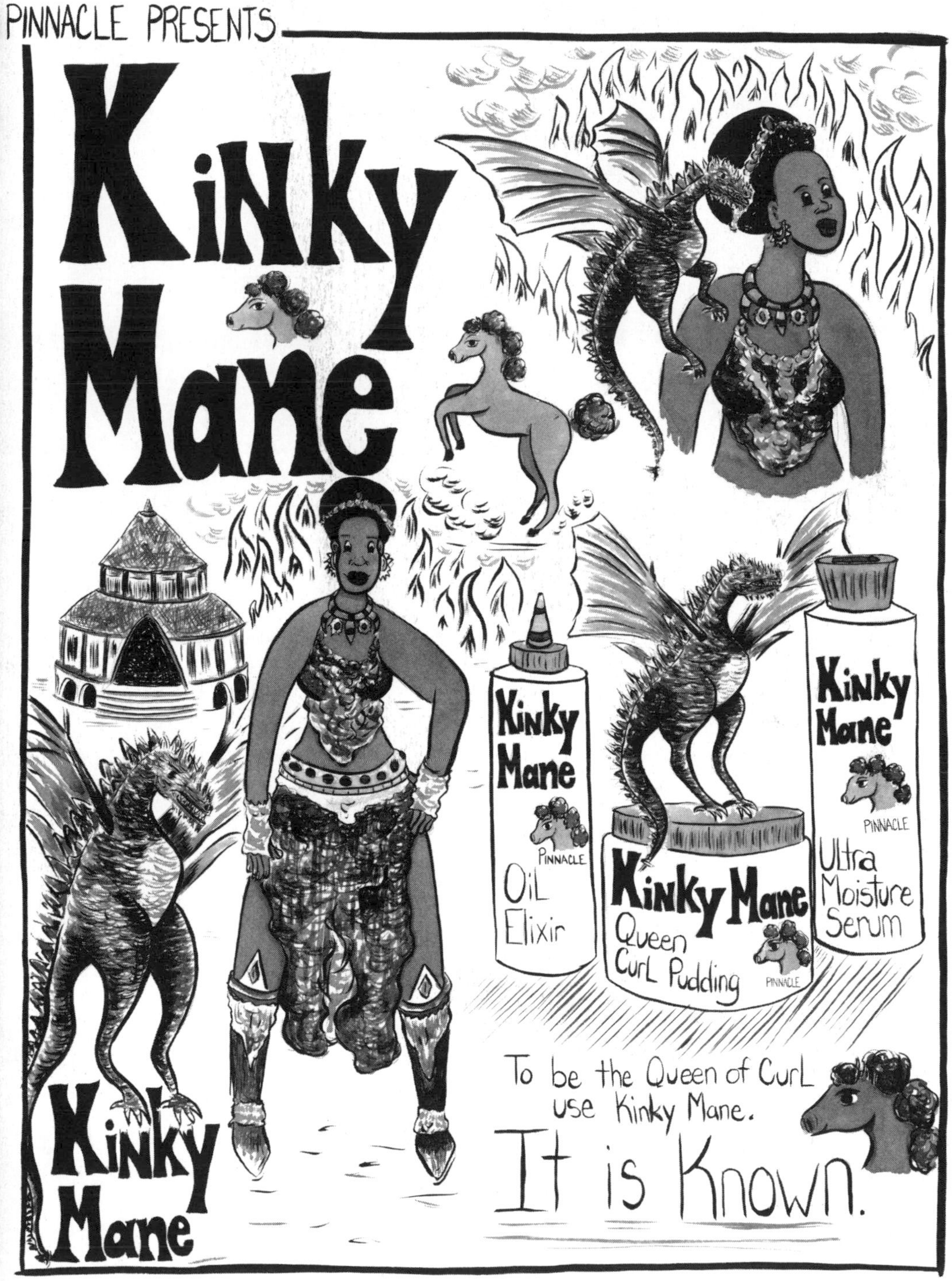
PINNACLE PRESENTS
Kinky Mane
Kinky Mane
Pinnacle
Oil Elixir
Kinky Mane
Queen Curl Pudding
Pinnacle
Kinky Mane
Pinnacle
Ultra Moisture Serum
Kinky Mane
To be the Queen of Curl use Kinky Mane.
It is Known.

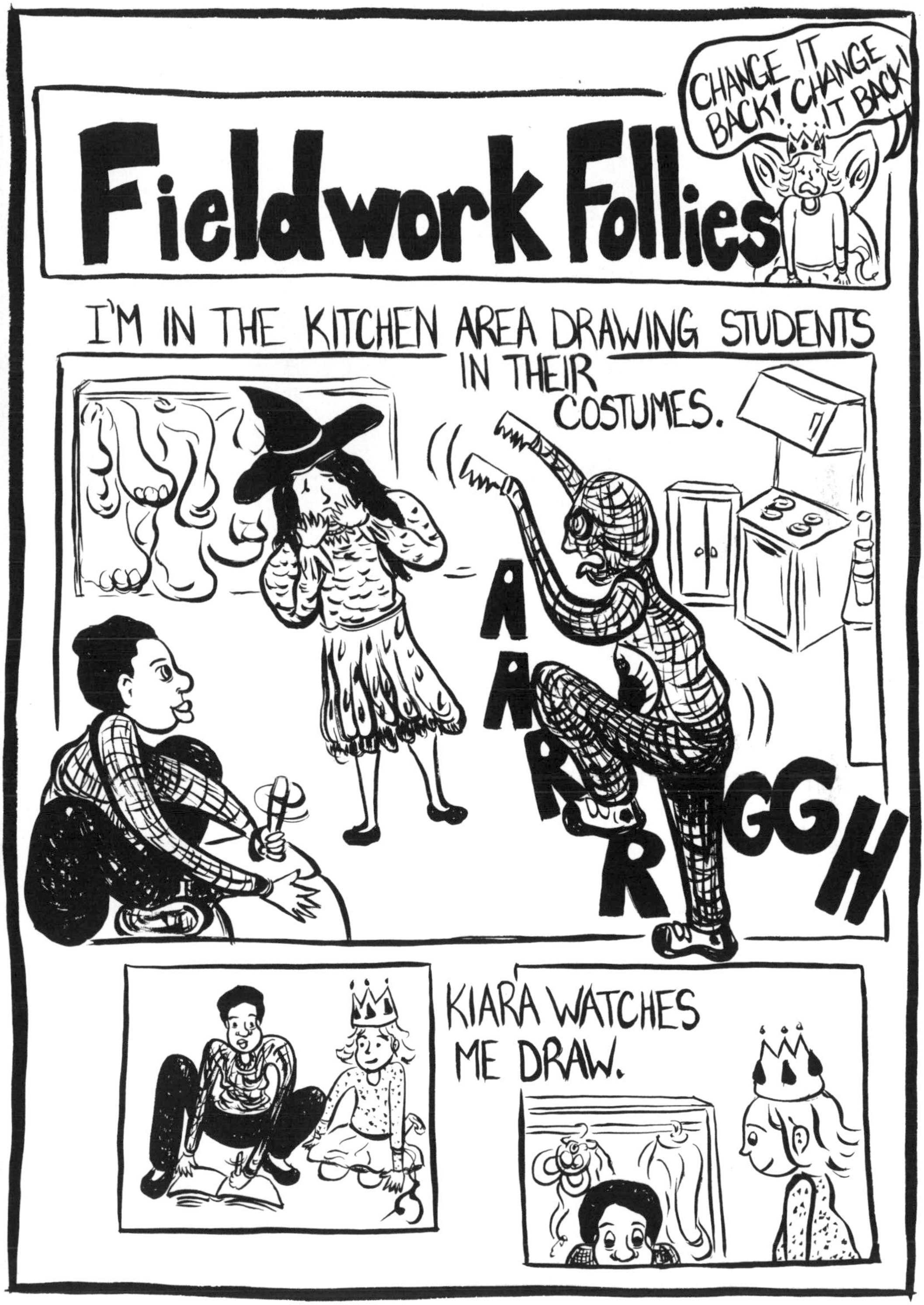
Fieldwork Follies
CHANGE IT BACK! CHANGE IT BACK!
I'M IN THE KITCHEN AREA DRAWING STUDENTS IN THEIR COSTUMES.
AARRRGGH
KIARA WATCHES ME DRAW.

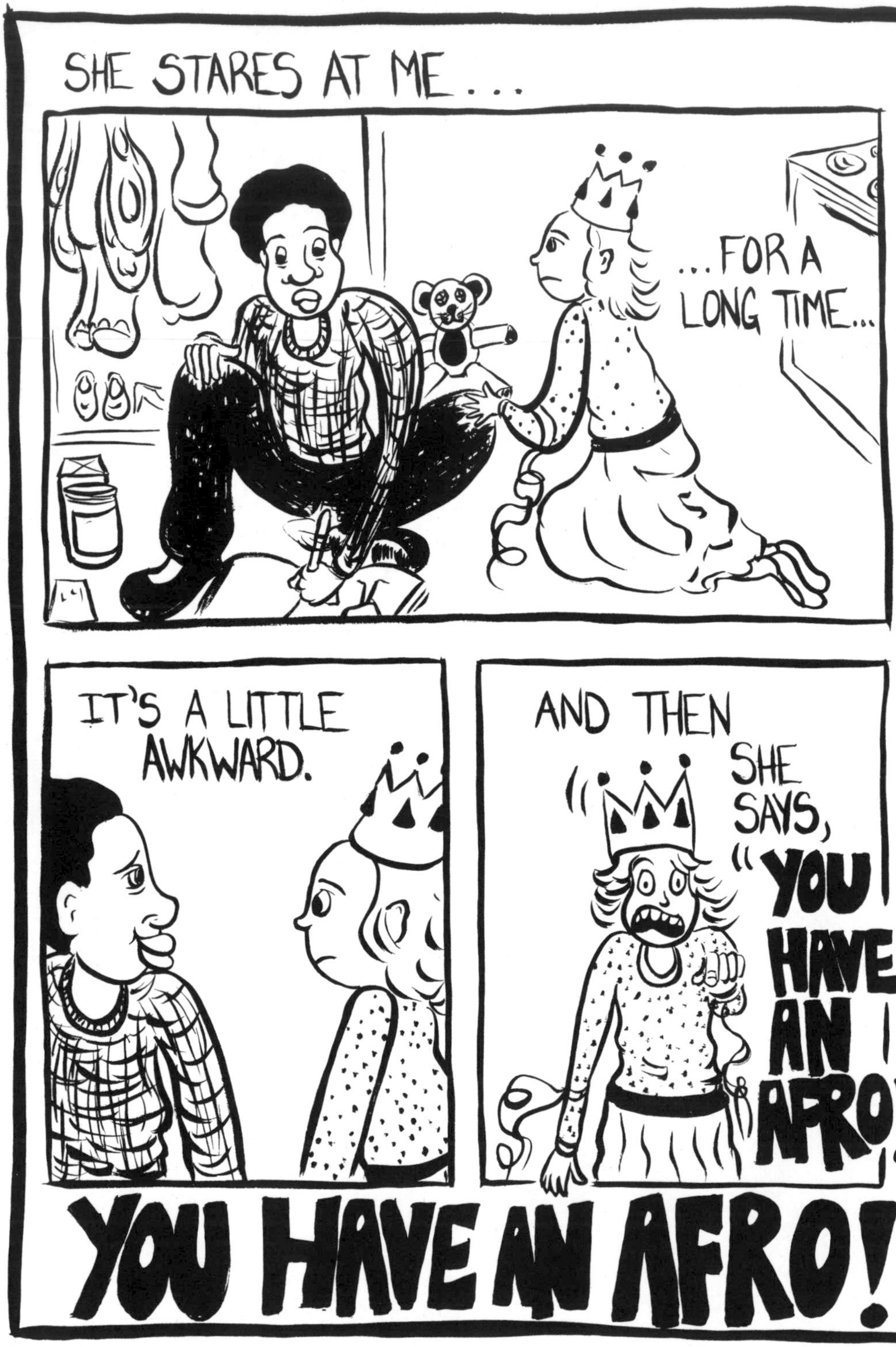

SHE STARES AT ME...
...FOR A LONG TIME...
IT'S A LITTLE AWKWARD.
AND THEN SHE SAYS, "YOU HAVE AN AFRO!"
YOU HAVE AN AFRO!

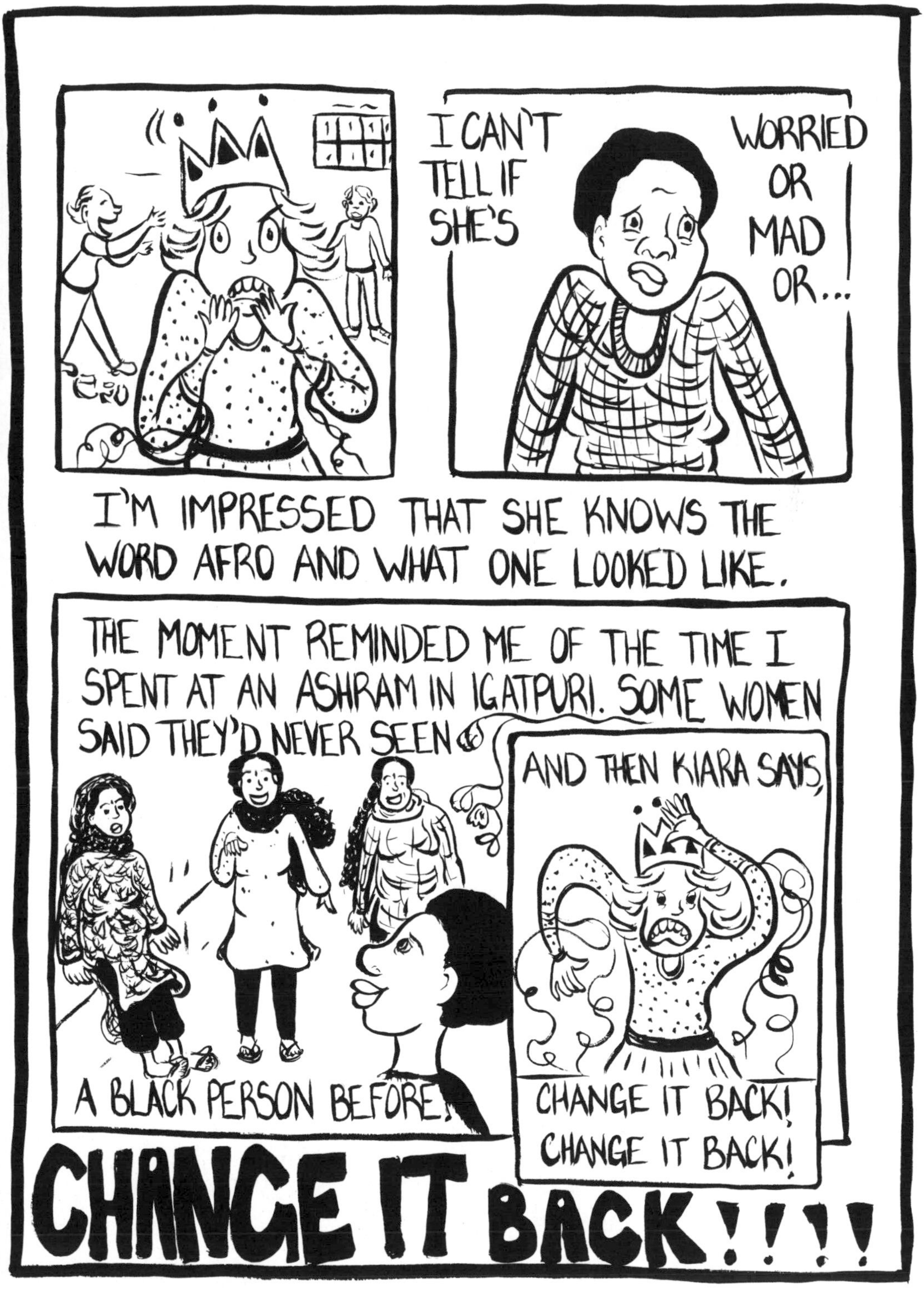

I CAN'T TELL IF SHE'S
WORRIED OR MAD OR...
I'M IMPRESSED THAT SHE KNOWS THE WORD AFRO AND WHAT ONE LOOKED LIKE.
THE MOMENT REMINDED ME OF THE TIME I SPENT AT AN ASHRAM IN IGATPURI. SOME WOMEN SAID THEY'D NEVER SEEN
A BLACK PERSON BEFORE.
AND THEN KIARA SAYS,
CHANGE IT BACK!
CHANGE IT BACK!
CHANGE IT BACK!!!!

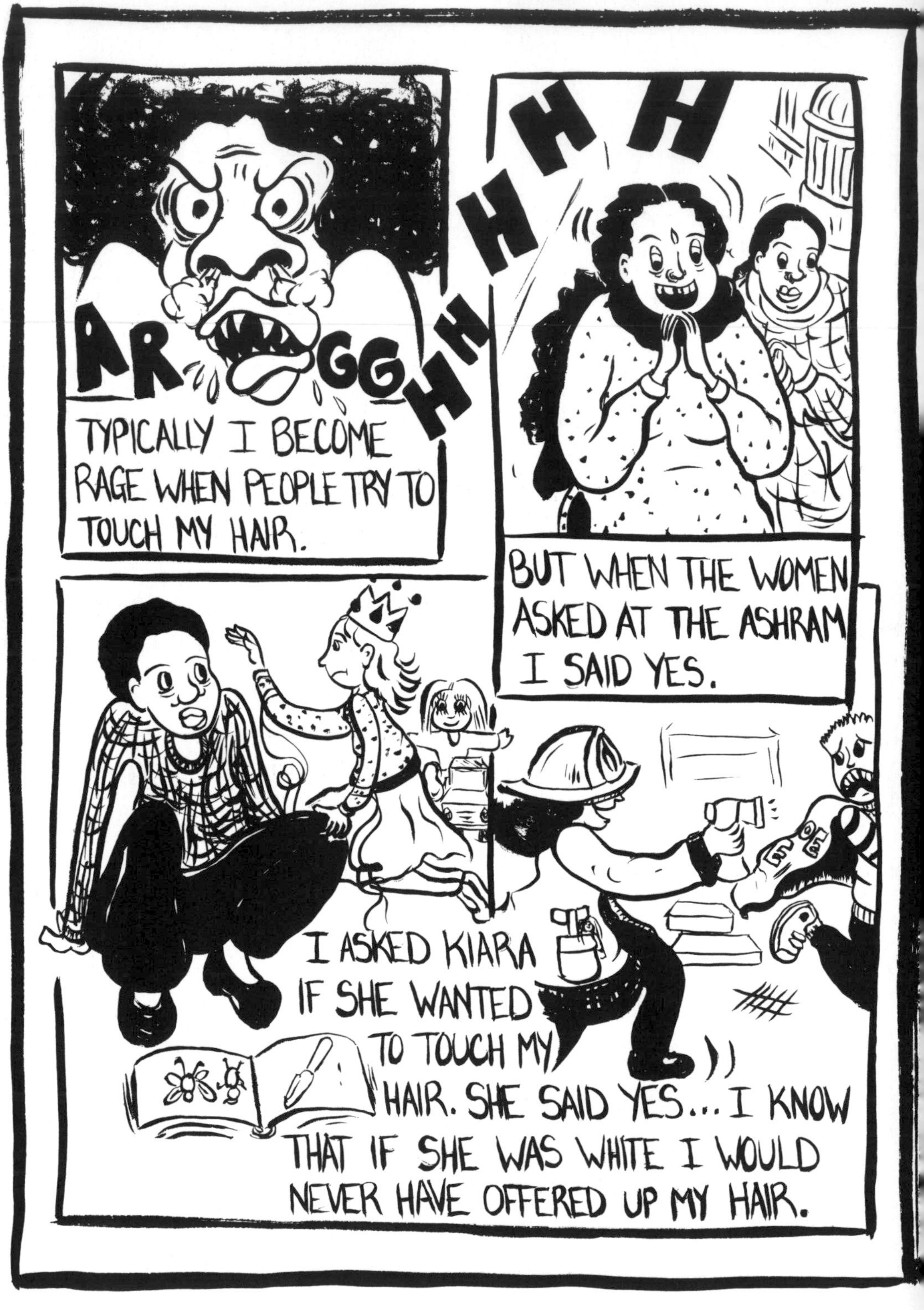
ARGGHHHHHHH
TYPICALLY I BECOME RAGE WHEN PEOPLE TRY TO TOUCH MY HAIR.
BUT WHEN THE WOMEN ASKED AT THE ASHRAM I SAID YES.
I ASKED KIARA IF SHE WANTED TO TOUCH MY HAIR. SHE SAID YES... I KNOW THAT IF SHE WAS WHITE I WOULD NEVER HAVE OFFERED UP MY HAIR.

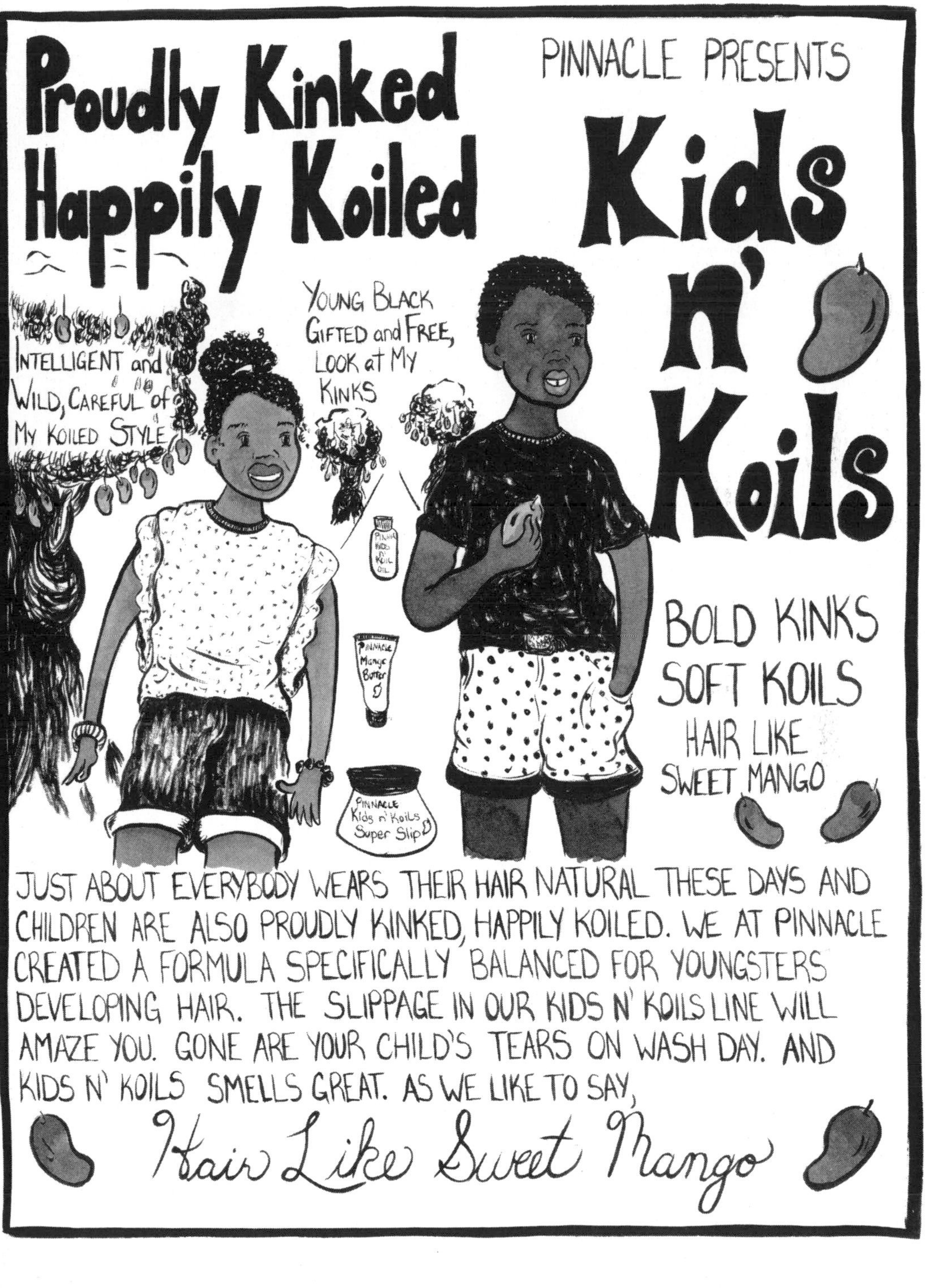
Proudly Kinked
Happily Koiled
PINNACLE PRESENTS
Kids n' Koils
INTELLIGENT and WILD, CAREFUL of My KOILED STYLE
YOUNG BLACK GIFTED and FREE, LOOK at My KINKS
PINNACLE Mango Butter
PINNACLE Kids n' Koils Super Slip
BOLD KINKS
SOFT KOILS
HAIR LIKE SWEET MANGO
JUST ABOUT EVERYBODY WEARS THEIR HAIR NATURAL THESE DAYS AND CHILDREN ARE ALSO PROUDLY KINKED, HAPPILY KOILED. WE AT PINNACLE CREATED A FORMULA SPECIFICALLY BALANCED FOR YOUNGSTERS DEVELOPING HAIR. THE SLIPPAGE IN OUR KIDS N' KOILS LINE WILL AMAZE YOU. GONE ARE YOUR CHILD'S TEARS ON WASH DAY. AND KIDS N' KOILS SMELLS GREAT. AS WE LIKE TO SAY,
Hair Like Sweet Mango

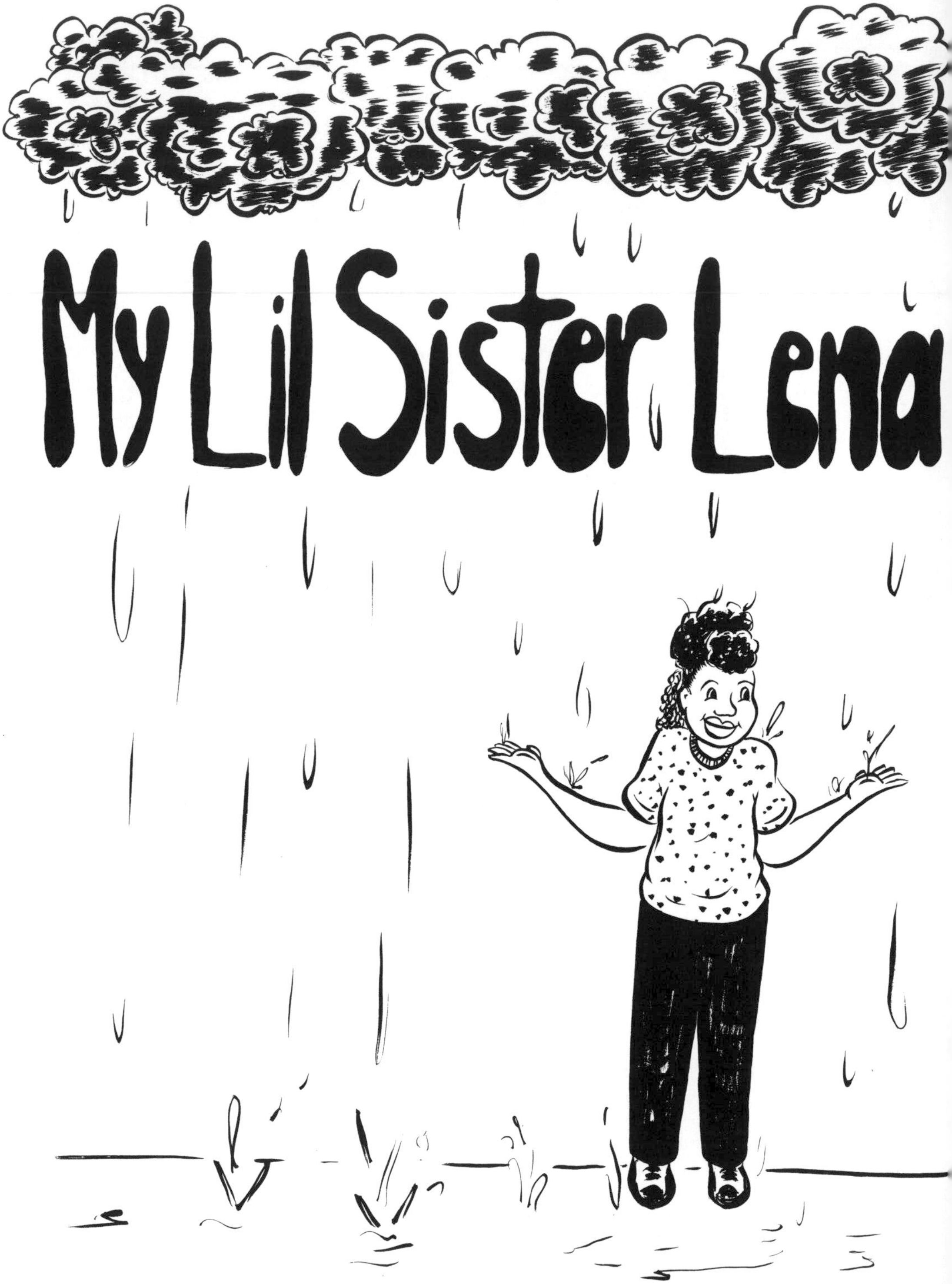
My Lil Sister Lena

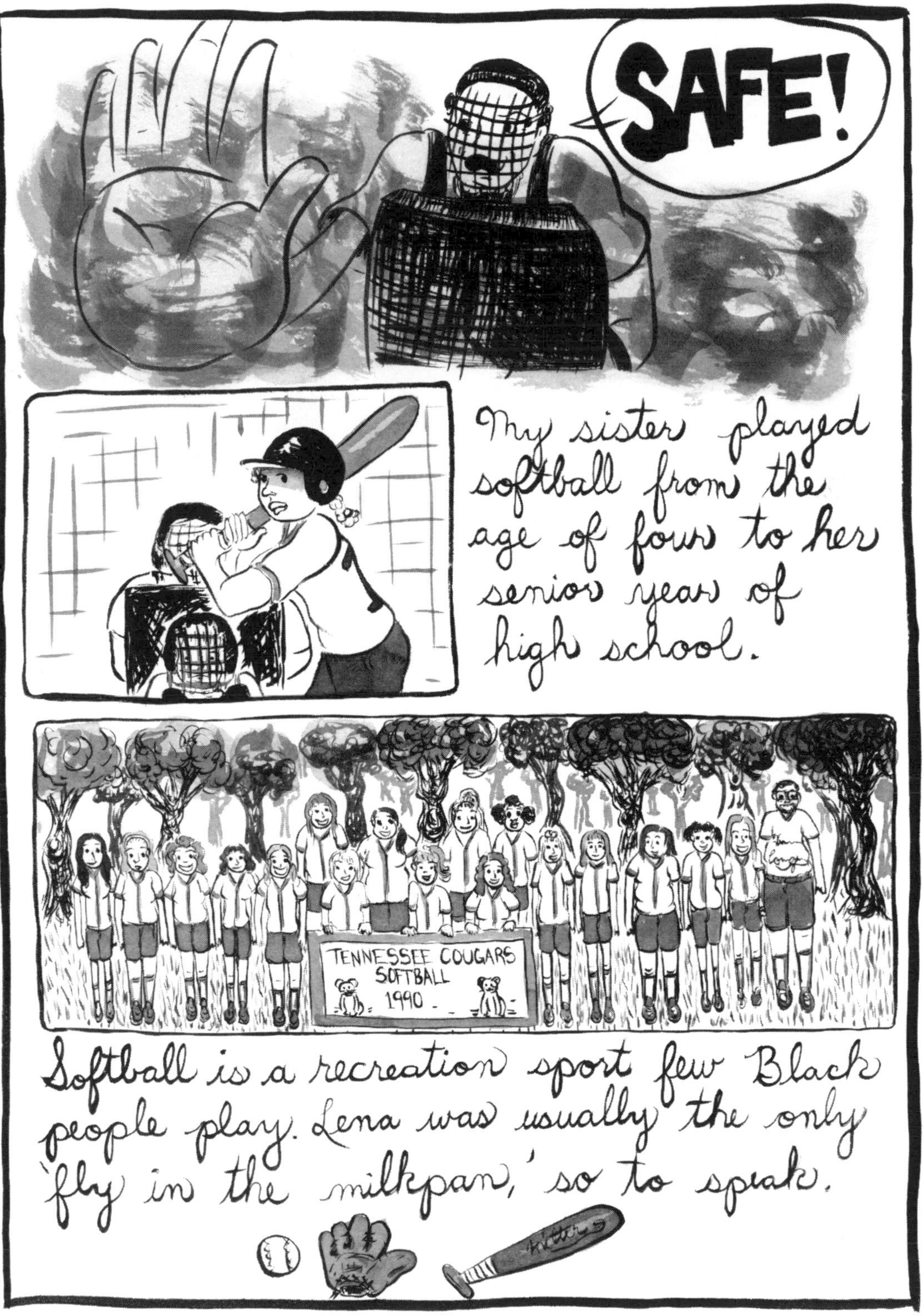
SAFE!
My sister played softball from the age of four to her senior year of high school.
TENNESSEE COUGARS SOFTBALL 1990
Softball is a recreation sport few Black people play. Lena was usually the only 'fly in the milkpan,' so to speak.

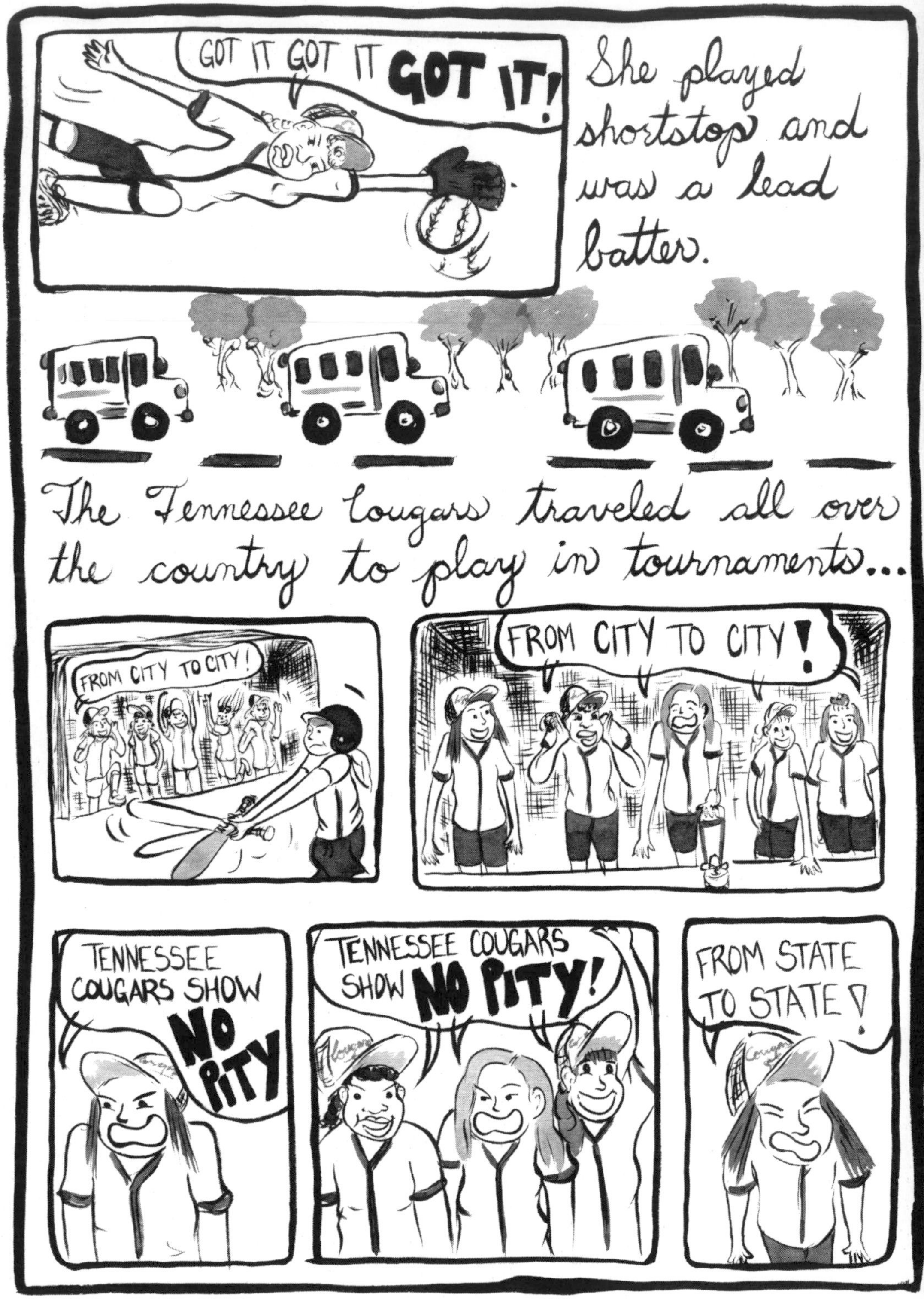
GOT IT GOT IT GOT IT!
She played shortstop and was a lead batter.
The Tennessee Cougars traveled all over the country to play in tournaments...
FROM CITY TO CITY!
FROM CITY TO CITY!
TENNESSEE COUGARS SHOW NO PITY
TENNESSEE COUGARS SHOW NO PITY!
FROM STATE TO STATE!

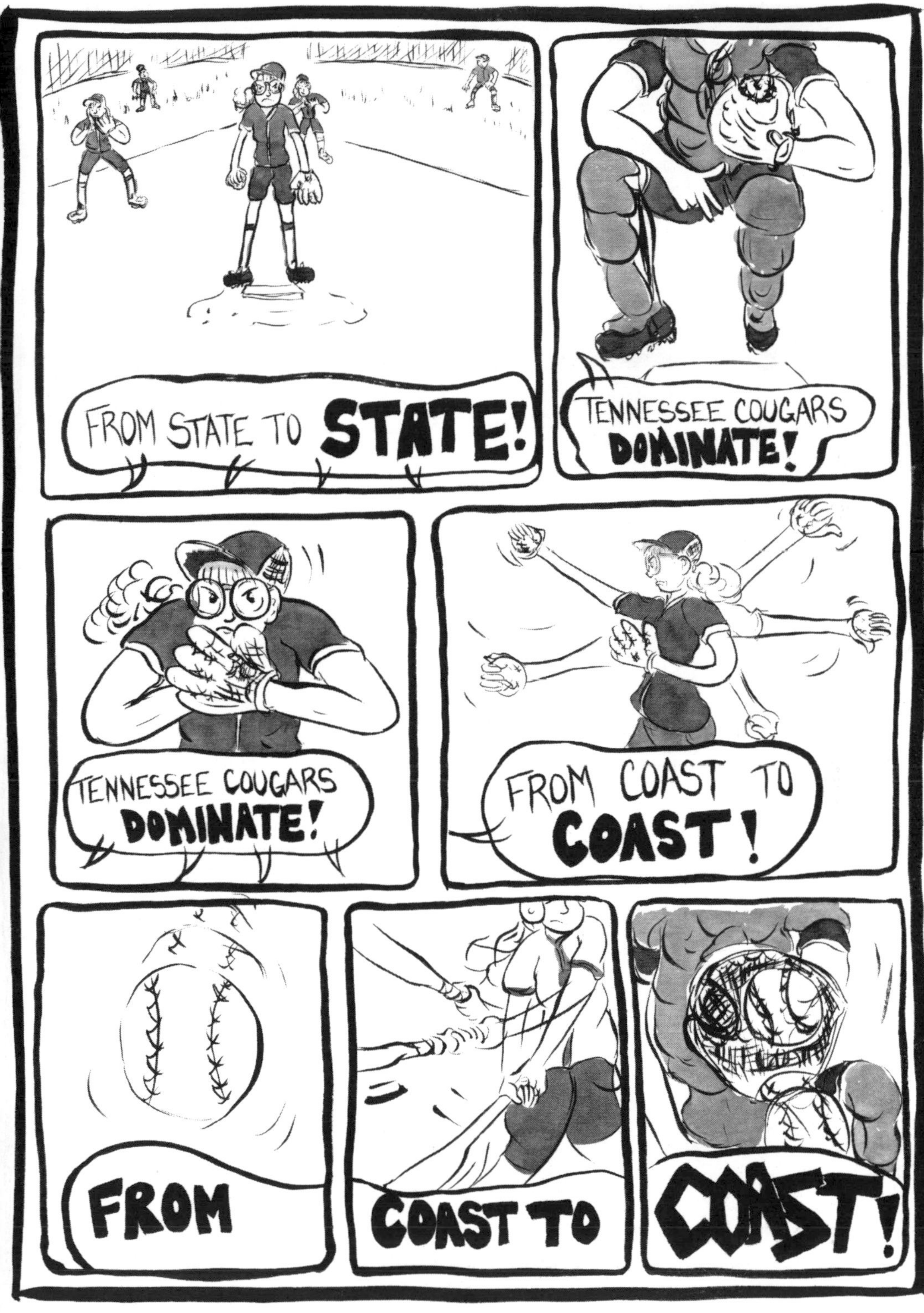
FROM STATE TO STATE!
TENNESSEE COUGARS DOMINATE!
TENNESSEE COUGARS DOMINATE!
FROM COAST TO COAST!
FROM
COAST TO
COAST!

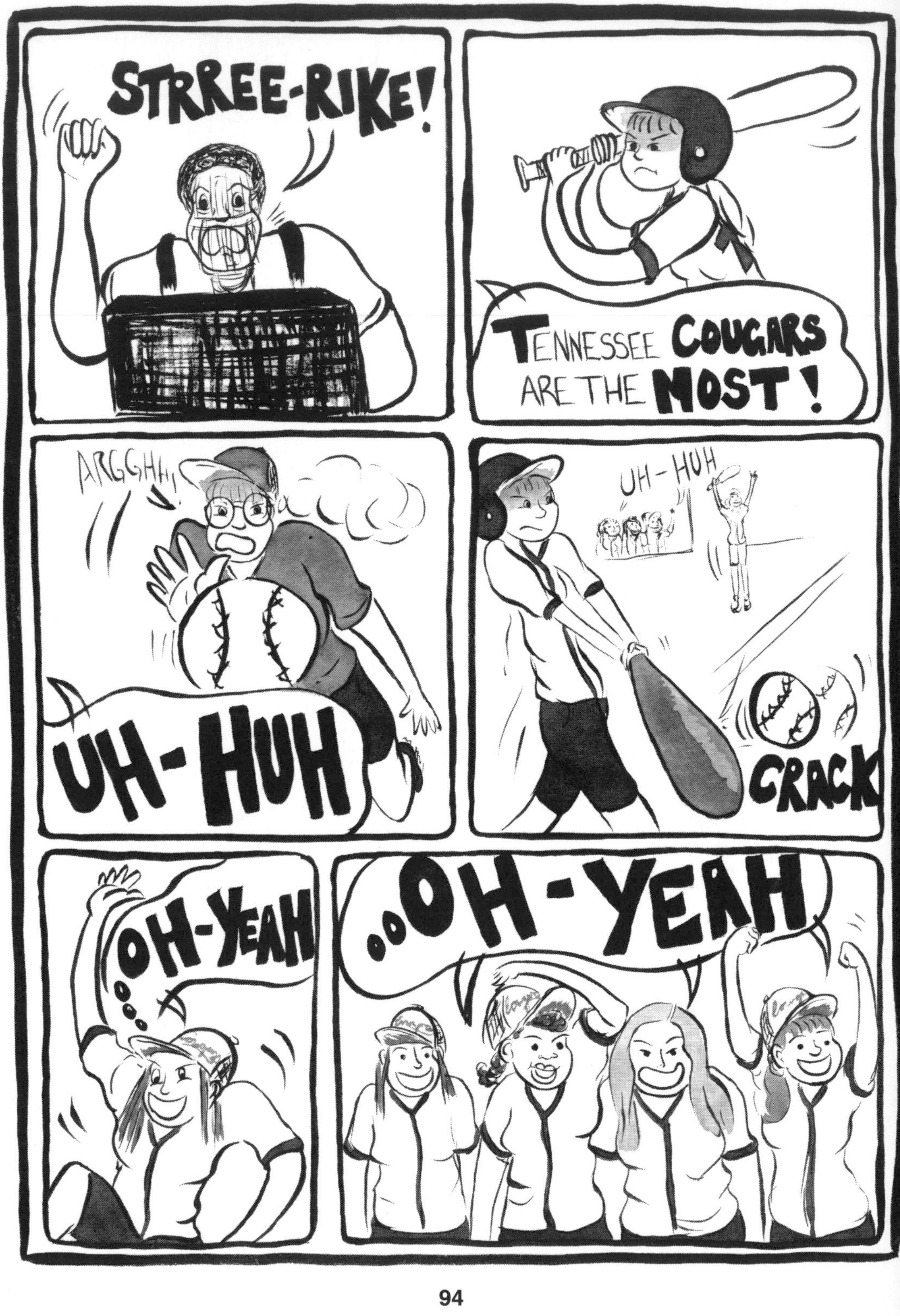
STRREE-RIKE!
TENNESSEE COUGARS ARE THE MOST!
ARGGHH
UH-HUH
UH-HUH
CRACK
OH-YEAH
OH-YEAH

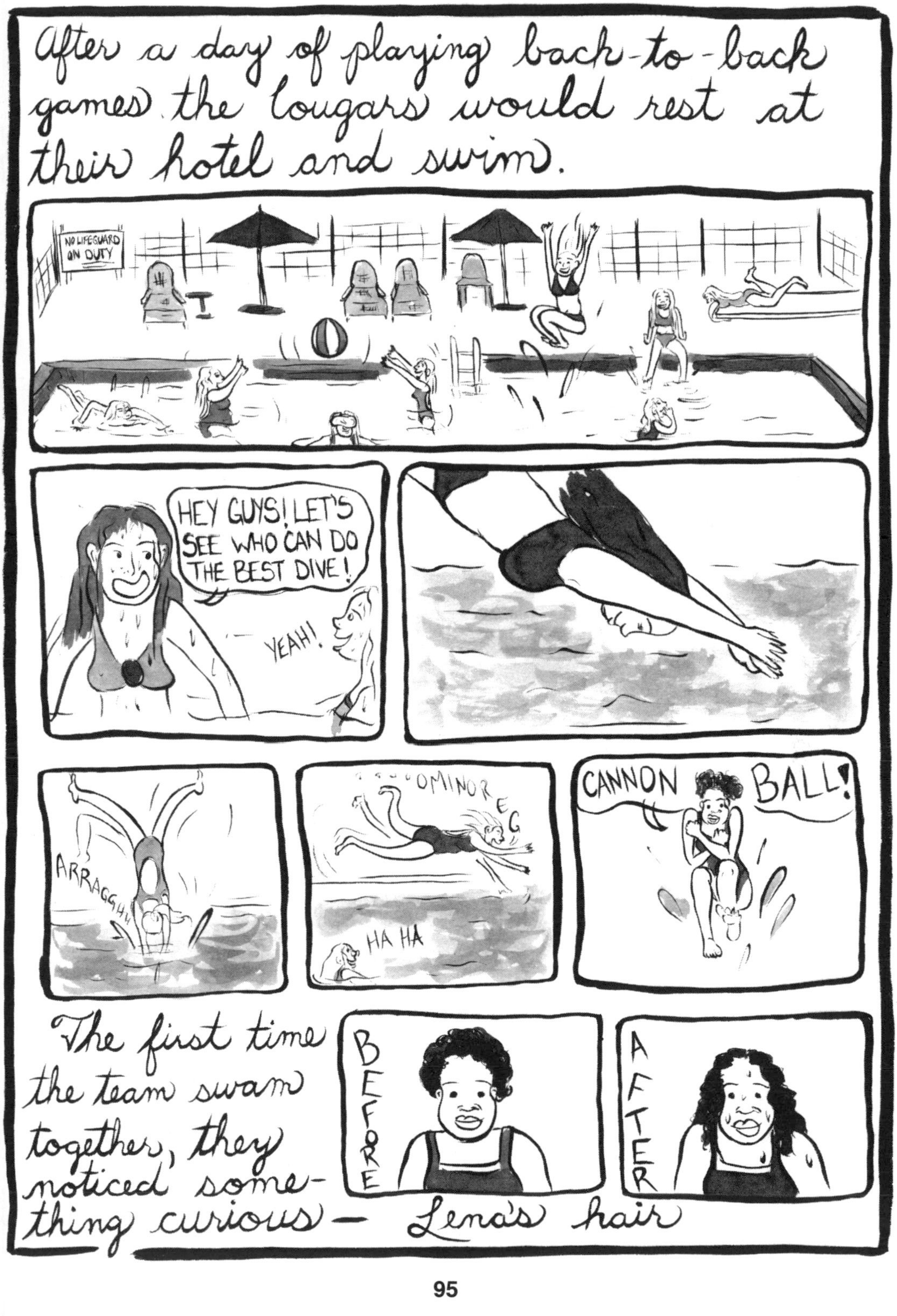
After a day of playing back-to-back games the Cougars would rest at their hotel and swim.
NO LIFEGUARD ON DUTY
HEY GUYS! LET'S SEE WHO CAN DO THE BEST DIVE!
YEAH!
ARRAGGHH
OMINOREG
HA HA
CANNON BALL!
The first time the team swam together, they noticed something curious — Lena's hair
BEFORE
AFTER

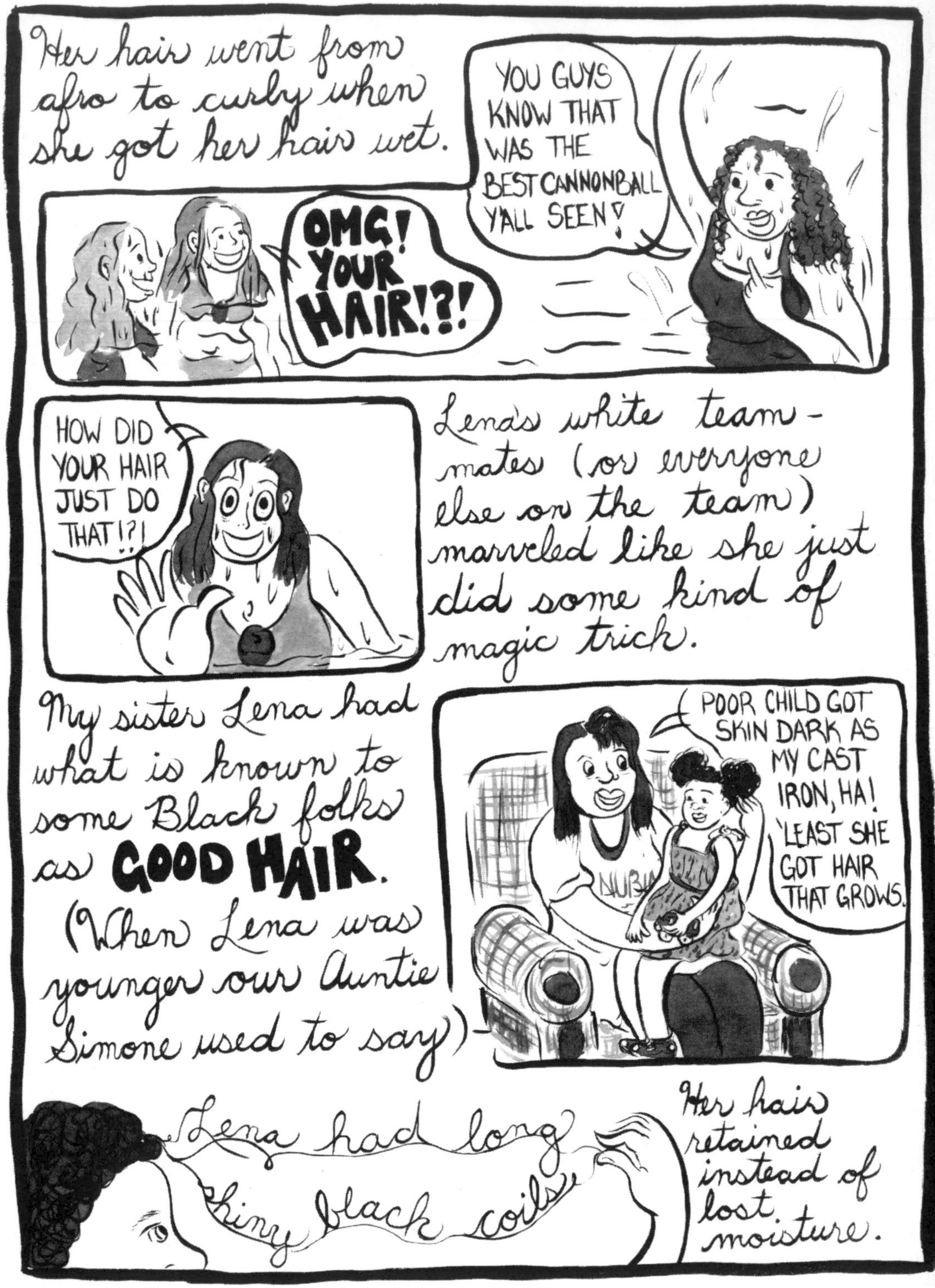

Her hair went from afro to curly when she got her hair wet.
YOU GUYS KNOW THAT WAS THE BEST CANNONBALL Y'ALL SEEN!
OMG! YOUR HAIR!?!
HOW DID YOUR HAIR JUST DO THAT!?!
Lena's white team-mates (or everyone else on the team) marveled like she just did some kind of magic trick.
My sister Lena had what is known to some Black folks as GOOD HAIR.
(When Lena was younger our Auntie Simone used to say)—
POOR CHILD GOT SKIN DARK AS MY CAST IRON, HA! 'LEAST SHE GOT HAIR THAT GROWS.
Lena had long shiny black coils.
Her hair retained instead of lost moisture.

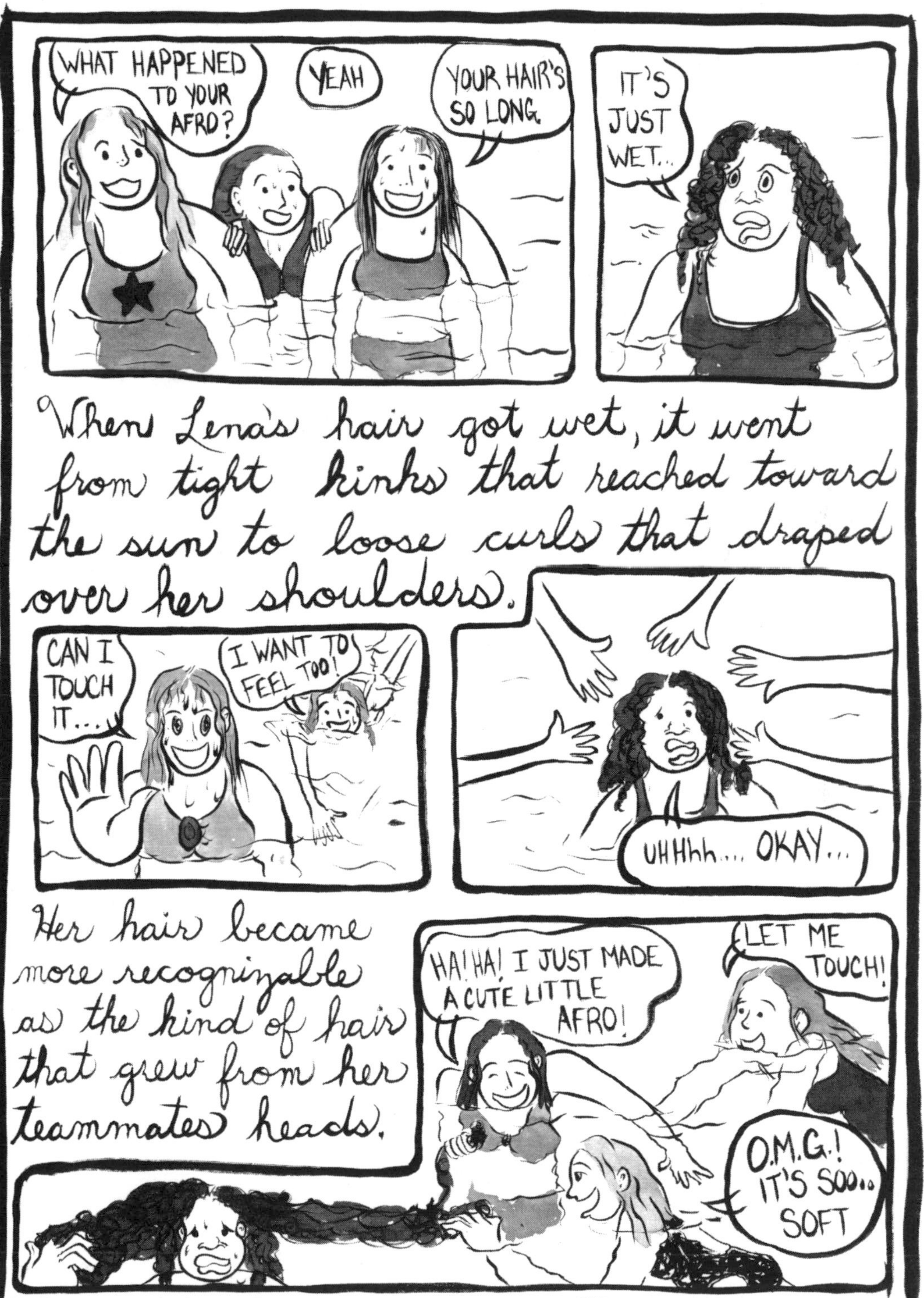
WHAT HAPPENED TO YOUR AFRO?
YEAH
YOUR HAIR'S SO LONG.
IT'S JUST WET...
When Lena's hair got wet, it went from tight kinks that reached toward the sun to loose curls that draped over her shoulders.
CAN I TOUCH IT...
I WANT TO FEEL TOO!
UHHhh.... OKAY...
Her hair became more recognizable as the kind of hair that grew from her teammates heads.
HA! HA! I JUST MADE A CUTE LITTLE AFRO!
LET ME TOUCH!
O.M.G.! IT'S SOO.. SOFT

The players floated towards her the way jellyfish sway in search of prey.

After the first time the Tennessee Cougars swam together, Lena's hair became their little curio.

WHY DON'T YOU WEAR YOUR HAIR OUT?

HUH?

EACH & EVERY...

Practice

GOOD GAME GOOD GAME GOOD GAME GOOD GAME GOOD GAME GOOD GAME GOOD GAME GOOD GAME

Game

Tennessee Cougars Softball

Tournament

Team Photo

GATORADE

Post-Game Celebration

and team social

the white girls watched and studied Lena's hair.

YOUR HAIR'S NICER THAN THIS BLACK GIRL'S IN MY MATH CLASS

YOU'RE DIFFERENT FROM OTHER BLACK GIRLS

WHY DO YOU ALWAYS HAVE YOUR HAIR BRAIDED?

WHY DOES YOUR HAIR ALWAYS SMELL LIKE CHOCOLATE?

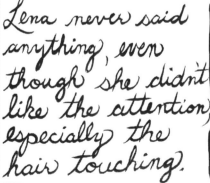

GIVE ME A T-

SO SOFT

—HUH!?!

And, of course they'd touch Lena's hair whenever they felt the urge, which was all the time.

Lena never said anything, even though she didn't like the attention, especially the hair touching.

NICE CATCH!

!?!

99

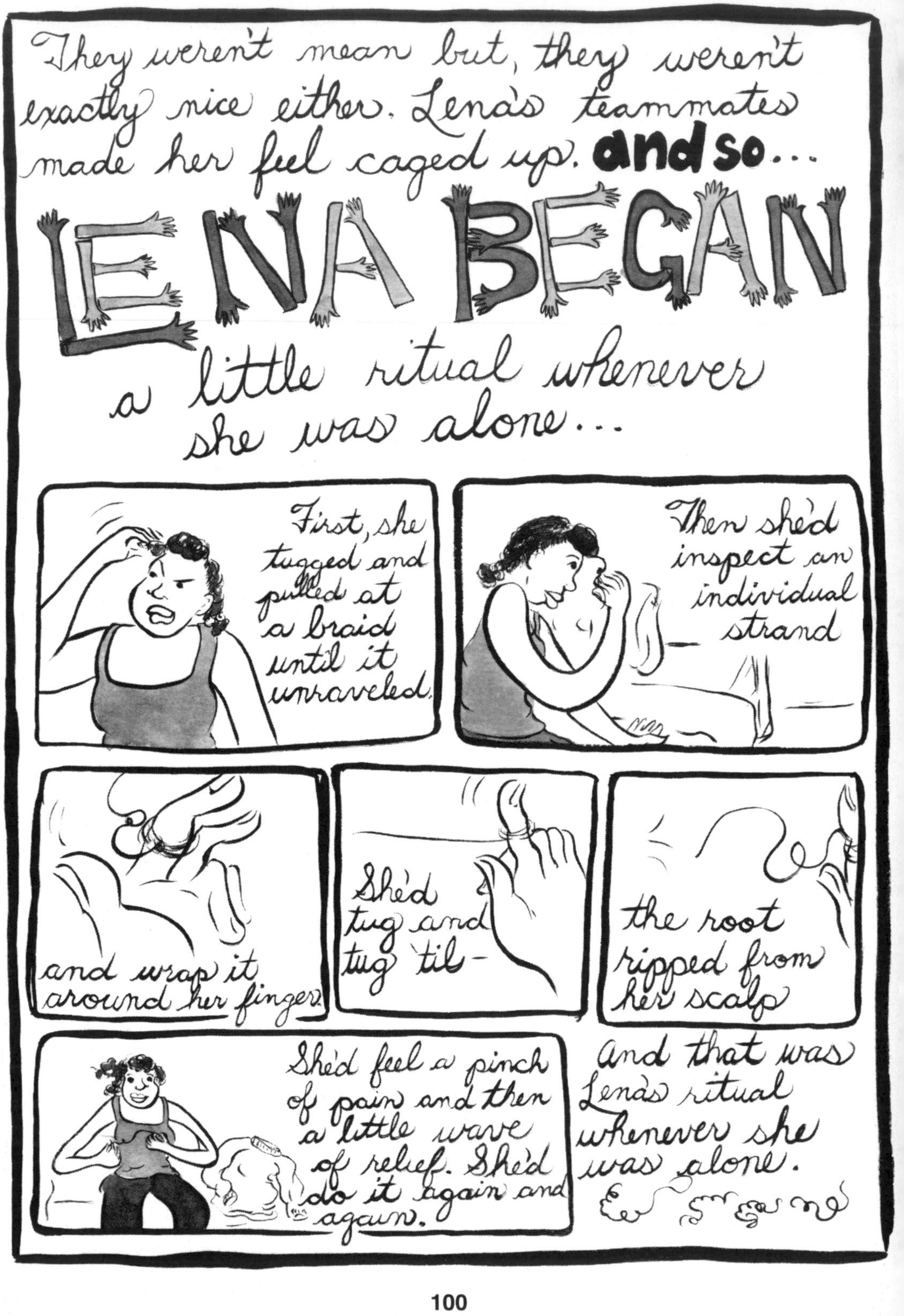

They weren't mean but, they weren't exactly nice either. Lena's teammates made her feel caged up. and so...
LENA BEGAN
a little ritual whenever she was alone...
First, she tugged and pulled at a braid until it unraveled.
Then she'd inspect an individual strand
and wrap it around her fingers
She'd tug and tug 'til-
the root ripped from her scalp
She'd feel a pinch of pain and then a little wave of relief. She'd do it again and again.
And that was Lena's ritual whenever she was alone.

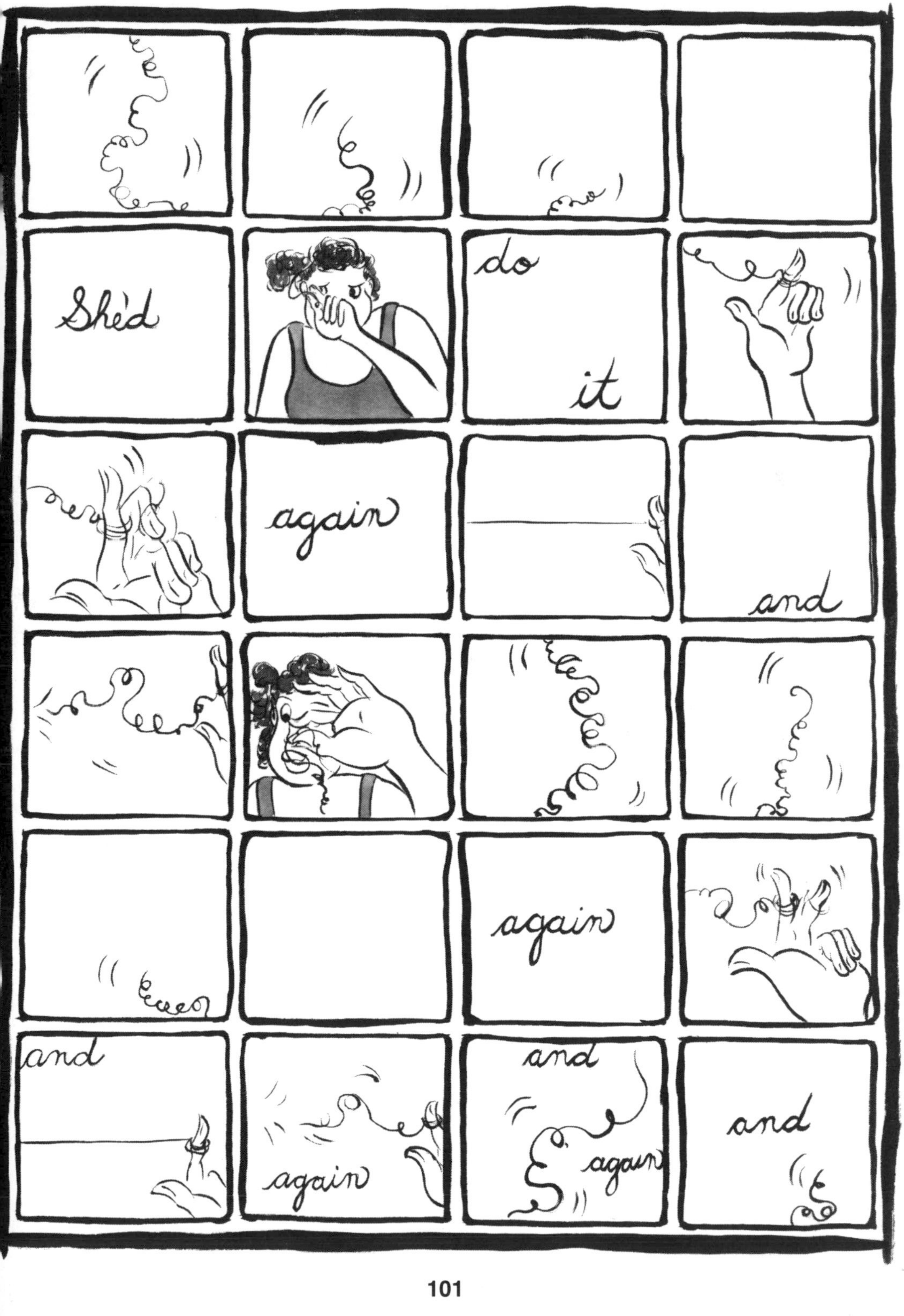
She'd
do
it
again
and
again
and
again
and
again
and

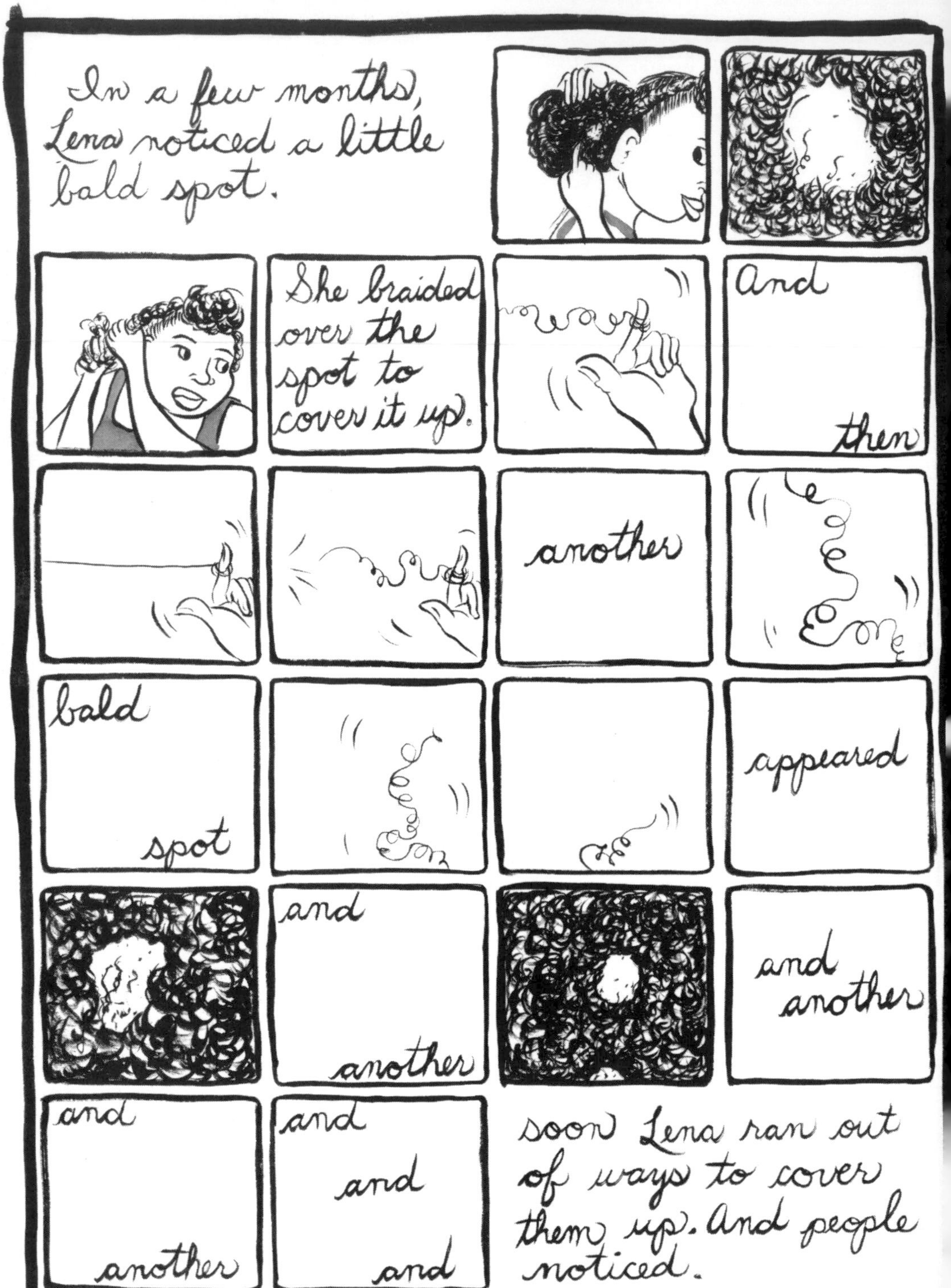
In a few months, Lena noticed a little bald spot.
She braided over the spot to cover it up.
And
then
another
bald
spot
appeared
and
another
and another
and
another
and
and
and
soon Lena ran out of ways to cover them up. And people noticed.

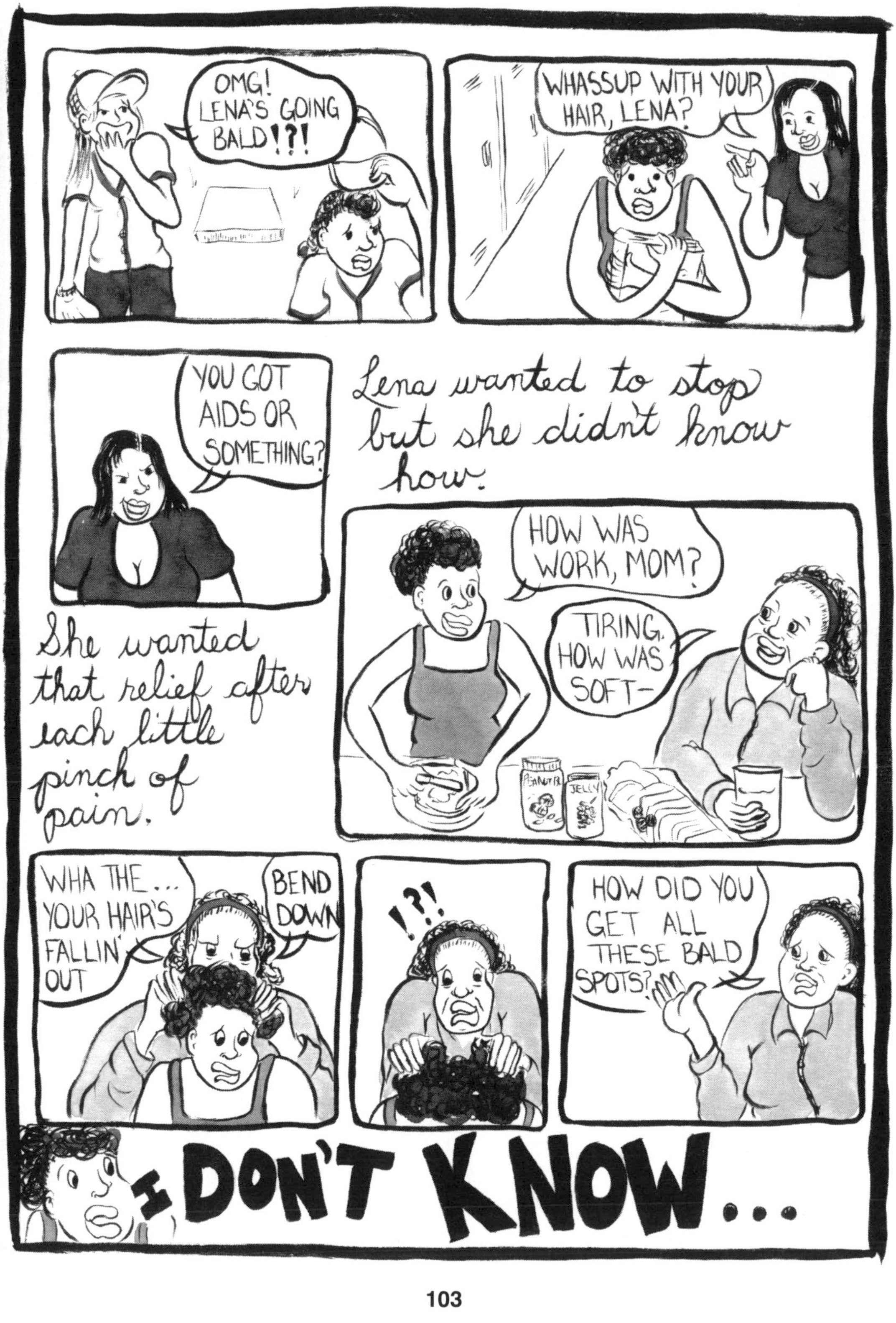
OMG! LENA'S GOING BALD!?!
WHASSUP WITH YOUR HAIR, LENA?
YOU GOT AIDS OR SOMETHING?
Lena wanted to stop but she didn't know how.
HOW WAS WORK, MOM?
TIRING. HOW WAS SOFT-
She wanted that relief after each little pinch of pain.
WHA THE... YOUR HAIR'S FALLIN' OUT
BEND DOWN
!?!
HOW DID YOU GET ALL THESE BALD SPOTS?
I DON'T KNOW...

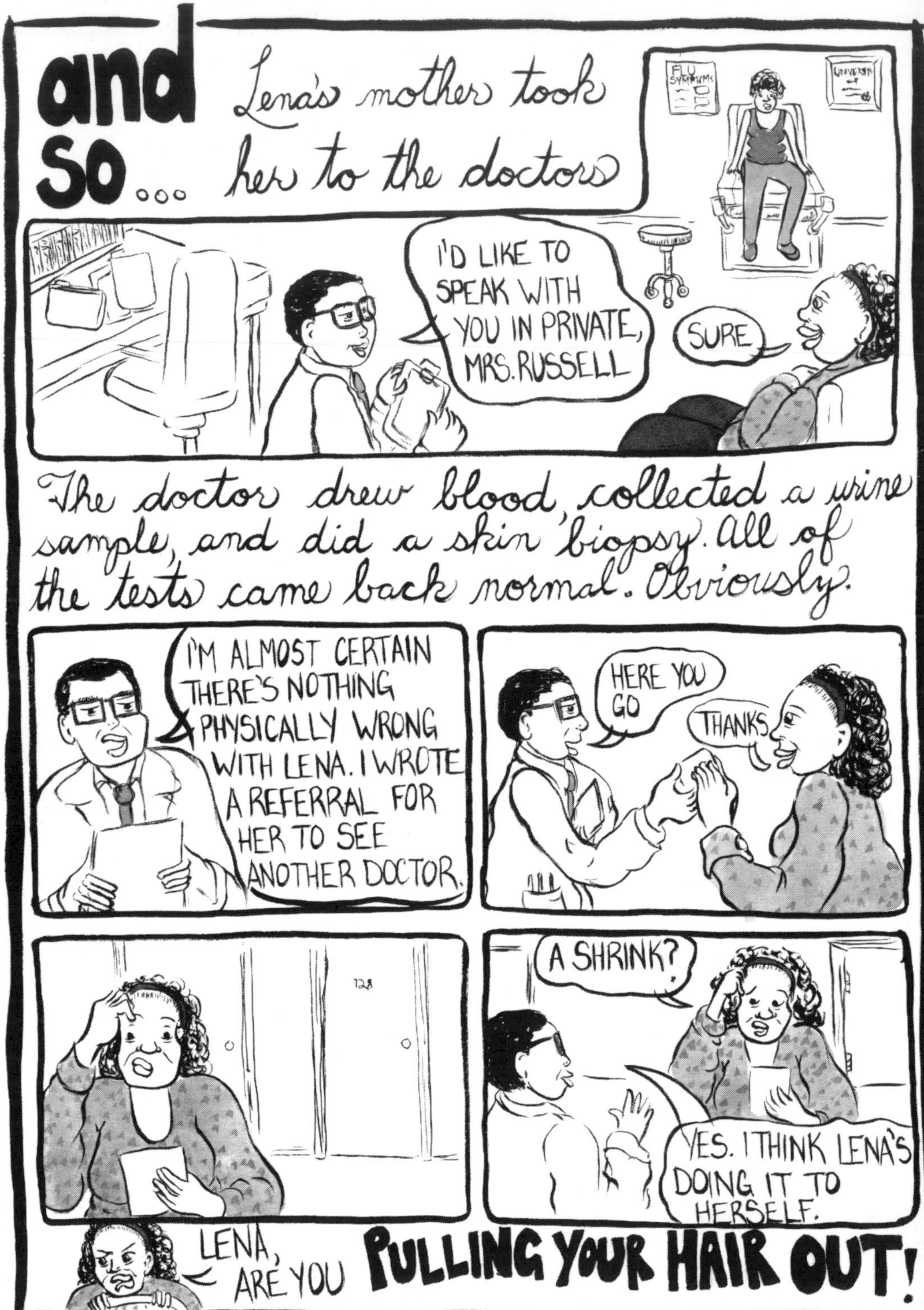
and so... Lena's mother took her to the doctors
FLU SYMPTOMS
UNIVERSITY
I'D LIKE TO SPEAK WITH YOU IN PRIVATE, MRS. RUSSELL
SURE
The doctor drew blood, collected a urine sample, and did a skin biopsy. All of the tests came back normal. Obviously.
I'M ALMOST CERTAIN THERE'S NOTHING PHYSICALLY WRONG WITH LENA. I WROTE A REFERRAL FOR HER TO SEE ANOTHER DOCTOR.
HERE YOU GO
THANKS
128
A SHRINK?
YES. I THINK LENA'S DOING IT TO HERSELF.
LENA, ARE YOU PULLING YOUR HAIR OUT!

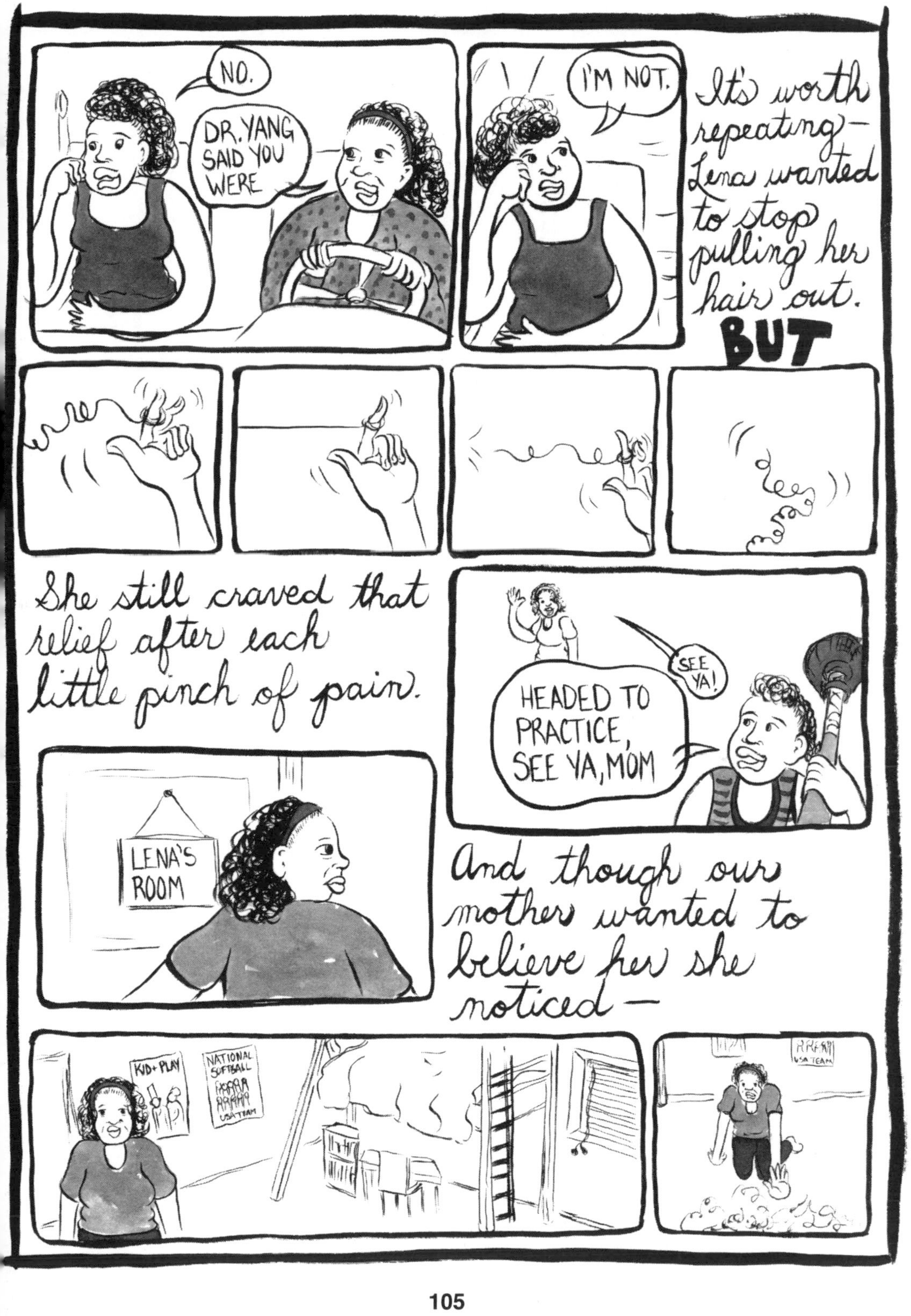
NO.
DR. YANG SAID YOU WERE
I'M NOT.
It's worth repeating— Lena wanted to stop pulling her hair out.
BUT
She still craved that relief after each little pinch of pain.
SEE YA!
HEADED TO PRACTICE, SEE YA, MOM
LENA'S ROOM
And though our mother wanted to believe her she noticed—
KID+PLAY
NATIONAL SOFTBALL
USA TEAM
USA TEAM

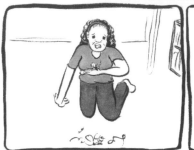

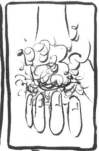

When Lena came back from practice, mom said –
YOU'RE GOING TO THE SHRINK TOMMORROW
BUT
NO BUTS!
WHAAAAWHAA
WHAAAWHA
During the first session, she said nothing,
the second she cried,
WHAAAA
WHAAAAA
I PULL MY HAIR OUT WHEN I'M ALONE
the third session was the same as the second,
and then at the fourth session she said one thing...

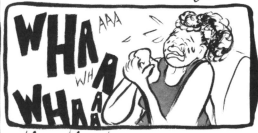

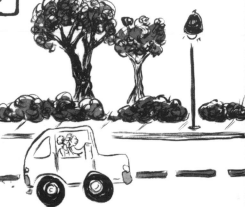

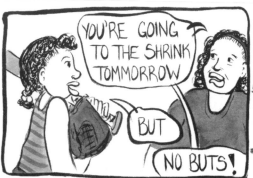

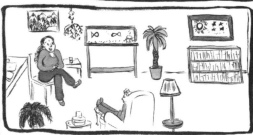

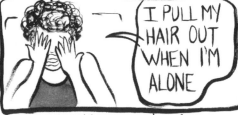

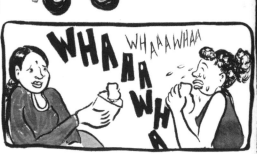

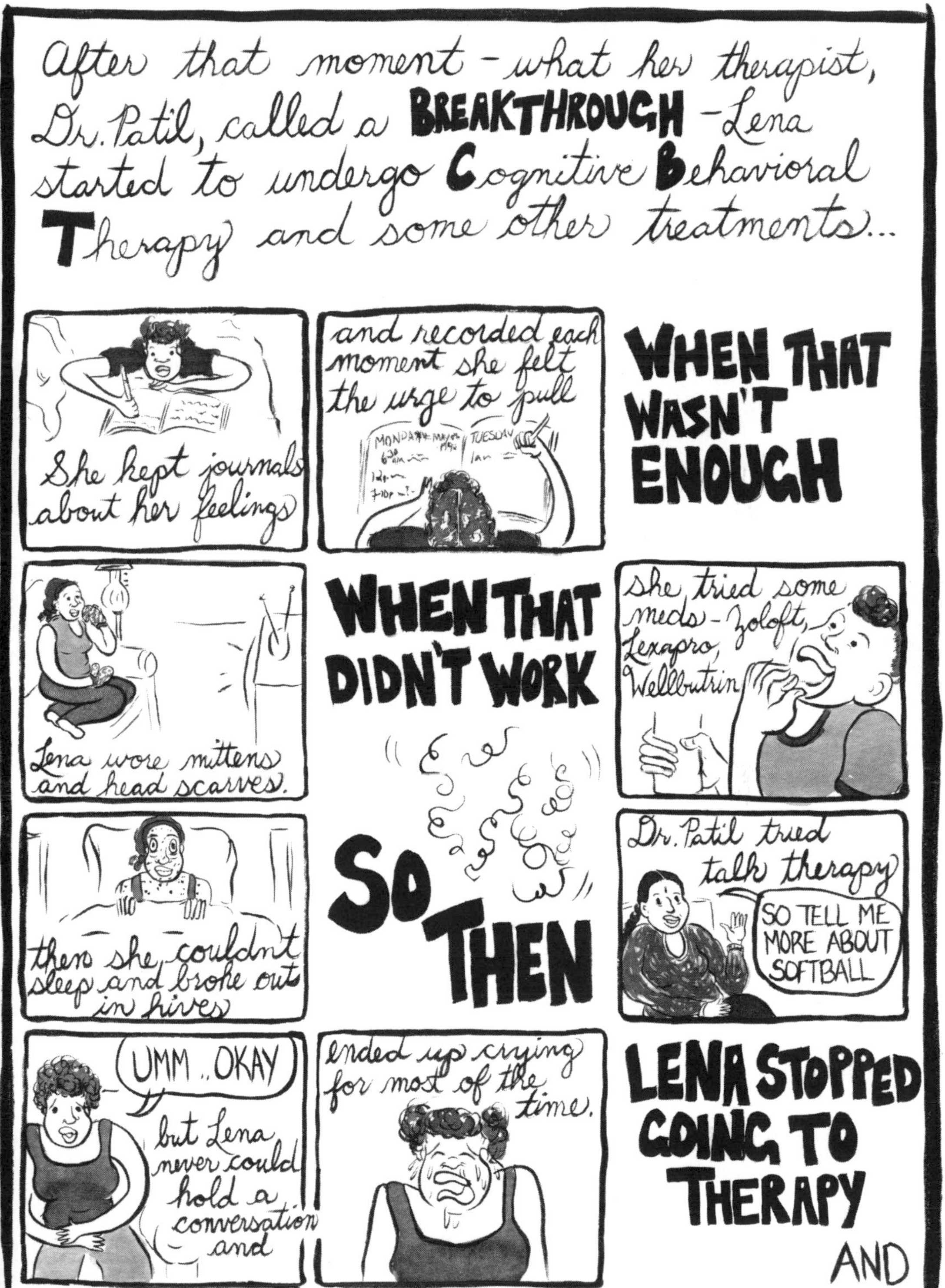
After that moment - what her therapist, Dr. Patil, called a BREAKTHROUGH - Lena started to undergo Cognitive Behavioral Therapy and some other treatments...
She kept journals about her feelings
and recorded each moment she felt the urge to pull
MONDAY
TUESDAY
WHEN THAT WASN'T ENOUGH
Lena wore mittens and head scarves.
WHEN THAT DIDN'T WORK
she tried some meds - Zoloft, Lexapro, Wellbutrin
then she couldn't sleep and broke out in hives
SO THEN
Dr. Patil tried talk therapy
SO TELL ME MORE ABOUT SOFTBALL
UMM..OKAY
but Lena never could hold a conversation and
ended up crying for most of the time.
LENA STOPPED GOING TO THERAPY
AND

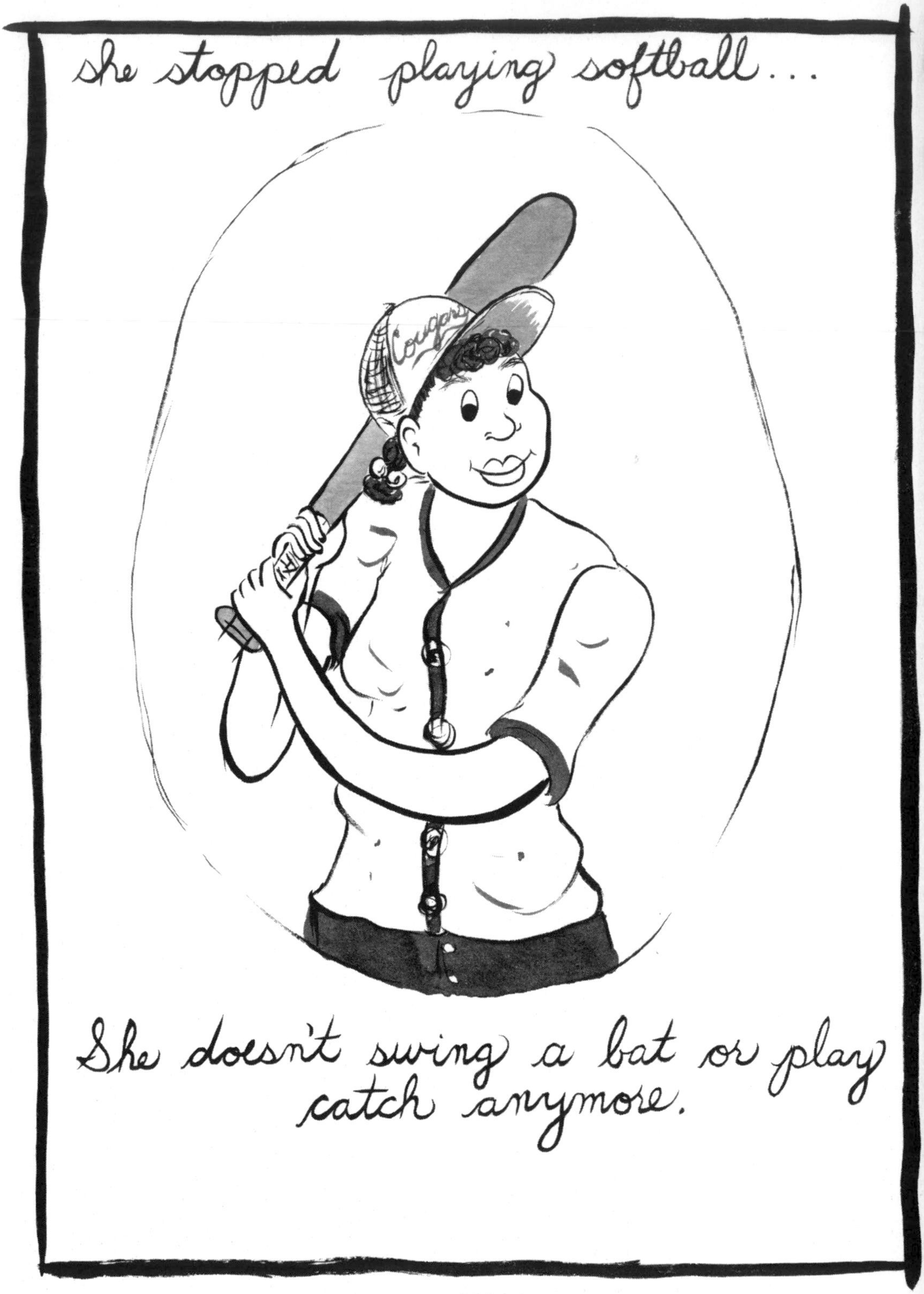
she stopped playing softball...
Cougars
She doesn't swing a bat or play catch anymore.

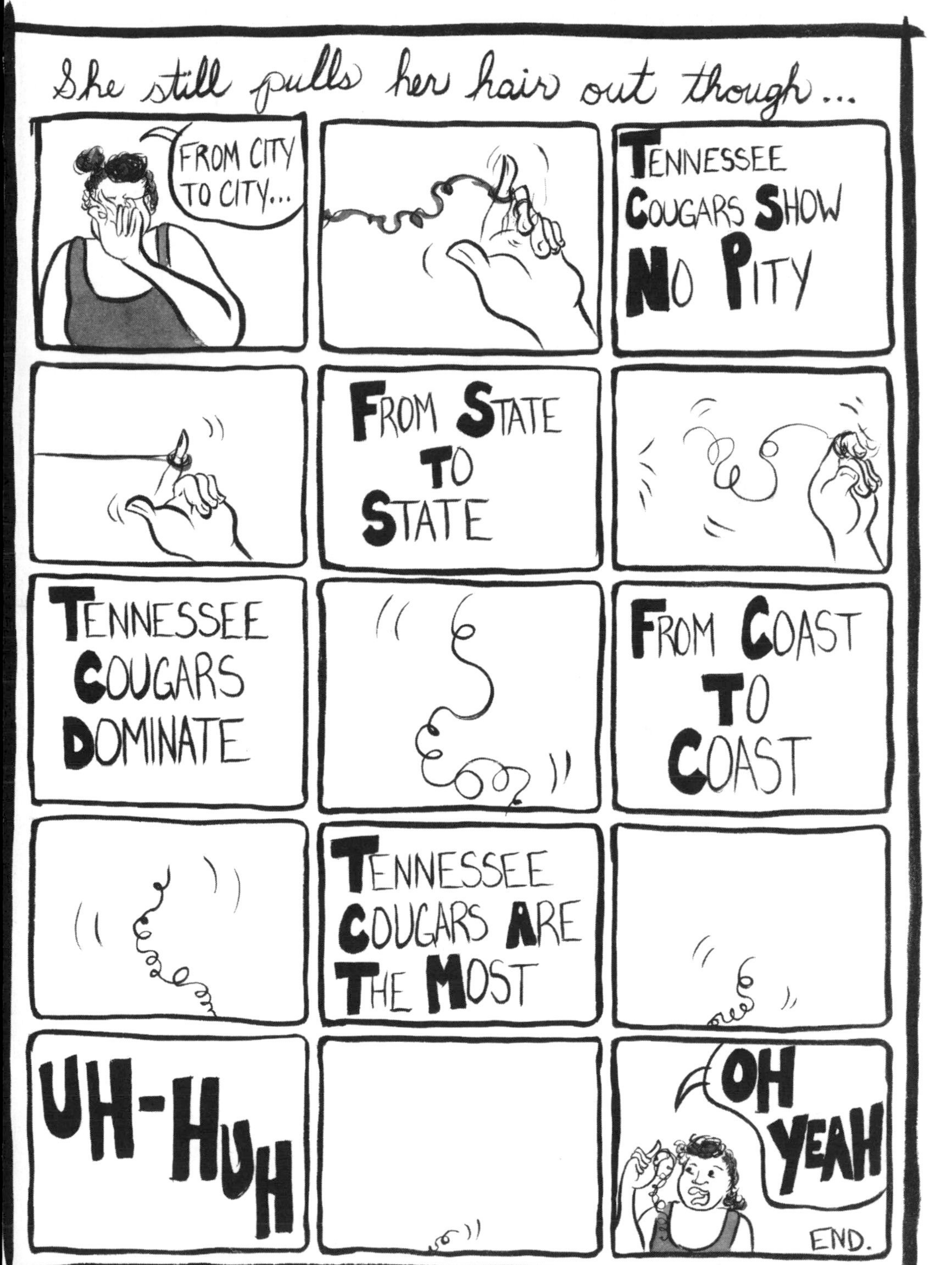
She still pulls her hair out though...
FROM CITY TO CITY...
TENNESSEE COUGARS SHOW NO PITY
FROM STATE TO STATE
TENNESSEE COUGARS DOMINATE
FROM COAST TO COAST
TENNESSEE COUGARS ARE THE MOST
UH-HUH
OH YEAH
END.

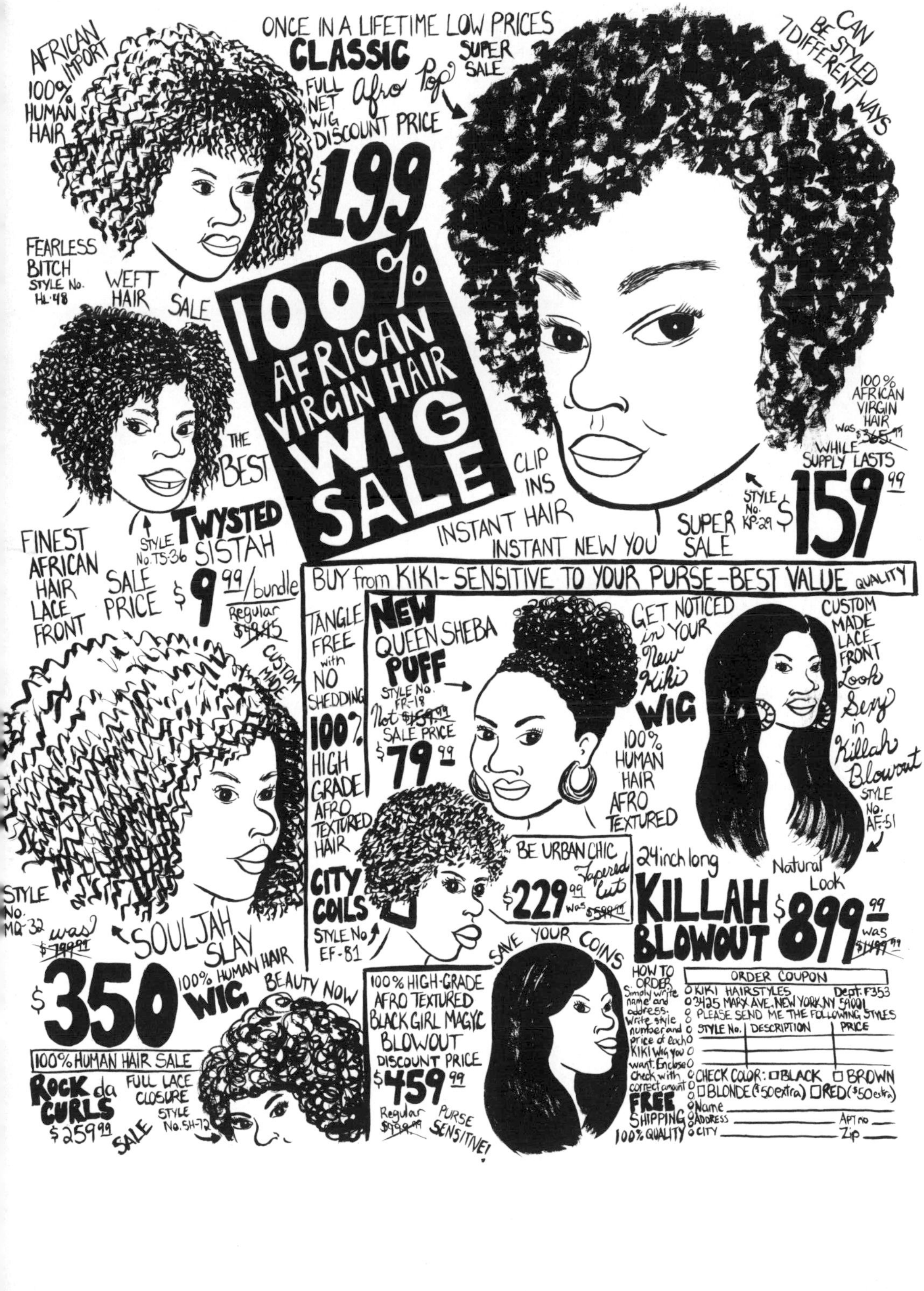
ONCE IN A LIFETIME LOW PRICES
CLASSIC
SUPER SALE
FULL NET WIG
Afro Pop
DISCOUNT PRICE
$199
AFRICAN 100% IMPORT
100% HUMAN HAIR
CAN BE STYLED 7 DIFFERENT WAYS
FEARLESS BITCH
STYLE No. HL-48
WEFT HAIR
SALE
100% AFRICAN VIRGIN HAIR WIG SALE
THE BEST
STYLE No. TS-36
TWYSTED SISTAH
FINEST AFRICAN HAIR LACE FRONT
SALE PRICE $9 99/bundle
Regular $49.95
CLIP INS
INSTANT HAIR
INSTANT NEW YOU
100% AFRICAN VIRGIN HAIR
Was $365.99
WHILE SUPPLY LASTS
STYLE No. KP-29
SUPER SALE
$159 99
BUY from KIKI - SENSITIVE TO YOUR PURSE - BEST VALUE QUALITY
CUSTOM MADE
TANGLE FREE with NO SHEDDING
100% HIGH GRADE AFRO TEXTURED HAIR
NEW QUEEN SHEBA PUFF
STYLE No. FR-18
Not $159.99
SALE PRICE
$79 99
GET NOTICED in YOUR New Kiki WIG
100% HUMAN HAIR AFRO TEXTURED
CUSTOM MADE LACE FRONT
Look Sexy in Killah Blowout
STYLE No. AF-51
STYLE No. MQ-32
was $799.99
SOULJAH SLAY
CITY COILS
STYLE No EF-81
BE URBAN CHIC
Tapered Cut
$229 99
was $599.99
24inch long
Natural Look
KILLAH BLOWOUT
$899 99
was $1499.99
$350
100% HUMAN HAIR WIG
BEAUTY NOW
100% HUMAN HAIR SALE
ROCK da CURLS
$259 99
FULL LACE CLOSURE
STYLE No. SH-72
SALE
SAVE YOUR COINS
100% HIGH-GRADE AFRO TEXTURED BLACK GIRL MAGYC BLOWOUT
DISCOUNT PRICE
$459 99
Regular $999.99
PURSE SENSITIVE!
HOW TO ORDER
Simply write name and address. Write style number and price of each KIKI Wig you want. Enclose check with correct amount
FREE SHIPPING
100% QUALITY
ORDER COUPON
KIKI HAIRSTYLES Dept. F353
3425 MARX AVE. NEW YORK, NY 59001
PLEASE SEND ME THE FOLLOWING STYLES
STYLE No. DESCRIPTION PRICE
CHECK COLOR: BLACK BROWN
BLONDE ($50 extra) RED ($50 extra)
Name
ADDRESS Apt no
CITY Zip

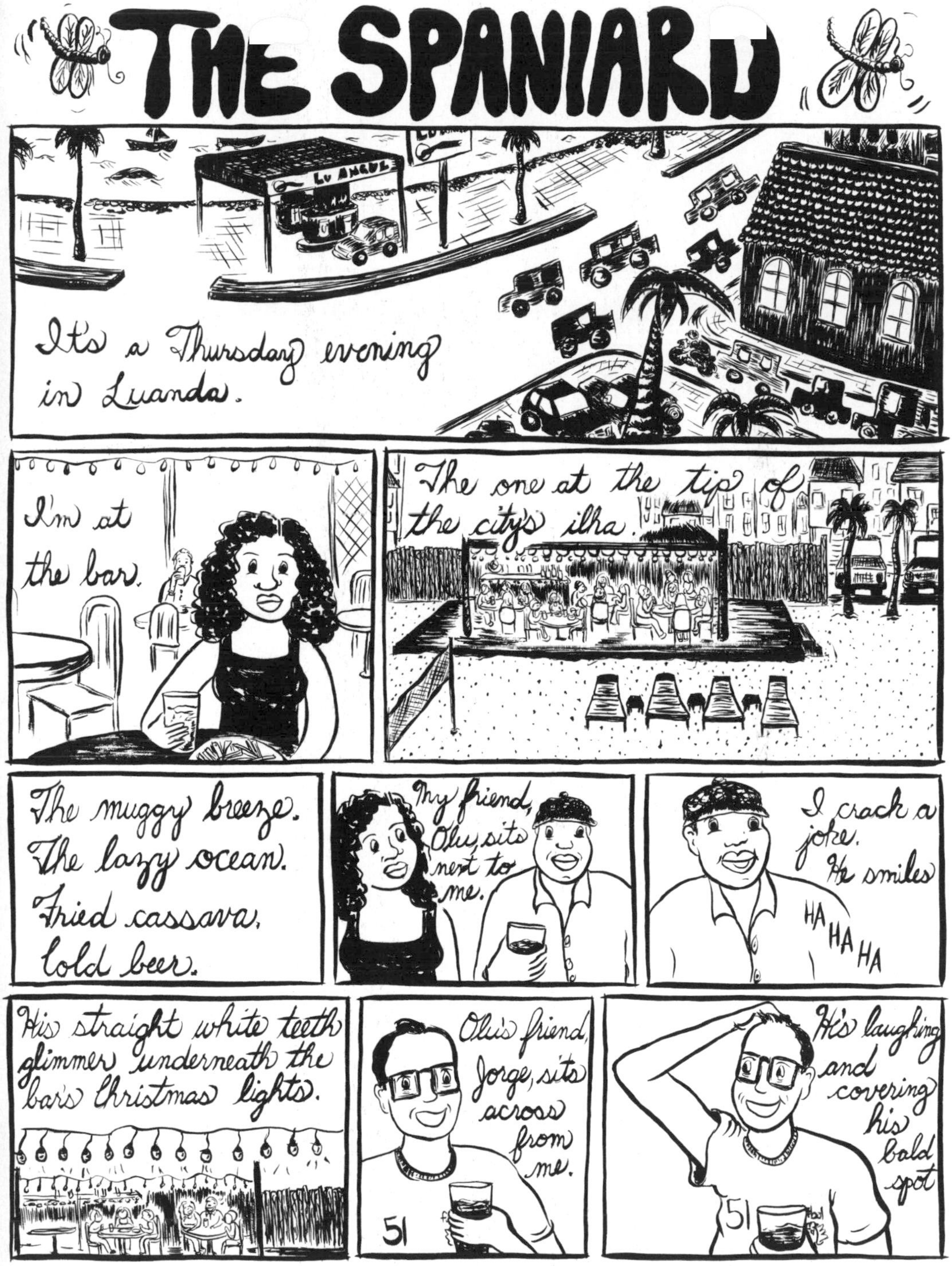
THE SPANIARD
It's a Thursday evening in Luanda.
I'm at the bar.
The one at the tip of the city's ilha.
The muggy breeze. The lazy ocean. Fried cassava. Cold beer.
My friend, Olu, sits next to me.
I crack a joke. He smiles
HA HA HA
His straight white teeth glimmer underneath the bar's Christmas lights.
Olu's friend, Jorge, sits across from me.
51
He's laughing and covering his bald spot
51

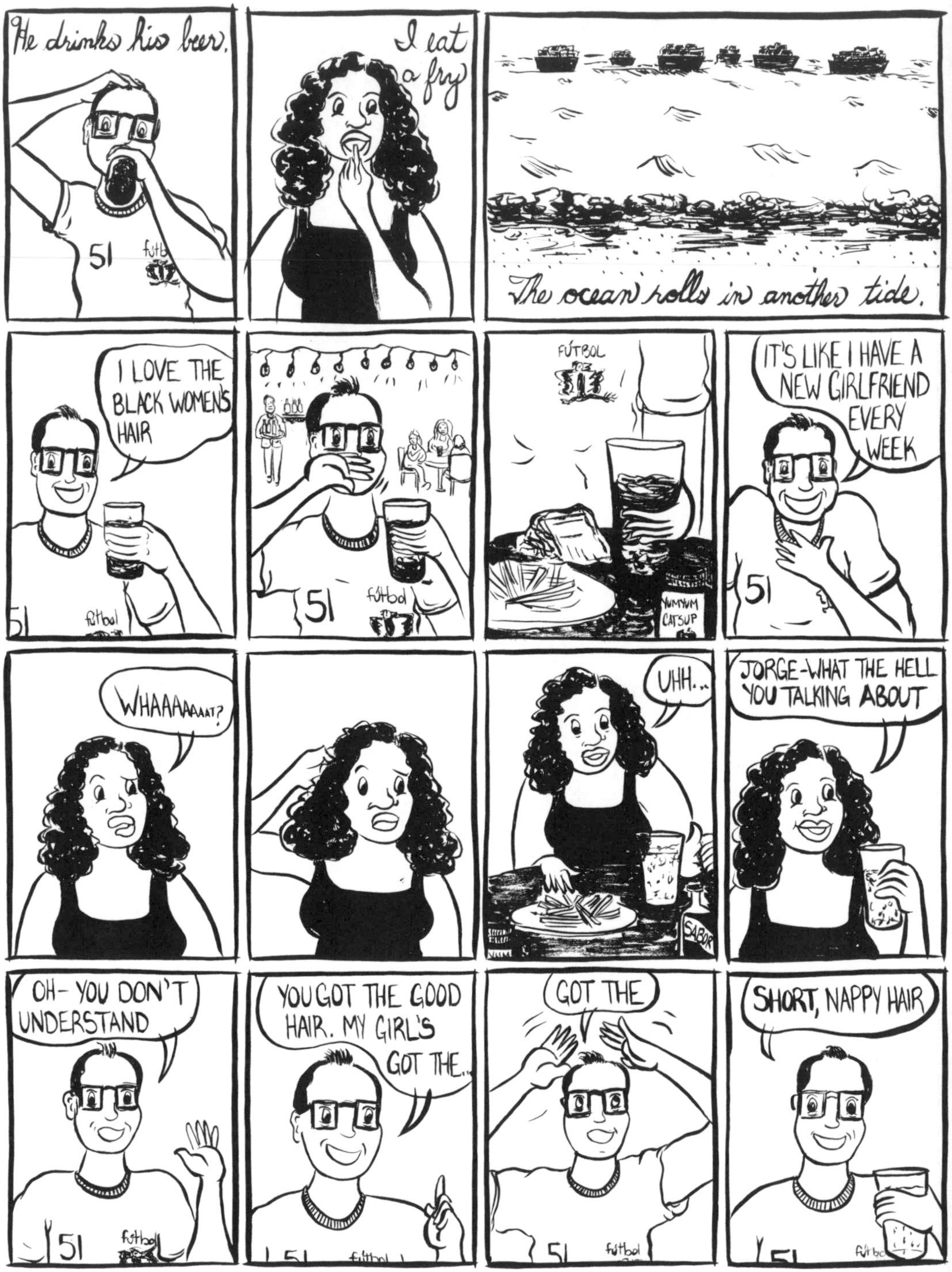
He drinks his beer.
I eat a fry
The ocean rolls in another tide.
I LOVE THE BLACK WOMEN'S HAIR
FÚTBOL
IT'S LIKE I HAVE A NEW GIRLFRIEND EVERY WEEK
WHAAAAAAAT?
UHH...
JORGE-WHAT THE HELL YOU TALKING ABOUT
OH- YOU DON'T UNDERSTAND
YOU GOT THE GOOD HAIR. MY GIRL'S GOT THE...
GOT THE
SHORT, NAPPY HAIR

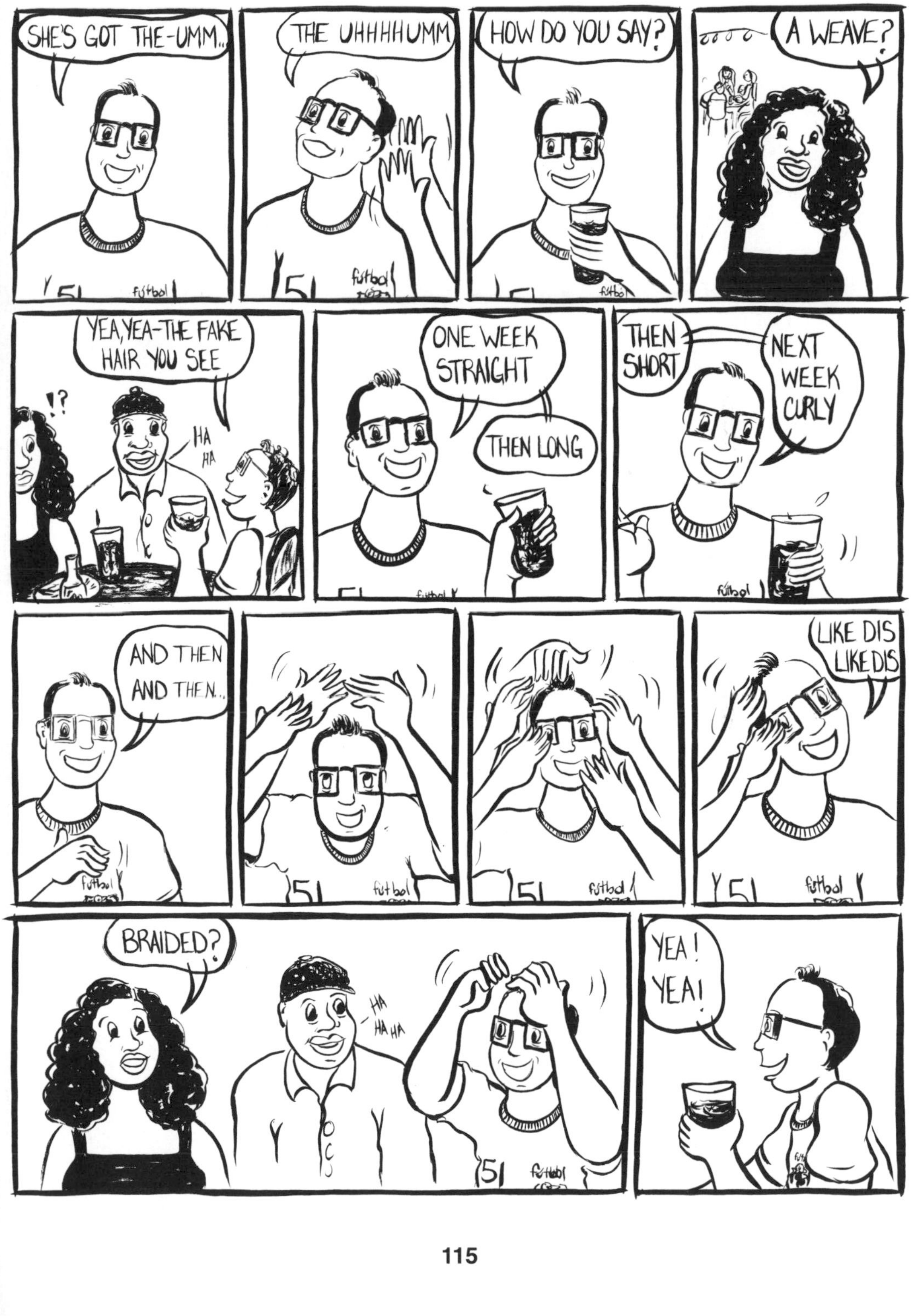
SHE'S GOT THE-UMM...
THE UHHHHUMM
HOW DO YOU SAY?
A WEAVE?
YEA, YEA-THE FAKE HAIR YOU SEE
!?
HA HA
ONE WEEK STRAIGHT
THEN LONG
THEN SHORT
NEXT WEEK CURLY
AND THEN AND THEN...
LIKE DIS LIKE DIS
BRAIDED?
HA HA HA
YEA! YEA!

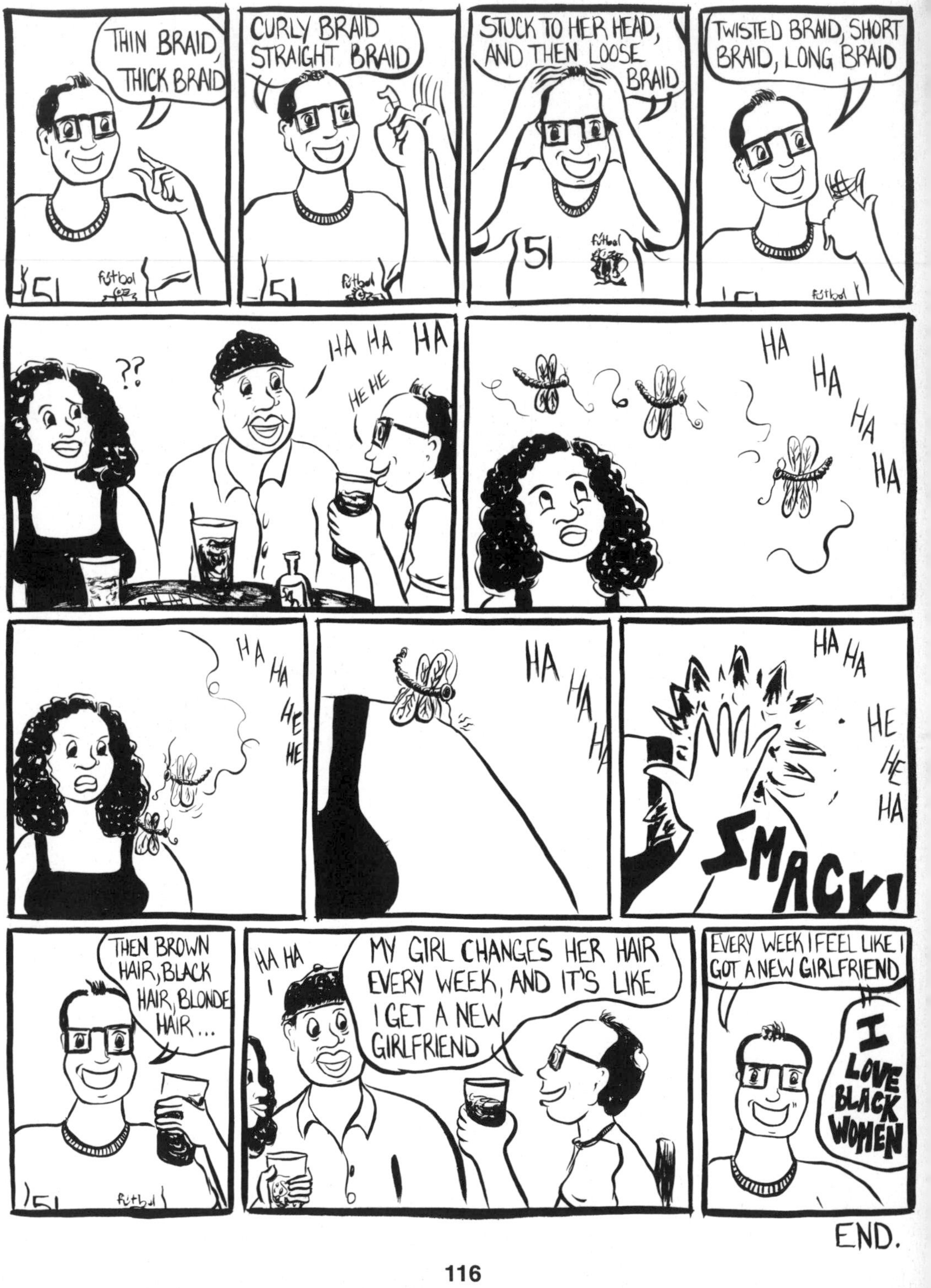
THIN BRAID, THICK BRAID
51
fútbol
CURLY BRAID STRAIGHT BRAID
51
fútbol
STUCK TO HER HEAD, AND THEN LOOSE BRAID
51
fútbol
TWISTED BRAID, SHORT BRAID, LONG BRAID
51
fútbol
??
HA HA HA
HE HE
HA
HA
HA
HA
HA
HA
HA
HE
HE
HA
HA
HA
HA
HA HA
HE
HE
HA
SMACK!
THEN BROWN HAIR, BLACK HAIR, BLONDE HAIR...
51
fútbol
HA HA
MY GIRL CHANGES HER HAIR EVERY WEEK, AND IT'S LIKE I GET A NEW GIRLFRIEND
EVERY WEEK I FEEL LIKE I GOT A NEW GIRLFRIEND
I LOVE BLACK WOMEN
END.

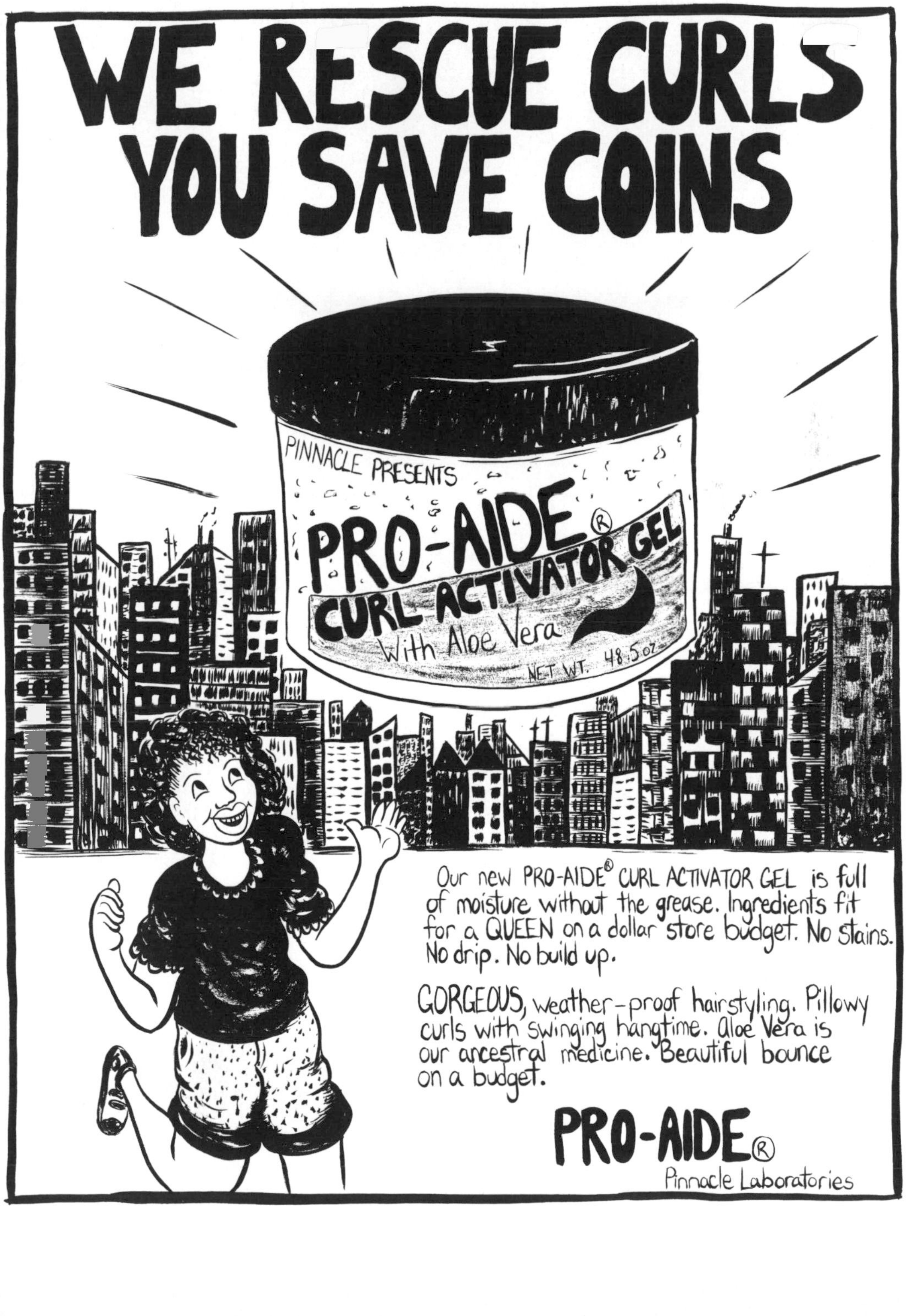
WE RESCUE CURLS
YOU SAVE COINS
PINNACLE PRESENTS
PRO-AIDE®
CURL ACTIVATOR GEL
With Aloe Vera
NET WT. 48.5 oz
Our new PRO-AIDE® CURL ACTIVATOR GEL is full of moisture without the grease. Ingredients fit for a QUEEN on a dollar store budget. No stains. No drip. No build up.
GORGEOUS, weather-proof hairstyling. Pillowy curls with swinging hangtime. Aloe Vera is our ancestral medicine. Beautiful bounce on a budget.
PRO-AIDE®
Pinnacle Laboratories

SISTERS & DAUGHTERS

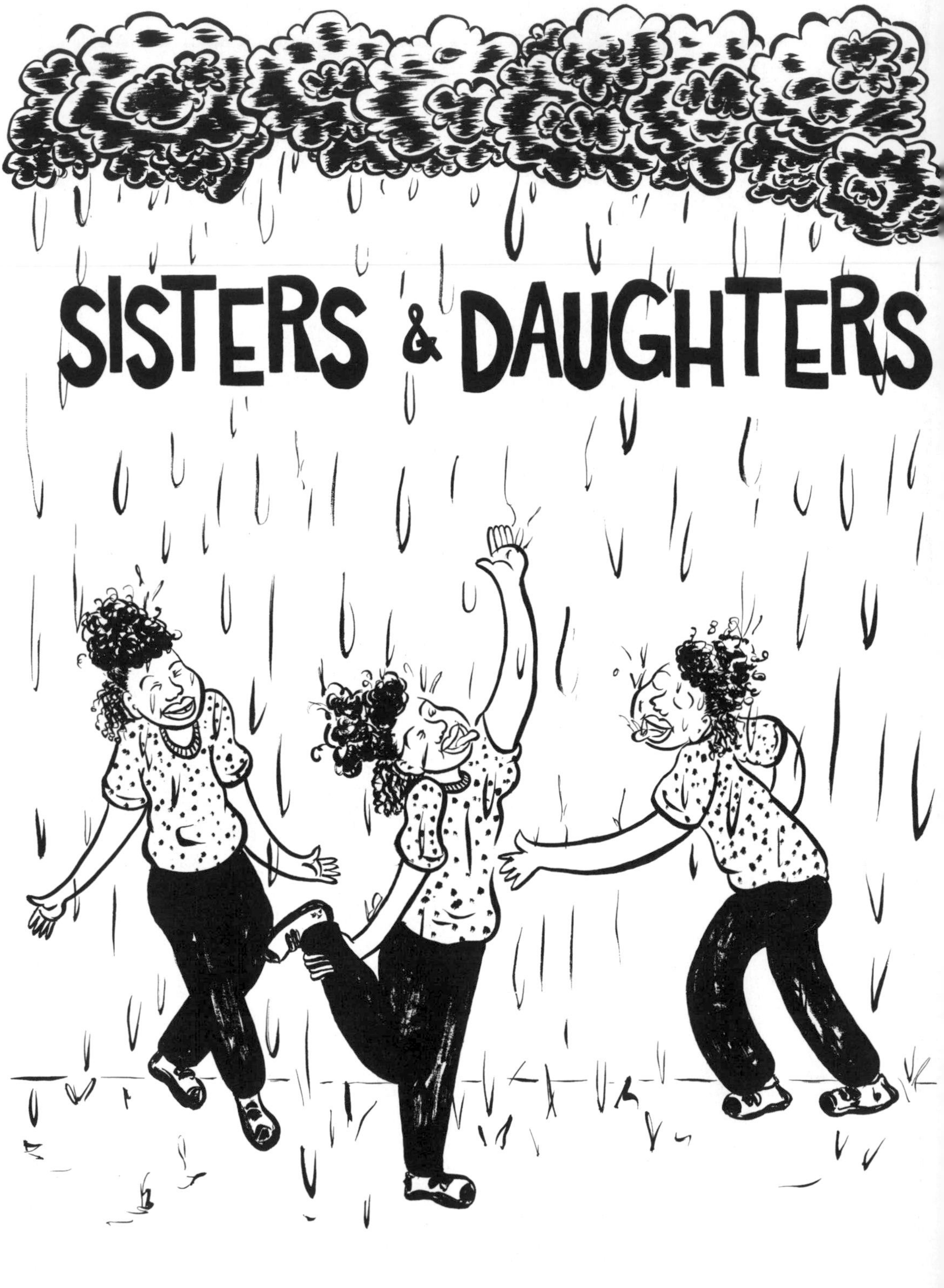

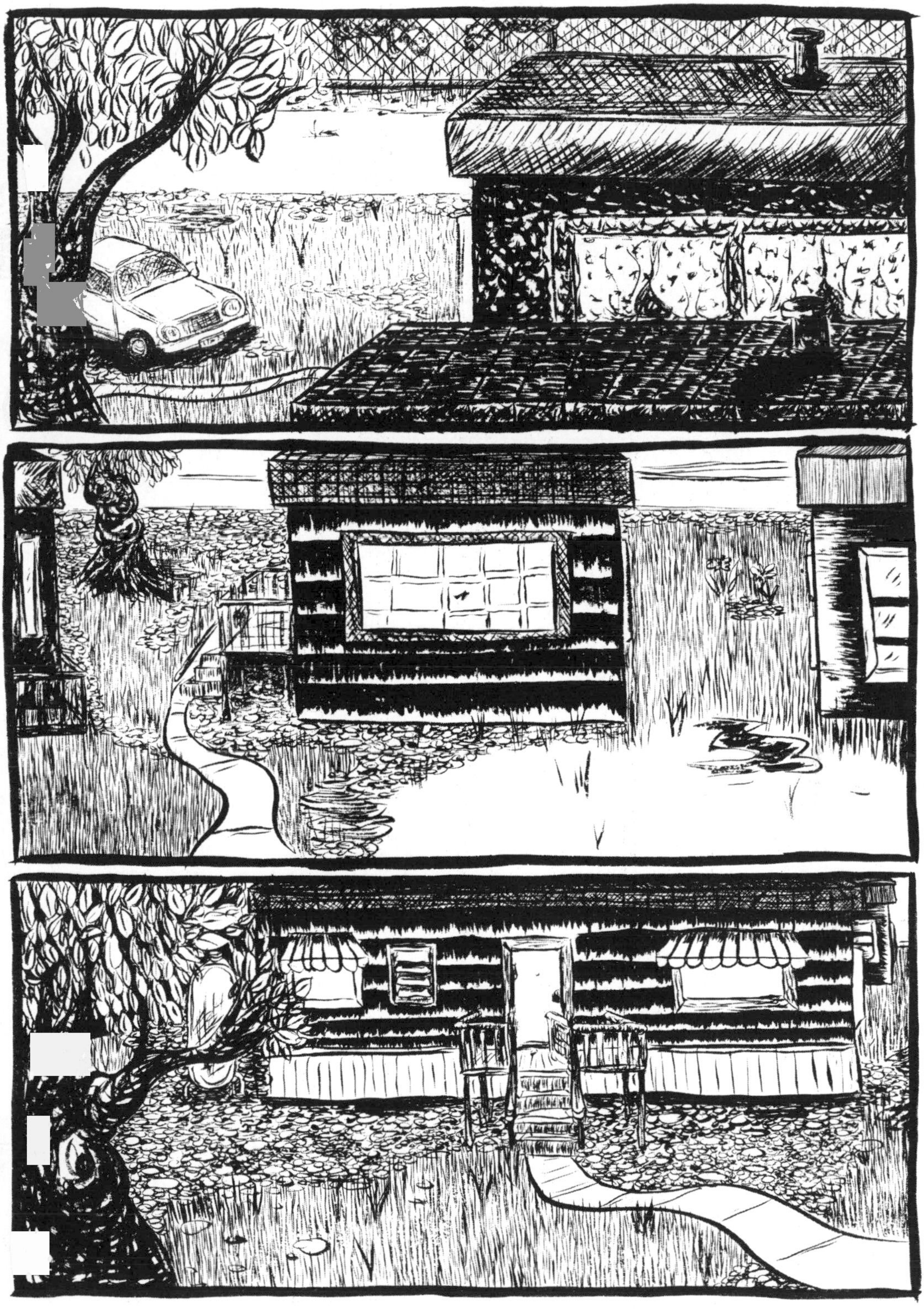

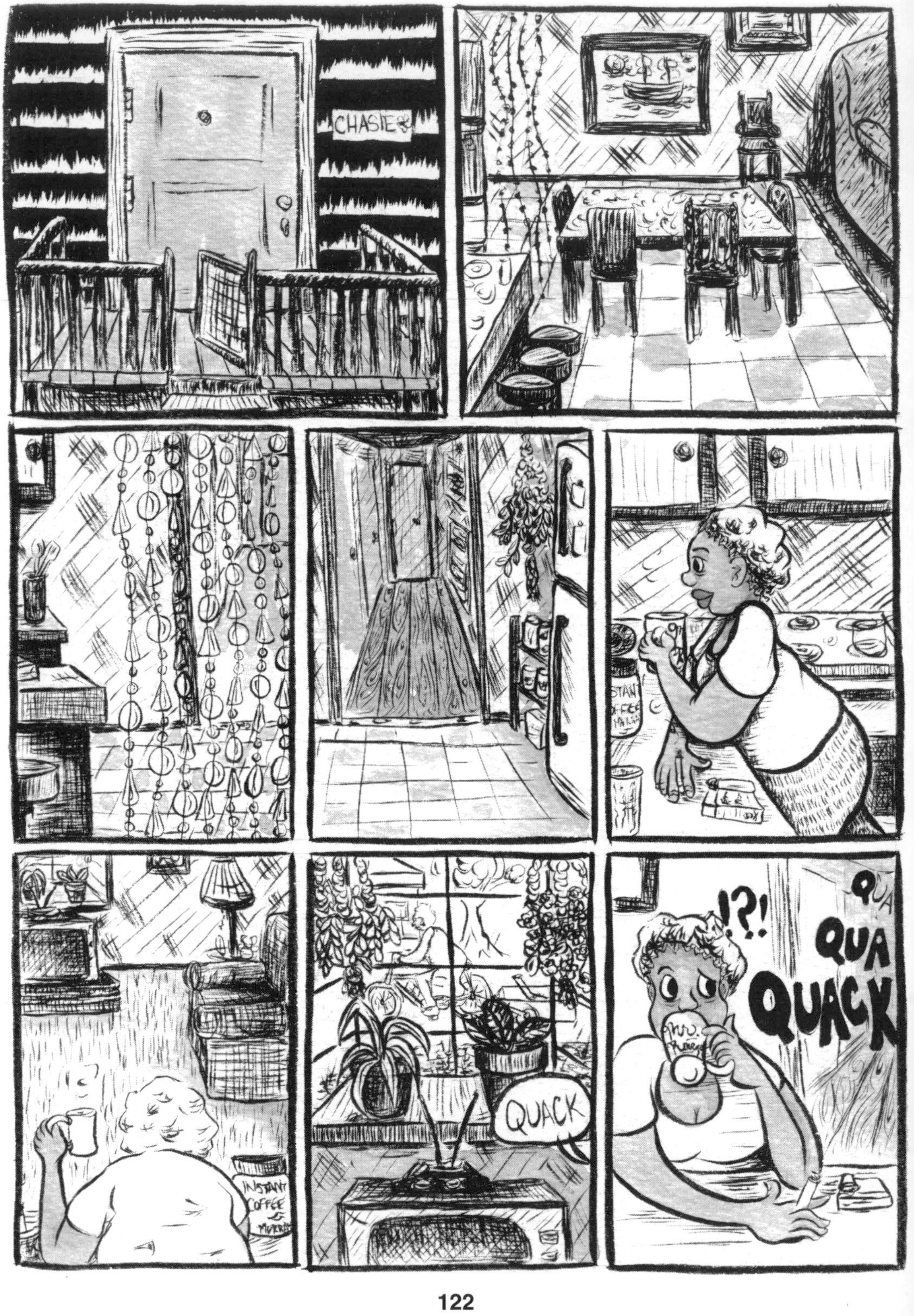
CHASIE
INSTANT COFFEE
QUACK
!?!
QUA
QUA
QUACK

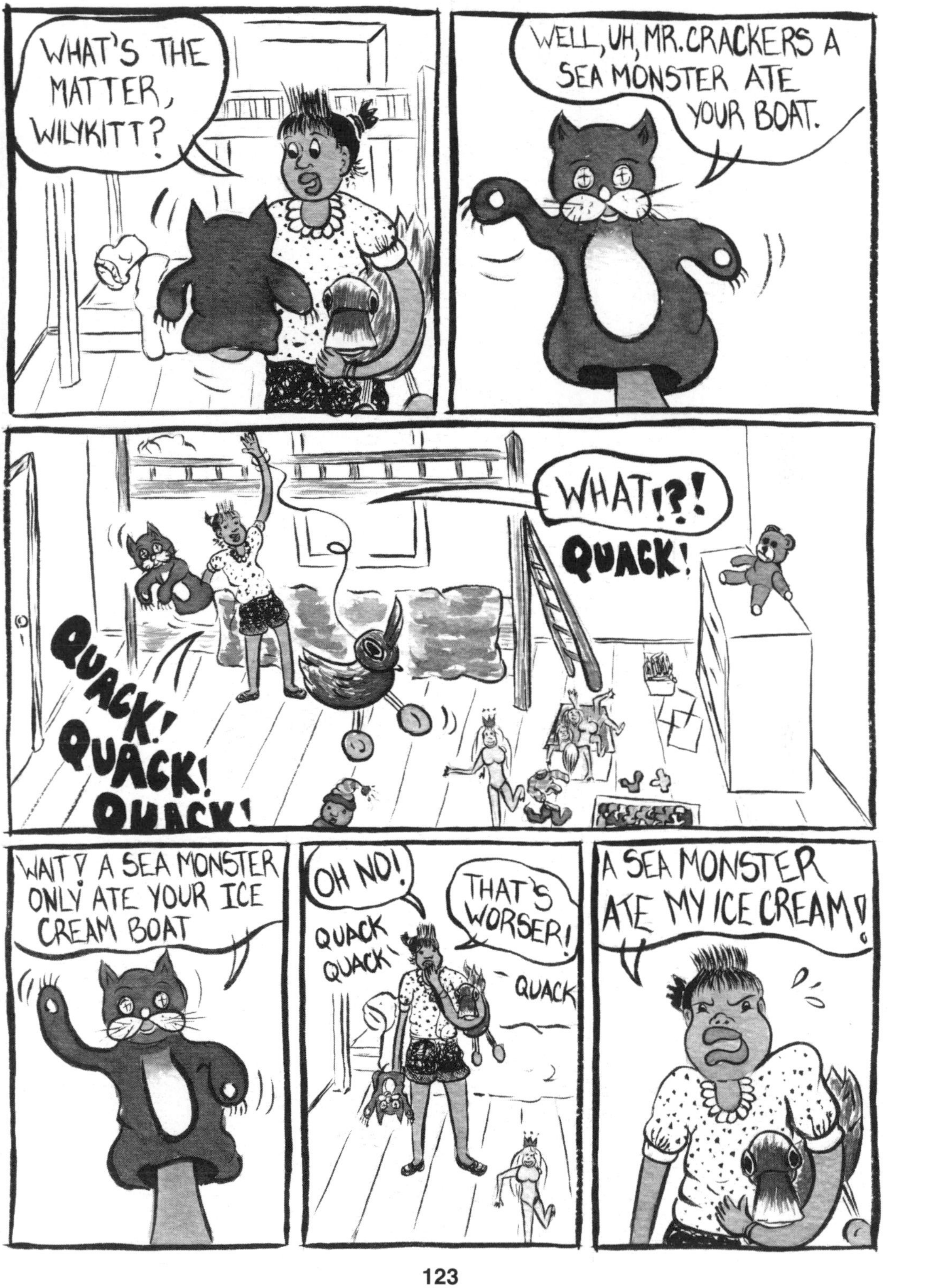
WHAT'S THE MATTER, WILYKITT?
WELL, UH, MR. CRACKERS A SEA MONSTER ATE YOUR BOAT.
WHAT!?!
QUACK!
QUACK!
QUACK!
WAIT! A SEA MONSTER ONLY ATE YOUR ICE CREAM BOAT
OH NO!
THAT'S WORSER!
QUACK QUACK
QUACK
A SEA MONSTER ATE MY ICE CREAM!

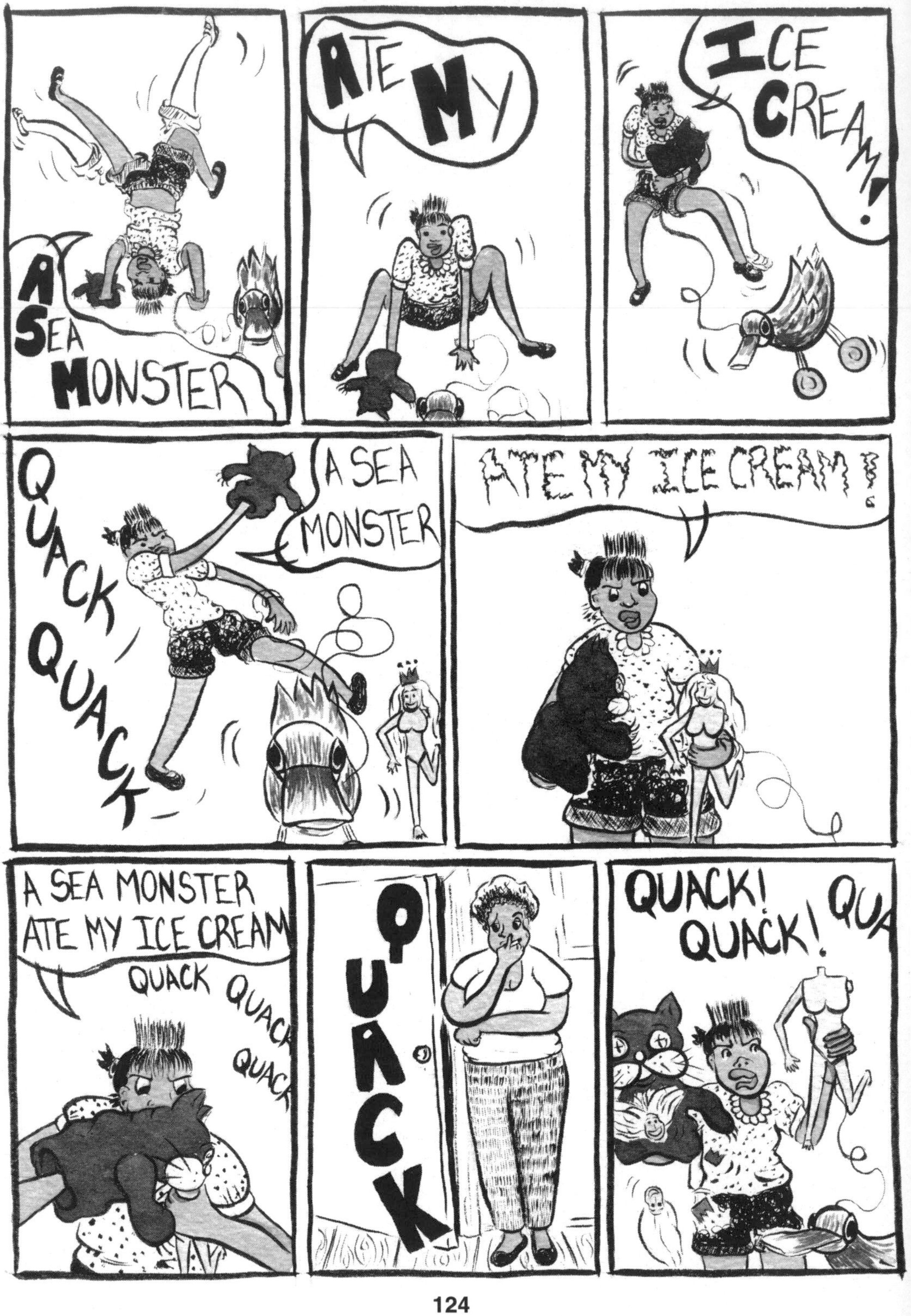
A SEA MONSTER
ATE MY
ICE CREAM!
QUACK QUACK QUACK
A SEA MONSTER
ATE MY ICE CREAM!
A SEA MONSTER ATE MY ICE CREAM
QUACK QUACK QUACK QUACK
QUACK
QUACK! QUACK!
QUA

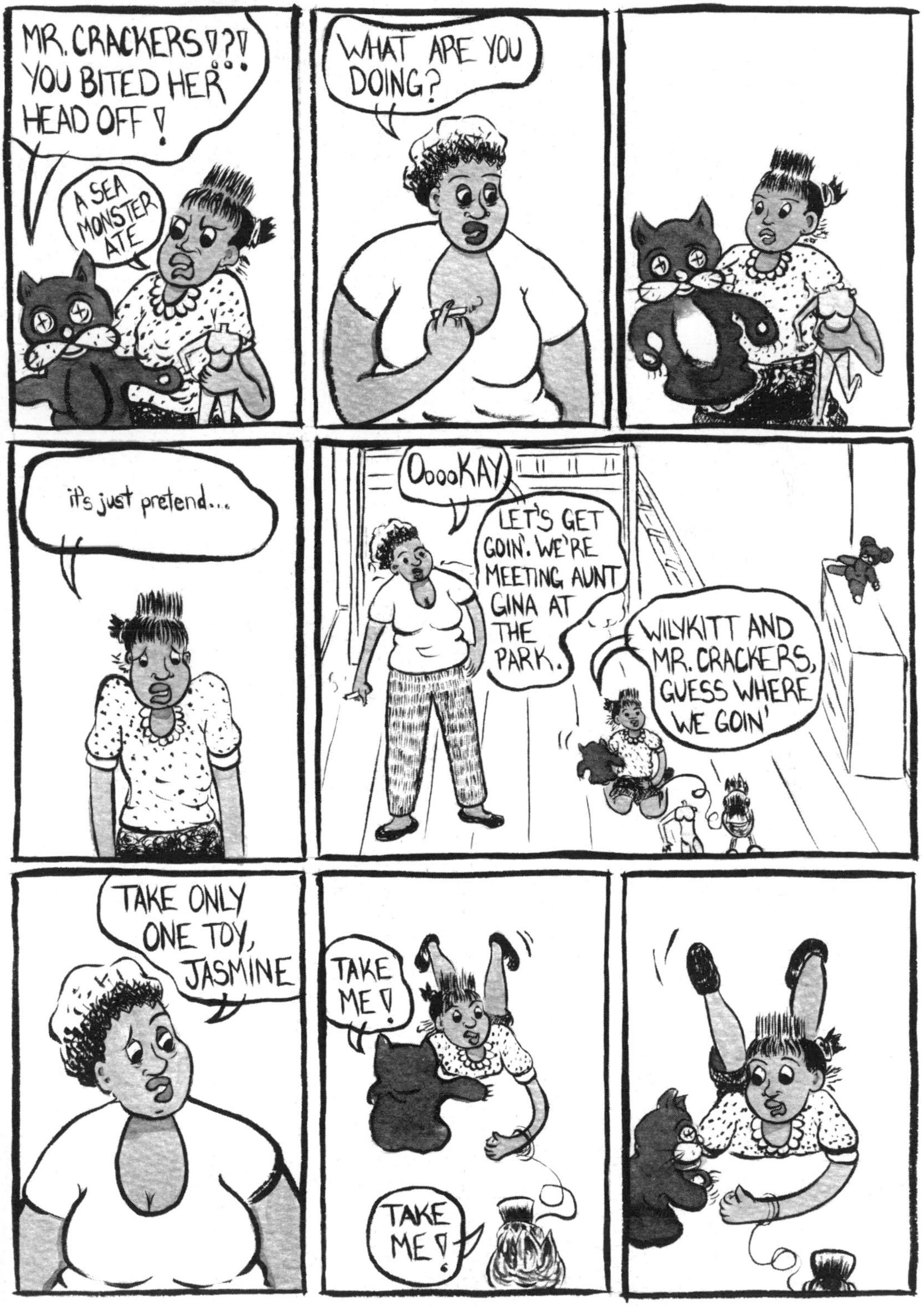
MR. CRACKERS!?!
YOU BITED HER
HEAD OFF!
A SEA MONSTER ATE
WHAT ARE YOU DOING?
it's just pretend...
OoooKAY
LET'S GET GOIN'. WE'RE MEETING AUNT GINA AT THE PARK.
WILYKITT AND MR. CRACKERS, GUESS WHERE WE GOIN'
TAKE ONLY ONE TOY, JASMINE
TAKE ME!
TAKE ME!

HURRY IT UP, JASMINE!
LET'S GO, MR. CRACKERS
BYE, WILYKITT
MOMMY, I ALMOST FORGOT MY CAPE!
GIANT FOOD STORE

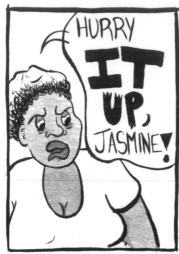

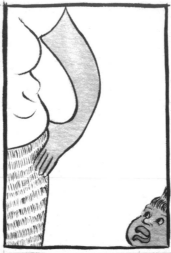

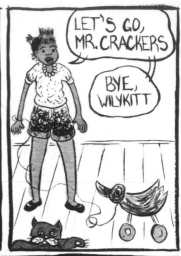

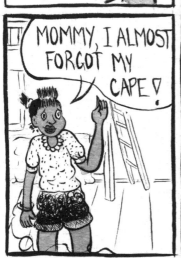

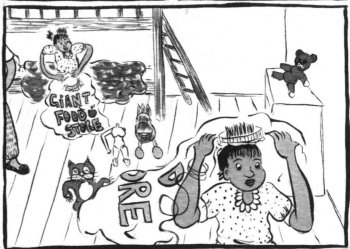

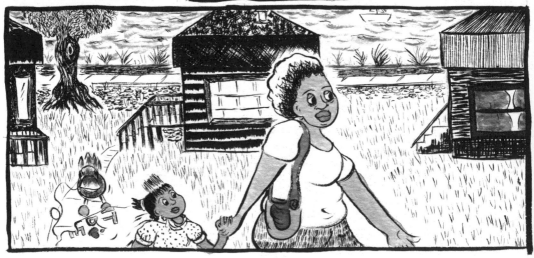

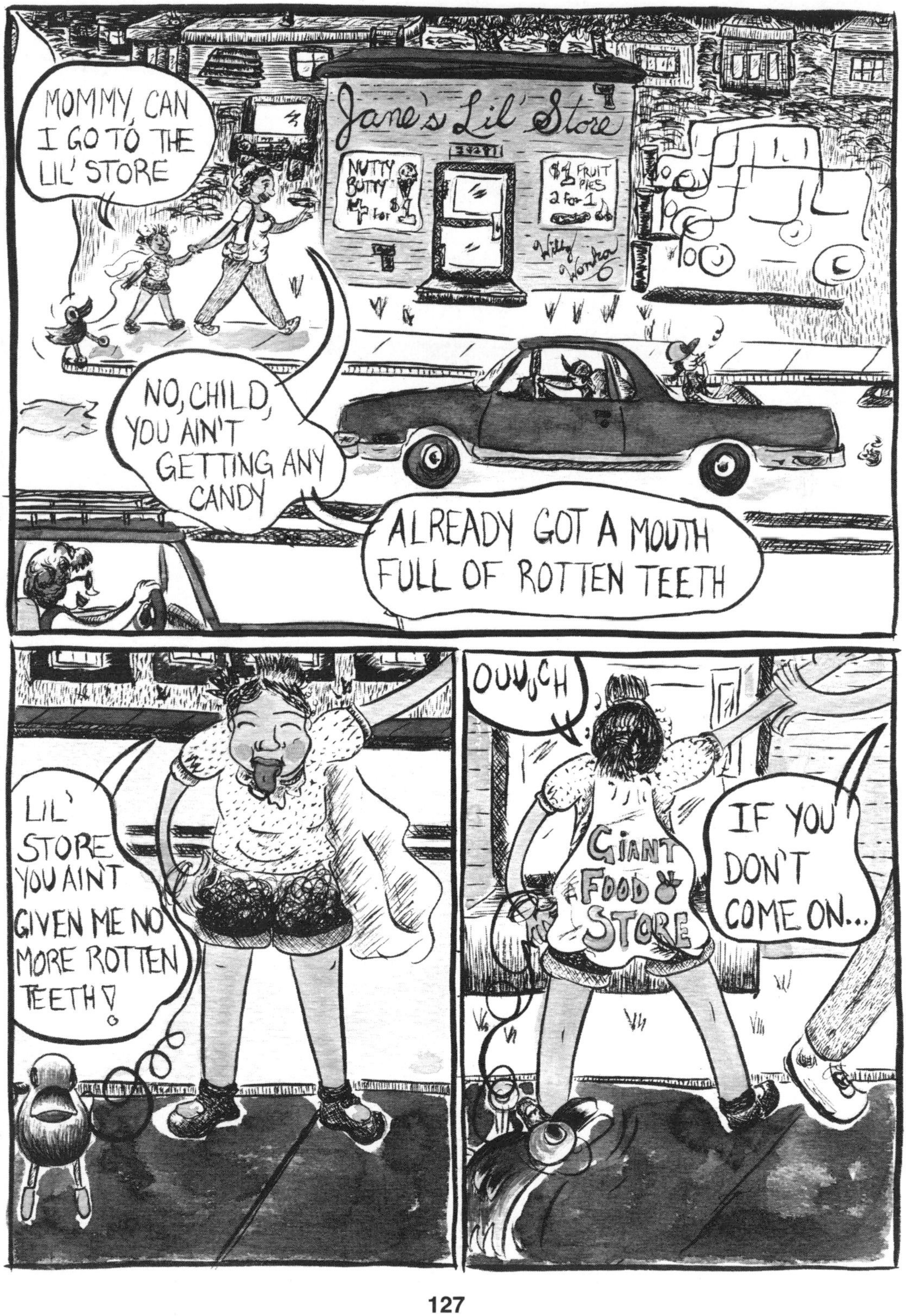
Jane's Lil' Store
NUTTY BUTTY
$1 FRUIT PIES 2 for 1
MOMMY, CAN I GO TO THE LIL' STORE
NO, CHILD, YOU AIN'T GETTING ANY CANDY
ALREADY GOT A MOUTH FULL OF ROTTEN TEETH
LIL' STORE YOU AIN'T GIVEN ME NO MORE ROTTEN TEETH!
OUUUCH
GIANT FOOD STORE
IF YOU DON'T COME ON...

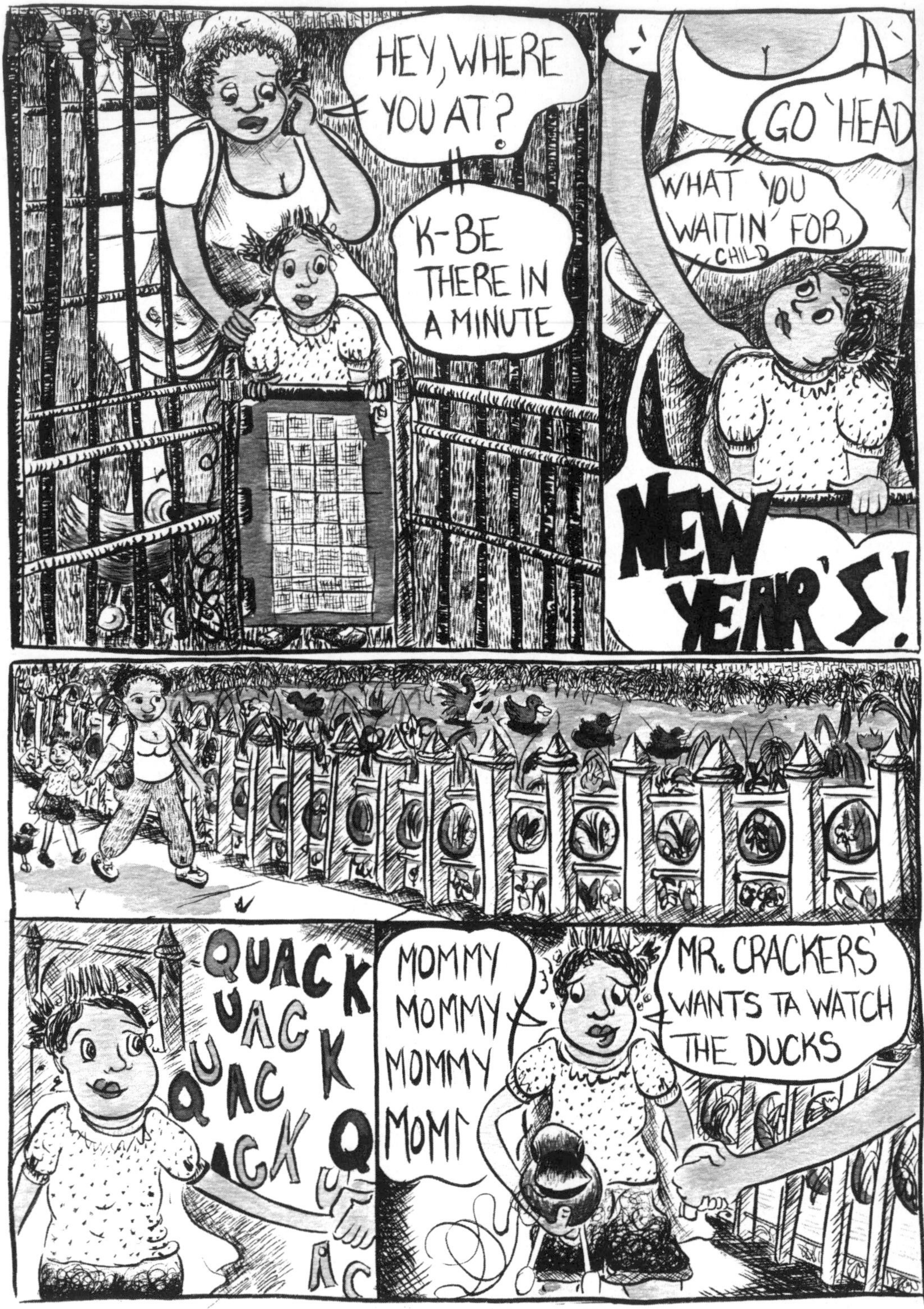
HEY, WHERE YOU AT?
'K-BE THERE IN A MINUTE
GO 'HEAD
WHAT YOU WAITIN' FOR, CHILD
NEW YEAR'S!
QUACK
UACK
QUAC K
ACK
MOMMY MOMMY MOMMY MOM
MR. CRACKERS' WANTS TA WATCH THE DUCKS

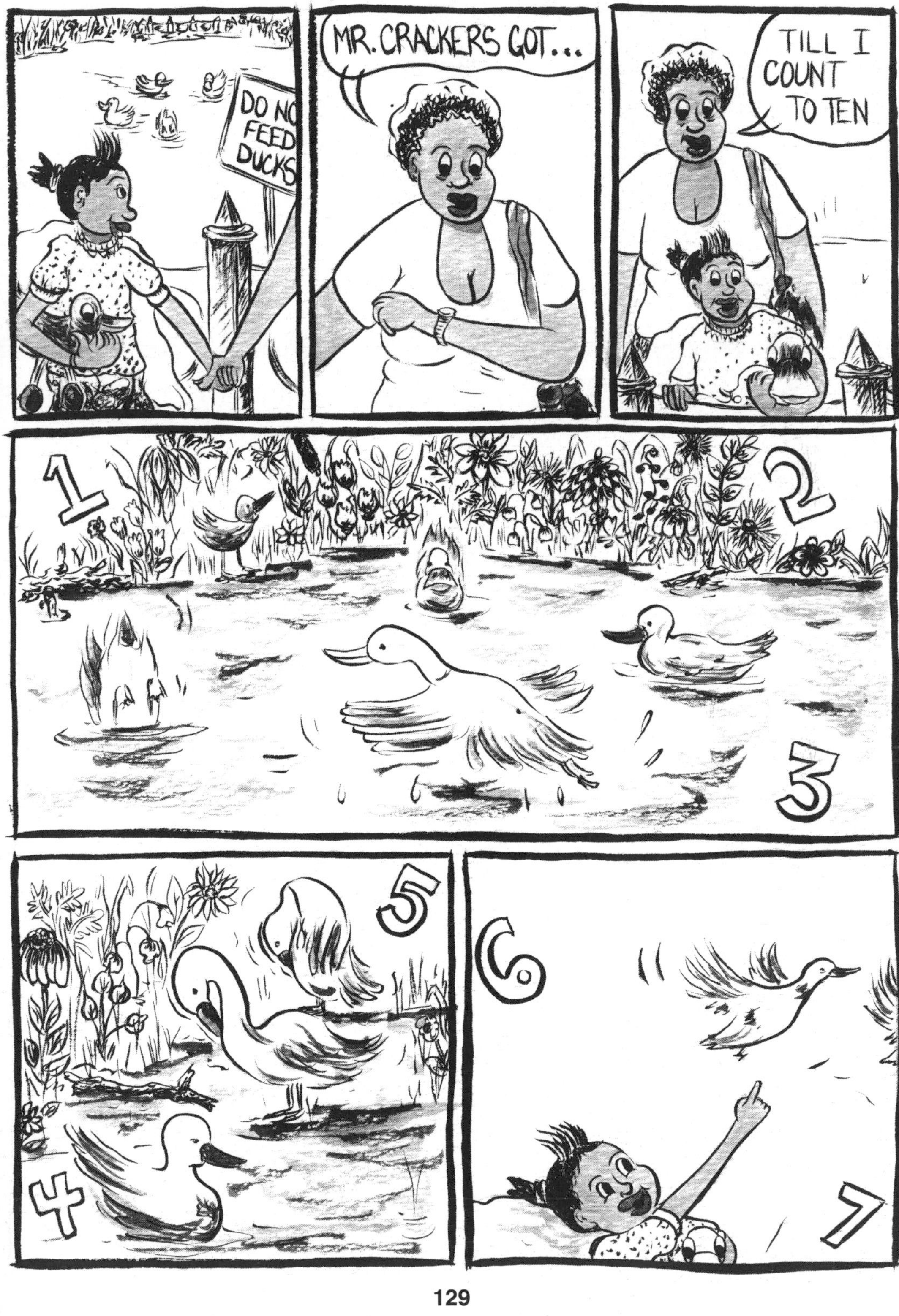
DO NOT FEED DUCKS
MR. CRACKERS GOT...
TILL I COUNT TO TEN
1
2
3
5
4
6
7

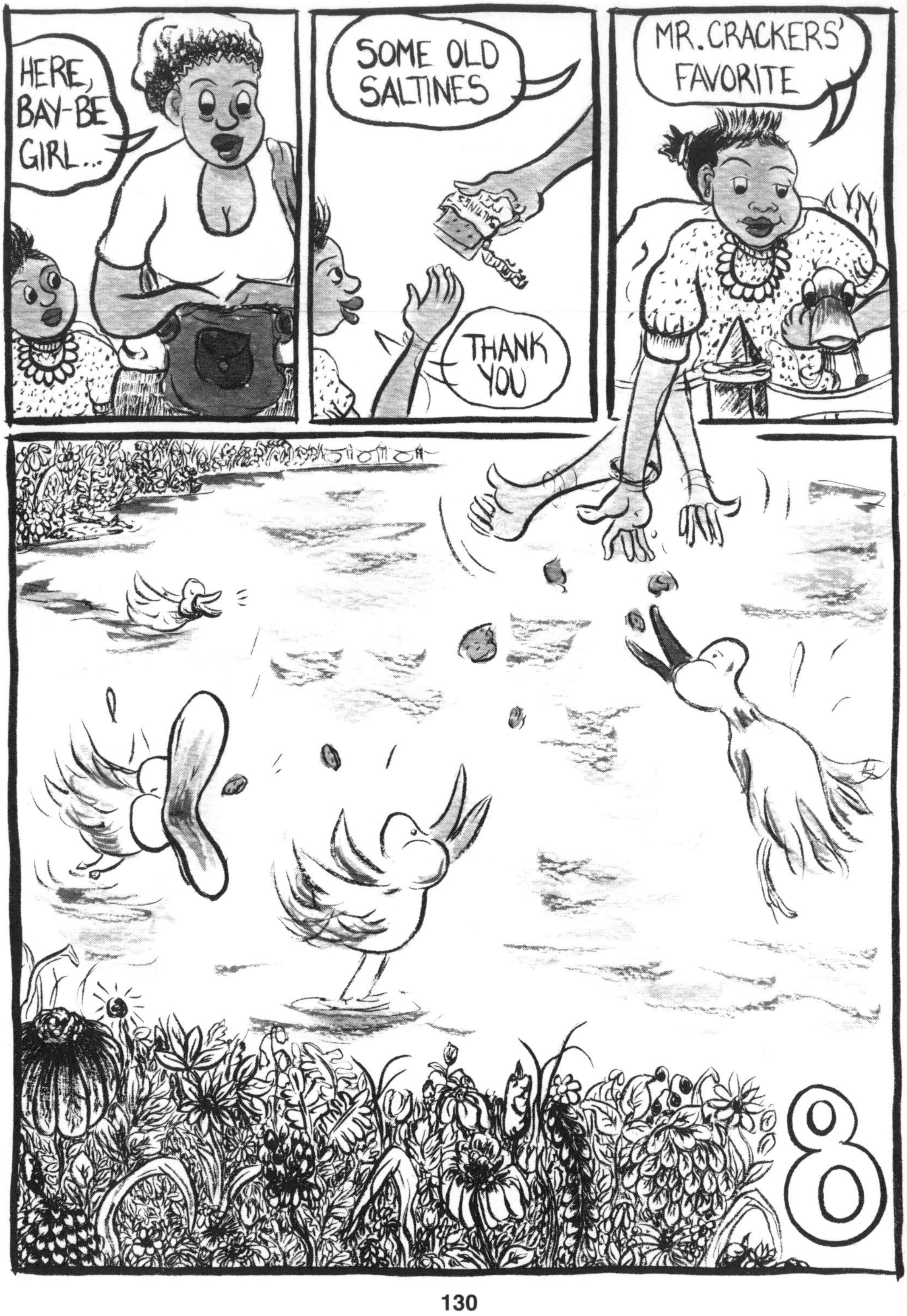
HERE, BAY-BE GIRL...
SOME OLD SALTINES
THANK YOU
MR. CRACKERS' FAVORITE
8

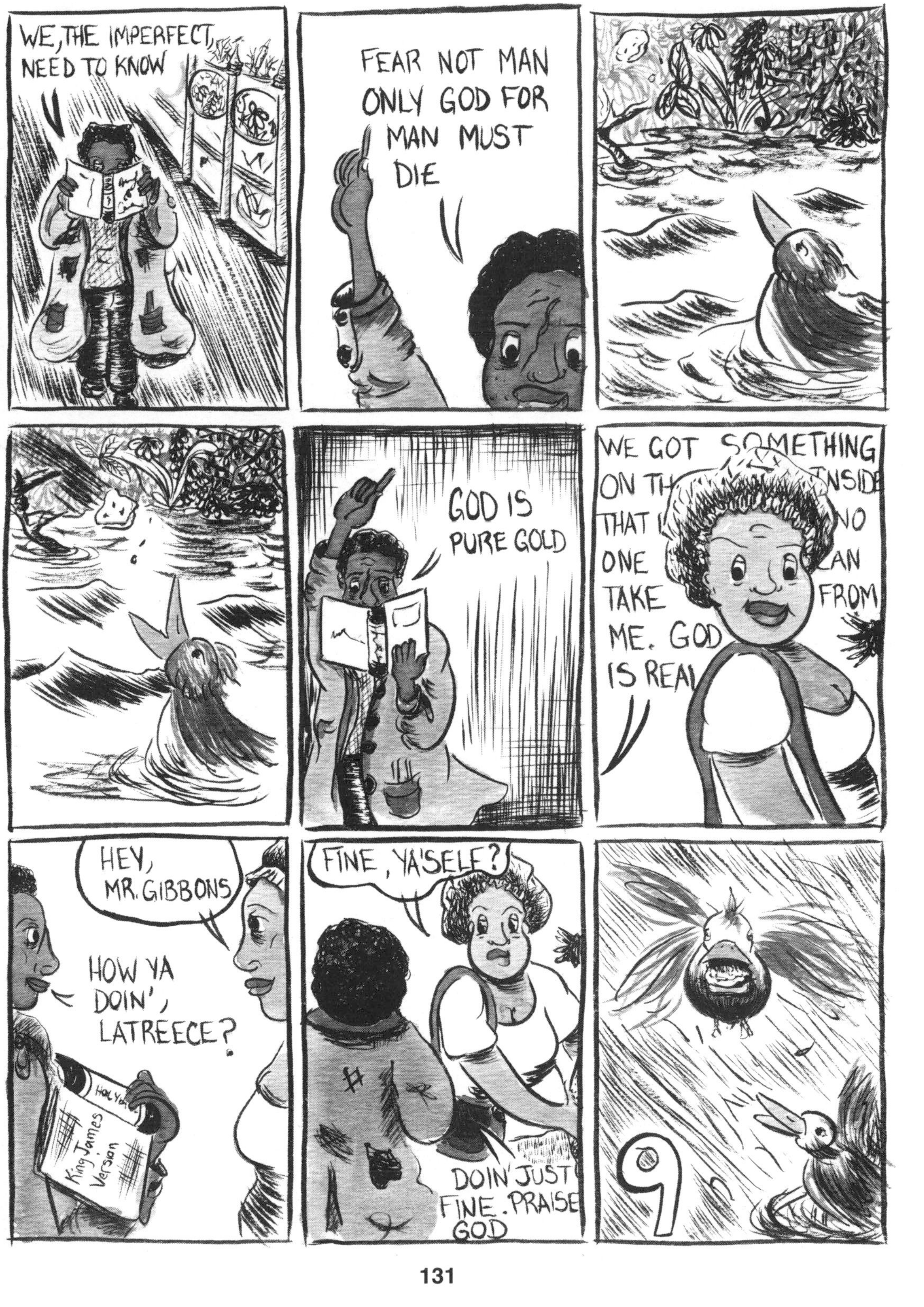
WE, THE IMPERFECT, NEED TO KNOW
FEAR NOT MAN ONLY GOD FOR MAN MUST DIE
GOD IS PURE GOLD
WE GOT SOMETHING ON TH INSIDE THAT NO ONE CAN TAKE FROM ME. GOD IS REA
HEY, MR. GIBBONS
HOW YA DOIN', LATREECE?
King James Version
FINE, YA'SELF?
DOIN' JUST FINE. PRAISE GOD

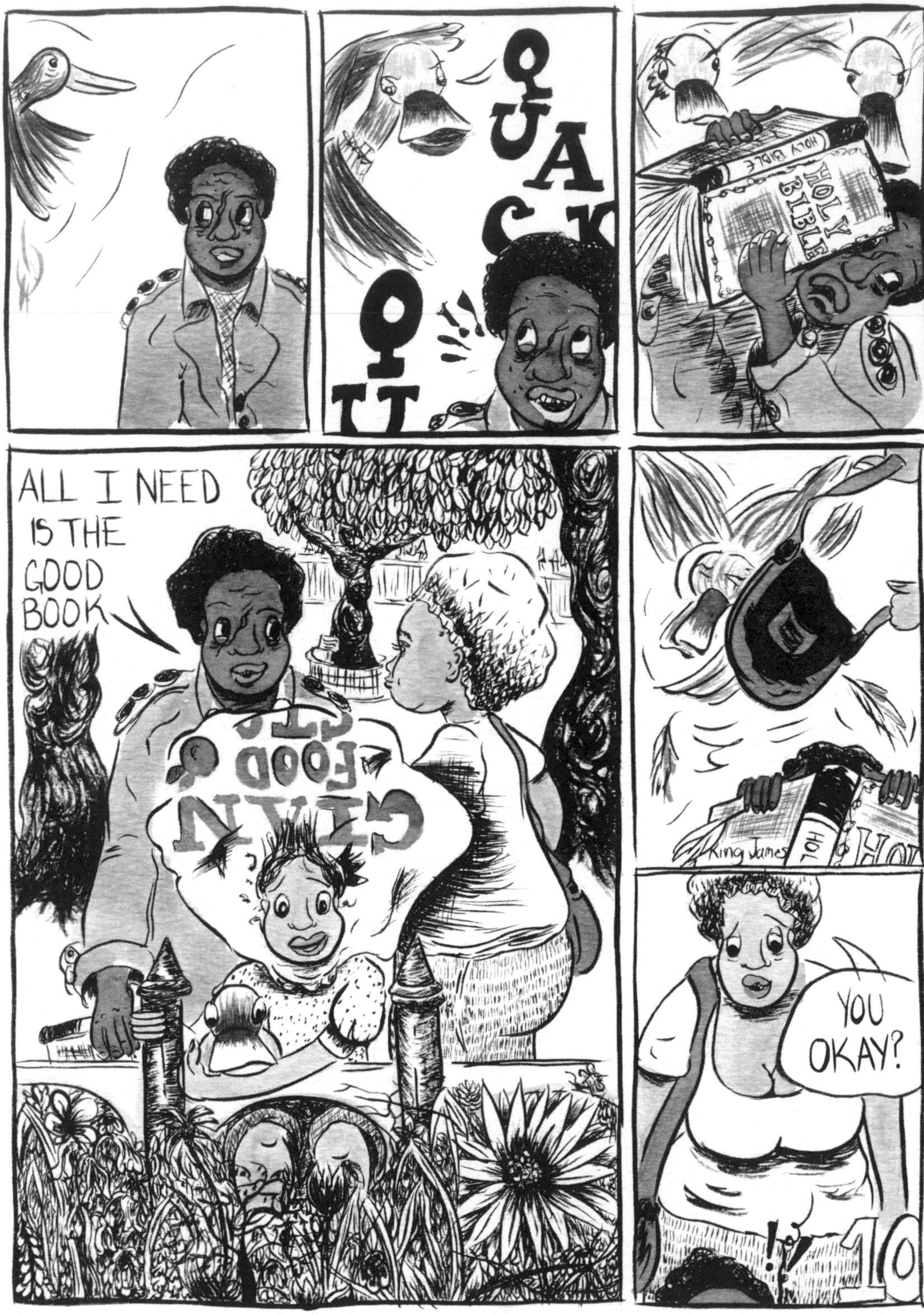
QUACK
HOLY BIBLE
ALL I NEED IS THE GOOD BOOK
King James
YOU OKAY?
!?
10

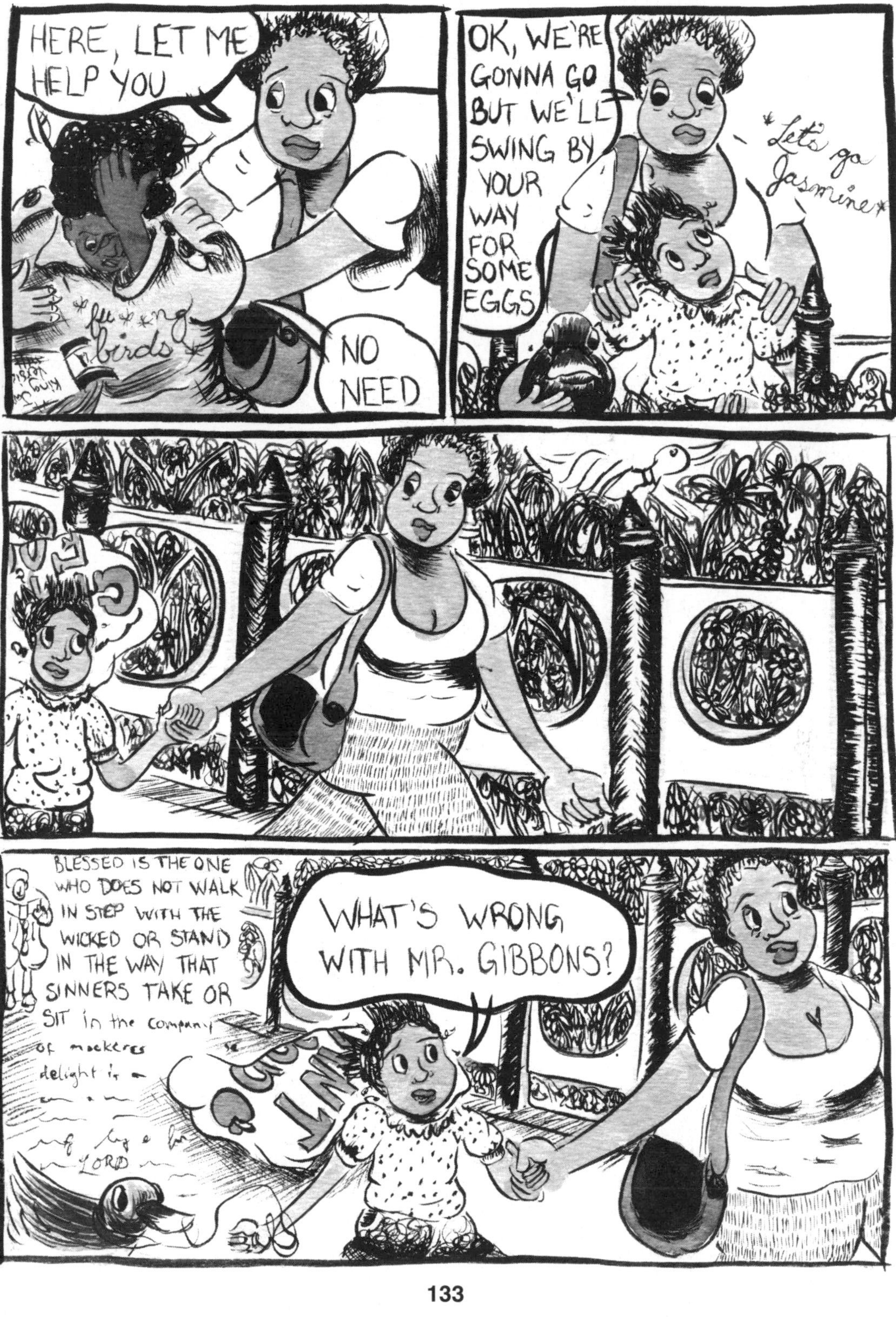
HERE, LET ME HELP YOU
NO NEED
OK, WE'RE GONNA GO BUT WE'LL SWING BY YOUR WAY FOR SOME EGGS
Let's go Jasmine
BLESSED IS THE ONE WHO DOES NOT WALK IN STEP WITH THE WICKED OR STAND IN THE WAY THAT SINNERS TAKE OR SIT in the company of mockers
LORD
WHAT'S WRONG WITH MR. GIBBONS?

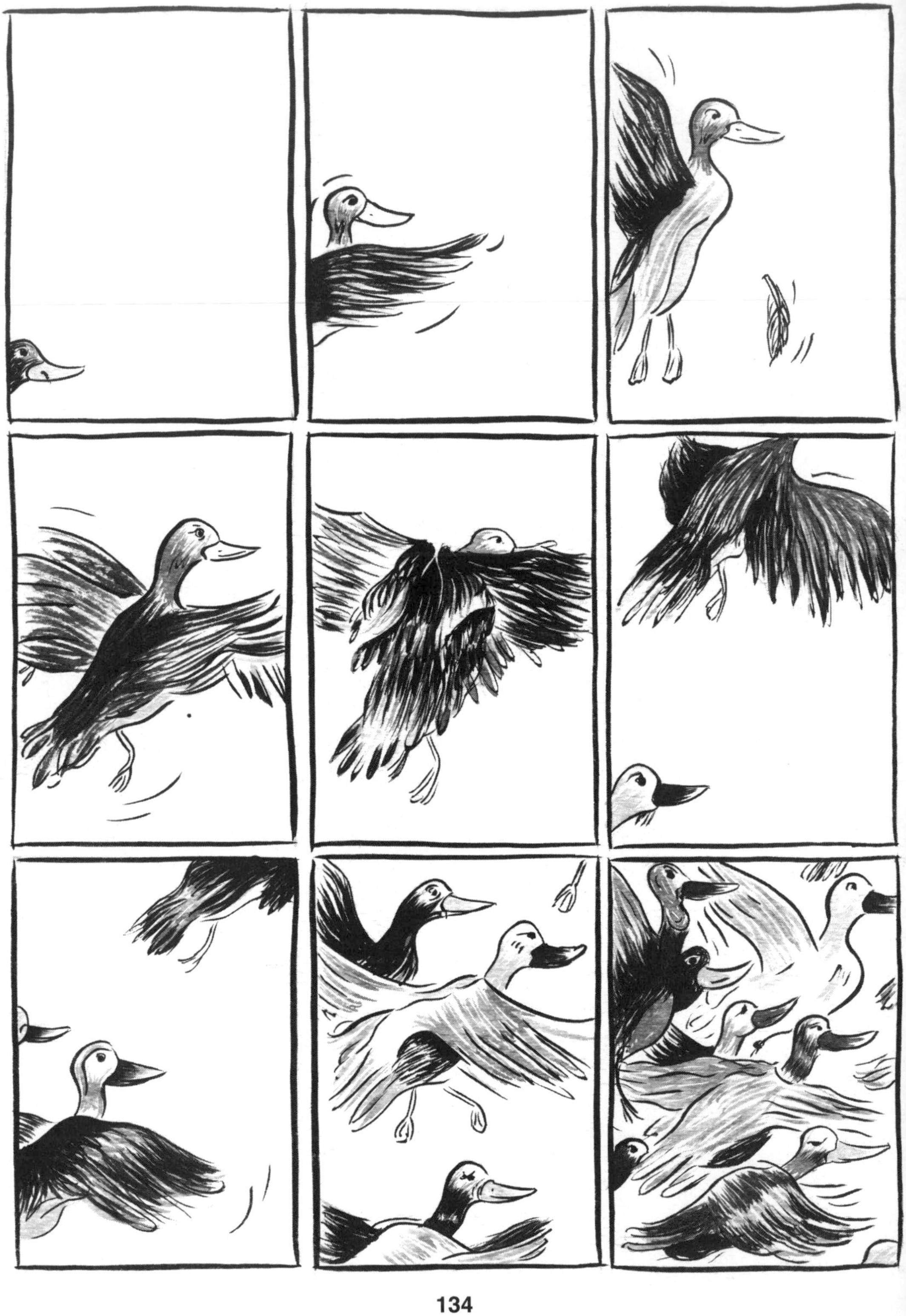

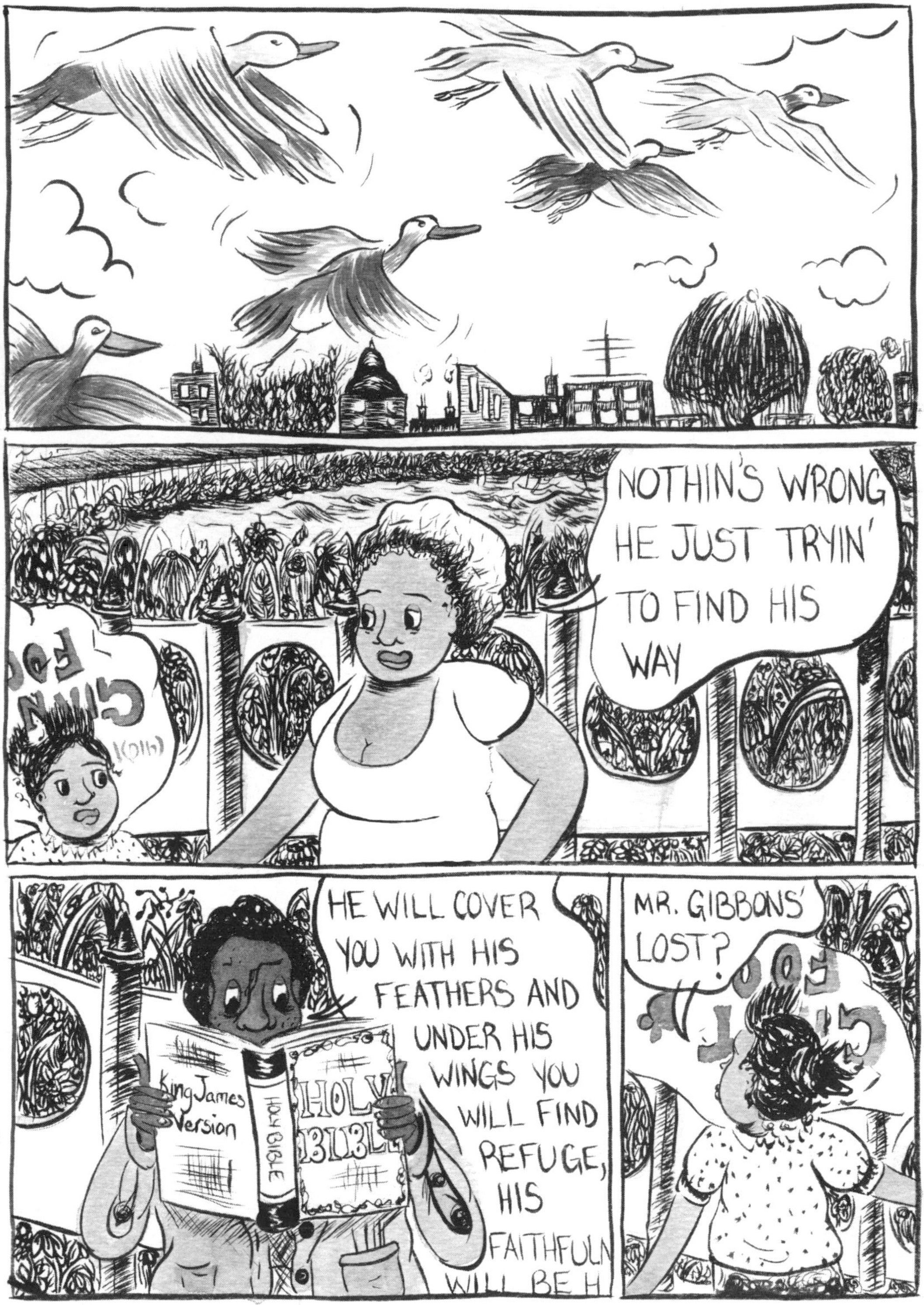
NOTHIN'S WRONG HE JUST TRYIN' TO FIND HIS WAY
HE WILL COVER YOU WITH HIS FEATHERS AND UNDER HIS WINGS YOU WILL FIND REFUGE, HIS FAITHFULN
WILL BE H
King James Version
HOLY BIBLE
HOLY BIBLE
MR. GIBBONS' LOST?

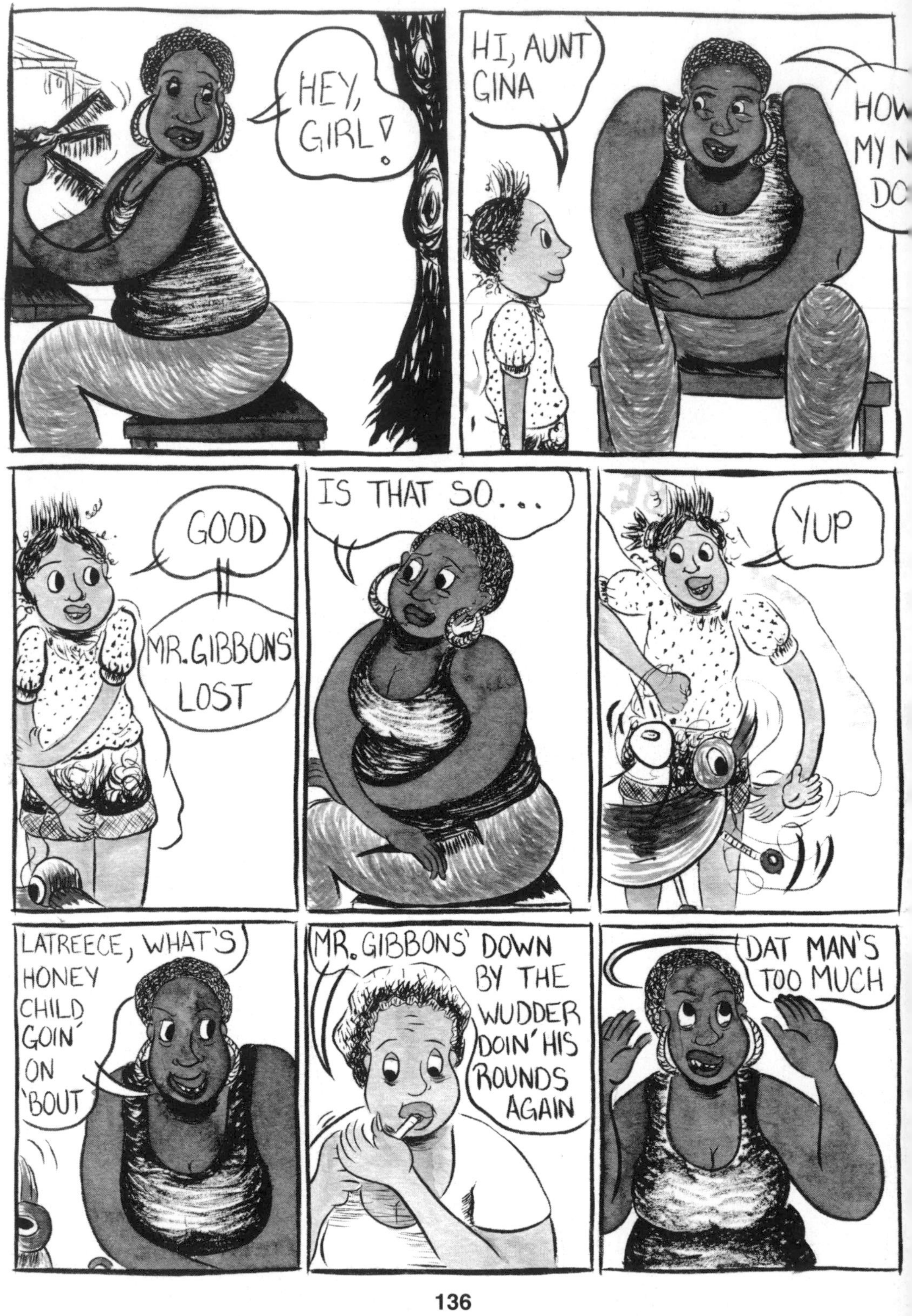
HEY, GIRL!
HI, AUNT GINA
HOW
GOOD
MR. GIBBONS' LOST
IS THAT SO...
YUP
LATREECE, WHAT'S HONEY CHILD GOIN' ON 'BOUT
MR. GIBBONS' DOWN BY THE WUDDER DOIN' HIS ROUNDS AGAIN
DAT MAN'S TOO MUCH

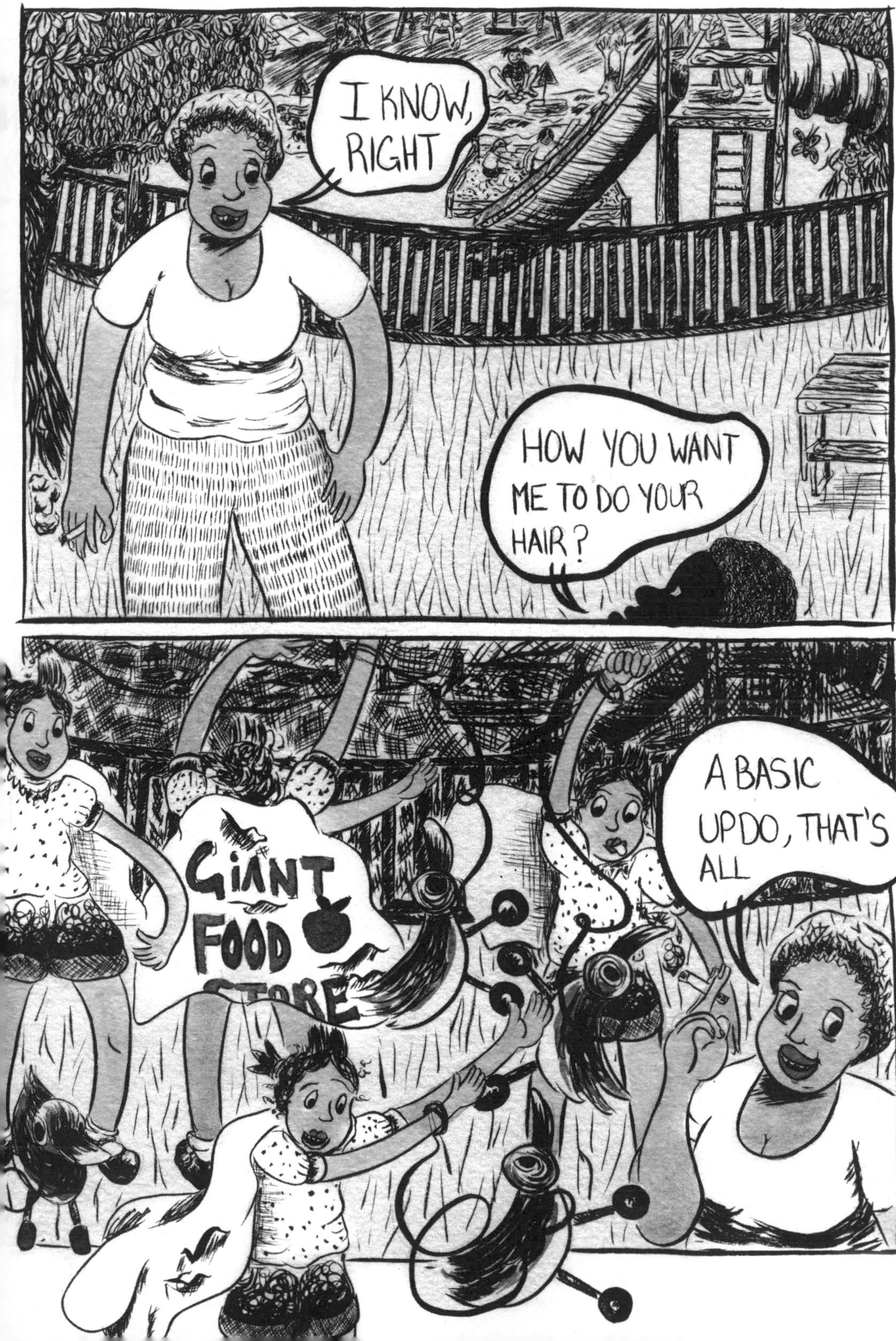
I KNOW, RIGHT
HOW YOU WANT ME TO DO YOUR HAIR?
GIANT FOOD STORE
A BASIC UPDO, THAT'S ALL

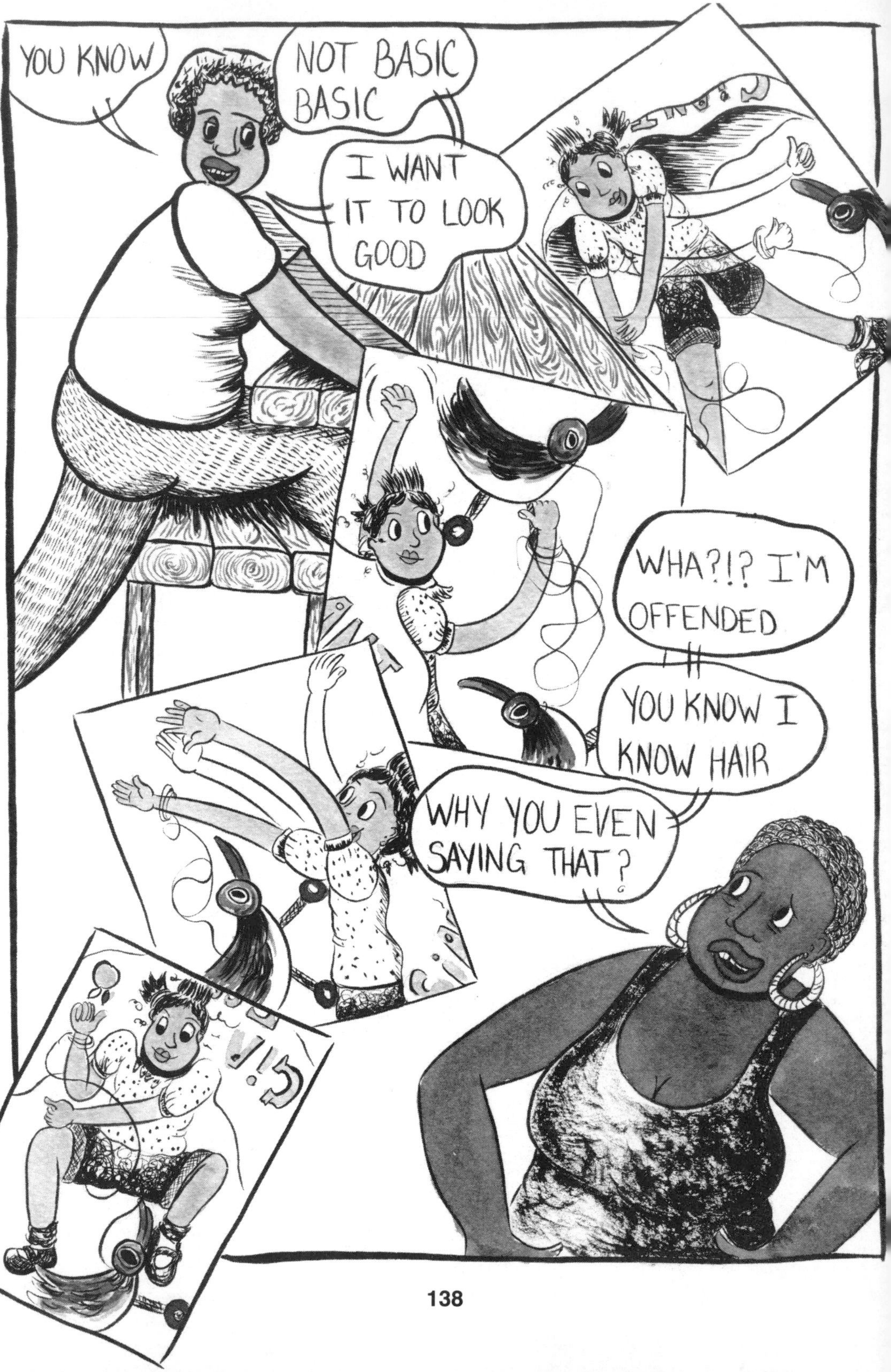
YOU KNOW
NOT BASIC BASIC
I WANT IT TO LOOK GOOD
WHA?!? I'M OFFENDED
YOU KNOW I KNOW HAIR
WHY YOU EVEN SAYING THAT?

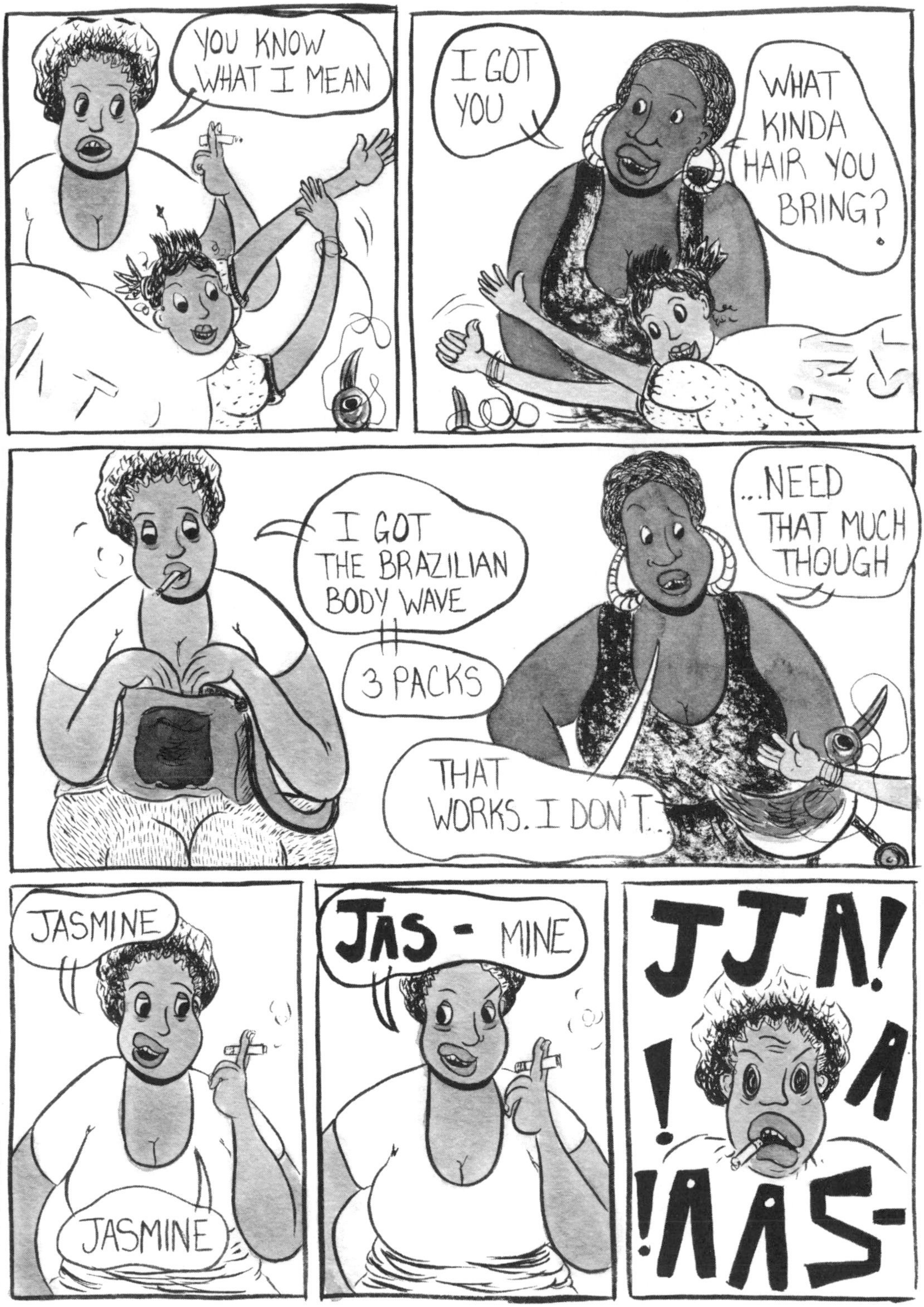
YOU KNOW WHAT I MEAN
I GOT YOU
WHAT KINDA HAIR YOU BRING?
I GOT THE BRAZILIAN BODY WAVE
3 PACKS
THAT WORKS. I DON'T...
...NEED THAT MUCH THOUGH
JASMINE
JASMINE
JAS - MINE

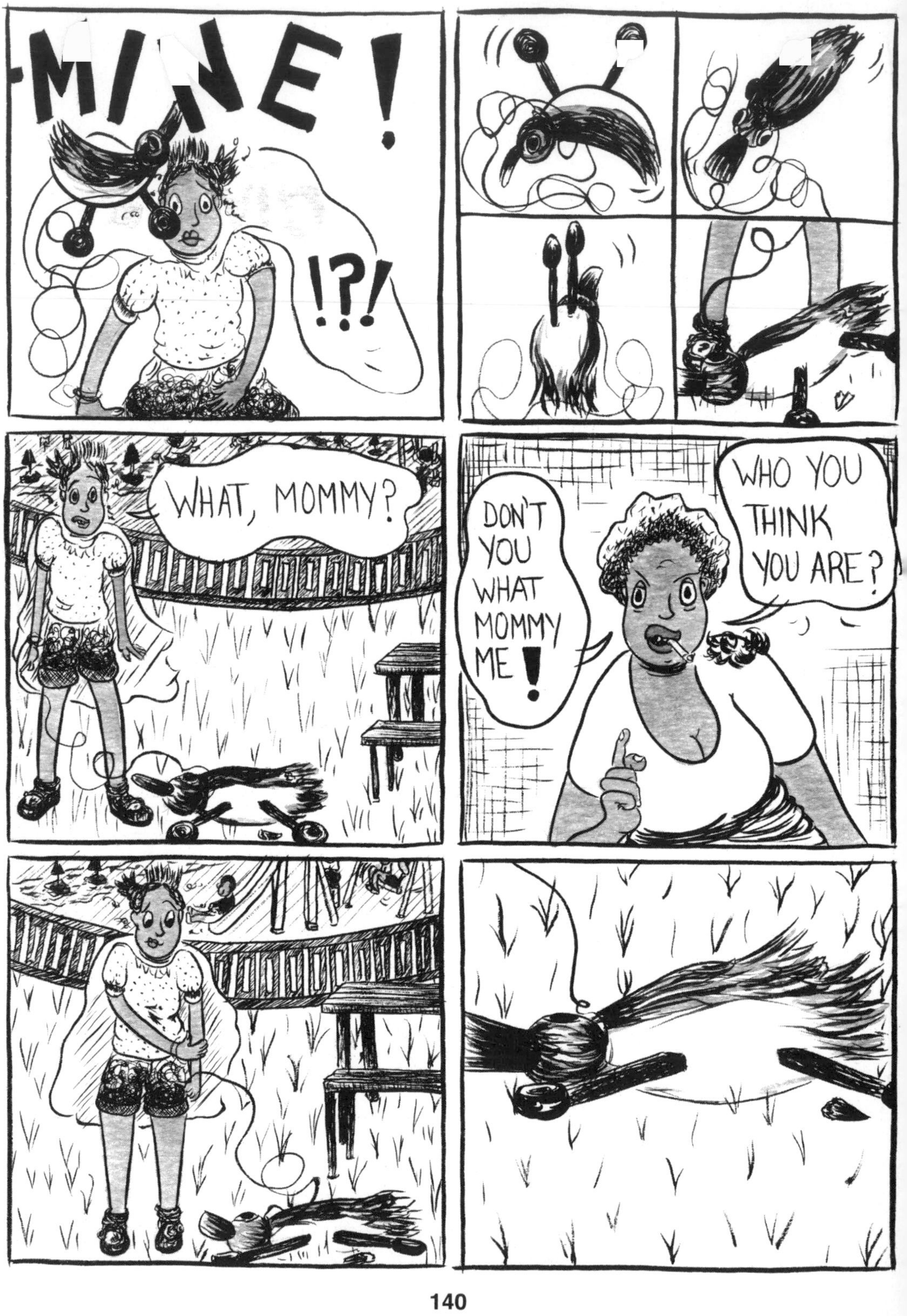

MINE!
!?!
WHAT, MOMMY?
DON'T YOU WHAT MOMMY ME!
WHO YOU THINK YOU ARE?

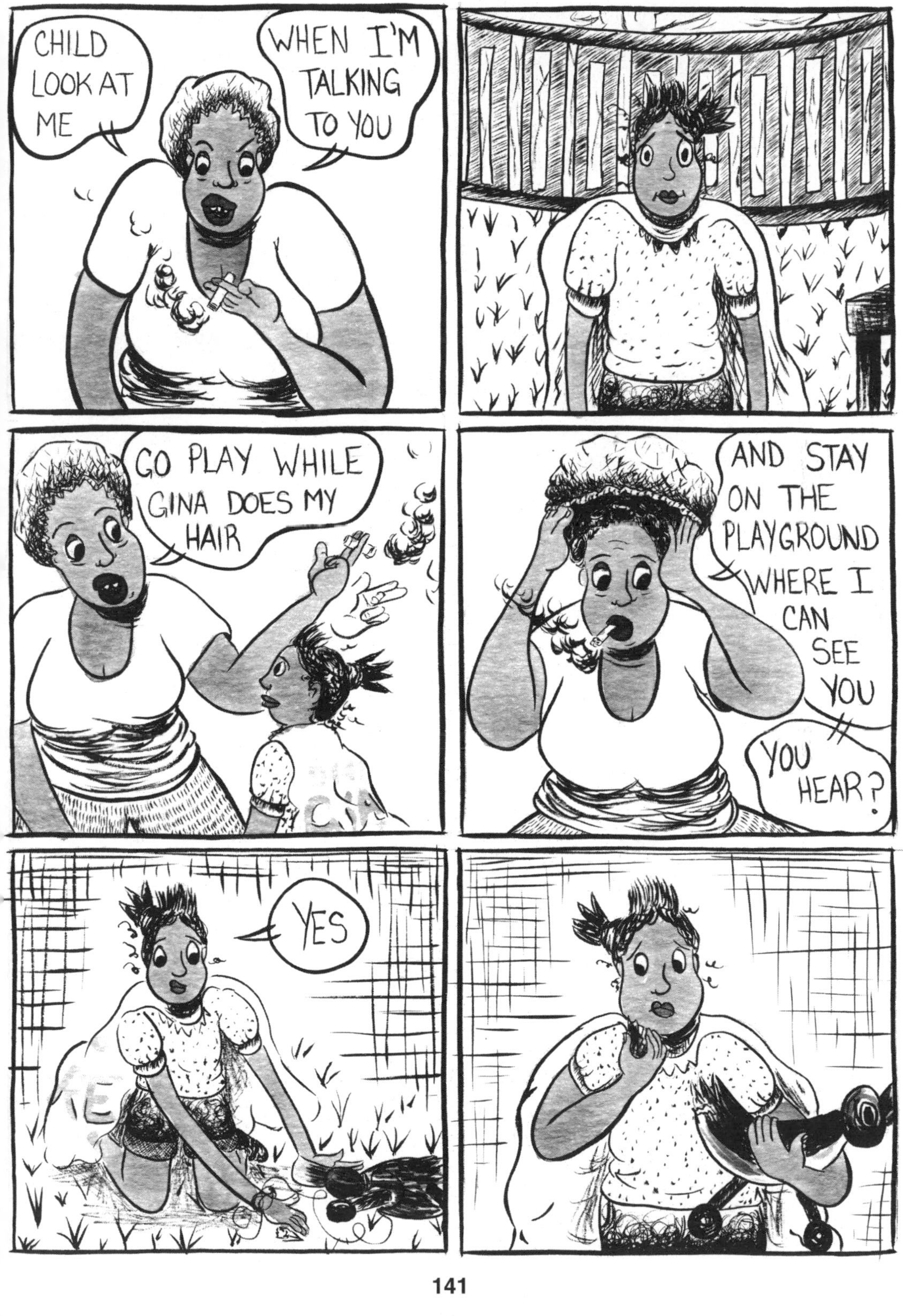
CHILD LOOK AT ME
WHEN I'M TALKING TO YOU
GO PLAY WHILE GINA DOES MY HAIR
AND STAY ON THE PLAYGROUND WHERE I CAN SEE YOU
YOU HEAR?
YES

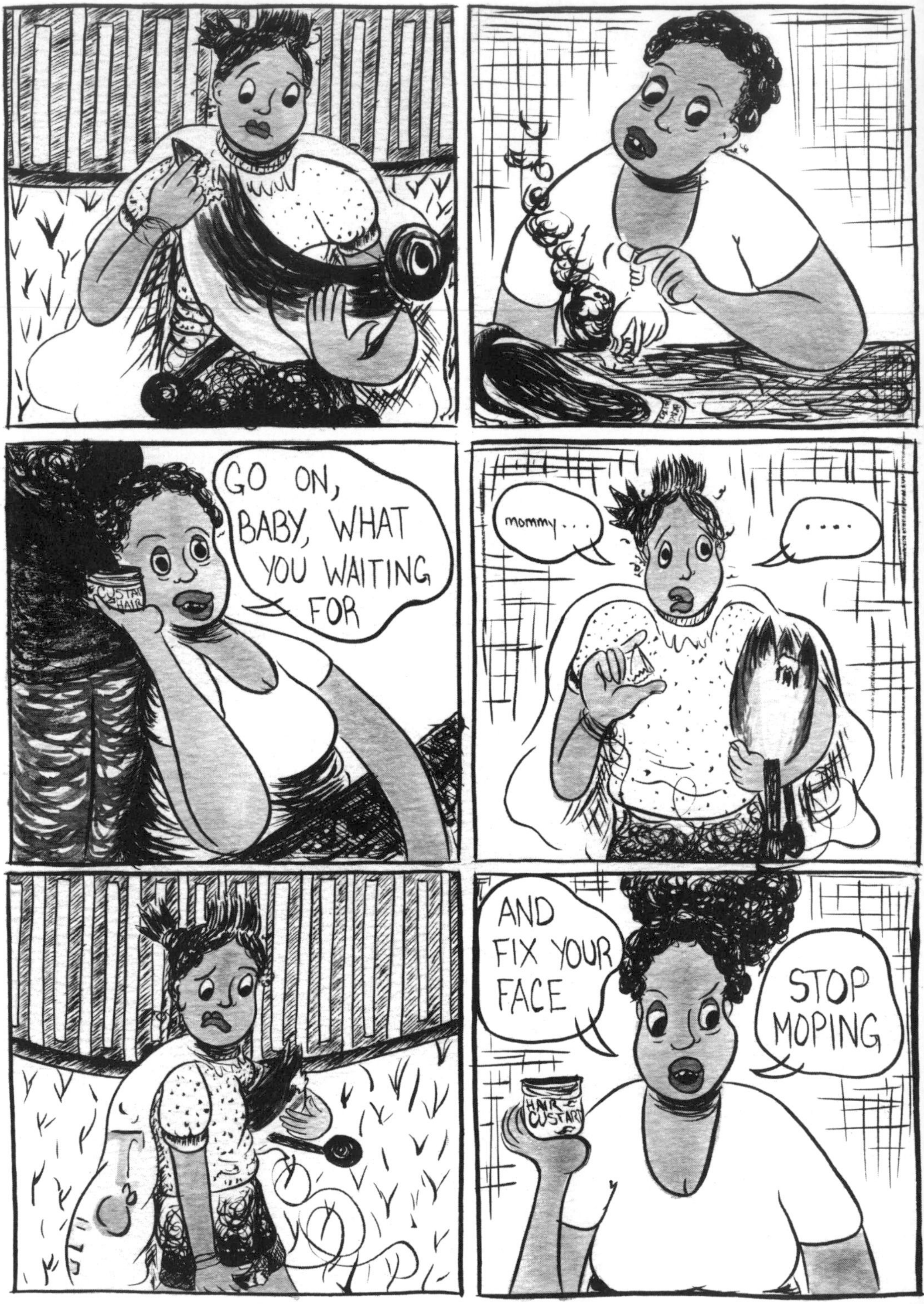
GO ON, BABY, WHAT YOU WAITING FOR
mommy . . .
. . . .
STOP MOPING
AND FIX YOUR FACE
HAIR CUSTARD

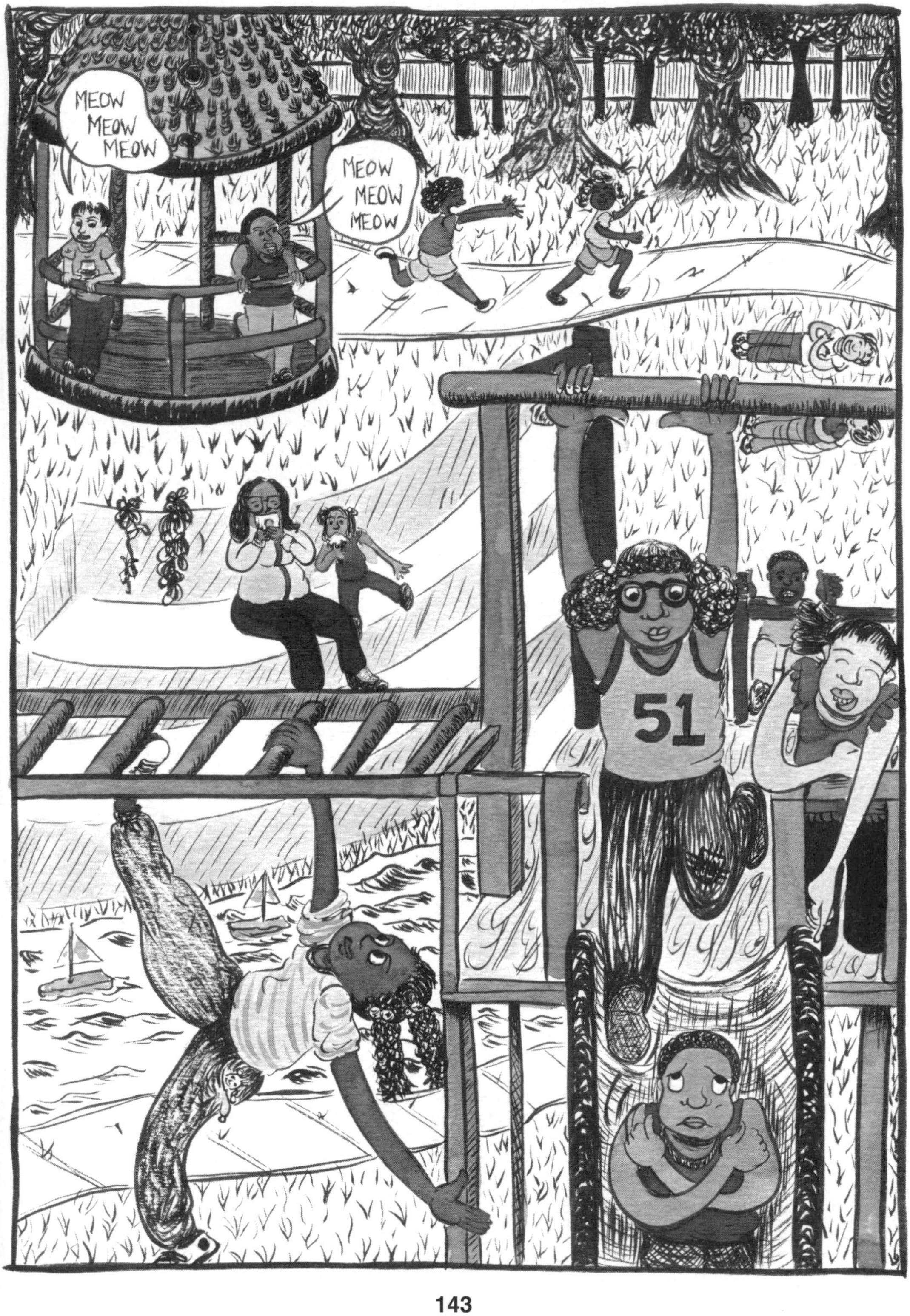
MEOW MEOW MEOW
MEOW MEOW MEOW
51

YOU CAN DO ALL T
NO PURPOSE OF
HAD HE
BUT NOW
EPENT
ASHES
MY COUSIN TOLD ME TO PUMP MY ARMS LIKE THIS
TO GET MY BLOOD MOVIN'
TO GET WHO TO MOVE WHAT?
HOLY BIBLE
ONE MORE MAN I GOT YOU I GOT YOU
I WON'T, MA!
DON'T GET YOUR HAIR WET!
LAY UP
NOPE
YOU SEE WHAT I GOTTA PUT UP WITH
CALM DOWN
AND LET ME DO YOUR HAIR
JASMINE'S ONLY SIX

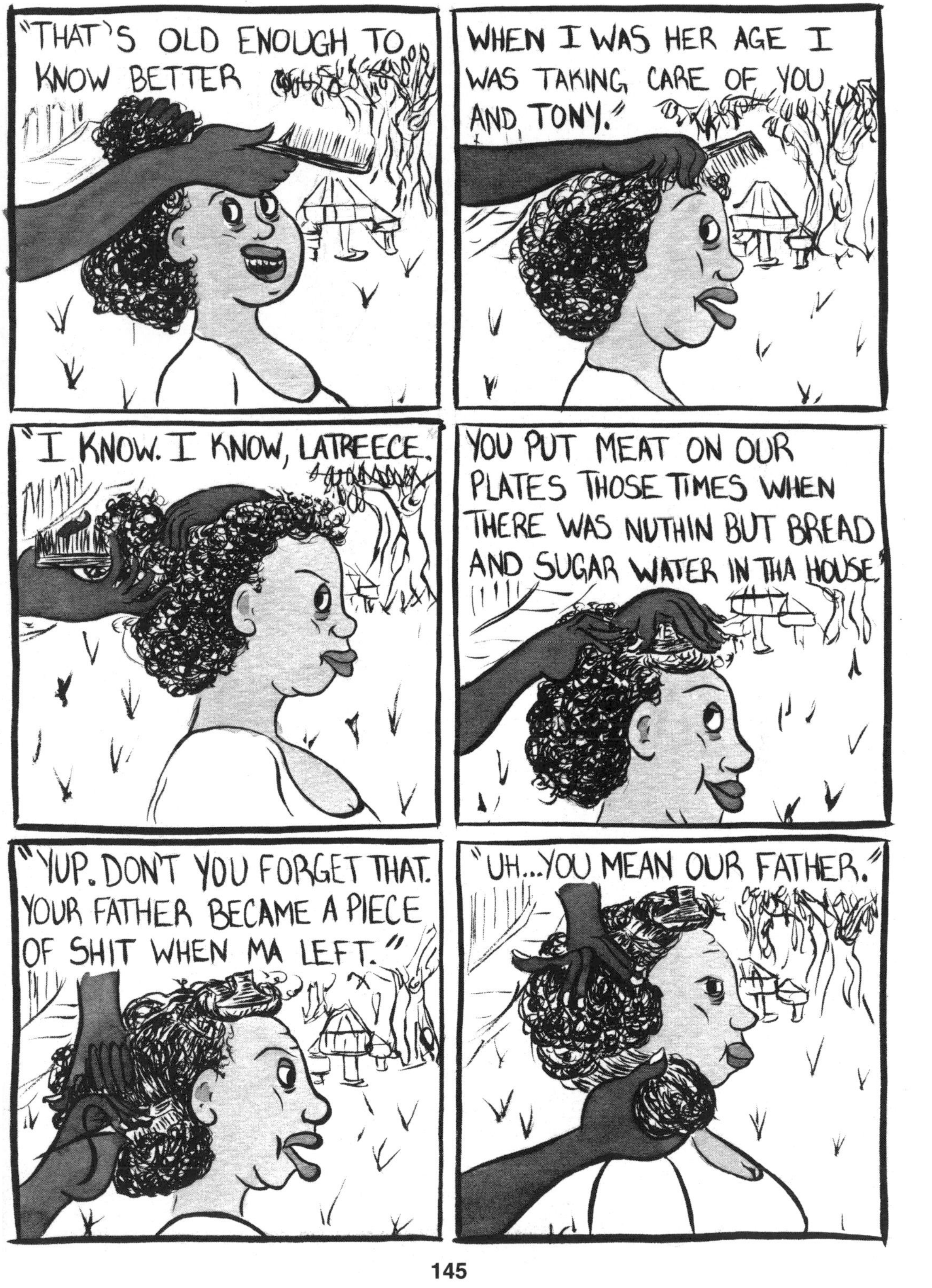
"THAT'S OLD ENOUGH TO KNOW BETTER
WHEN I WAS HER AGE I WAS TAKING CARE OF YOU AND TONY."
"I KNOW. I KNOW, LATREECE.
YOU PUT MEAT ON OUR PLATES THOSE TIMES WHEN THERE WAS NUTHIN BUT BREAD AND SUGAR WATER IN THA HOUSE."
"YUP. DON'T YOU FORGET THAT. YOUR FATHER BECAME A PIECE OF SHIT WHEN MA LEFT."
"UH...YOU MEAN OUR FATHER."

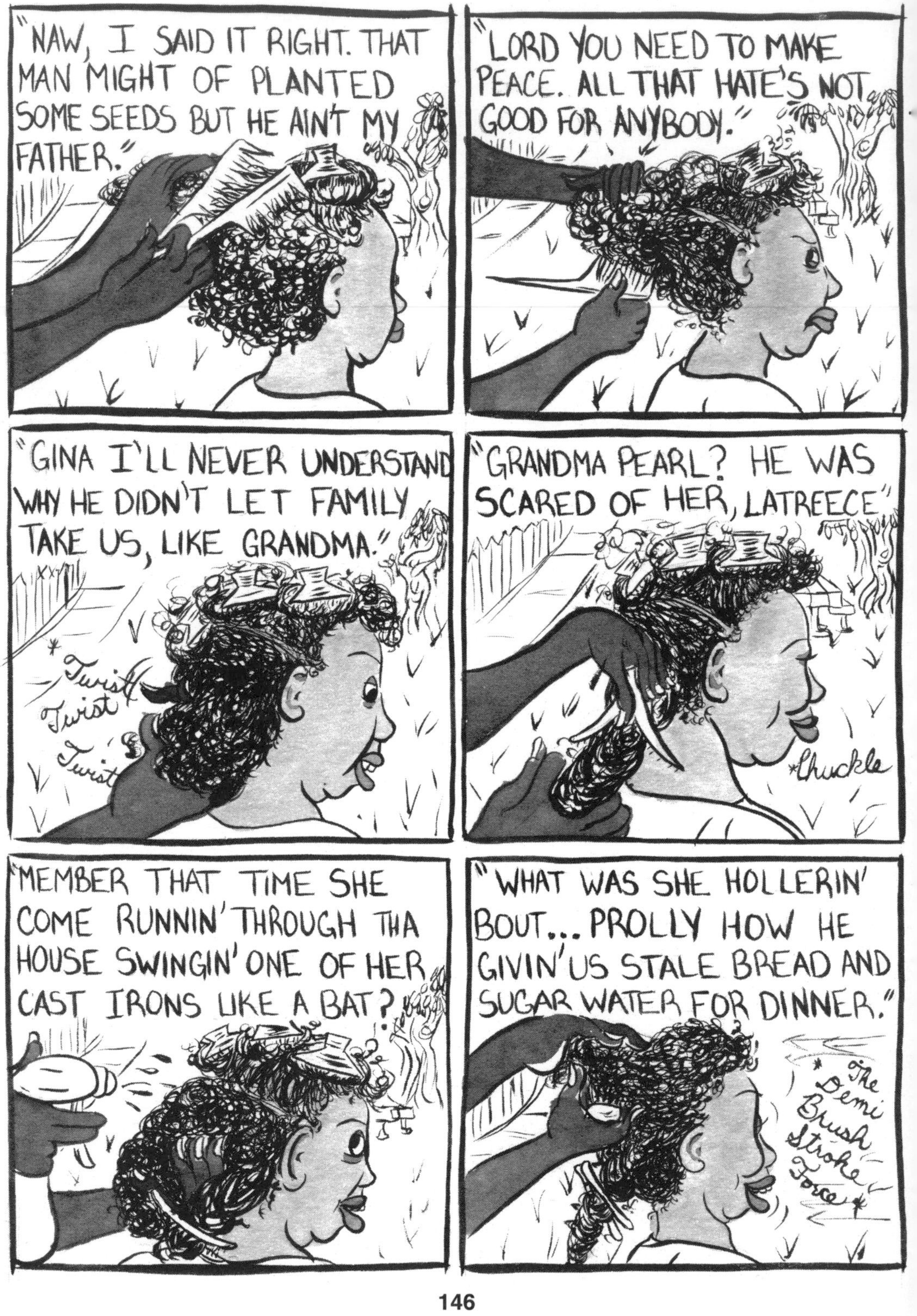
"NAW, I SAID IT RIGHT. THAT MAN MIGHT OF PLANTED SOME SEEDS BUT HE AIN'T MY FATHER."
"LORD YOU NEED TO MAKE PEACE. ALL THAT HATE'S NOT GOOD FOR ANYBODY."
"GINA I'LL NEVER UNDERSTAND WHY HE DIDN'T LET FAMILY TAKE US, LIKE GRANDMA."
*Twist Twist Twist
"GRANDMA PEARL? HE WAS SCARED OF HER, LATREECE"
*Chuckle
"MEMBER THAT TIME SHE COME RUNNIN' THROUGH THA HOUSE SWINGIN' ONE OF HER CAST IRONS LIKE A BAT?
"WHAT WAS SHE HOLLERIN' BOUT... PROLLY HOW HE GIVIN' US STALE BREAD AND SUGAR WATER FOR DINNER."
The Demi Brush Stroke Force

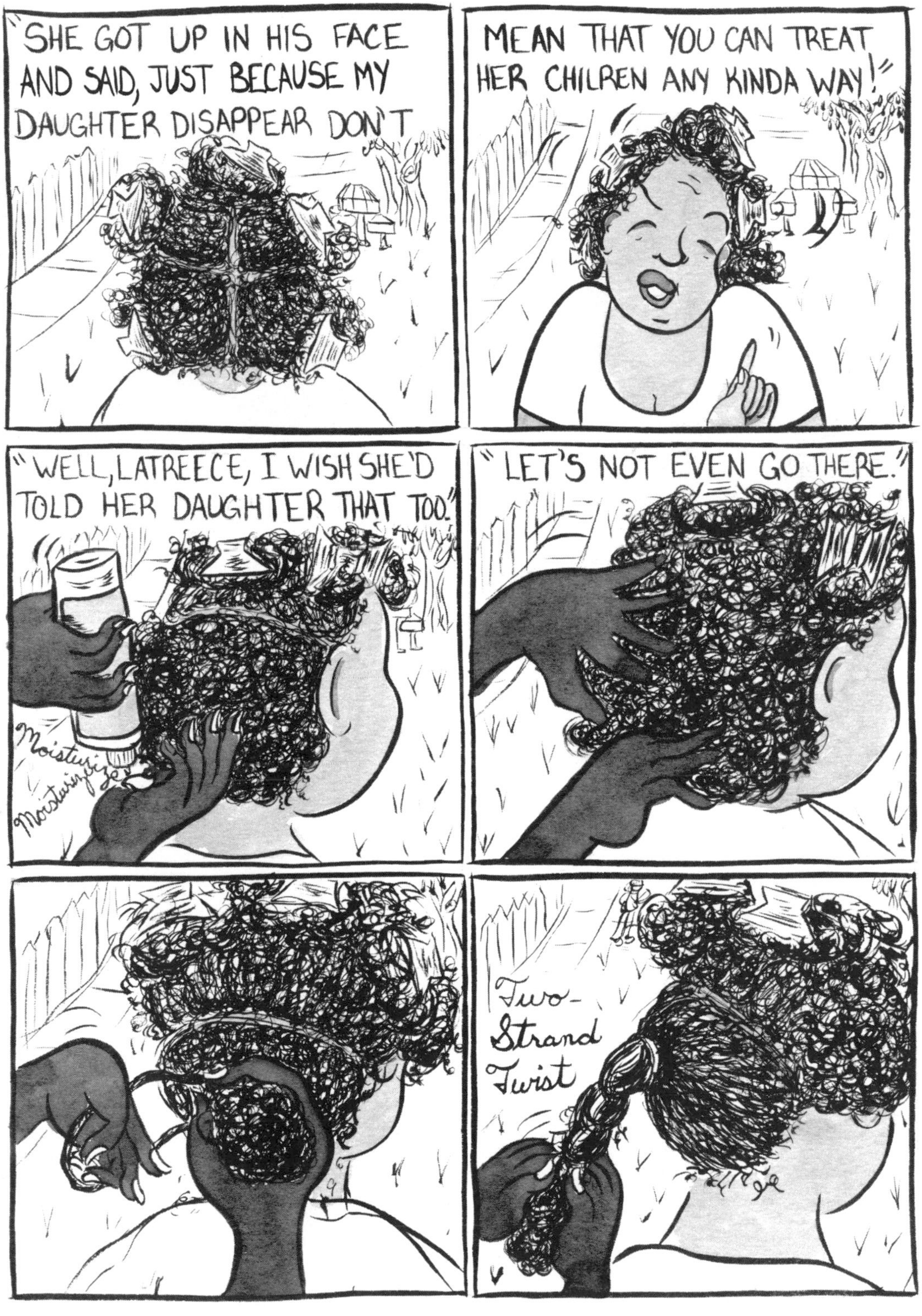
"SHE GOT UP IN HIS FACE AND SAID, JUST BECAUSE MY DAUGHTER DISAPPEAR DON'T
MEAN THAT YOU CAN TREAT HER CHILREN ANY KINDA WAY!"
"WELL, LATREECE, I WISH SHE'D TOLD HER DAUGHTER THAT TOO."
"LET'S NOT EVEN GO THERE."
Two-Strand Twist

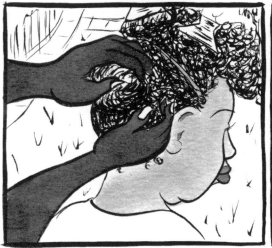

"JASMINE DON'T KNOW HOW LUCKY SHE GOT IT."

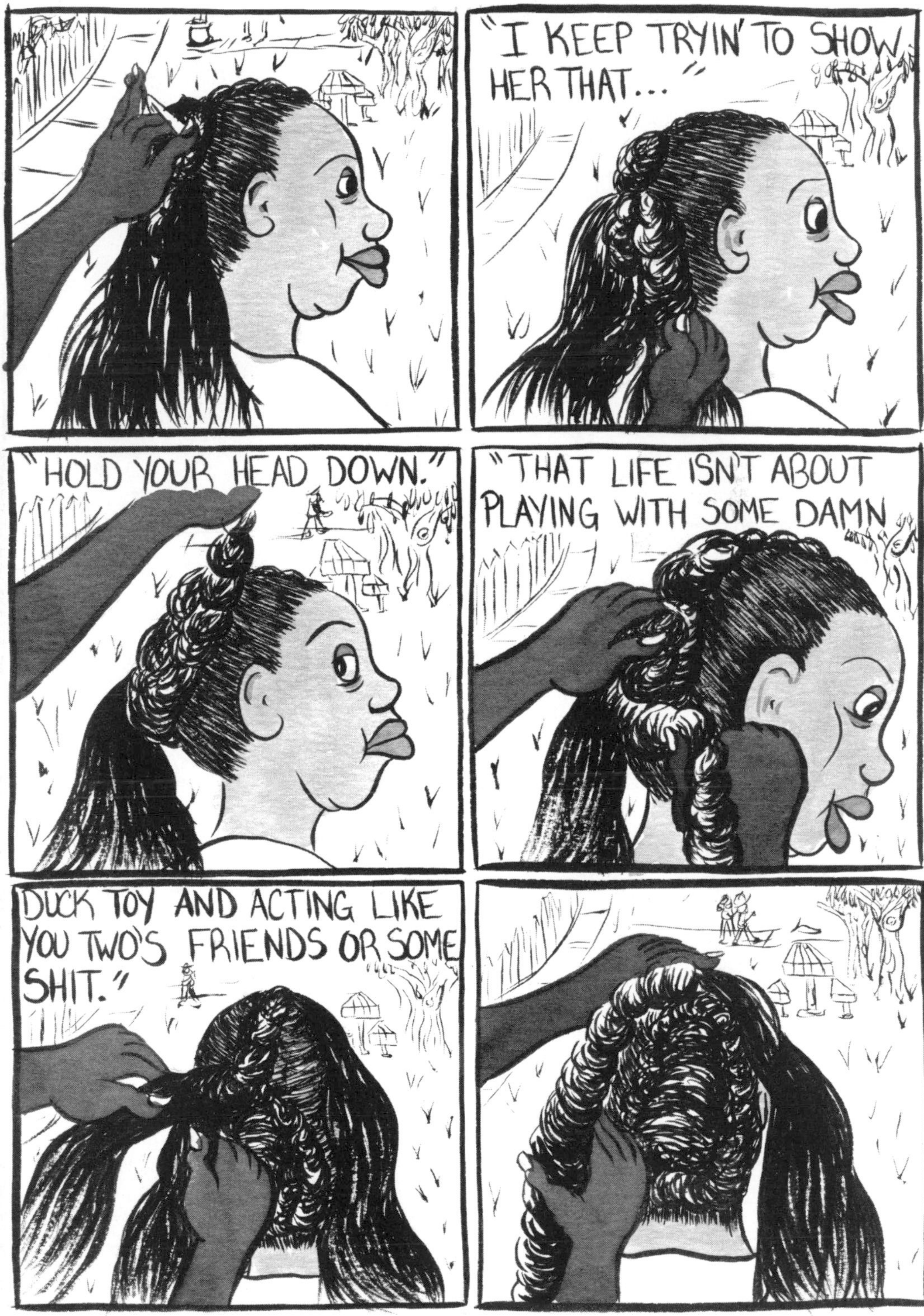
"I KEEP TRYIN' TO SHOW HER THAT..."
"HOLD YOUR HEAD DOWN."
"THAT LIFE ISN'T ABOUT PLAYING WITH SOME DAMN
DUCK TOY AND ACTING LIKE YOU TWO'S FRIENDS OR SOME SHIT."

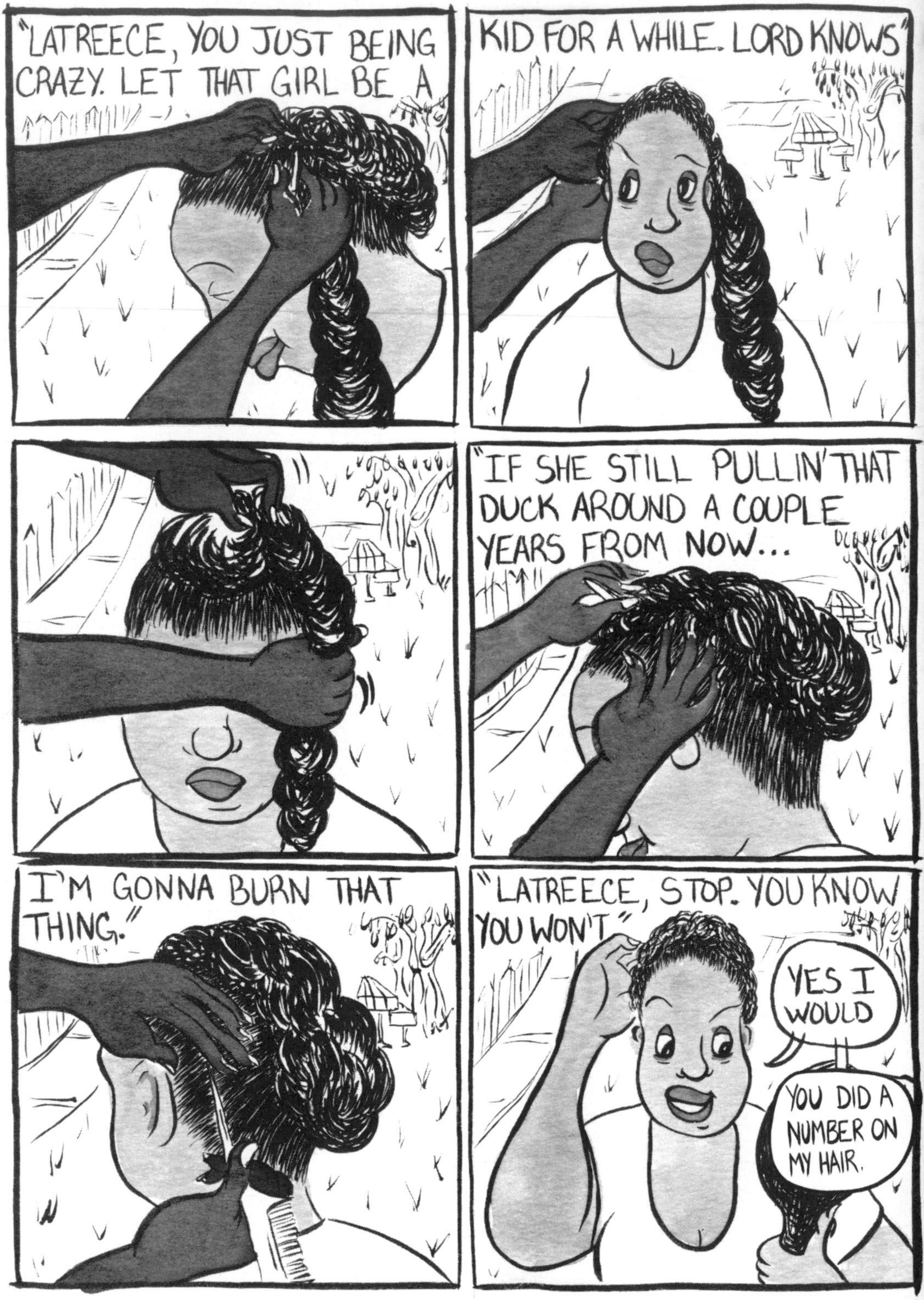
"LATREECE, YOU JUST BEING CRAZY. LET THAT GIRL BE A
KID FOR A WHILE. LORD KNOWS"
"IF SHE STILL PULLIN' THAT DUCK AROUND A COUPLE YEARS FROM NOW...
I'M GONNA BURN THAT THING."
"LATREECE, STOP. YOU KNOW YOU WON'T"
YES I WOULD
YOU DID A NUMBER ON MY HAIR.

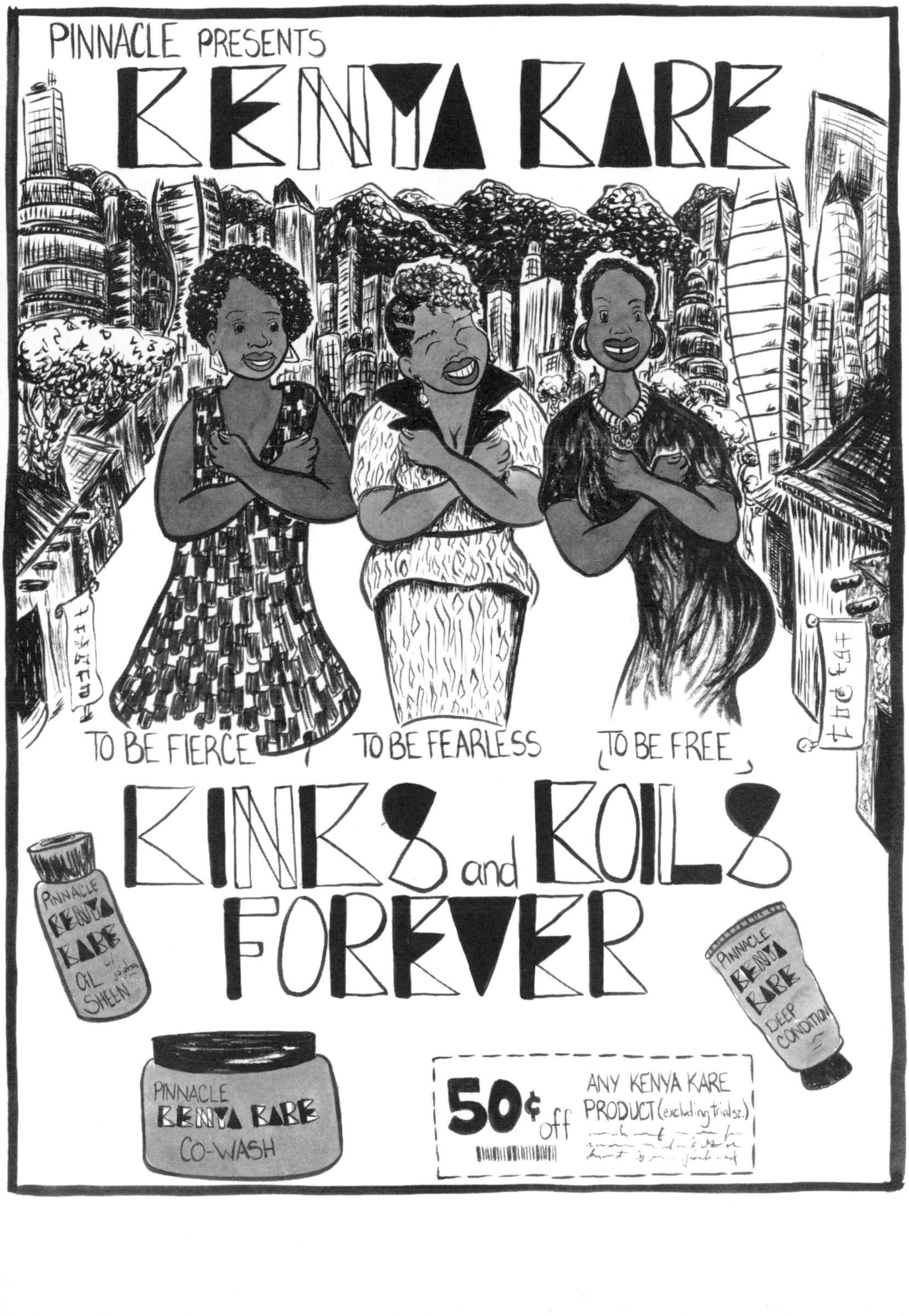
PINNACLE PRESENTS
KENYA KARE
TO BE FIERCE
TO BE FEARLESS
TO BE FREE
KINKS and KOILS FOREVER
PINNACLE KENYA KARE OIL SHEEN
PINNACLE KENYA KARE DEEP CONDITION
PINNACLE KENYA KARE CO-WASH
50¢ off
ANY KENYA KARE PRODUCT (excluding trial sz.)

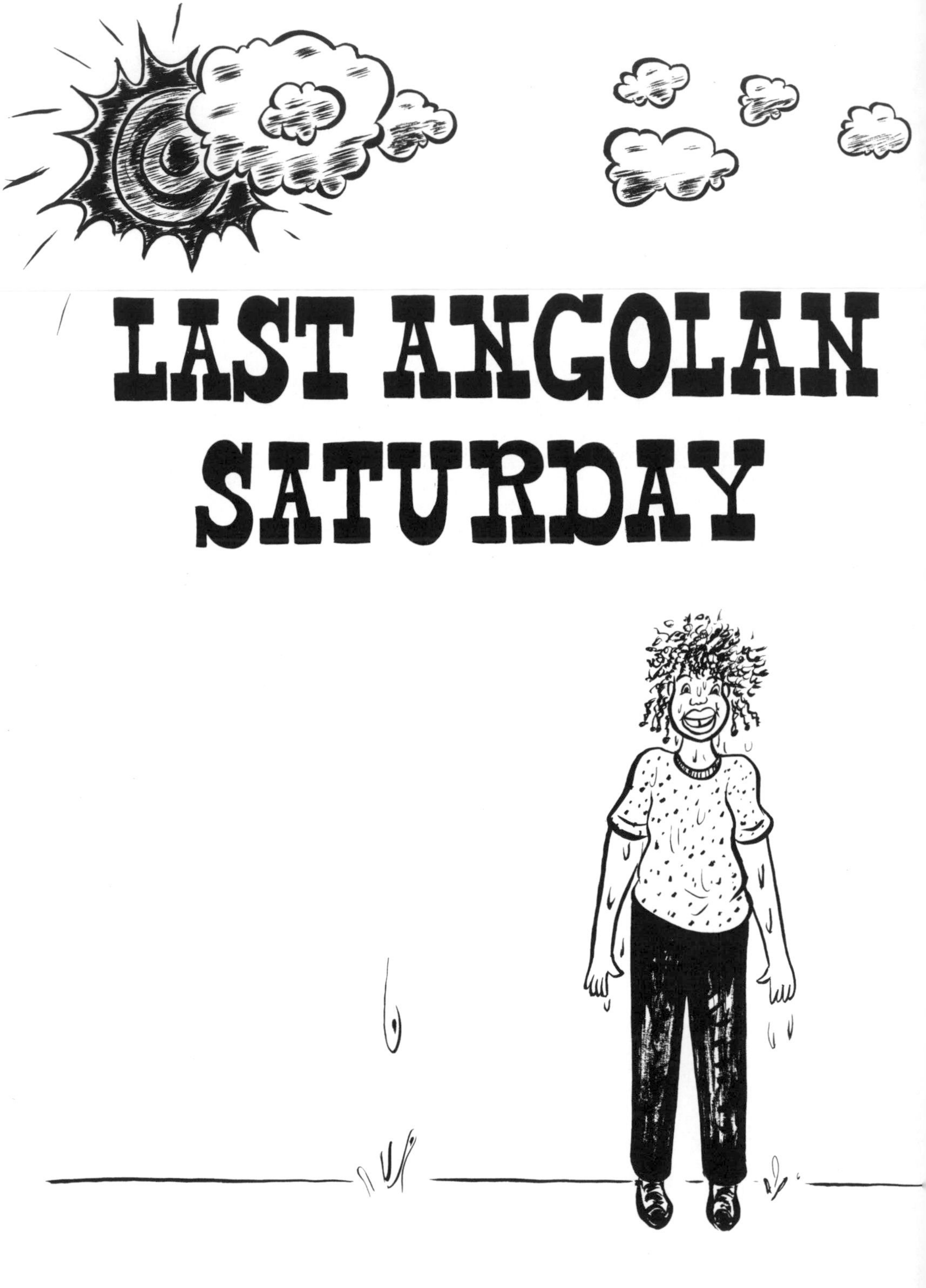
LAST ANGOLAN SATURDAY

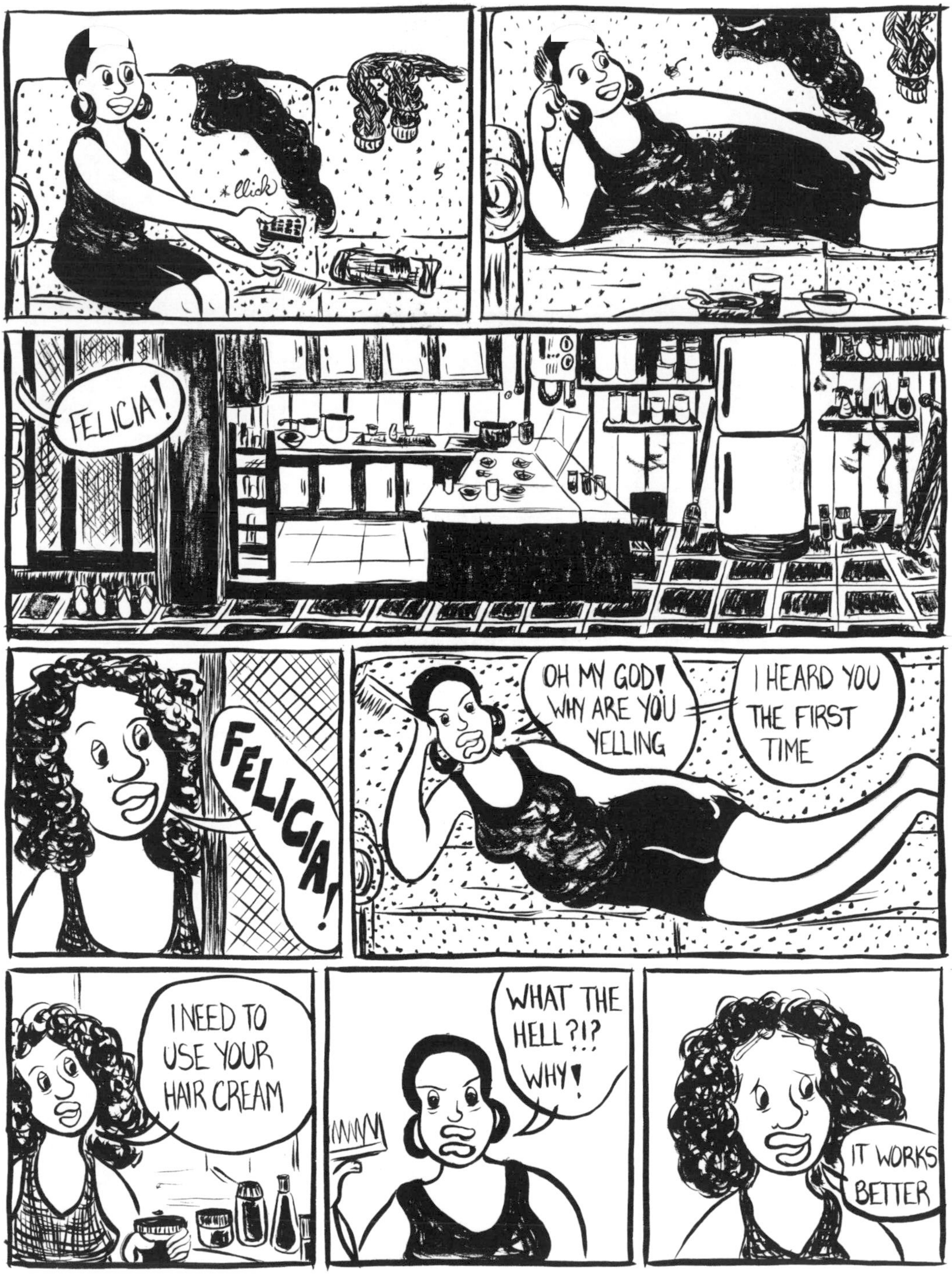
*click
FELICIA!
FELICIA!
OH MY GOD! WHY ARE YOU YELLING
I HEARD YOU THE FIRST TIME
I NEED TO USE YOUR HAIR CREAM
WHAT THE HELL?!? WHY!
IT WORKS BETTER

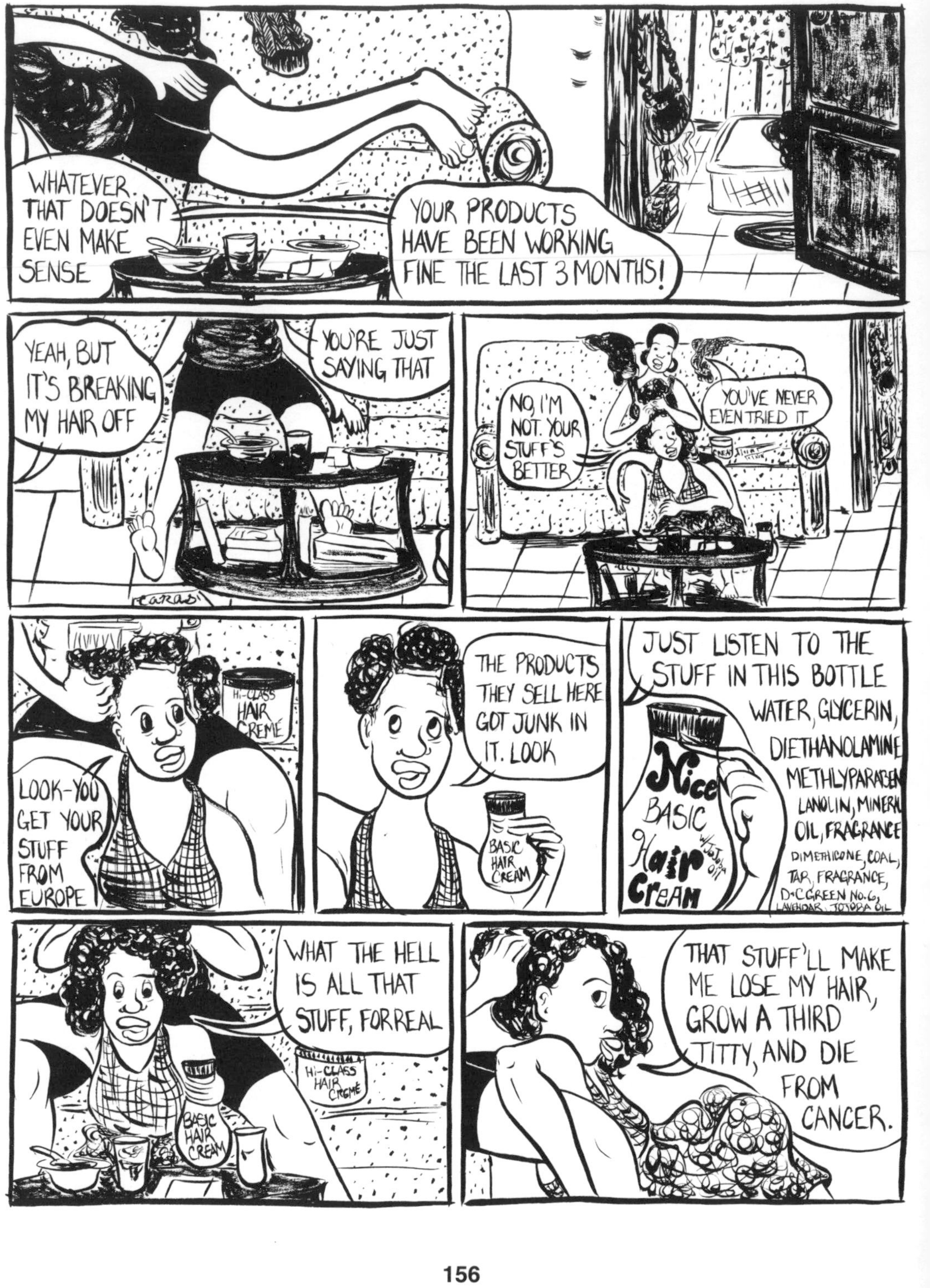
WHATEVER. THAT DOESN'T EVEN MAKE SENSE
YOUR PRODUCTS HAVE BEEN WORKING FINE THE LAST 3 MONTHS!
YEAH, BUT IT'S BREAKING MY HAIR OFF
YOU'RE JUST SAYING THAT
NO, I'M NOT. YOUR STUFF'S BETTER
YOU'VE NEVER EVEN TRIED IT
Hi-CLASS HAIR CREMÉ
LOOK-YOU GET YOUR STUFF FROM EUROPE
THE PRODUCTS THEY SELL HERE GOT JUNK IN IT. LOOK
BASIC HAIR CREAM
JUST LISTEN TO THE STUFF IN THIS BOTTLE
Nice BASIC Hair Cream w/ JoJoba Oil
WATER, GLYCERIN, DIETHANOLAMINE METHLYPARABEN LANOLIN, MINERAL OIL, FRAGRANCE DIMETHICONE, COAL TAR, FRAGRANCE, D+C GREEN No. 6, LAVENDAR, JOJOBA OIL
WHAT THE HELL IS ALL THAT STUFF, FORREAL
Hi-CLASS HAIR CREMÉ
BASIC HAIR CREAM
THAT STUFF'LL MAKE ME LOSE MY HAIR, GROW A THIRD TITTY, AND DIE FROM CANCER.

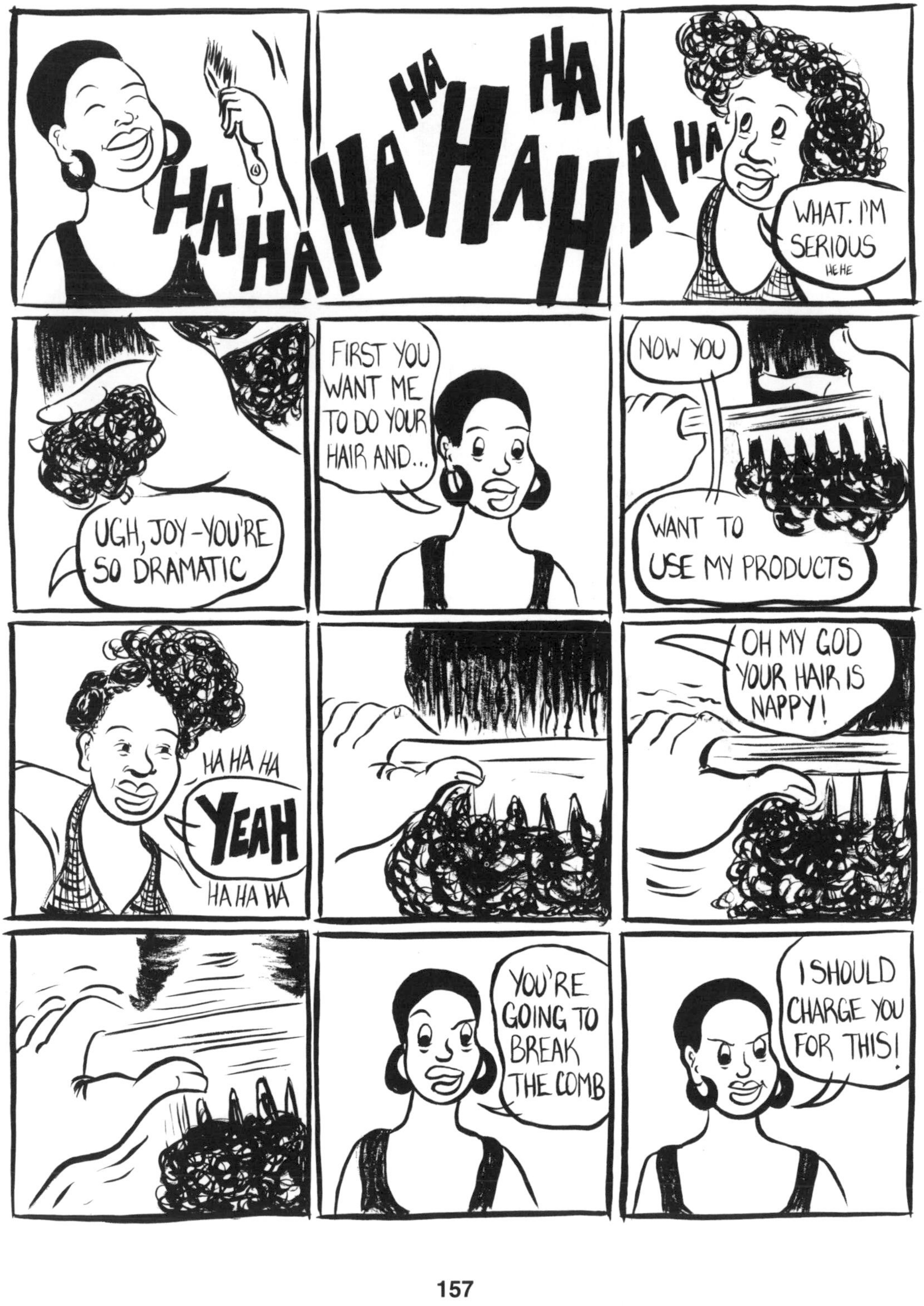
HA HA HA HA HA HA HA HA HA HA HA
WHAT. I'M SERIOUS HEHE
UGH, JOY-YOU'RE SO DRAMATIC
FIRST YOU WANT ME TO DO YOUR HAIR AND...
NOW YOU
WANT TO USE MY PRODUCTS
HA HA HA
YEAH
HA HA HA
OH MY GOD YOUR HAIR IS NAPPY!
YOU'RE GOING TO BREAK THE COMB
I SHOULD CHARGE YOU FOR THIS!

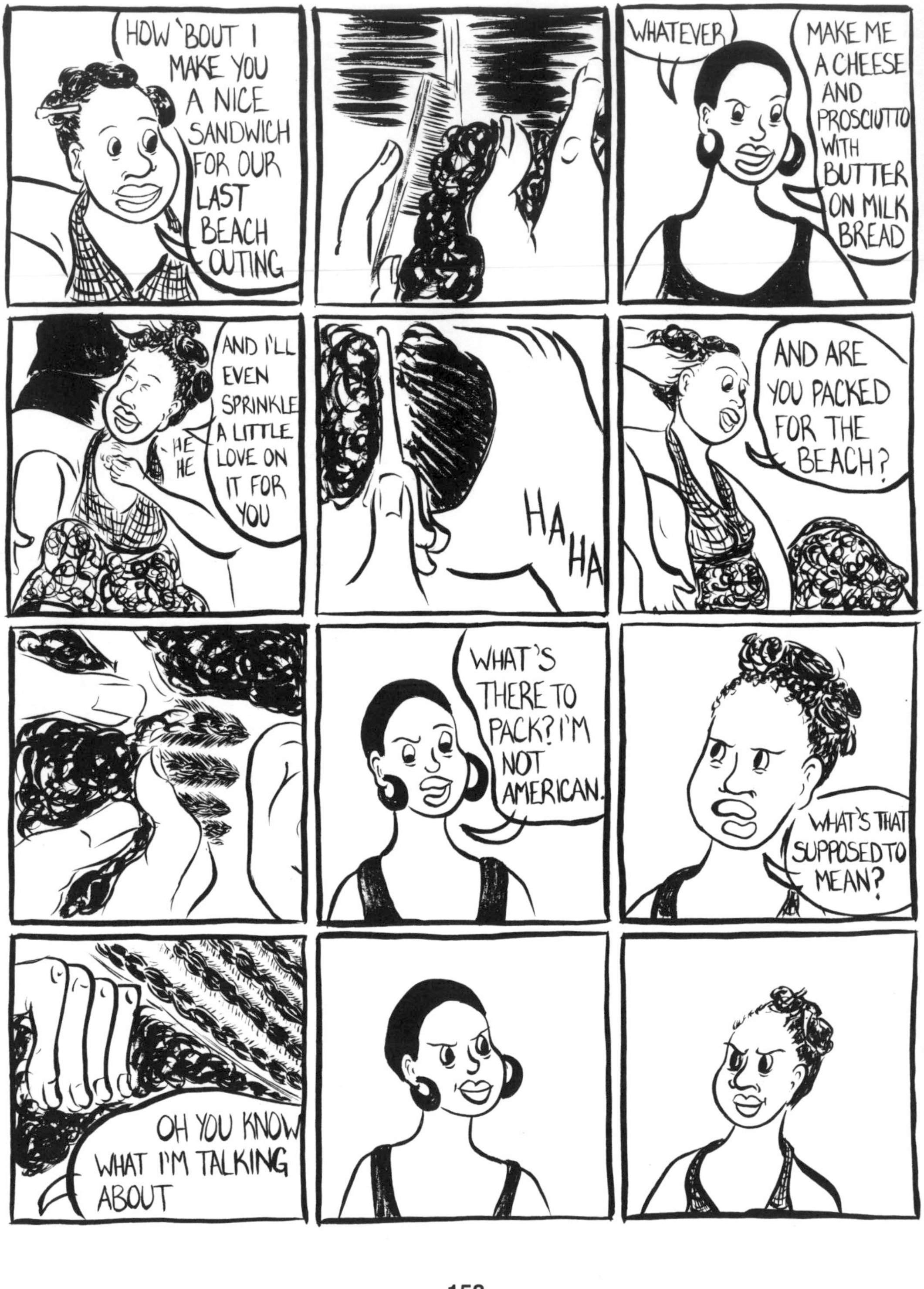
HOW `BOUT I MAKE YOU A NICE SANDWICH FOR OUR LAST BEACH OUTING
WHATEVER
MAKE ME A CHEESE AND PROSCIUTTO WITH BUTTER ON MILK BREAD
AND I'LL EVEN SPRINKLE A LITTLE LOVE ON IT FOR YOU
HE HE
HA HA
AND ARE YOU PACKED FOR THE BEACH?
WHAT'S THERE TO PACK? I'M NOT AMERICAN.
WHAT'S THAT SUPPOSED TO MEAN?
OH YOU KNOW WHAT I'M TALKING ABOUT

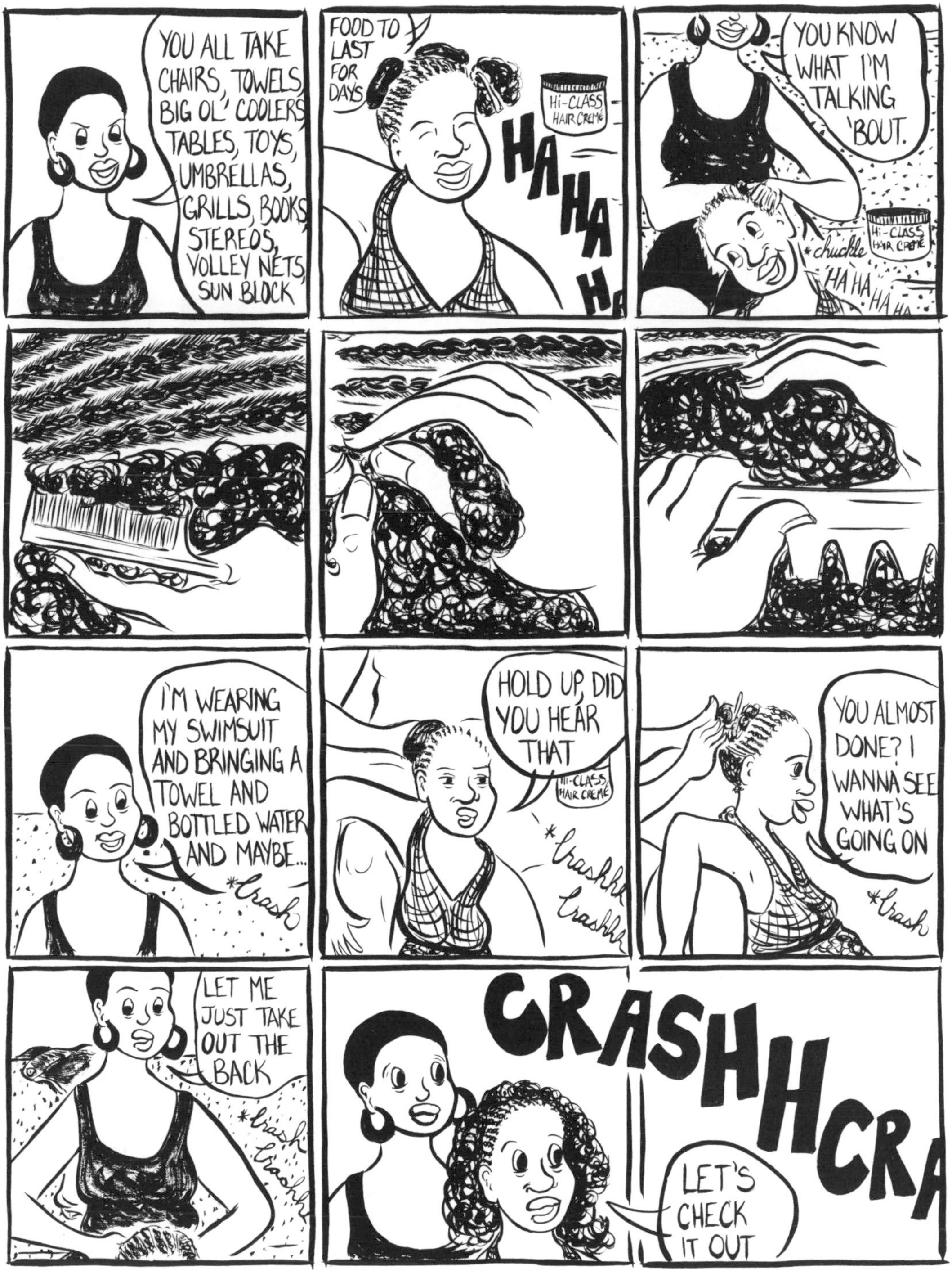
YOU ALL TAKE CHAIRS, TOWELS, BIG OL' COOLERS, TABLES, TOYS, UMBRELLAS, GRILLS, BOOKS, STEREOS, VOLLEY NETS, SUN BLOCK
FOOD TO LAST FOR DAYS
Hi-CLASS HAIR CREME
HA HA HA HA
YOU KNOW WHAT I'M TALKING 'BOUT.
Hi-CLASS HAIR CREME
*chuckle
HA HA HA HA
I'M WEARING MY SWIMSUIT AND BRINGING A TOWEL AND BOTTLED WATER AND MAYBE...
*crash
HOLD UP, DID YOU HEAR THAT
Hi-CLASS HAIR CREME
*crashhh crashhh
YOU ALMOST DONE? I WANNA SEE WHAT'S GOING ON
*crash
LET ME JUST TAKE OUT THE BACK
*crash crashh
CRASHHCRA
LET'S CHECK IT OUT

A decisão...
que nos
últimos meses
ém practicado...
realizada segunda-feira
YOUR STATUE LOOKS LIKE SHE'S ABOUT TO PEE HERSELF.
CRASH
LEAVE MY STATUE ALONE JOY
CRASH
YOU KNOW IT'S TRUE
CRASHHHH
NO MATTER, SHE'S JUST HOLDING HER WRAP
HAHA SSURRE
CRASH
CRASH
SOUNDS LIKE SOMEONE'S SMASHING CARS
OR DOING CONSTRUCTION

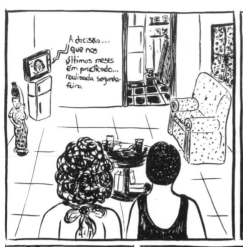

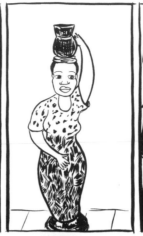

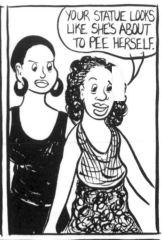

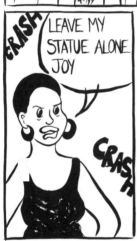

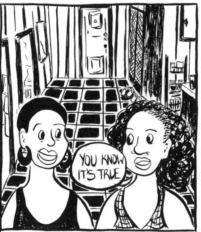

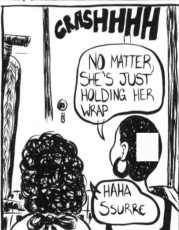

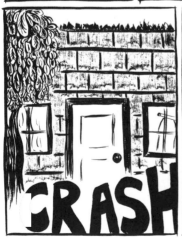

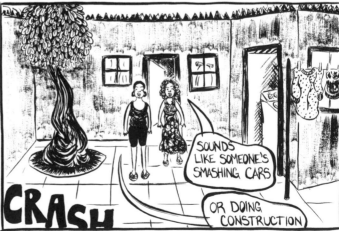

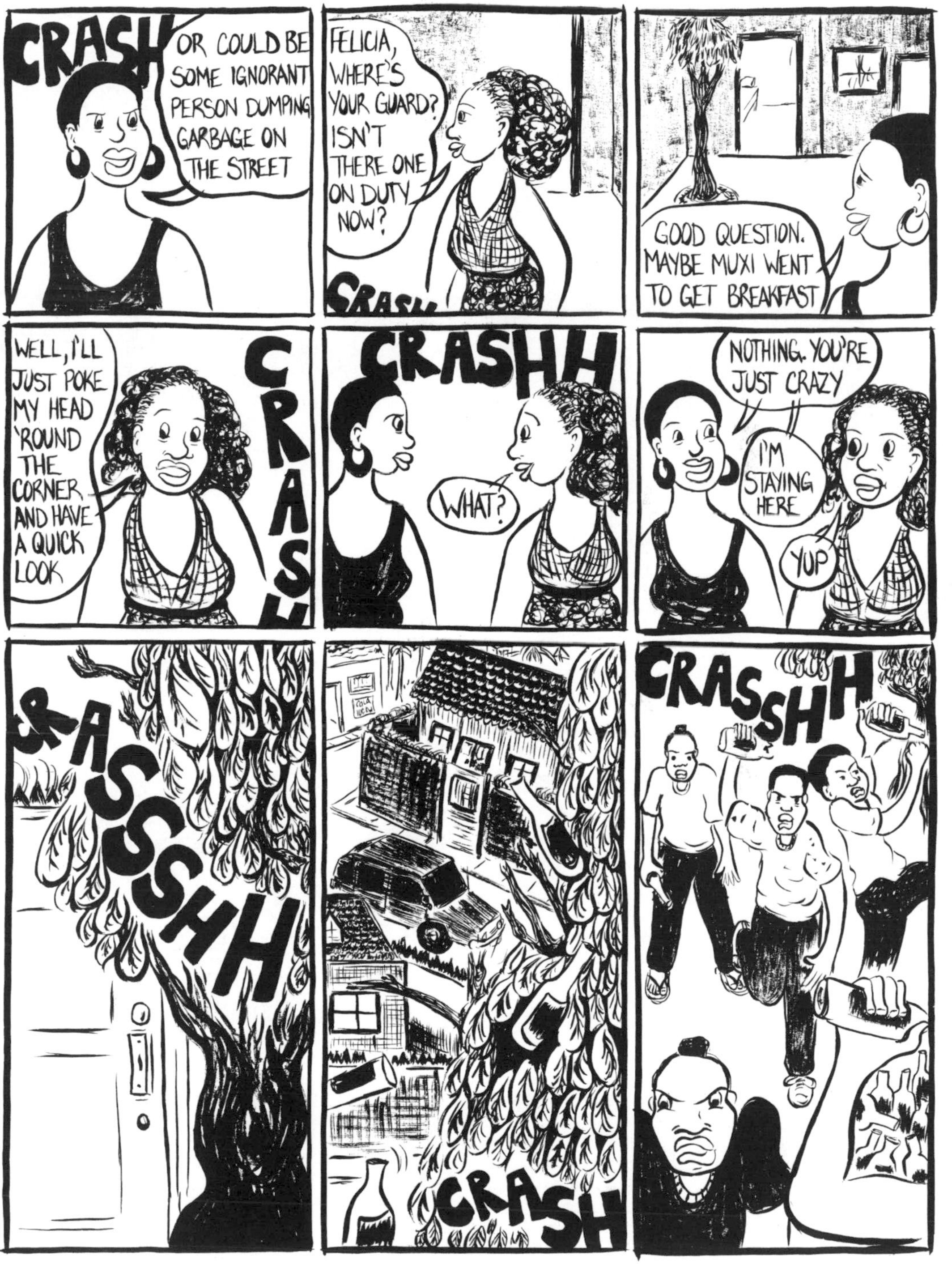
CRASH
OR COULD BE SOME IGNORANT PERSON DUMPING GARBAGE ON THE STREET
FELICIA, WHERE'S YOUR GUARD? ISN'T THERE ONE ON DUTY NOW?
CRASH
GOOD QUESTION. MAYBE MUXI WENT TO GET BREAKFAST
WELL, I'LL JUST POKE MY HEAD 'ROUND THE CORNER AND HAVE A QUICK LOOK
CRASH
CRASHH
WHAT?
NOTHING. YOU'RE JUST CRAZY
I'M STAYING HERE
YUP
CRASSHH
CRASH
CRASSHH

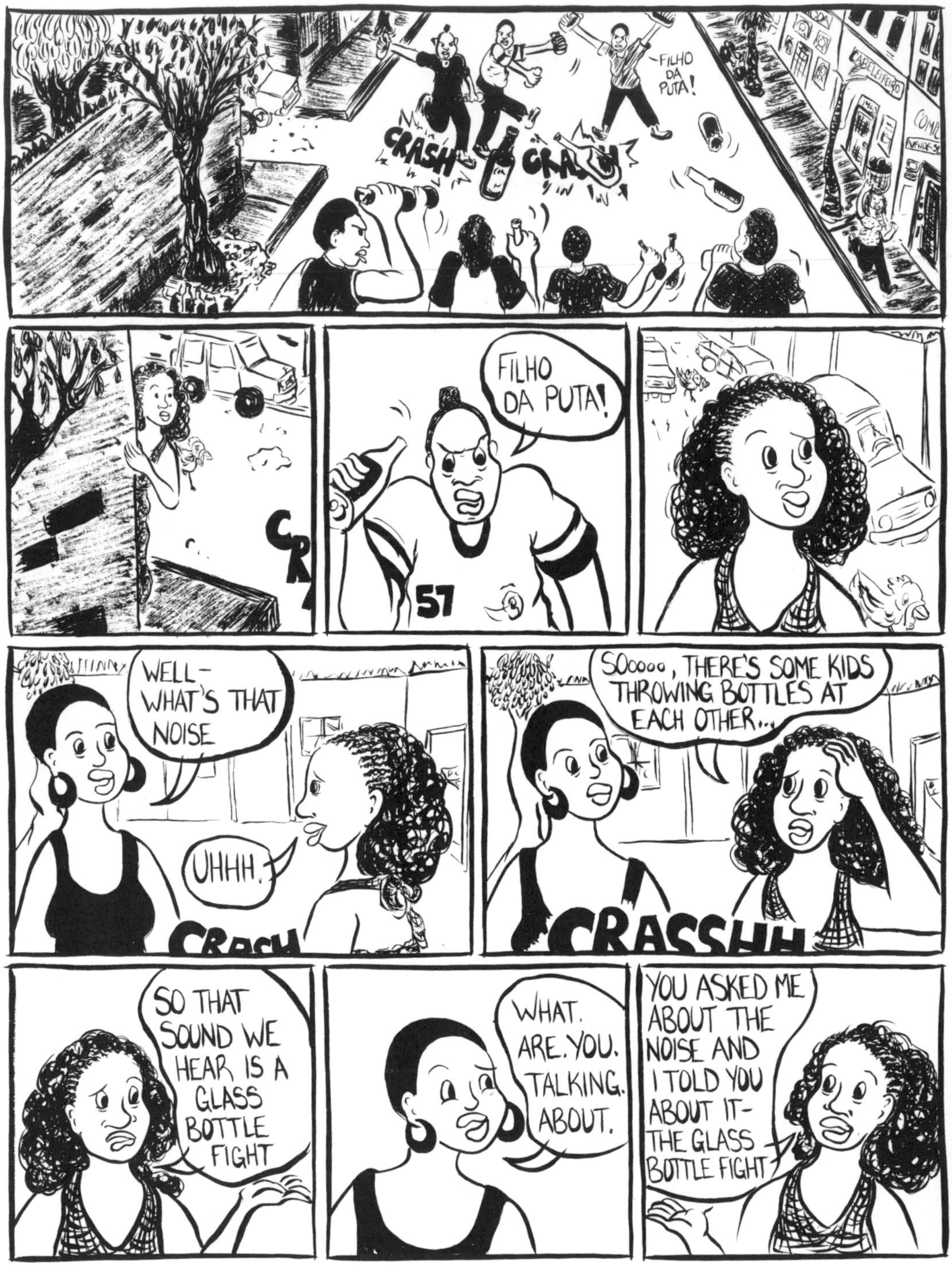
FILHO DA PUTA!
CRASH
CRASH
FILHO DA PUTA!
57
WELL- WHAT'S THAT NOISE
UHHH.
CRASH
SOoooo, THERE'S SOME KIDS THROWING BOTTLES AT EACH OTHER...
CRASSHH
SO THAT SOUND WE HEAR IS A GLASS BOTTLE FIGHT
WHAT. ARE. YOU. TALKING. ABOUT.
YOU ASKED ME ABOUT THE NOISE AND I TOLD YOU ABOUT IT- THE GLASS BOTTLE FIGHT

YEAH, OKAY BUT WHAT DOES THAT MEAN?
I DON'T KNOW
BASICALLY, IT MEANS WE HAVE TO TURN DOWN THE OTHER STREET WHEN WE PICK UP KENYATTA AND GO TO THE BEACH
GLASS BOTTLE FIGHT IS SO RANDOM THOUGH
CRASH
I KNOW RIGHT
THEY ARE THE BEBE KIDS OF LUANDA
HAHA HA HA HA HAH HAHA HA
YOU'RE SO MEAN
HAHAHA HA
LET ME CALL KENYATTA AND TELL HER WE'RE ON OUR WAY
COOL, I'M GOING TO MAKE OUR SANDWICHES
I WANT MINE ON MILK BREAD

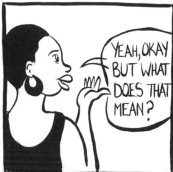

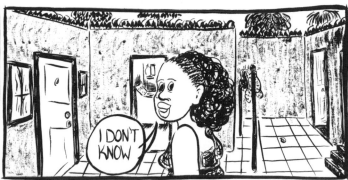

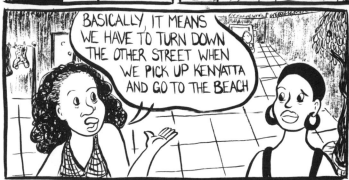

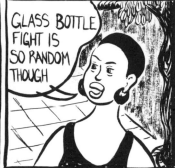

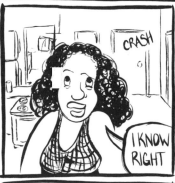

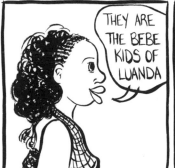

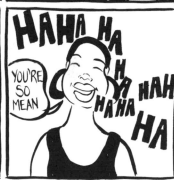

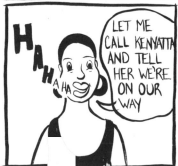

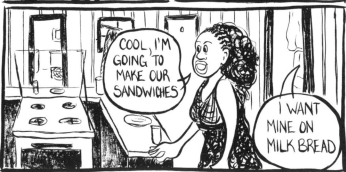

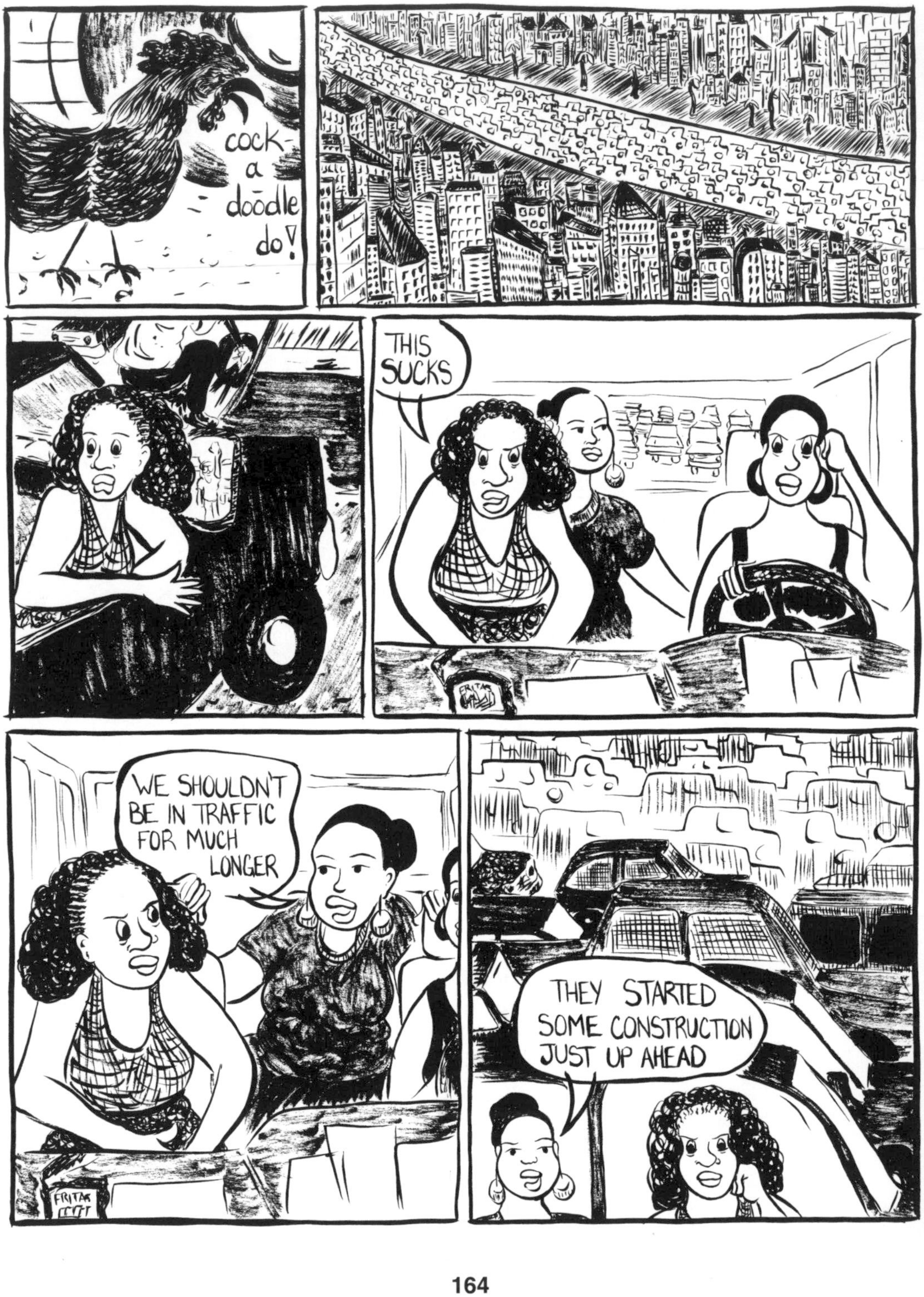
cock-a-doodle do!
THIS SUCKS
WE SHOULDN'T BE IN TRAFFIC FOR MUCH LONGER
THEY STARTED SOME CONSTRUCTION JUST UP AHEAD

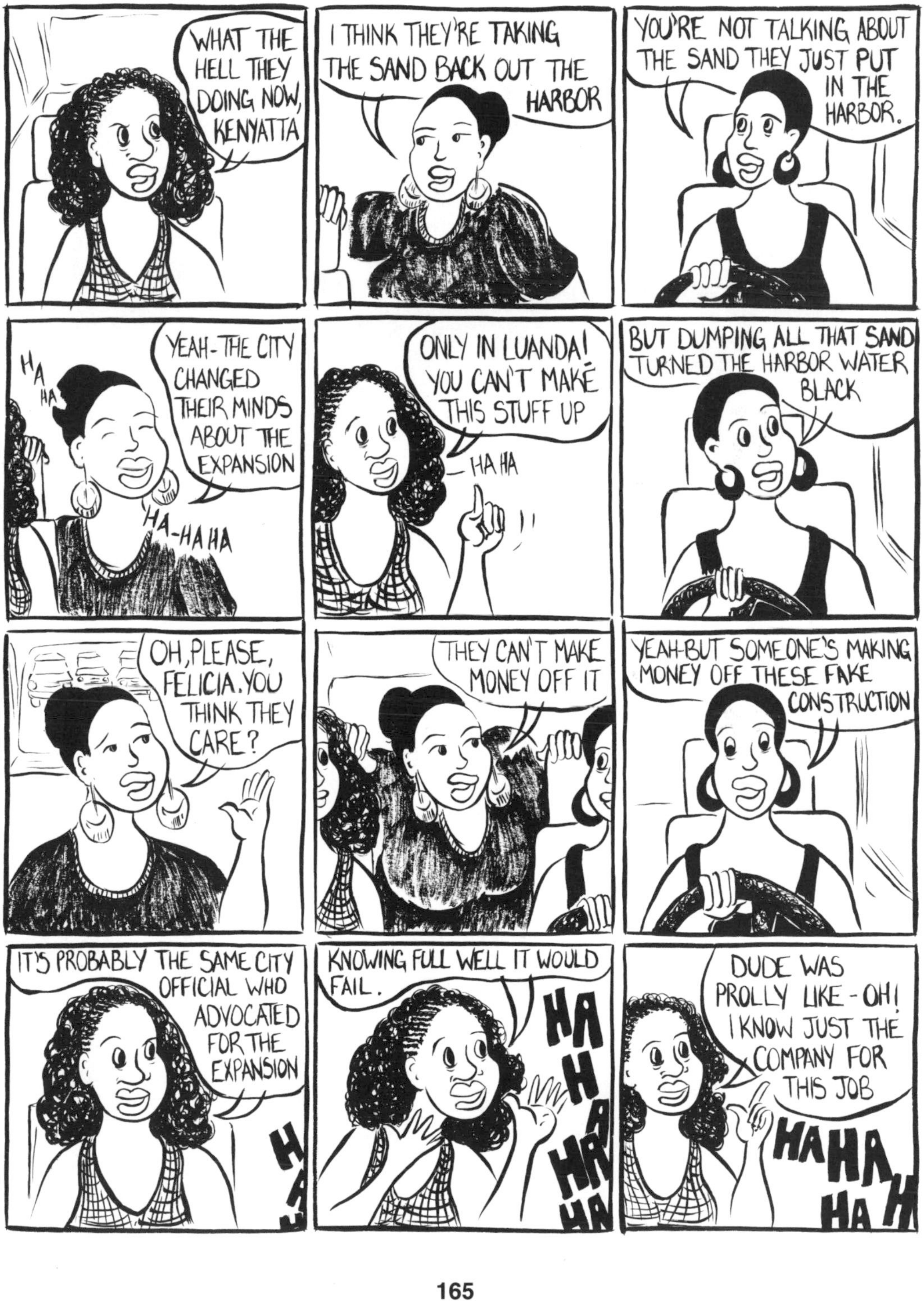
WHAT THE HELL THEY DOING NOW, KENYATTA
I THINK THEY'RE TAKING THE SAND BACK OUT THE HARBOR
YOU'RE NOT TALKING ABOUT THE SAND THEY JUST PUT IN THE HARBOR.
HA HA
YEAH- THE CITY CHANGED THEIR MINDS ABOUT THE EXPANSION
HA-HA HA
ONLY IN LUANDA! YOU CAN'T MAKE THIS STUFF UP
HA HA
BUT DUMPING ALL THAT SAND TURNED THE HARBOR WATER BLACK
OH, PLEASE, FELICIA. YOU THINK THEY CARE?
THEY CAN'T MAKE MONEY OFF IT
YEAH-BUT SOMEONE'S MAKING MONEY OFF THESE FAKE CONSTRUCTION
IT'S PROBABLY THE SAME CITY OFFICIAL WHO ADVOCATED FOR THE EXPANSION
KNOWING FULL WELL IT WOULD FAIL.
HA HA HA HA HA
DUDE WAS PROLLY LIKE - OH! I KNOW JUST THE COMPANY FOR THIS JOB
HA HA HA

HAHA HAHAHA
HAHA
HA HA
HA HA
HAHA
Oooo POPCORN!
NO
Y'ALL WANT SOME?
GET ME A BAG
MOÇO
MOÇO
MOÇO
BOM DIA- FAZ FAVOR
DOIS SACOS DE PIPOCAS
COM SAL
SIM BOM DIA SIM
PIPOCAS

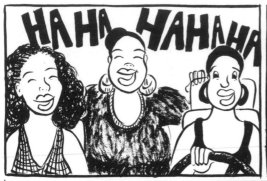

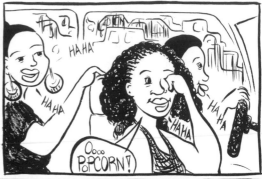

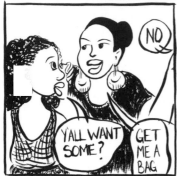

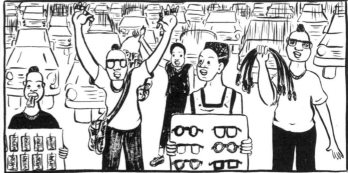

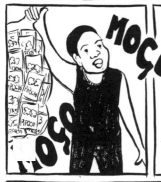

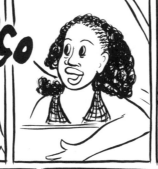

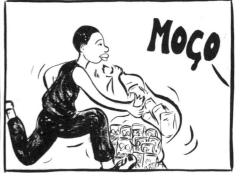

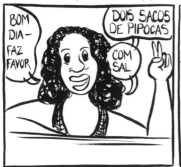

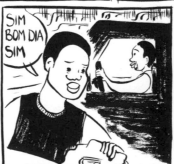

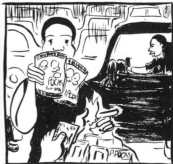

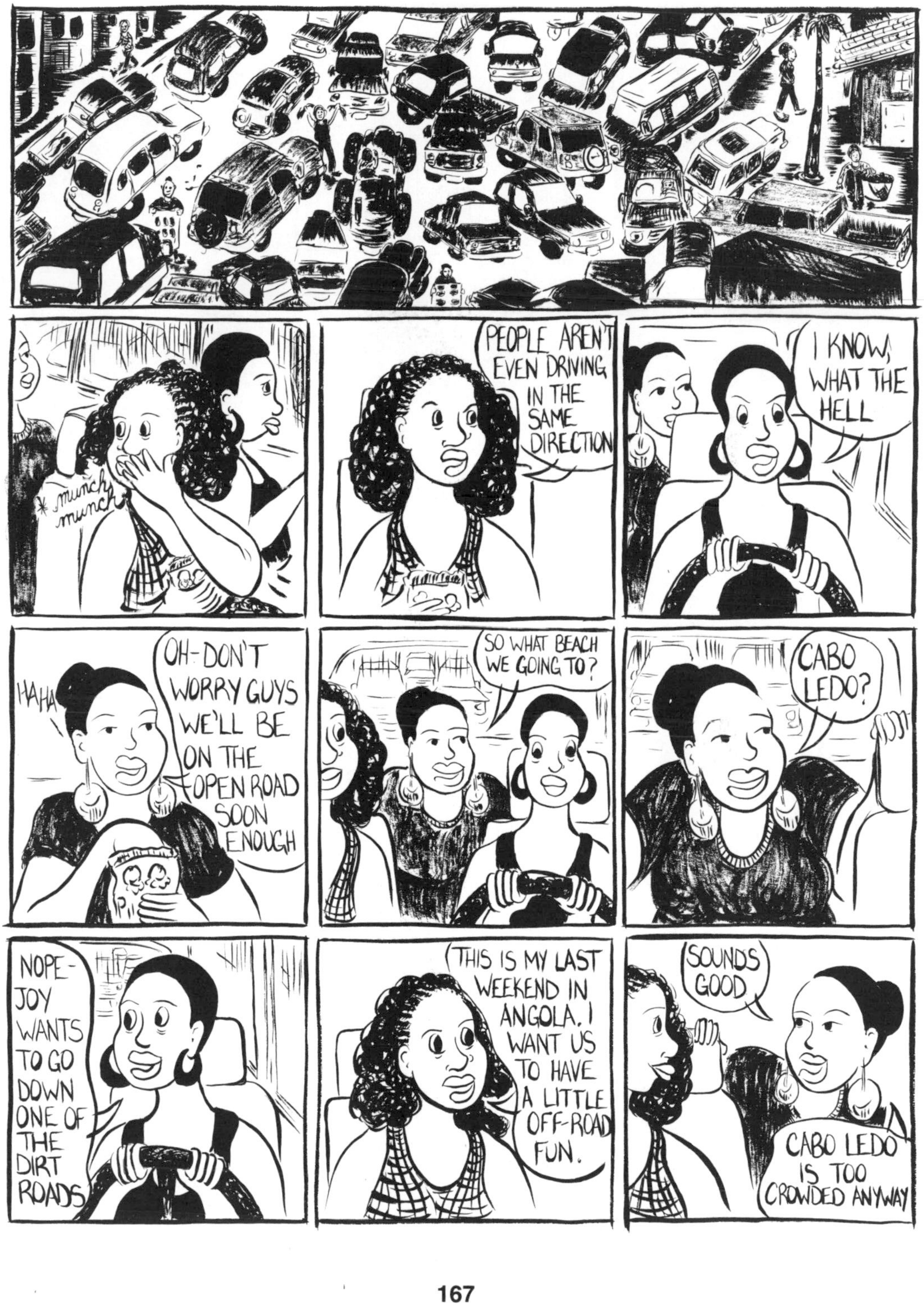

munch munch
PEOPLE AREN'T EVEN DRIVING IN THE SAME DIRECTION
I KNOW, WHAT THE HELL
HAHA
OH- DON'T WORRY GUYS WE'LL BE ON THE OPEN ROAD SOON ENOUGH
SO WHAT BEACH WE GOING TO?
CABO LEDO?
NOPE- JOY WANTS TO GO DOWN ONE OF THE DIRT ROADS
THIS IS MY LAST WEEKEND IN ANGOLA. I WANT US TO HAVE A LITTLE OFF-ROAD FUN.
SOUNDS GOOD
CABO LEDO IS TOO CROWDED ANYWAY

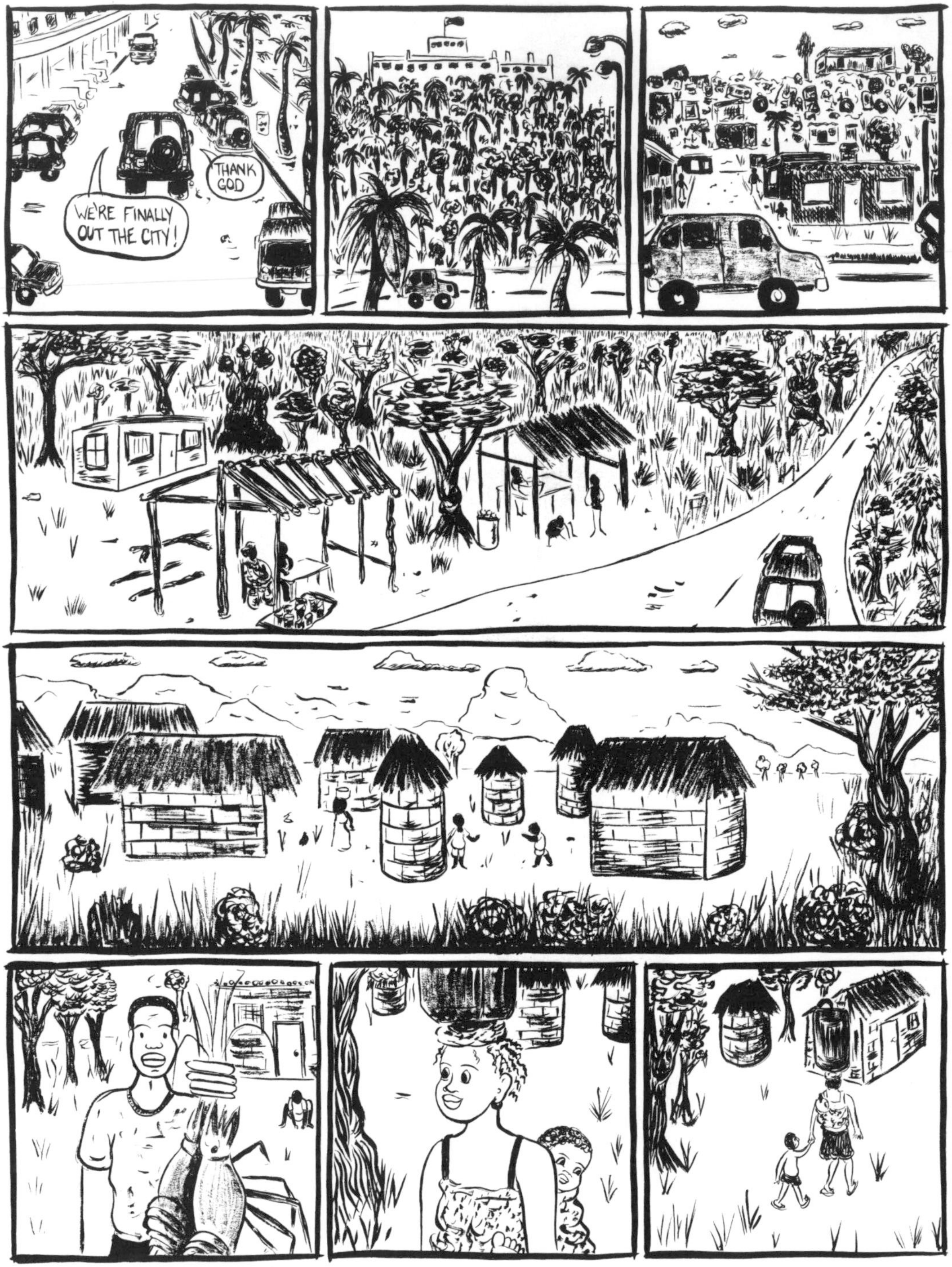
WE'RE FINALLY OUT THE CITY!
THANK GOD

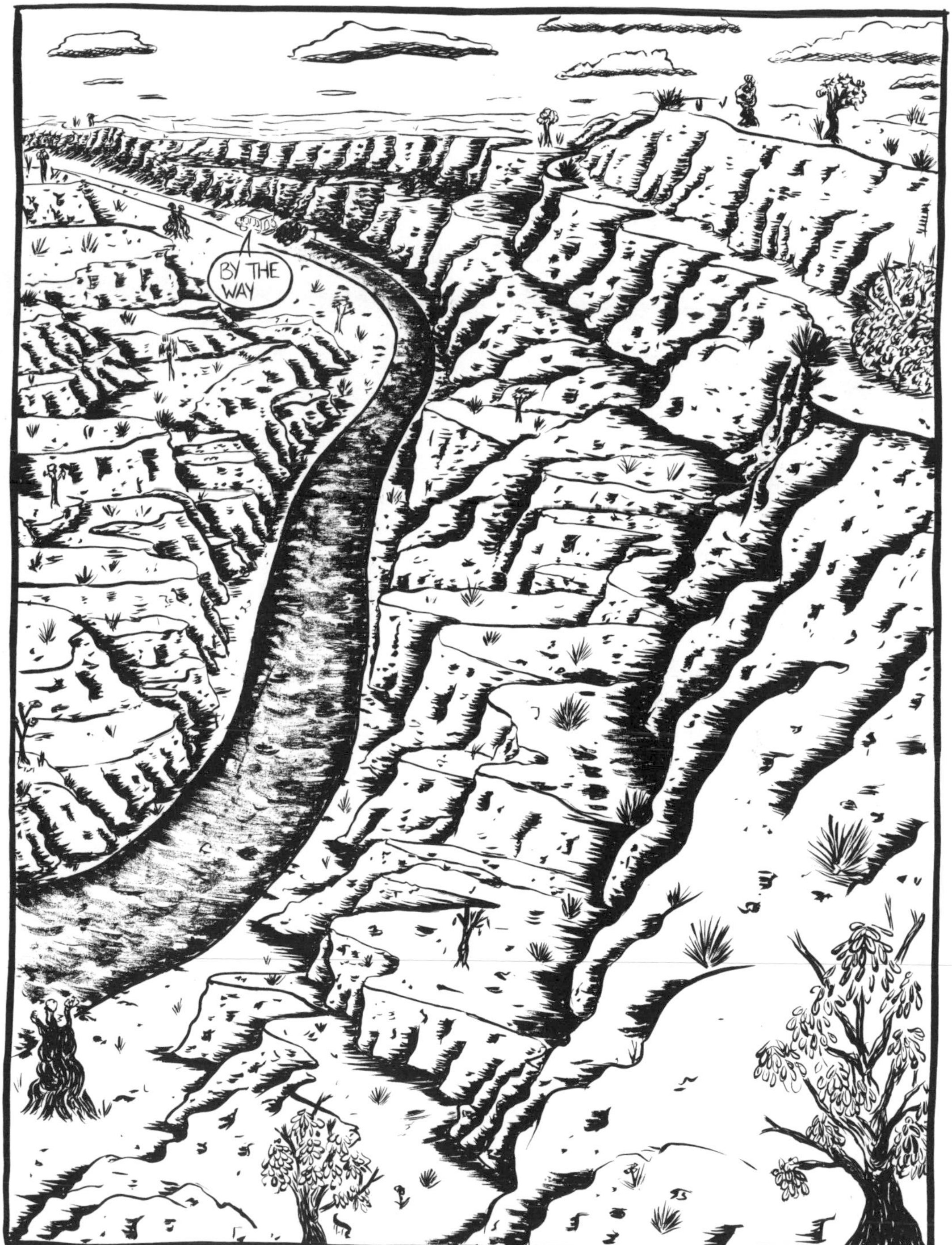
BY THE WAY

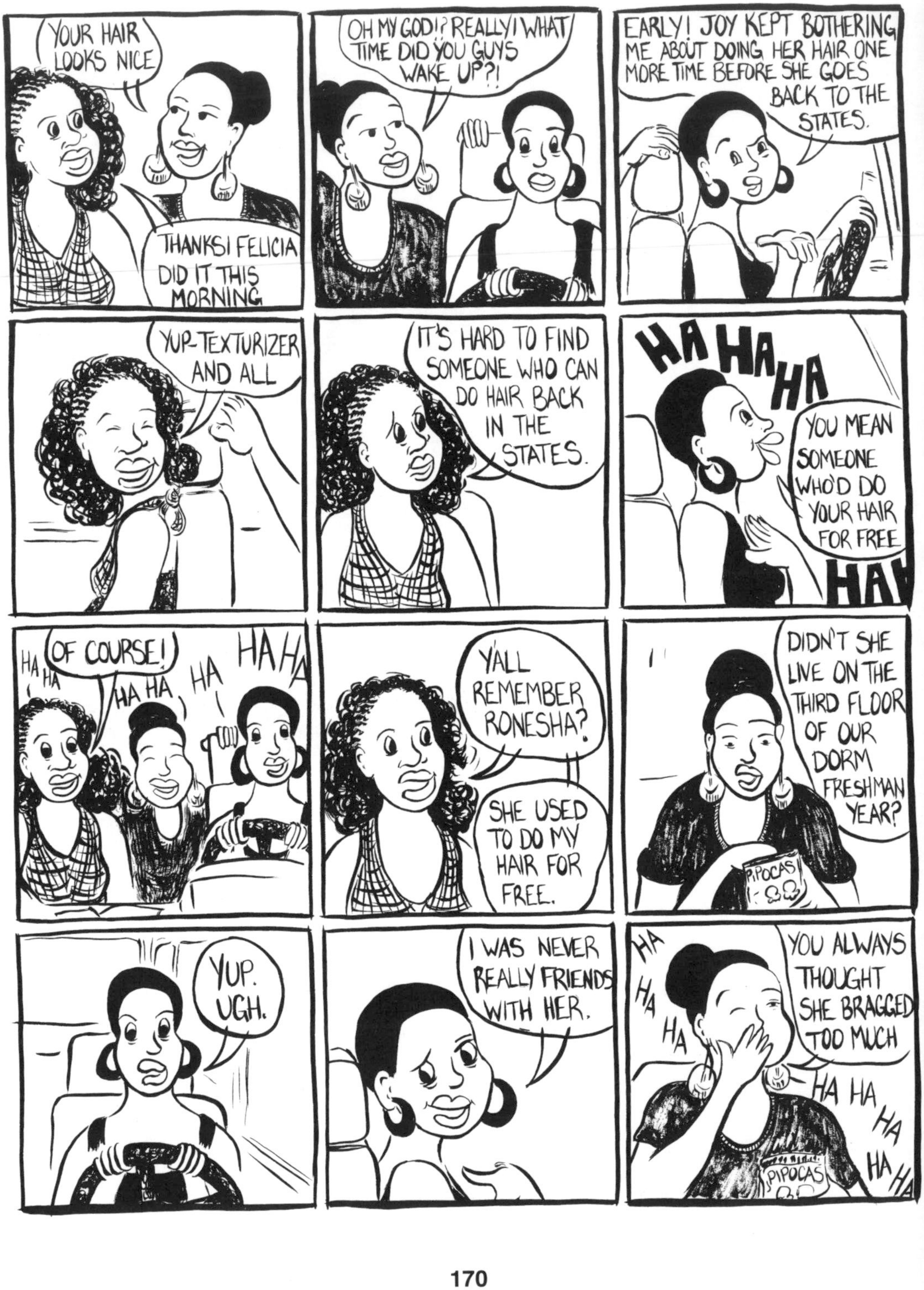
YOUR HAIR LOOKS NICE
THANKS! FELICIA DID IT THIS MORNING
OH MY GOD!? REALLY! WHAT TIME DID YOU GUYS WAKE UP?!
EARLY! JOY KEPT BOTHERING ME ABOUT DOING HER HAIR ONE MORE TIME BEFORE SHE GOES BACK TO THE STATES.
YUP-TEXTURIZER AND ALL
IT'S HARD TO FIND SOMEONE WHO CAN DO HAIR BACK IN THE STATES.
HA HA HA HA
YOU MEAN SOMEONE WHO'D DO YOUR HAIR FOR FREE
HA
HA HA
OF COURSE!
HA HA, HA HA HA
Y'ALL REMEMBER RONESHA?
SHE USED TO DO MY HAIR FOR FREE.
DIDN'T SHE LIVE ON THE THIRD FLOOR OF OUR DORM FRESHMAN YEAR?
PIPOCAS
YUP. UGH.
I WAS NEVER REALLY FRIENDS WITH HER.
HA HA HA
YOU ALWAYS THOUGHT SHE BRAGGED TOO MUCH
HA HA HA HA HA
PIPOCAS

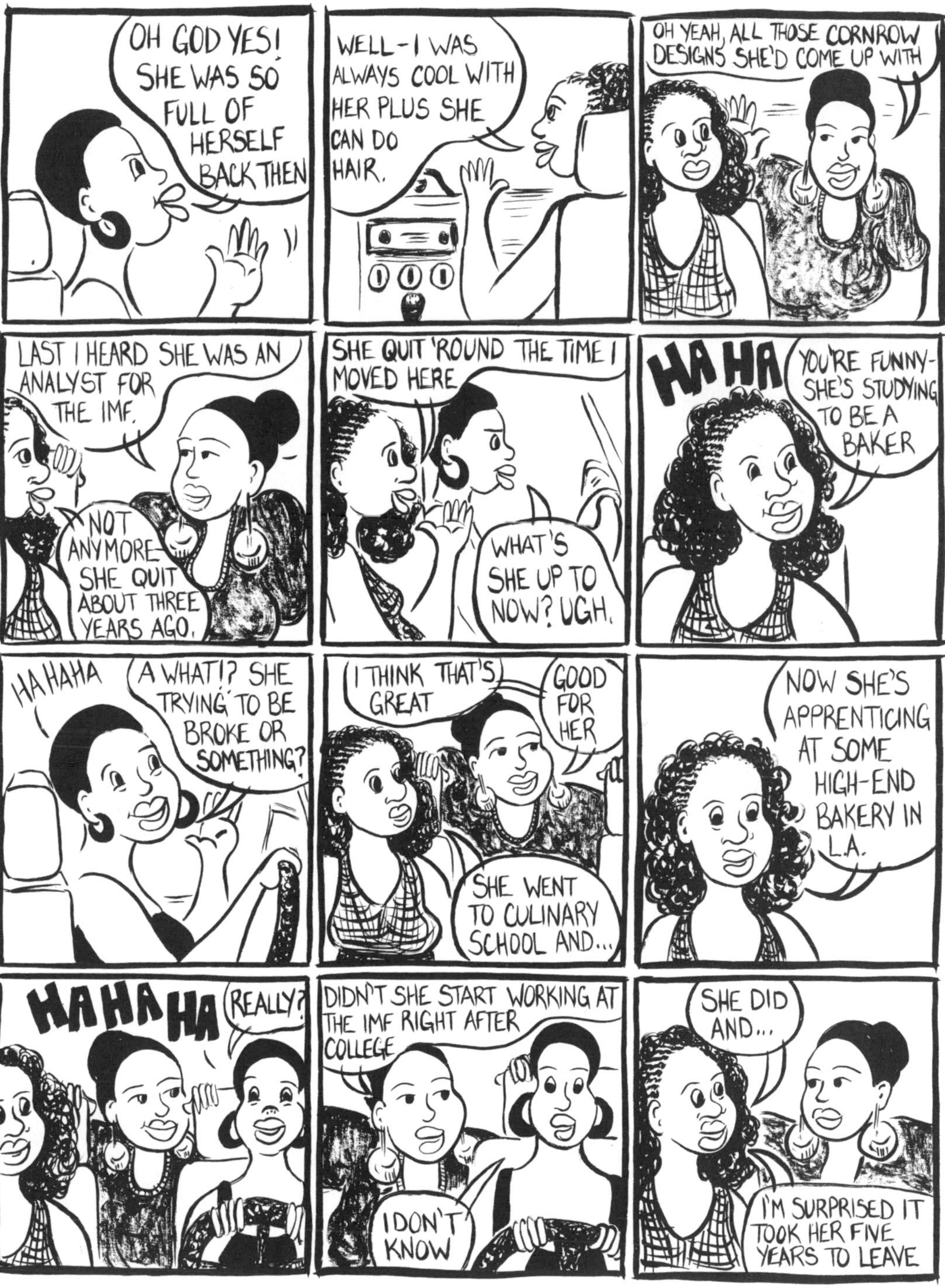
OH GOD YES! SHE WAS SO FULL OF HERSELF BACK THEN
WELL - I WAS ALWAYS COOL WITH HER PLUS SHE CAN DO HAIR.
OH YEAH, ALL THOSE CORNROW DESIGNS SHE'D COME UP WITH
LAST I HEARD SHE WAS AN ANALYST FOR THE IMF.
NOT ANYMORE - SHE QUIT ABOUT THREE YEARS AGO.
SHE QUIT 'ROUND THE TIME I MOVED HERE
WHAT'S SHE UP TO NOW? UGH.
HA HA
YOU'RE FUNNY - SHE'S STUDYING TO BE A BAKER
HAHAHA
A WHAT!? SHE TRYING TO BE BROKE OR SOMETHING?
I THINK THAT'S GREAT
GOOD FOR HER
SHE WENT TO CULINARY SCHOOL AND...
NOW SHE'S APPRENTICING AT SOME HIGH-END BAKERY IN L.A.
HAHAHA
REALLY?
DIDN'T SHE START WORKING AT THE IMF RIGHT AFTER COLLEGE
I DON'T KNOW
SHE DID AND...
I'M SURPRISED IT TOOK HER FIVE YEARS TO LEAVE

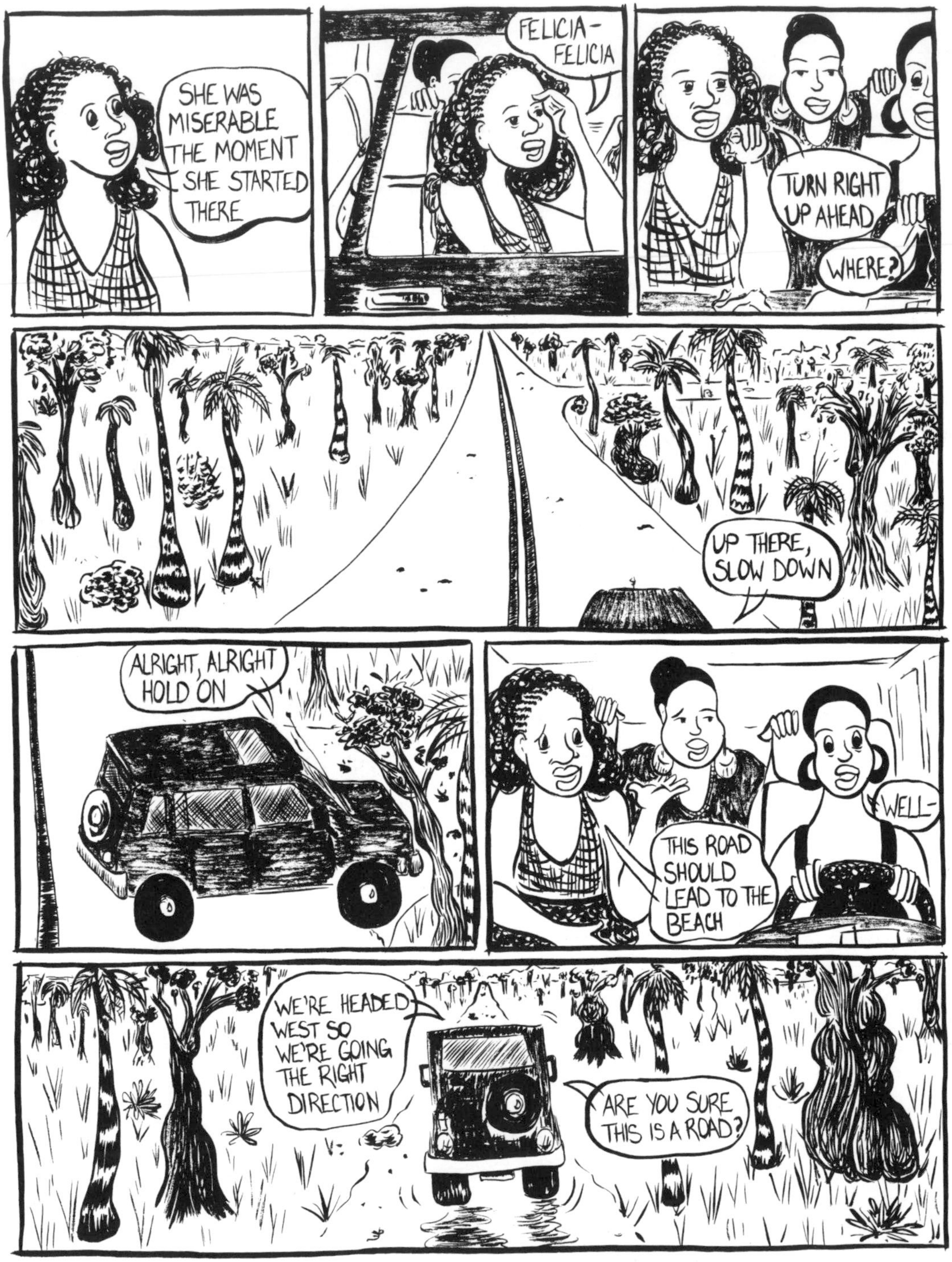
SHE WAS MISERABLE THE MOMENT SHE STARTED THERE
FELICIA- FELICIA
TURN RIGHT UP AHEAD
WHERE?
UP THERE, SLOW DOWN
ALRIGHT, ALRIGHT HOLD ON
WELL-
THIS ROAD SHOULD LEAD TO THE BEACH
WE'RE HEADED WEST SO WE'RE GOING THE RIGHT DIRECTION
ARE YOU SURE THIS IS A ROAD?

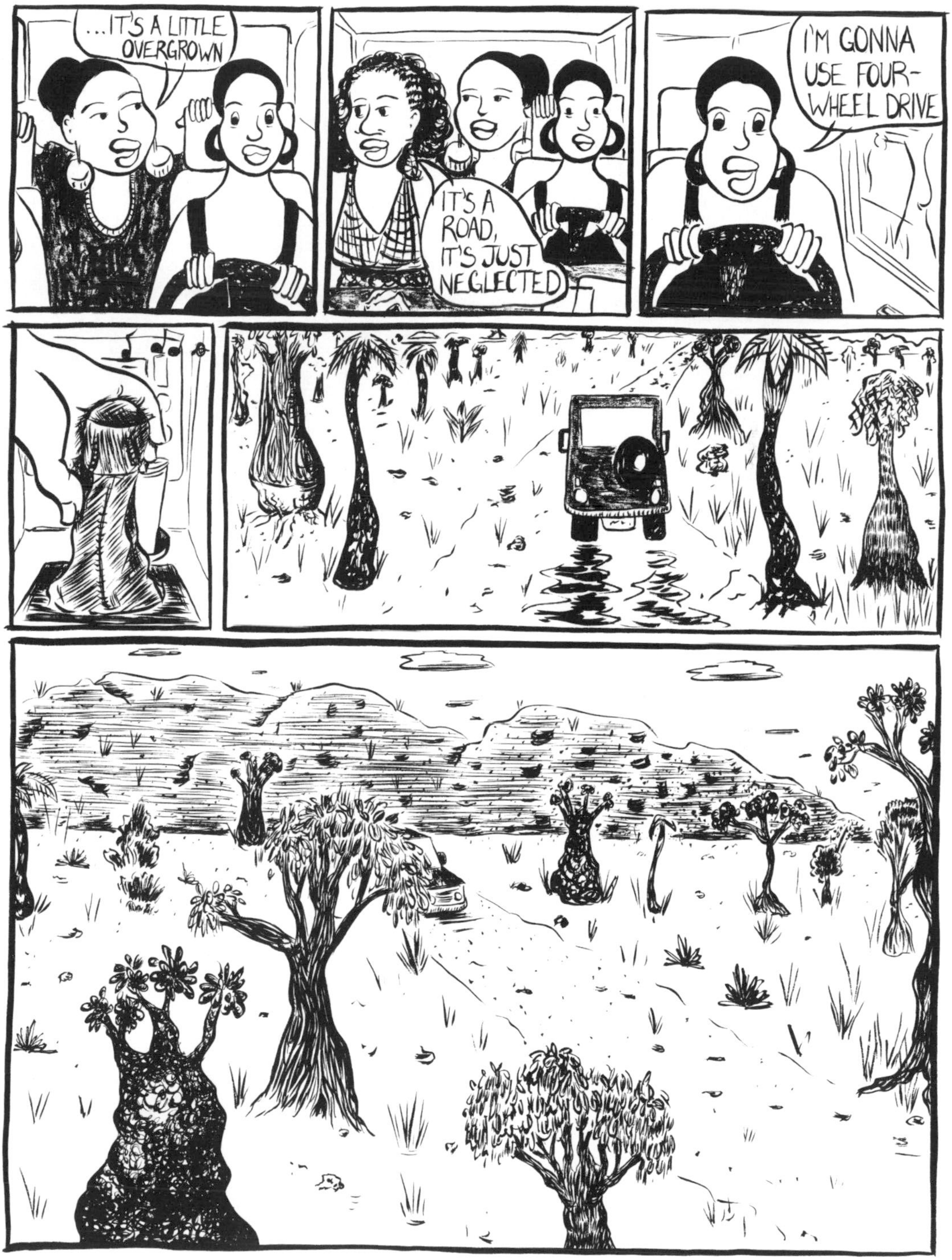
...IT'S A LITTLE OVERGROWN
IT'S A ROAD, IT'S JUST NEGLECTED
I'M GONNA USE FOUR-WHEEL DRIVE

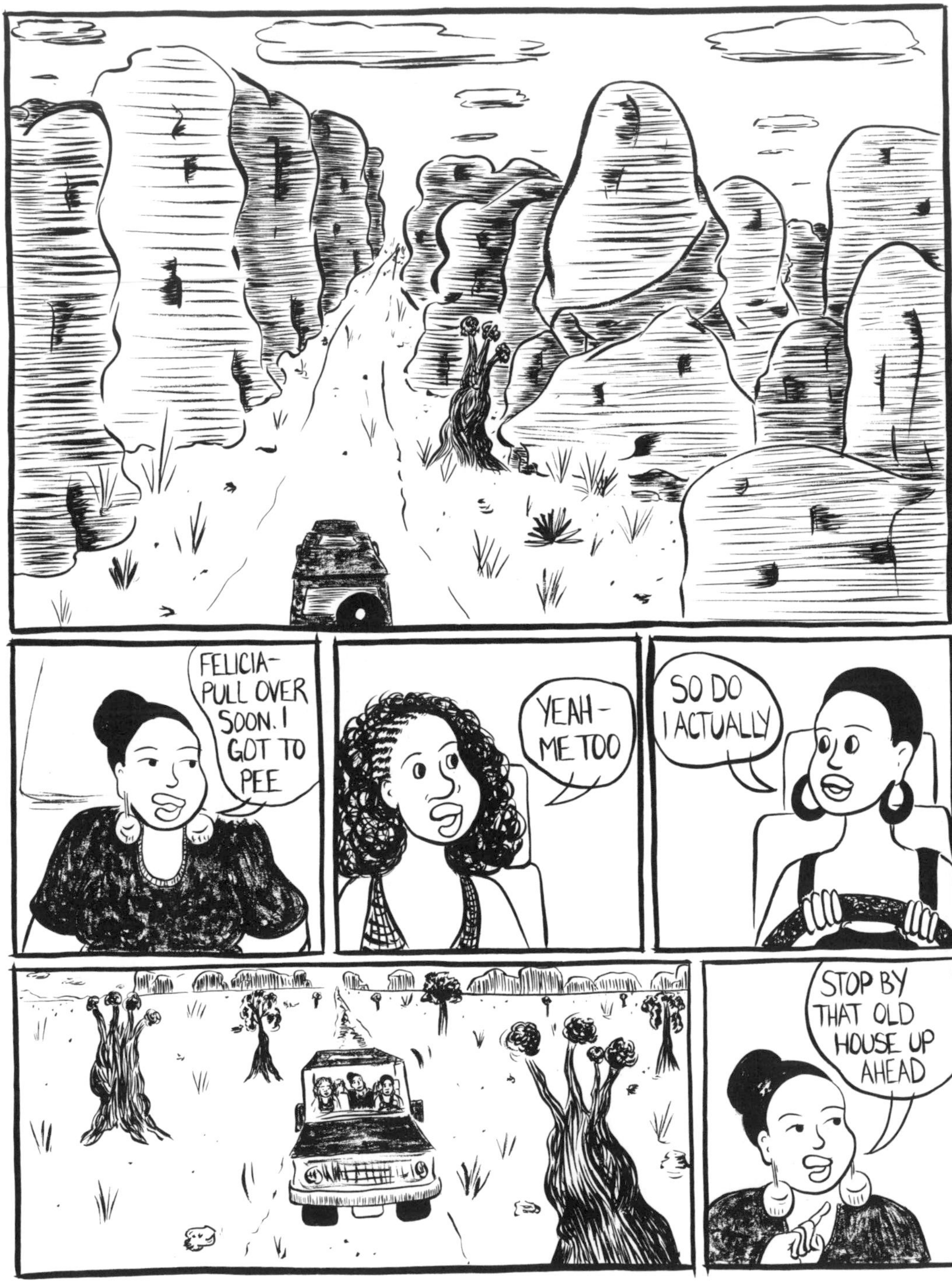
FELICIA-
PULL OVER
SOON. I
GOT TO
PEE
YEAH-
ME TOO
SO DO
I ACTUALLY
STOP BY
THAT OLD
HOUSE UP
AHEAD

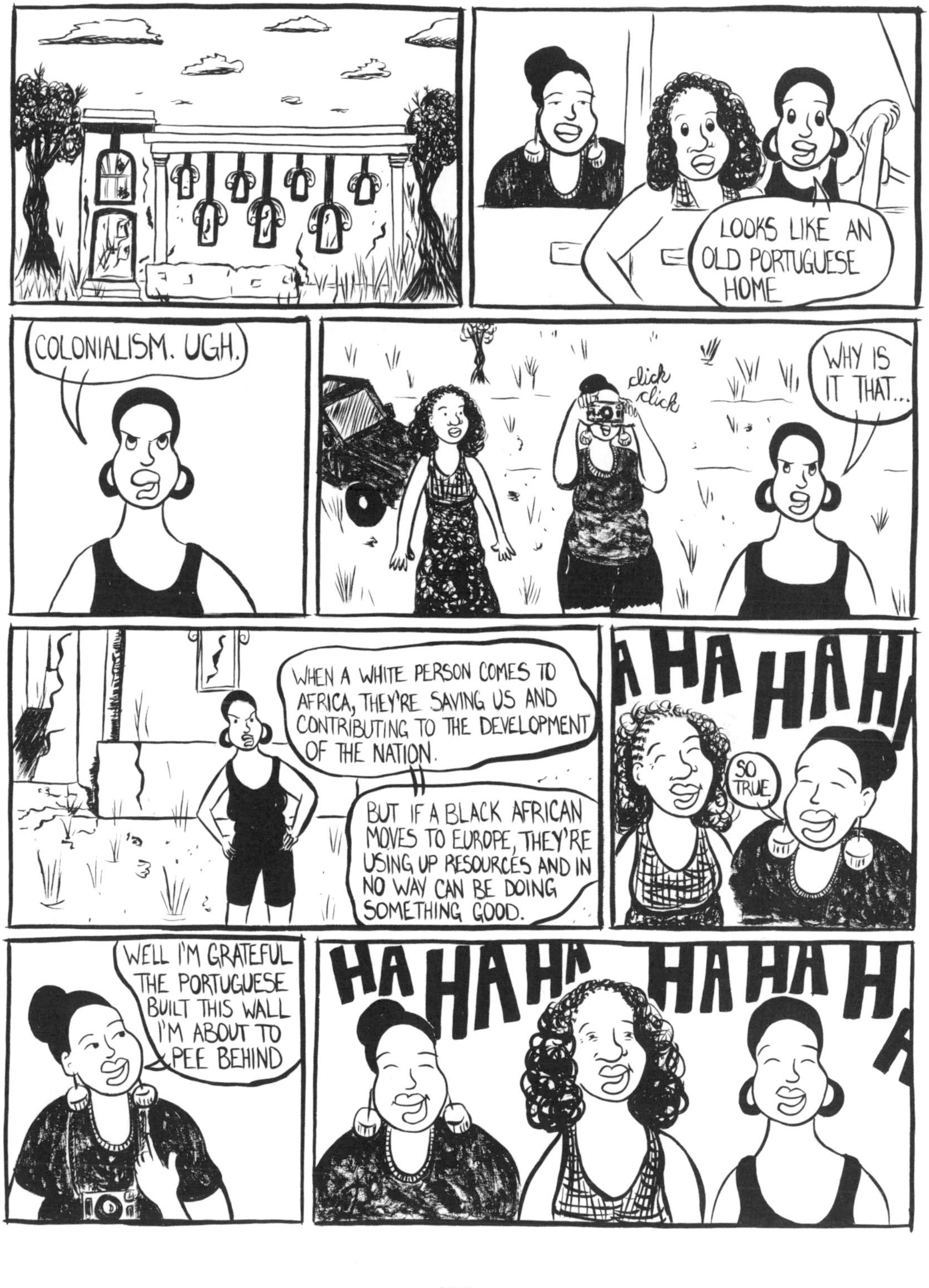
LOOKS LIKE AN OLD PORTUGUESE HOME
COLONIALISM. UGH.
click click
WHY IS IT THAT...
WHEN A WHITE PERSON COMES TO AFRICA, THEY'RE SAVING US AND CONTRIBUTING TO THE DEVELOPMENT OF THE NATION.
BUT IF A BLACK AFRICAN MOVES TO EUROPE, THEY'RE USING UP RESOURCES AND IN NO WAY CAN BE DOING SOMETHING GOOD.
HA HA HA HA
SO TRUE
WELL I'M GRATEFUL THE PORTUGUESE BUILT THIS WALL I'M ABOUT TO PEE BEHIND
HA HA HA HA HA HA H

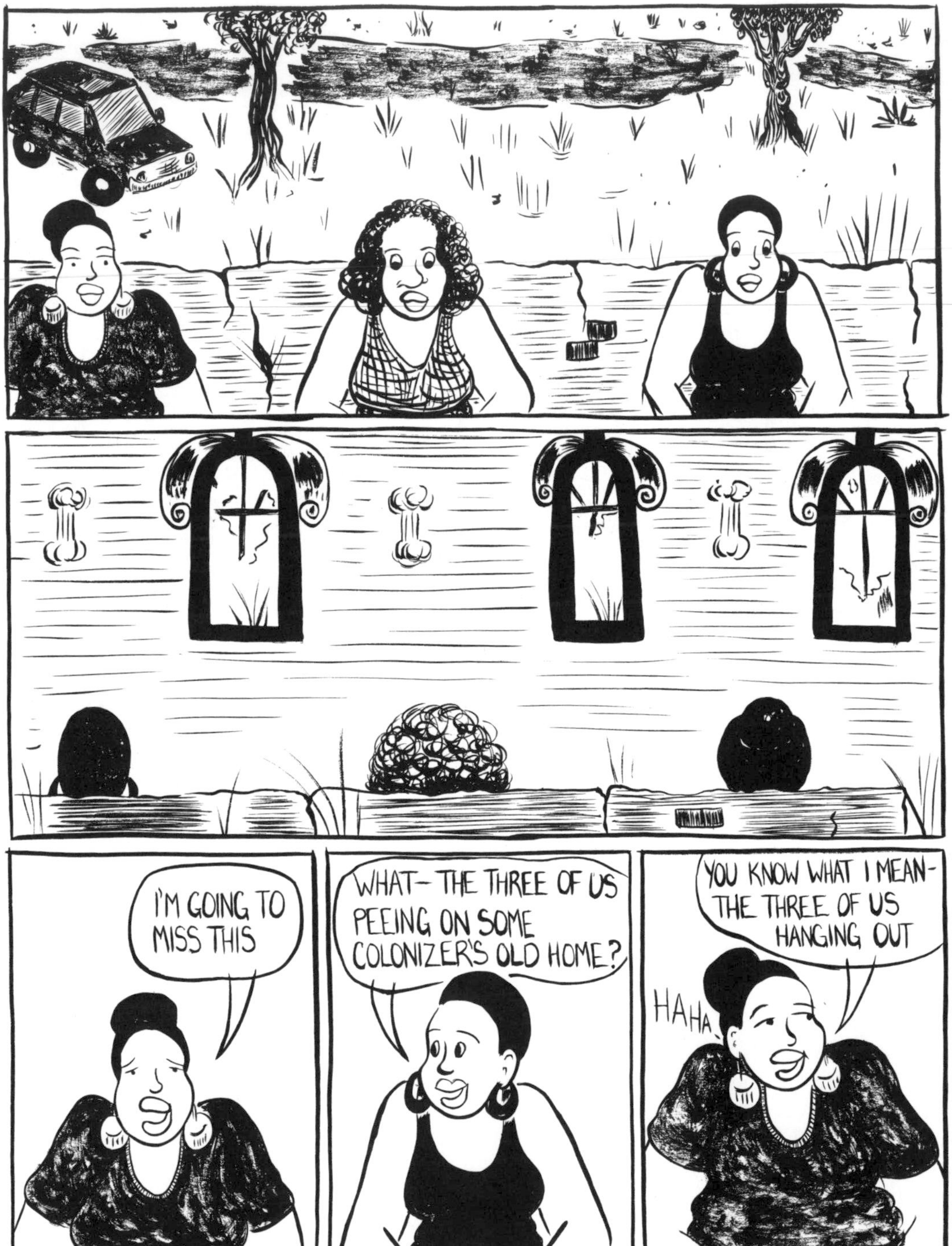
I'M GOING TO MISS THIS
WHAT- THE THREE OF US PEEING ON SOME COLONIZER'S OLD HOME?
YOU KNOW WHAT I MEAN- THE THREE OF US HANGING OUT
HAHA

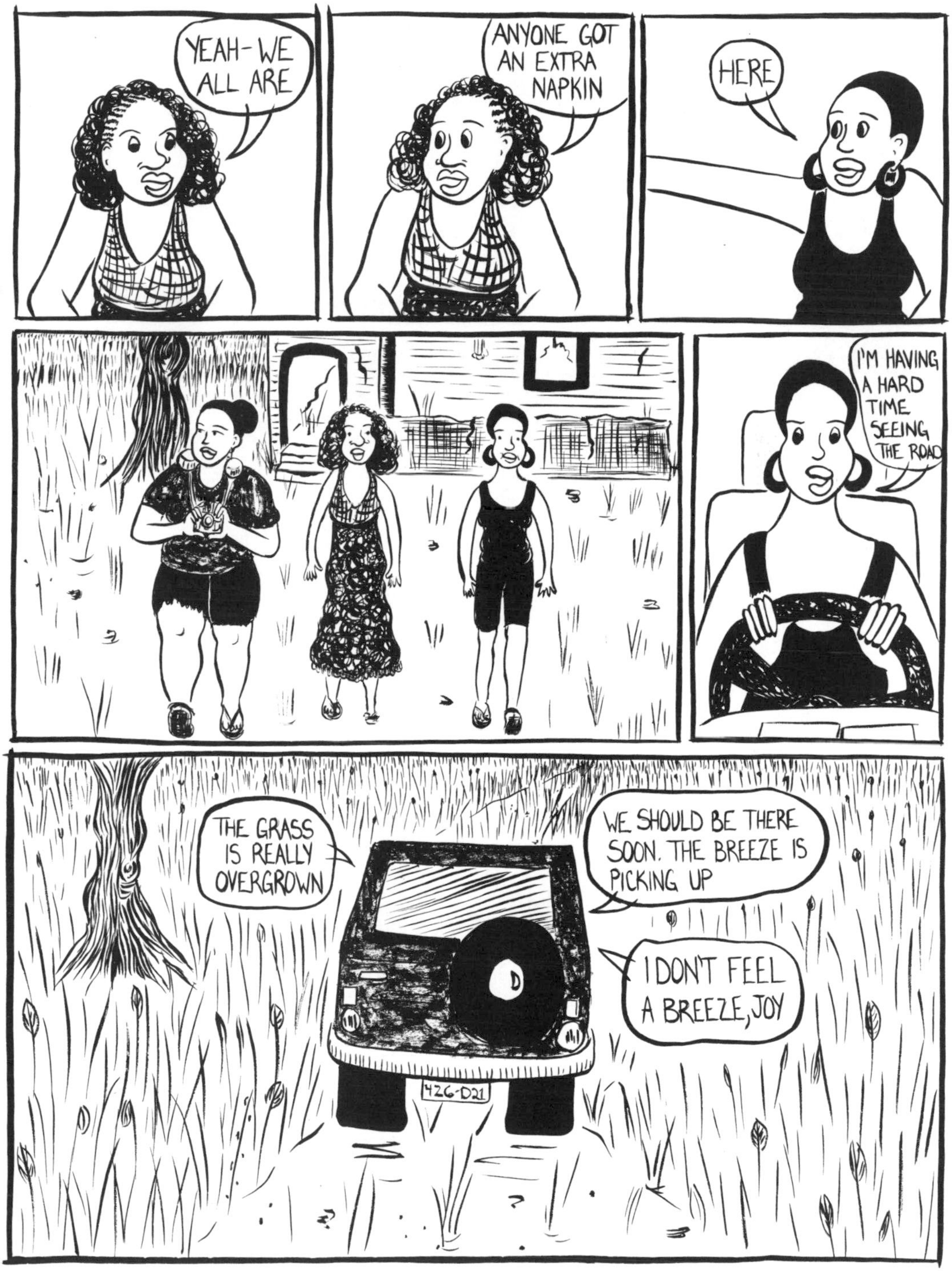
YEAH- WE ALL ARE
ANYONE GOT AN EXTRA NAPKIN
HERE
I'M HAVING A HARD TIME SEEING THE ROAD
THE GRASS IS REALLY OVERGROWN
WE SHOULD BE THERE SOON. THE BREEZE IS PICKING UP
I DON'T FEEL A BREEZE, JOY
426-D21

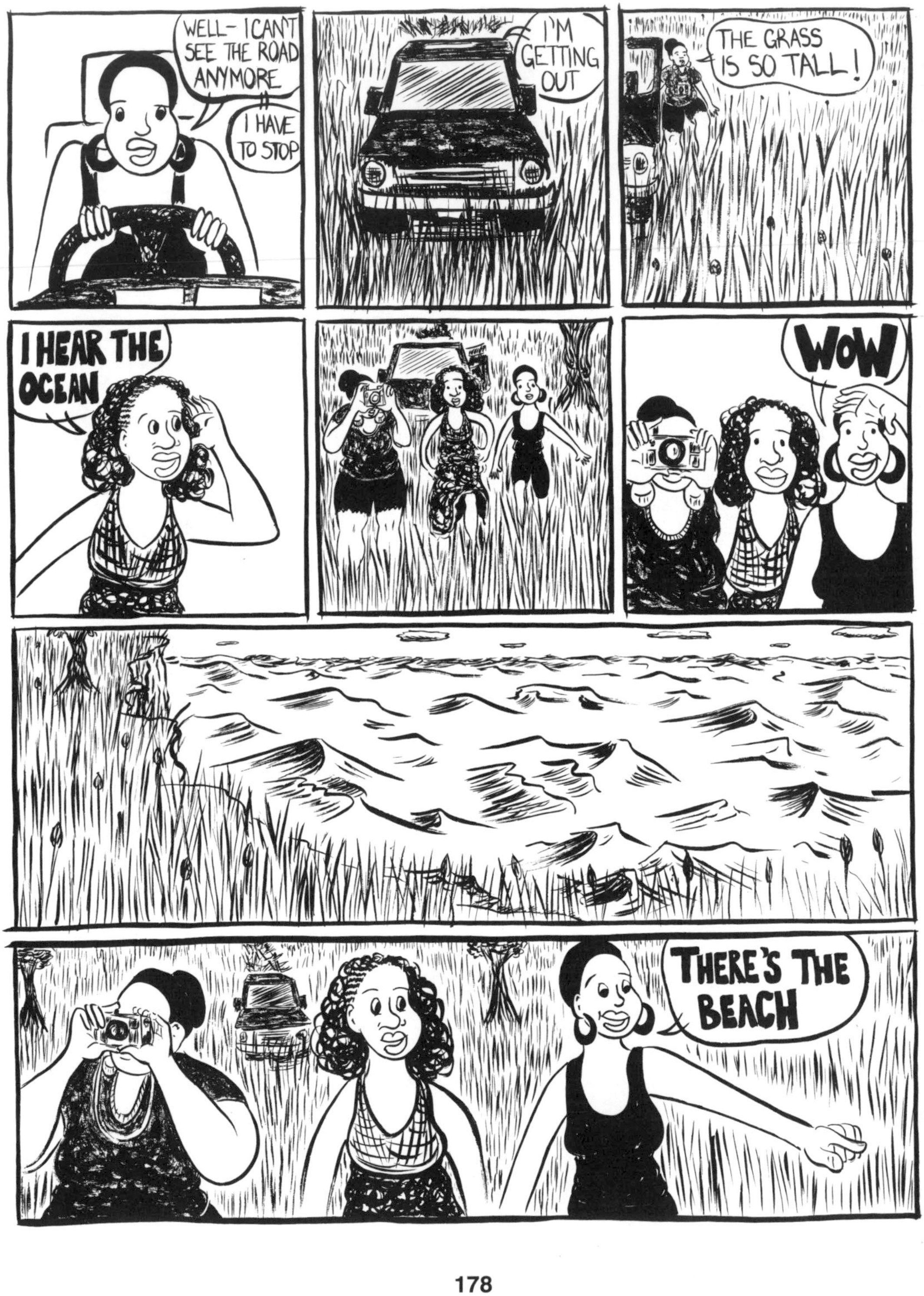
WELL- I CAN'T SEE THE ROAD ANYMORE
I HAVE TO STOP
I'M GETTING OUT
THE GRASS IS SO TALL!
I HEAR THE OCEAN
WOW
THERE'S THE BEACH

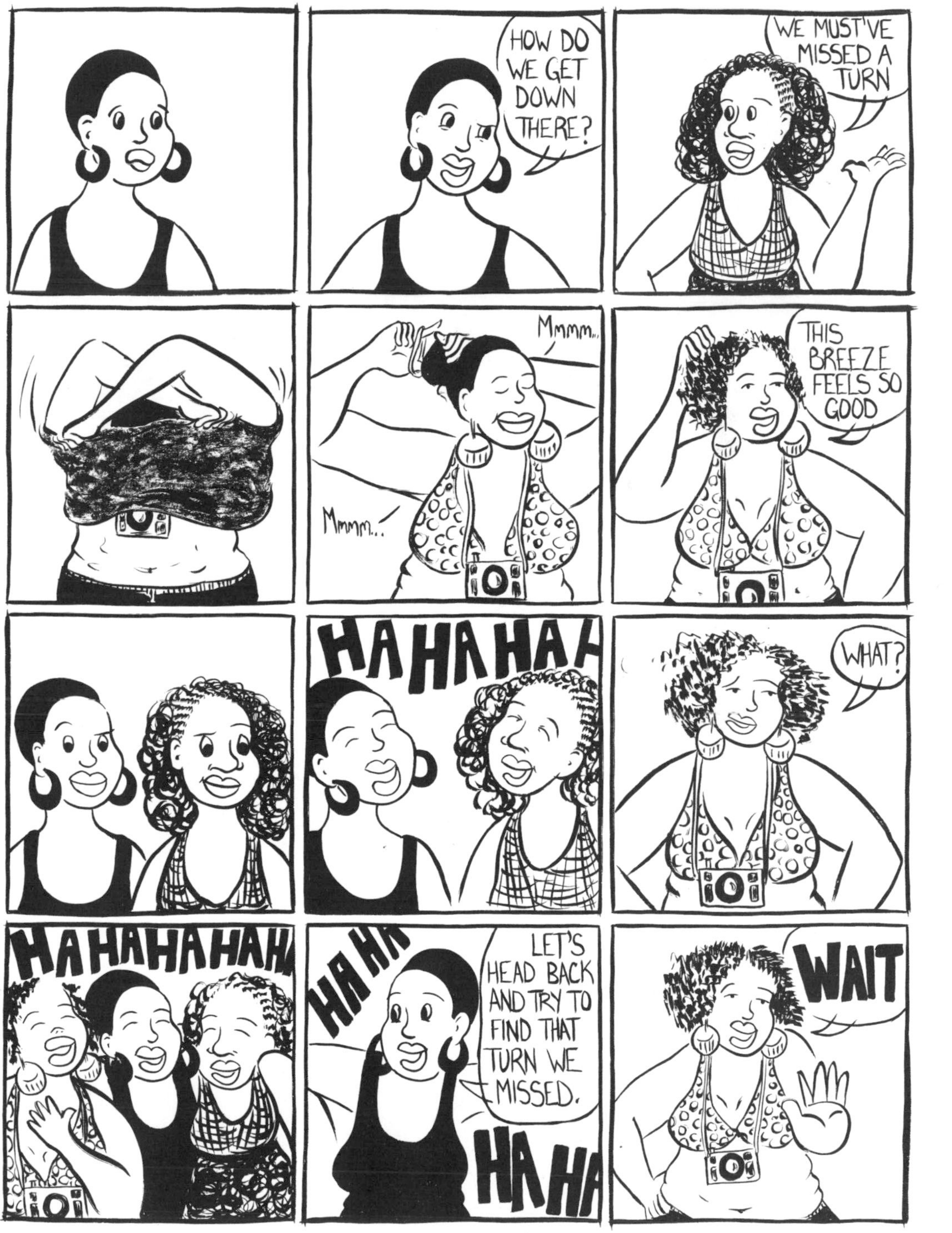
HOW DO WE GET DOWN THERE?
WE MUST'VE MISSED A TURN
Mmmm...
Mmmm...
THIS BREEZE FEELS SO GOOD
HAHAHAH
WHAT?
HAHAHAHAHA
HA HA
LET'S HEAD BACK AND TRY TO FIND THAT TURN WE MISSED.
HAHA
WAIT

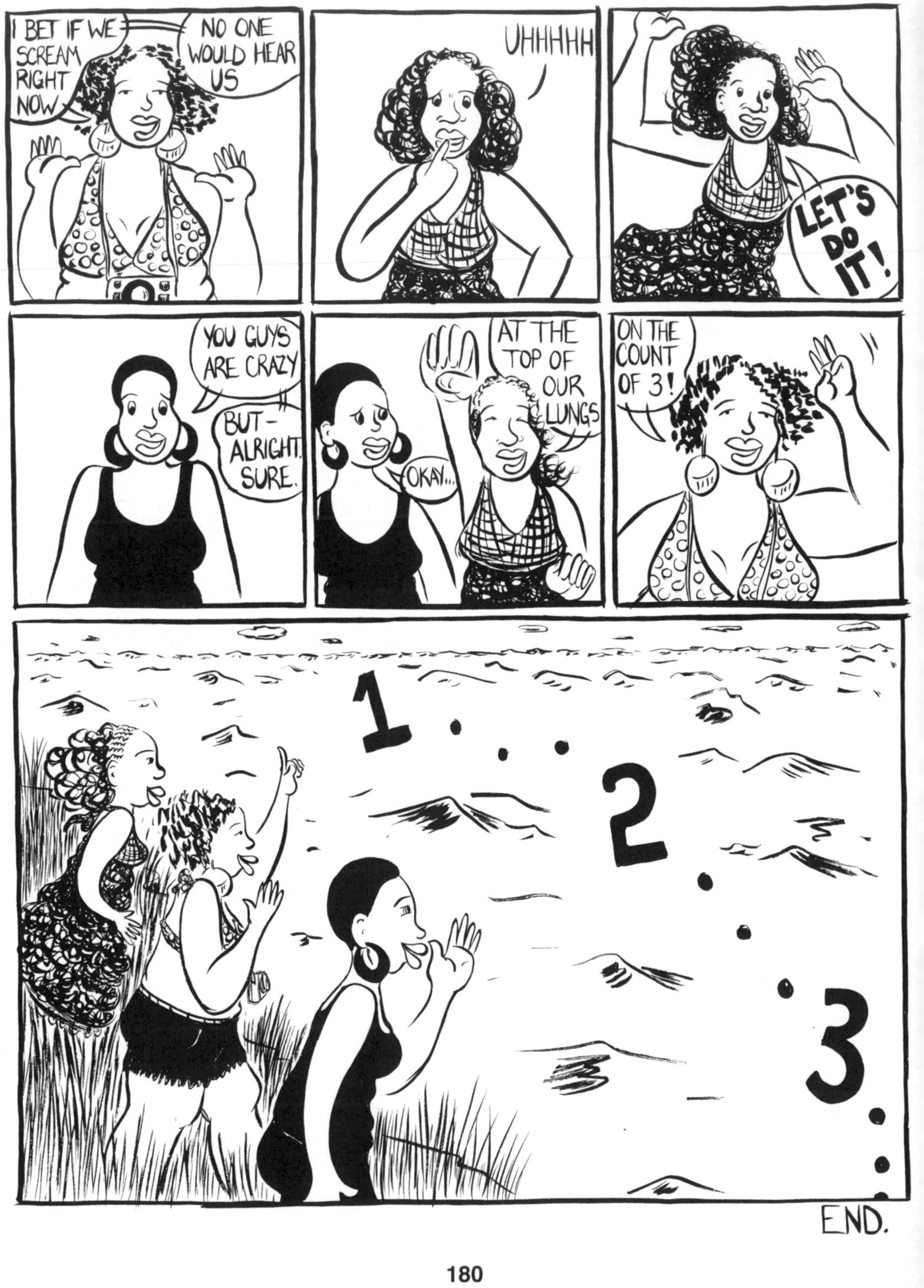
I BET IF WE SCREAM RIGHT NOW
NO ONE WOULD HEAR US
UHHHHH
LET'S DO IT!
YOU GUYS ARE CRAZY
BUT- ALRIGHT. SURE.
AT THE TOP OF OUR LUNGS
OKAY...
ON THE COUNT OF 3!
1 . . .
2 . . .
3 . . .
END.

drawnandquarterly.com | ebonydrawsflowers.com

ISBN 978-1-77046-348-6
First edition: May 2019 | Printed in Canada | 10 9 8 7 6 5 4 3 2 1

Cataloguing data available from Library and Archives Canada

Published in the USA by Drawn & Quarterly, a client publisher of Farrar,
Straus and Giroux. Orders: 888.330.8477. Published in Canada by Drawn
& Quarterly, a client publisher of Raincoast Books. Orders: 800.663.5714.
Published in the United Kingdom by Drawn & Quarterly, a client
publisher of Publishers Group UK. Orders: info@pguk.co.uk

Acknowledgments

I'm grateful to Tracy Hurren and Peggy Burns for all their work to help this book come to life.

Thanks to Julia Pohl-Miranda and the rest of the Drawn+Quarterly staff.

Support from the Rona Jaffe Foundation and Penland School of Crafts allowed me to have more time, creative space, and materials to finish my book. Thank you. Jill Eberle-you are an excellent teacher.

Thanks to my fellow cartooning friends-Dawn Wing, Liz Kozik, and KC Councilor.

Love to Lynda Barry. You taught me how to discover the writing in drawing and the drawing in writing. You turned me into a cartoonist and education researcher.

Love to my friends, family, and Remi.

Thanks for reading!

Ebony Flowers was born and raised in Maryland.
She holds a BA in Biological Anthropology from
the University of Maryland College Park and a PhD
in Curriculum and Instruction from the University
of Wisconsin-Madison, where she wrote her
dissertation as a comic (mostly). Ebony is a 2017
Rona Jaffe Award recipient. This is her first
collection of short stories.